'*The Egyptologist* soars so high, into clouds of such bright comic invention, that Phillips achieves a hilarity equal to anything in *Prague* ... A novel very much worth reading'

—*New York Times Book Review* (Editor's Choice)

omic ... clever ... [Phillips] demonstrates great zest in mixing fact and fiction, istory and satire, to concoct a rollicking narrative that's one part Evelyn Waugh, one part H. Rider Haggard, one part *World Book Encyclopaedia*'

—*New York Times*

A tour de force of plotting and narrative technique ... one of the most horrendously, hideously humorous endings in modern fiction. It will knock you out'

—*Washington Post*

'Wildly inventive ... Phillips' pitch-perfect ventriloquism is a wonder'

—*Time Out New York*

'*The Egyptologist* is a wonder, a work of imaginative prowess ... It's ambitious. It's inventive. It's challenging ... What remains perfectly clear ... is Phillips' rapid ascension as a novelist of complexity, depth and vast imagination'

—*San Francisco Chronicle* (Editor's Recommendation)

'Opium-addicted heiresses, sexy columnists, Australian detectives and real-life figures ... heighten the novel's dazzling complexity'

—*The Washington Post*

An intricately built whodunit for the King Tut lover in all of us'

—*Esquire*, (The Big Important Book of the Month)

[A] cleverly crafted whodunit ... *The Egyptologist* is complicated, ull of characters'

—N

A suave, elegant novel ... Phillips' formidable research and witt this one well worth your time ... a major novelist in the making'

—K

Also by Arthur Phillips

PRAGUE

THE EGYPTOLOGIST

Duckworth

THE EGYPTOLOGIST

a novel

ARTHUR PHILLIPS

First published in the UK in 2005 by
Gerald Duckworth & Co. Ltd.
90-93 Cowcross Street, London EC1M 6BF
Tel: 020 7490 7300
Fax: 020 7490 0080
inquiries@duckworth-publishers.co.uk
www.ducknet.co.uk

First published in the US
by Random House, an imprint
of the Random House Publishing Group

ISBN 0-7156-3399-6

ILLUSTRATIONS © BY JACKIE AHER
BOOK DESIGN BY BARBARA M. BACHMAN

Printed in Great Britain by
Creative Print and Design, Ebbw Vale

FOR JAN, OF COURSE

CONTENTS

Reproduction: Cartouche of King Atum-hadu | xi

Reproduction: First page of journal of Ralph Trilipush | xiii

Map of Egypt | 1

Documents compiled by Laurence Macy III, 1955 | 3

- Correspondence:
  Ralph Trilipush and Margaret Finneran, 1922

- Correspondence:
  Harold Ferrell to Laurence Macy III, 1954–1955

- Journals of Ralph Trilipush, 1922

- Correspondence:
  Ralph Trilipush and Chester Crawford Finneran, 1922

- Correspondence:
  Beverly Quint to Ralph Trilipush, 1922

- Correspondence:
  Hugo Marlowe to Beverly Quint, 1918

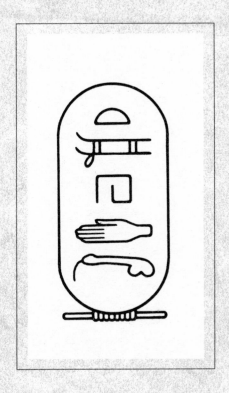

Royal cartouche of King Atum-hadu

(King "Atum-Is-Aroused"), final (?) king (?) of Egypt's XIIIth Dynasty,

1660 (?)–1630 (?) B.C.

HOTEL OF THE SPHINX

TELEGRAPH: hotsphinxcairo

Tuesday, 10 October, 1922
Hotel of the Sphinx, Cairo.

Journal : Arrival in Cairo via rail from
Alexandria. Set to work immediately. Have
scheduled five days in Cairo for logistics and
background writing prior to heading south
to site.

Book Notes : To begin at its proper beginning,
the completed book must have a frontispiece,
protected by a transparent onion-skin overlay.

Frontispiece : "The Royal Cartouche of King
Atum-hadu, final king of Egypt's Middle
Kingdom, XIII th Dynasty, 1660-1630 B.C."
Assume only scholarly readership? No—
clarify for general readers that a cartouche
is the royal seal, one of the king's five names
(the Son of Ra name) written in hieroglyphs
and enclosed in an oval.

Epigraph after the frontispiece :
"It is the intelligence and resolution of
man in overcoming physical difficulty
which are to be the source of our

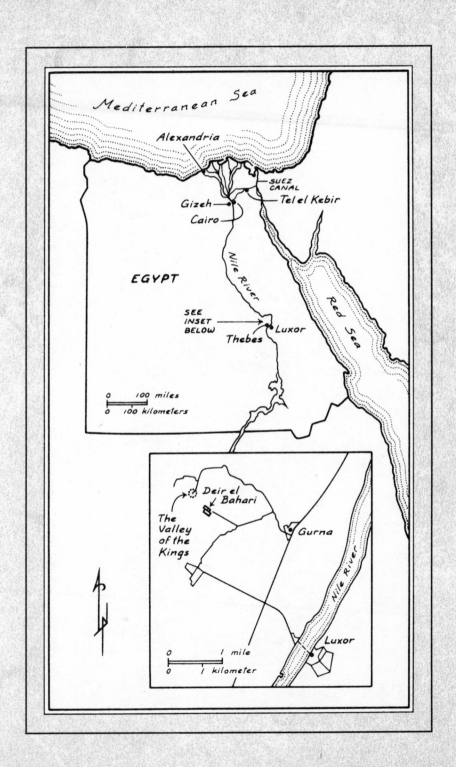

31 Dec. Sunset. Outside the tomb of Atum-hadu. On the Victrola 50: "I'm Sitting on the Back Porch Swing (Won't You Come Sit by Me, Dear?)."

My darling Margaret, my eternal Queen whose beauty astonishes the sun,

Your father and I are heading home tomorrow, back to you—the luxurious riverboat north to Cairo, a night at that city's Hotel of the Sphinx, then by rail to Alexandria, and from there we have booked victorious passage on the Italian steamer *Cristoforo Colombo*, ports of call Malta, London, New York, from where we shall catch the very first train to you in Boston. You shall embrace your fiancé and your father by 20 January.

Upon my return, our wedding will, of course, be our most pressing business. Then, after refreshed preparations, I shall lead a second expedition back here to Deir el Bahari to conduct a photographic survey of the wall paintings and clear the artefacts and treasures from the tomb. All that remains this evening is to seal up the tomb's front, leaving my find exactly as I discovered it. And then posting you this package. My messenger is due here presently.

Nothing stands in our way now, my darling. My success here, your father's reinstated blessing—all is precisely as I promised. You will be relieved to know that your father and I are again fast friends. (Thank you for your "warning" cable, but your father's misplaced anger back in Boston could never have survived his time here in my company!) No, he congratulates me on my find ("*our* find, Trilipush!" he corrects me), sleepily sends you his love, and sheepishly begs you to disregard those foolish things he told you of me. He was under terrible strain, surrounded by jealousy and intriguers, and now he is simply delighted that I have forgiven him for succumbing, even for an instant, to such corrosive lies. And now we are returning to you, just as you will return to me.

Of course, if you are reading this letter, then I have not, for reasons I can only speculate, made it safely back to Boston and your embrace. I did not arrive trailing clouds of immortal glory, did not drape around your white throat this strand of whitest gold I am bringing you from Atum-hadu's tomb. And I did not, taking you gently aside, under the double-height arched windows of your father's parlour, brush away your tears of joy at my safe return, and quietly ask you to give me as soon as it arrives a package (this package), that you would be receiving from me shortly, stamped with the alluring postage of far-off Egypt, addressed to me in your care, to be opened by you only in case of my extended and inexplicable absence.

No, events will proceed just as I have foretold, and you will not read this letter. I shall arrive before it, shall gently take it from you before you open it, and all of this will be unread, unnecessary, a precaution known to no one but me.

But. But, Margaret. But. You have seen as clearly as anyone the malevolence of those who would have us fail, and one never knows when fatal accidents or worse might befall one. And so I am taking the liberty of sending to you the enclosed journals. Dear God, may it all arrive safely.

Margaret, you are now holding, if the besuckered tentacles of my enemies have not yet slithered into the Egyptian postal system, three packets, arranged chronologically in order of composition. They open 10 October, with my arrival in Cairo at the Hotel of the Sphinx, thoughts of you and our engagement party still effervescent in my head. Journal entries never meant for publication are intermingled with those that were, and with elements of the finished work. Much of the journal is a letter to you, the letter I never found the right moment to send until now. I intend to untangle all that back in Boston. The second packet begins when I exhausted my supply of the hotel's stationery and in its place relied on the generosity of colleagues at the Egyptian

Government's Antiquities Service; several score pages are on the letter-head of the Service's Director-General. Finally, I have nearly filled one very handsome Lett's #46 Indian and Colonial Rough Diary, the preferred journals of British explorers whilst working in faraway heat and sand, advancing knowledge at the risk of their very hides. Do not worry: the pages torn from its back are none other than the pages of this letter. Together the three documents compose the rough draft of my indisputable masterwork, *Ralph M. Trilipush and the Discovery of the Tomb of Atum-hadu.*

Also, I am enclosing the letters you have sent me here, your words, kind and cruel intermingled. Seven letters, two cables, and the cable I sent you that was thrown in my face yesterday. And your father's cables to me.

I just replaced the stylus, my last but one. This is a lovely song.

I am trusting a boy to serve as my messenger to the post.

Over time, Margaret, there is erosion. Sands abrade, rubble obscures, papyri crumble, paints decay. Some of this is, of course, destructive. But some erosion is clarifying, as it scours away false resemblances, uncharacteristic lapses, confusing and inessential details. If, in the course of writing my notes, I have made here and there a wrong turn, misunderstood or badly described something I saw or thought I saw, well, at the time one thinks, No matter, I shall edit when I return home. And I shall. But, of course, should I be beaten to death and shoved inside a gangly Earl's travelling trunk and then hacked to pieces and my shreds lazily flipped overboard to peckish sharks, well, then, a pity indeed that I did not edit my work when I had the chance. I shall then need a brilliant and courageous redactor who can puff away dusty speculation to reveal stark, cold, obsidian and alabaster truth. You will provide that clarifying erosion.

We come to the crucial task I am entrusting to you, my muse-become-executrix. You are now the guardian-goddess of all that I have accomplished. These writings are the story of my discovery, my trouncing of doubters and self-doubt. I am entrusting to you nothing less than my *immortality.* I am relying on you, despite everything, for whom else do I have? If something should happen to my body, then you are now responsible—by opening this package, by reading these words—to ensure that my name and the name of Atum-hadu never perish. It is the least you can do for me, Margaret.

You will oversee the publication of this, my last work. Insist on a large printing from a prestigious university press. Stamp your pretty foot and demand shelf space in all major university libraries, as well as with the major Egyptological museums in the USA, Britain, France, Germany, Italy, and in Cairo. And the general public! Cover your ears, Maggie! For there will be a clamour like no one has ever heard when the news escapes. But hold them all at bay until you are ready. Do the work as I am telling you, insist that the book be printed exactly as I say, and give the vultures nothing else.

I do not have time to edit just at the moment; events are moving too fast here. And we leave tomorrow. So I shall do it myself when I arrive safely home, but, allow me to provide contingent guidance if events should unwind elsewise.

For example, as I look at them now, certainly some of the early sketches seem not to have been entirely complete. The eye plays tricks in dim light, when one is hurried, but the final drawings are unquestionably precise, so those first efforts can go. And you will extract my ongoing letter to you, my private or overly candid diary entries here and there. What is only for you and what is for all the world fall away from each other; the division is an easy one to see, if you are careful. I was overeager as a diarist and as your correspondent at the beginning. There is no need to publish anything about you and me, the parties and the partnerships. I was excited, and for good reason, Margaret, as history will attest. And I see now also some stray meditation, releasing a little scholarly steam here and there, my second guesses allowed some room to stumble about only to suffocate in the open air. A careful reading, I beg of you, a careful reading in private, careful editing, and then find a typist (call Vernon Collins), use my illustrations from the notebooks, just the last group of them, when Atum-hadu's paradoxes were all clear, and I at last understood what I was seeing.

If you must be my widow, M., then you will also be my wind. You will gently erode away the inessential. I started crossing bits out just now, but I do not have time, and I might cut into bone, so look here: I shall make your work as simple as I can: the relevant material in order: Kent, Oxford, the discovery of Fragment C with my friend, his tragic end, you and I falling in love, your father's investment, Atum-hadu's tomb in all its splendour, the insightful solution to his Tomb Paradox, sealing up our find for a later return, your father and I heading home, our unfortunate murder. Or not, of course. It could not be clearer. Burn the rest as the marginalia of a scholar's early drafts.

The sunset here is unlike anything I have ever seen. The colour as the sun melts into the changing desert cliffs — such colours do not exist in Boston or Kent. These are the hills and cliffs where my life's story is indelibly etched.

Last stylus. I do love this song.

If, Margaret, you are reading this letter, sobbing, horrified at your double loss but girding yourself and your pen for the vital tasks ahead of you, then I do not hesitate to accuse from here, before the commission of the dreadful crime itself, the maniacal Howard Carter, whose name you may perhaps have heard in recent weeks, the half-mad, congenitally lucky bumbler who tripped over a stair and fell into the suspiciously well-preserved tomb of some minor XVIIIth-Dynasty boy-kinglet named Trite-and-Common and who, in his crippling jealousy, has several times threatened my person in the past months, both whilst sober and whilst intoxicated on a variety of local narcotic inhalants. If I have neglected to note in my professional journals Carter's unceasing attitude of hostility and barely contained violence towards me, such delicacy is only a pained professional courtesy to a once-great explorer, and is, moreover, an example of that certain bravura I have always displayed and you have always admired. Thus I have ignored his repeated threats to make me and my "noble patron, Mr. Chester Crawford Finneran, disappear inexplicably." Obviously, should your father and I not step off the *Cristoforo Colombo* in the port of New York, you may be quite certain that we were done in by Carter or one of his thugs, like his money-man, a lanky English Earl, whose mild manner frays and scarcely covers a vicious character, stretch it though he does, or by their hideous orange-haired confederate, whom you know only too well.

Most beautiful Margaret, these months have not lacked in misunderstanding between us. But for all the harsh letters and harsher silence you sent me, I know that your love for me remains just as my love for you; there is nothing in this life that I value more highly than your embrace. The gramophone recording has come to an end again and now only wheezes in exhaustion.

That was my last stylus from the hundreds I brought with me. The thought that I have seen you for the last time, that I shall never again hold you, trembling in the breezes that dance through your ballroom when the windows swing open to the garden, that the pallor of your throat and the colour of your limbs will never again be revealed to me seizes me so roughly that I can scarcely write now. I cannot bear the thought that I shall never see you again. I cannot bear it. I cannot bear that you will think of me as your father described me, not as I really am, as I know you saw me, at the start. Please think of me at our happiest, when you were most proud of me, when you found the hero you had so long been seeking, the only man you could imagine, when we talked of the world at our feet. Please think of me like that, my darling darling. I love you more than you can know, in ways you will never imagine.

> I will see you soon, my love.
> Your Ralph

Sunset on the Bayview Nursing Home
Sydney, Australia
December 3, 1954

Dear Mr. Macy,

I am in receipt of your letter of the 13th November and I'm delighted to make your acquaintance, if only by post. I'm sickened to hear of your lovely aunt Margaret's passing. It's my dearest wish that she thought of me fondly now and again. We met in times of crisis, high drama. You never forget those, I can tell you. She was a beautiful, vibrant woman when I saved her back in '22. I never saw her again after I brought to justice the man who caused her suffering.

I'm certainly most intrigued by your "small request to tap into [my] no doubt excellent memory." True enough, sir, it is still excellent, and I'll make an extra effort to prove it to you. In my day, I was known for having perfect recall.

I might also add that you're no insignificant sleuth yourself to have tracked me here to this hellhole of a pensioners' house, this human wastebin, thirty years after the facts, young Mr. Macy. Should the investigative field ever interest you professionally, I think you well-suited, and that's high praise, that is, coming from me. Of course, maybe you're the sort of fellow who doesn't have to work at all, eh?

To answer your first question, which maybe was only politeness showing off your breeding, even in a letter to a stranger, but nevertheless, the answer is: bored. Bored nearly to death, thanks, which I suspect is the idea behind these places. Drink up the last of our savings and then bore us to death to open up the narrow, sagging bed and one of the few stinking pots to piss in, 'cause the next old fellow's crossing his legs for it.

I can't tell you how pleased I am at your request to hear about my greatest case, to help fill the blank spaces of your "private Macy family history." And you're in luck: see, I brought very little with me to this damnable place, not one for fine clothes or possessions, me, a simple man, always ready to move fast if circumstances demanded, but when I saw for certain that I was heading here, I said to myself, "Ferrell, you'll be a royal fool if you don't haul your files along and write down your case histories in your many spare hours. It'll be a bright, shining warning to the criminal types out there, a fine teaching tool for other detectives, and a gripping yarn for the general reader." Which is why your letter pleases me so very much.

You want clear recollections? Well, I'm historical truth on two legs, I am, but I need a fellow just like you if I'm going to stop sitting on these dynamite tales and pop them into the public eye. I'm safe in assuming you know people in New York publishing, yes? True-crime magazines maybe? Let's give that some thinking. I know you said you're only asking for "personal family history," but I'm too close to the finish line to play fancy-dress games, Mr. Macy. I see where we can go on this, and I think we've a winner. See, I kept notes, wrote everything out verbatim, as they say, just as soon as I could after interviews. We didn't have the machines they have now to make a taped recording, so we compensated. Young detectives today with their magnetic recorders don't even know what they don't know how to do anymore, but in our day, we had good memories and we wrote fast. If I don't have every last word right here in front of me, well, I have a fine memory of the sort of thing people said or meant to say, so I can reconstruct just fine. It just needs colour, quotation marks, literary frills, typewriting. I'll provide the heroics, you do the rest, eh?

Even if, at the end, some of it wasn't crystal clear to me, still I think this case is my finest, so if you're ready to be my Mr. Watson, let's begin here, and after this one, let's figure I've another dozen at least for us to pull together.

Now, you say you have documents which "may shed light on lingering questions" I might have, and that's a rich piece of bait to dangle in front of a bloke like me. I am who I am, and even thirty years on, I'm curious to hear anything you'd care to disclose. When you refer to finding Margaret's private papers after her death, what does that include, I wonder. What did she say about me? She wasn't above stretching the truth for a story, that one.

When I knew your family back in '22, you weren't even born yet, I don't suppose. When did your aunt meet your uncle? You know, she was a little keen on me, your aunt. She ever tell you this? I suppose not, and I'm sure your uncle was an excellent fellow. But when I met her, she was engaged to that devilish toff poofter explorer, and I think I seemed like just the thing to her—a man of unimpeachable honour, always after the truth, putting the truth first always.

What even to call this case? Think about it: it started as an odd-duck inheritance task, then it was a missing-person case with a dozen different clients, then a double murder, a prenuptial background investigation, then a debt-collection case, and suddenly quite a different double murder. With the imprisonment of the damned Arab (I can't remember his name, oddly), we settled at least the final crime, but much inside this coconut don't slosh when I shake it, even now. You should track down that Arab; he's probably still rotting in some Gippo jail. Maybe he's finally ready to reveal where he stashed the bodies and the treasure.

All right, off we go: the case opens in Mayfair, London, May 1922, according to the notes in my dossier here. There, a very rich man named Barnabas Davies, the proprietor of Davies Brewery, learnt from his sawbones that he hadn't but a few weeks or months to live. Tragic. This Davies, he's an older bloke, but he has a lovely young wife and a couple of little children. Death on its way, Davies settles his affairs with his solicitors. Spick and span, sign on the line, the widow and kids are filthy rich and some junior partner's going to run the brewery show. But then a week later, Davies, still alive, calls his solicitors back and says he's decided to do a few more things he hadn't thought of before.

This is June 7th now. The solicitors come back to Davies's house, sip more of his brandy, and take their notes as the old man bashes their ears: the family and the business are one thing, but now he realises more should be done. He wants the world to know the Davies name for its permanent power to do good. He wants his money to go to a professor's chair in his name at a university, he wants his money to build a hospital, he wants his name on a museum wing filled with paintings by artists receiving Davies Foundation Modern Art Stipends, he's going to fund a monument to some regiment that lost near every damn man in it in the War, and Davies wants the block stuck in the new Davies Gardens, and a football club out in some little town is going to be the Davies FC, and he has an architect called in to start drawing up plans for a zoo shaped like a big D, even as he's on the verge of taking to his bed, perhaps for the last time. Davies, Davies, Davies everywhere.

And then he instructs the solicitors in something very odd, indeed. Apparently, Mr. Davies has risen quite far in this world. He was in the merchant navy as a younger fellow, before he'd had his bit of luck here and there and built the empire that kept the pommies in not-bad amber fluid. You've probably not heard of Davies Ale, son. I think it was bought by another brewer after the Second War, and the name was changed. I recall a bottle with a boat on it, maybe a pirate. Either way, old dying Davies, he presents the solicitors with a list—a rather long list, see—of *women* all over the world. Women from Canada, the USA, Ecuador and Peru, Australia, even Russia, and the dates he *thinks* he was last in these places, the last time he'd seen these women. The dates go back to the start of his merchant navy days, a good forty years in some cases, fifteen in the most recent. And here we go: Mr. Davies tells the solicitors that some or many or maybe all of these women might very likely have had children by Mr. Davies.

Find the birds, he says, and find out for certain if they *have* had his brats. If they have, don't say another word, just thank the mothers and go find the children. Talk to the children and present them with this offer: Davies will leave them each some money—good money, when you consider all they had to do for it was get themselves born out of matrimony, which isn't that hard a trick—if they agree to two things: (a) don't pester the Davies family back in England for one more penny, seeing as legal family is still a cut above, even to this maniac, and (b) agree to take the name Davies as their own. That's right, Mr. Macy, change their names. The oldest will be forty years old, right? But if a bastard wants his cash, he'll change his name. How much cash? The amount's negotiable, Davies tells the lawyers as he presents them with a chart he's made: ideally the children take the bottom figure, but the lawyers can go up to the higher sums, depending on nationality, and whether the children have accomplished something noteworthy, or seem like they might. There's equations on his chart, I was told. A Frenchie in a profession is worth 3.5× as much as an Argentine sailor, for example.

Not surprisingly, the solicitors put up a bit of a fuss. They point out that if nobody's come for old Davies so far, and he is—no use dancing around it—about to meet St. Pete anyway, there's no need to go scraping around for old problems to dig up. Besides, says one sane solicitor, it puts Davies at a disadvantage to have these illegitimates suddenly taking his good name. "Not at all," says Davies, "you're quite missing the point, chappies. These children are mine, and everything they accomplish in this world is mine, too, and should bear my name, because I'm proud of them. I want the Davies name to live on in them and in what they do. We're all Davieses," says the old fellow, getting himself into quite a sweat about it, "my dynasty." "Well, we're just solicitors," say the solicitors, "and tracking down your abandoned brats in the four corners of the earth isn't our affair," although they don't put it quite so hard to their wealthy client as that, I shouldn't think. But he won't listen: "Get detectives to do it, I don't care how you do it, just do it, make it legal, put it in a document, and I'll sign the thing, but do it fast, 'cause time's at stake here, isn't it just? If I have to, I'll sign blank ones and you can fill in the children's names later" is more or less how Mr. Davies puts it.

And I hear you ask: "Just how many possible mothers were there?" Well, Davies's first list turned out to be rather preliminary. The final tally kept swelling over the next few days, as the fat brewer calls back the solicitors to add names when he recollects them, or when he finds another lady's signature at the bottom of some old love note he's burning before signing off for his lunch date with the almighty. When HQ contacted me in Sydney Branch, the 21st of June, 1922, the tally of potential Davies spawn was at thirty-eight and still climbing.

Now "Sydney Branch" and "London HQ": I should clarify those. I'd run my own proprietorship, Ferrell Detection, until March 1922, just a few months before this case, *The Case of the Promiscuous Brewer and the Murders in the Desert*, eh? Catches you? It wasn't a particularly lucrative venture, Ferrell Detection, but I'd a knack for disguise and getting people to tell the truth or at least show it when they were lying. I was a brave little bastard and that's a fact. I knew my Sydney, top and bottom, and I had no time for criminals who thought they were geniuses, because not a one of them ever is, Mr. Macy. There ain't more than three types of people in this world, I can tell you after my years of dealing with them, and maybe not even three.

Then, March '22, I received an offer to become part and parcel of Tailor Enquiries Worldwide, a growing concern in London and ready to put some truth in that "Worldwide." I did a little looking into their business. They were run by a Nicholas Tailor, who was really a Hungarian named Miklos Szabo, who'd done well in England, making of himself the gentleman's confidential enquirer sort of bloke, with a vague continental accent and an air of worldly know-how. Good enough for me, and like that, for an exchange of monetary units and a discussion with their representative as to who paid what to whom and when, I took down my Ferrell Detection sign and had a bloke I knew pop round with one saying Tailor Enquiries Worldwide, Sydney Branch.

And not long after our transaction, I had my orders on the Davies case. I received the same letter that Tailor's men received all over the wide world, explaining our assignment from the London solicitors who'd engaged Mr. Tailor's agency. For, sure enough, one of good Mr. Davies's ports of call had been Sydney, and I was to track a lady named Eulalie Caldwell, who as of 1890 or '91 or 1892 or maybe '93 (as best as Davies could remember) had been a nice-looking young woman with no attachments, living on her own in Kent Street (a very rough part of Sydney), making a temporary living doing some washing up. End of information.

Mr. Macy, sir, it is not every day a detective begins to look for a lost heir and instead solves two double murder cases, one a full four years old. But that is precisely what I accomplished. If I savour the details of this triumph from a long and difficult career, I trust you'll understand.

Kent Street was a dismal hole in the 1890s, and it wasn't much improved by '22. But I wasn't unfamiliar with slums like it, could hardly avoid such things in my chosen field of endeavour. And, with that knowledge, I certainly didn't share Mr. Davies's illusion that his lovely young lass had been stopping there temporarily on her way to better things. If she was alive, she wouldn't be far. This would take no time at all, and I was only curious to see how I could bill London HQ for the maximum time and expense, since it all went back to the solicitors and Mr. Davies in the end.

Public records, asking around, not too hard to get the drum on something like this. Two days later, June 24th, and I'm in a nasty tenement not in Kent Street proper, but two streets over. What a sight, the way these poor bastards lived. I almost felt a bit of a saint—these folks needed Davies's money and I was there to help at least one of them say the right things to get some. You know what people like that want? A little space just to be alone, get some quiet sleep, get clean in. A little privacy. You've no idea, Mr. Macy, in your great big mansion in New York. Compassion, you see, I don't lack for it.

So there I am in a crowded room, trying like hell to shake sense out of a woman who looks about sixty-five or seventy, toothless and ghastly, nose like a rotted cabbage, no shape to the rest of her at all. Mr. Davies must have been one lonely merchant sailor, even thirty years earlier, because she says she's Eulalie Caldwell. (Although she gives me a birth date that would make her forty-nine. Women are like that.)

The place looks and smells like rodents come and go as the mood hits them, and the noise from the other families in the courtyard and upstairs makes your teeth rattle. If Davies has a brat in this crowd, it would be about thirty, and there are a few who might fit that bill, but who can say, because there are people everywhere, barging in and out, yelling, bringing in or hauling off this or that piece of rubbish. There are kids no older than thirteen, others are strapping angry fellows who claim they do standover work, but my nose says they're into something underhand. A couple of young women, filthy things, who I recognised as practitioners of a discreet profession. There's no way to tell who's related to who or who even lives there. My notes from the day read "Dirty animals," but I don't know if I meant vermin or house pets or these people.

I stand there trying to get Eulalie to listen to me. Plainly she isn't suited to do any work anymore, if she ever was. She's useless, and I'm just praying to squeeze some of the last brain activity out of her when in comes a short, skinny, sickly looking black-haired fellow in shirtsleeves who takes a piece of brown bread out of his tucker bag, pulls the hard crust off it, and drops it in the old lady's lap. She looks down at it and nods, like at an old friend. The fellow stands behind her and watches me. He seems a likely candidate for my heir. I ask my question: "Do either of you know a Mr. Barnabas Davies?"

Eulalie goggles at me, but then just gnaws at her bread and looks at her feet. The bloke opens the negotiations with "What if we do?" and I counter with the industry-standard "Well, then I have another question for you." He has to pose a bit more, so we get a "Who are you anyway?" which always earns a "That depends, don't it?" Finally, we arrive at "She might know of Davies. But if he wants her now, it's a little late, isn't it?"

"You never know, son, I work for very powerful men," and he chews on that for a bit, and away we go: yeah, yeah, Davies is a name the young fellow knows, but still Eulalie don't say a word, just takes a bottle of beer from her young man.

The fellow starts coughing up pieces of the story, here and there, for me to gather up and fit together. This one, Tommy, is one of Eulalie Caldwell's brats, one of eleven that saw the light of day and cleared their first year. Tommy knows the name Barnabas Davies only because Eulalie used to "babble on and on" about Barnabas when Tommy was a boy. "Barnabas: the one true love of her life, the man who would've made her a happy woman in London, but it wasn't meant to be. Christ, what a song." I'm thinking, That was an easy case, I have my boy and now we get on to changing his name, job done. But no: her *next* man was Tommy's father, and he stayed around longer than Davies had, living with her and the kids for a few months of Tommy's life, even returning later on to father child number four, but he was never of the "quality" of the mysterious Davies, come and gone like the wind, promising, as he set off to sea, to return for the lovely nineteen-year-old he'd spent a weekend with (on). No, it turns out Tommy is child number two. He has a full sister (child four), and there's a flock of half siblings, tragic stories he now wants to share with me since I'm there and he thinks I asked, and to which I listened with no interest as they had no bearing on my business: a long and tedious recital of stillborns, hunger, broken promises of advancement from this or that lying toff, here an unwilling but profitable prostitute, there a nasty marriage, one boy killed at Gallipoli, another working at a station in the north, all the way down to the thirteen-year-old girl standing right there in front of me (no name in my records).

Of course, how damned dull this all was, like poverty always is, and when Tommy was done singing all this, we worked back to the main question. Where was Tommy's older sibling, sired by Davies, Eulalie's child number one? And only then does Eulalie look up at me, and she starts to make an odd noise and then she's crying, by which I mean her nose is dripping like a tap and her lips are shaking, but no tears are coming. "Oh, Paul," she says, and you can't even imagine how angry Tommy looks—not at me, but at the drunk hag sitting in front of him who only now has managed to put two words together. "Shut your mouth, why don't you? Get off your date and clean something, you bloody bitch," and the crying woman manages to shuffle out of the room, with the youngest girl following her out, calling Tommy nasty names.

Back to the raging, wheezing little man's tale: Paul Barnabas Caldwell was a "year or two older" than Tommy, so that meant born in 1892 or 1893, which fit my bill. Tommy hated Paul. He grew up loving him, of course—he's your older brother, you love him, and you feel sorry for him when he gets smacked by Mum or by the man of the house (a rotating title, apparently) or by Bowlex (Dowlex? I think I'm reading that right)—but Paul grew up fast and started throwing his weight around too: he started to hit Eulalie back, before he ran away for the last time. And Paul was good at school, surprising thing, even when he was a little fellow. Tommy don't like that, though: Paul was the only one who'd had a chance at school, a real chance, since Eulalie could still work a bit back then, could make a little money, and so Paul got to go to school "regular, not just now and again," while the others were in and out, helping their mum with work, quitting the books as soon as the state said they were through. Worse though, Eulalie always told Tommy and the other kids that Paul was special because Paul's dad was something special, and she'd throw that at Tommy's dad too: "You aren't Barnabas Davies." Tommy told me with a quiet, angry amazement, "But Paul wasn't even grateful for that," he used to call Eulalie a whore and a disgrace, would say she wasn't his mother, wasn't a proper woman at all, and he'd be off out the door to visit his other friends, "and he never took me," says Tommy, "never once took me, never showed me his books and pictures, looked at me like I was dirt because my dad wasn't your Mr. Davies, but was just poor old Tom from down the pub. But I got him once"— Tommy laughs, showing his few teeth—"I got him good. I once snatched one of his library books, a real nasty one, took it and showed it to Rowler (Bowlex?). Paul had the devil whipped out of him that day. That was something to see."

Well, Mr. Macy, you can imagine that this was quite a tiresome spectacle—vengeful lies, self-pitying misunderstood memories—but it was something I could understand and put up with as long as I got my job done. Had to listen to a heap of this before I could get young Tom calm enough to answer me: where was Paul Davies *now*? My mistake triggered another storm: "He isn't Paul *Davies*, he's Paul *Caldwell*, you hear? The Caldwell name is good enough for him, he's lucky to have it." "Fine, Paul Caldwell then, Tom—where is he?" Turns out Paul's been gone since Tommy was thirteen or fourteen. Not one word when he left. "That broke Eulalie," says Tommy. "She needed him. He was going to be the man of this house, and now I still have to bloody well hear how I'm not Barnabas Davies's son."

"And since then, since, let's say, 1907?"

"Yeah, that Bolshie, what's her name, the crazy library lady, she came by one day, in '18 or '19, prim and proper and disgusted by us, and shows us the letter from the Army saying Paul was missing, a corporal he was, and 'no further information' known. We didn't even know he went off to the War. Him missing and Mick dead on that Turkish beach, God damn, Eulalie cried for a bleeding month. Now what in Christ's name do you *want* with us?"

My notes say, "Two and a half hours with those animals. Bill London for ten hours." No crime that, Macy, since London turns around and bills the solicitors for twenty and they bill Davies for forty, and that's about right for this bastard, leaving women in distress like he did. Can you imagine, Macy? All over the world, detectives like me were prying around in the open sores of unhappy families and abandoned women. There must have been a whole city's worth of pathetic, screaming scenes like this one going on all over the world right then, at that very moment, because old Mr. Davies had been a wolf as a young man and wanted to be loved for it as an old man.

My notes also say, "Engaged by Tommy Caldwell to bring back any word of Paul Caldwell's address or grave, payable on contingency." I had my second client on what was now the Paul Davies/Paul Caldwell case, though I highly doubted his intention to pay.

Mr. Macy, I slept like a baby last night, not the old nightmare, nor a toss or a turn. For this alone I thank you. Just knowing that you and I are working together on this memoir, opening up the old case, explaining its logic and structure, letting the world know what I achieved. I feel a new man. I even ate a full breakfast this morning, choked down all this poison and it tasted just fine. Last night, before I nodded off, I pulled out my other boxes of files from under the iron bed, and I read through a couple of the finest, though the rotter next to me whinged about the light and even called in one of the toughs to force me to douse the glim—it hardly matters. After you and I do this one, I think the one I call *The Beautiful Dead Girl* would do well with our readers. ("Don't miss another Ferrell and Macy adventure, coming next month!")

So, the Barnabas Davies case was closed, eh? We had the name of Davies's Sydney child: Paul Caldwell, born 1893. We had a personality sketch of him up to the age of fourteen: possibly above-average intelligence, but with the anger of the abandoned child trapped in poverty. Beyond that, we don't know what kind of son Mr. Davies left behind when he tripped onto his boat and buttoned up his trousers. We know the boy went off to fight in the War and he didn't come home. *Missing*, Mr. Macy, meant they couldn't sort out the pulped-up bodies in the French mud or on the Turkish beach or in the Suez Canal. And Melbourne just called you dead after a while being missing. I think it was in '19 or '20 they said *no one* was missing anymore—all the *missing* files got relabelled as *killed*. So as far as official records had it, Paul was dead, though for some reason no one had got around to telling Eulalie and Tommy yet. Either way, case closed, I reckoned.

But then, I reckoned again, Mr. Macy, and a canny and dramatic moment it was, as you and our readers shall see. *Why* close this case? I could spin away heaps of hours trying to get details of Paul Caldwell's life and military service to send back to his proud papa. True, no heir to give money to, probably, but "missing" isn't *quite* "dead," so why not see what I could find? And if he was dead, maybe he was a war hero, and he could be renamed posthumously, become brave Paul *Davies*, gallant martyr of the Ardennes, so the fat, dying brewer would buy himself a nice dead hero-son, and what was *that* worth on his chart, and who picked up the cash legacy for it? My mind was moving fast, the old game was afoot, and the final tab in London was going to pay for a nice holiday.

Now I had to pull strings to get a squiz at Caldwell's military dossier. It was locked up tight in Melbourne, not even families were allowed to see the files. Still can't today. Even Davies in London as next of kin would be allowed only a short letter declaring death and final rank. But if it's detection you want, Mr. Macy, you need a network of helpful individuals. With that, simplest thing in the world: bloke owes me a favour, knows another bloke who manages some girls in Melbourne, and one of them worked for a man who knew a bloke working in the office of the historian at Defence and that bloke owed the first man a favour, or the first man would mention to Defence that the second bloke had been spending intimate time with this or that inappropriate (not to say outright Aboriginal) girl, and a little money (billable as a Barnabas Davies expense, no question) moved (shrinking as it went) down along this long line of nameless but helpful individuals, and some scribbled notes made their way back along it, and now it's the 7th of July, when I copy the notes neatly into my file and add my own first questions, all of which reads, verbatim:

Paul Caldwell. Born 1890 (Tommy said 1893). Volunteered for infantry (why?) October 1916, with determination made (by whom?) that his service be limited entirely to Egypt for as long as AIF has presence there, due to special knowledge and circumstances (which?). Entered as private (if he had special knowledge, why only private?). Dispatched to infantry at Tel el Kebir, Egypt. Promoted twice and cited for distinctive service twice with commendatory letter included in file from Brit. Capt. H. S. Marlowe. (Why a British captain bothering with an Aussie digger?) Missing while on leave, 12 November 1918. Natives far south at Deir el Bahari (500 miles away from his camp), subsequently discover Caldwell's rifle, identity disks of Caldwell and aforementioned Marlowe. (A pommy officer and a digger on leave together?) Rank at end of service: corporal. Missing status changed to Dead in final records closing, June 29, 1919.

Because he was a British officer, Captain Marlowe's file was conveniently located in London, so we have to be satisfied with this for now, my good Watson. Now, the questions I jotted down in my notes that day are only a few of what should occur to a clear-eyed investigator presented with this synopsis. I'll leave it to you to try to count up the puzzles hidden in those hundred and eight words, because they breed fast, the little rabbits. Here's a gift, though, in case your history's not too strong: the War ended on the 11th of November, 1918, the day *before* Paul vanished.

One more item from the boy's file: "Next of kin: Mrs. Emma Hoyt, in care of Flipping Hoyt Brothers Entertainment, Ltd., Sydney." So much for Eulalie Caldwell and brother Tommy; no wonder they'd had to hear the news from a third party: they weren't mentioned when Paul enlisted. Kin seems to have been a complicated question for our boy. I'd have to ask the lawyers: might his Davies inheritance belong to this new next of kin, if Paul Caldwell was dead and somehow retroactively rechristened Paul Davies?

Good morning, Mr. Macy! Shall we continue? Good.

Of course I remembered the Flipping Hoyt Brothers Circus—but first, I hear impatient Mr. Macy whingeing, "What's this ripping yarn got to do with my poor mistreated auntie and vanished great-uncle?" Everything, Mr. Macy, everything. Patience. Have some faith in your storyteller, eh?

Now then, of course I remembered the Flipping Hoyt Brothers Circus, but I was surprised to find it still in existence when I went enquiring after Emma Hoyt at the circus's ticket booth, the 8th of July, 1922.

"She's about to go on," says the bald, shirtless, moustached man at the booth. "She's available for admirers after the performance, but here's a tip, mate: she'll be more likely to talk to you if she knows you saw her show."

"It's on *now*?" I asked, looking around the field surrounding us and the sagging yellow tent, three or four people milling about some caravans.

"Starts in five minutes. You're a lucky man." I paid for a front-row seat, and the bald man emerged to tear the ticket he'd just sold me, then showed me to my place, pulling the canvas shut behind us. I counted the audience: I was one of eight, though there were empty benches and risers and a row of large divans with tables, seats for 300 or some. My usher sat me, then continued down the empty aisle, stepped over the flaking red wooden wall in front of me, opened a gate in the high metal fence circling the sandy pit, locked the gate behind him, and picked up a megaphone. His red velvet trousers were white at the seat. "Ladies and gentlemen," he yelled, walking in circles, looking high over my head at long-ago crowds.

His opening remarks finished, he unwound his whip and lifted a hatch at the back of the cage. Three monstrous tigers slunk in. Our bald man lazily attended to making them leap over each other, roll on their backs, spring through a metal ring, all of which they performed sluggishly but with sudden bursts of snarling rebellion, which the whip didn't shut up too quickly. For his finale, he had the tigers lie down, not without resistance, and he opened the hatch at the back of the cage again. There, dramatically lit from behind, was a strange little profile, and then in waddled a penguin. The bird circled the prone tigers once, promenaded up and down their backs, and then "logrolled" them, walking in place on their bellies as the tigers rolled underneath him. Finally, the penguin stepped off, took a turn of the ring for applause, and approached the three tigers to kiss each of them on the nose (previously sprayed with herring scent, no doubt). The children gasped and laughed. It was a neat display, I'd imagine. When it worked.

Today, though, the third cat had had enough: as the fish-stinking kiss brushed his twitching, whiskered muzzle, there was a blur of orange-and-black paw and the penguin looked down at the three red stripes on his white breast with the surprise of a rich man who's spilled claret on his evening shirt. He raised his beaked head, astonished. He looked to the lazy tiger keeper who'd trained him, talked him into this twice-daily escapade, and was himself stunned at the tiger's break in discipline, and now was raising his whip and shouting at the cat, but too late. The paw flashed again, and the suddenly headless penguin rocked in place but didn't tip over, because the cat's other paw was pinning the flipper feet to the sand. The tiger was about to enjoy the snack he'd just uncorked when he felt the lash bite his back, and he turned with a roar on the man who'd both whipped and fed him since his tiger-cub days. "You don't snarl at me, boy-o!" shouted my ticket vendor, flogging with a fury. Only now did the two children in the audience realise the penguin whose antics they'd just been admiring wasn't well, as its head, beady-eyed and baffled, had come to rest on the red wooden wall a few rows in front of them.

For reasons Mrs. Hoyt later explained to me as a matter of discipline for the beasts and safety to their master, the cats were required to perform their entire routine again, without fail, before they could be allowed out of the cage for their meat reward. While the two children sobbed and their parents told them, "Now, now, it's all just a trick," the tigers, growling and irritable, reviewed their tasks and swatted at their man. Again the leaping, the rolling, the springing through rings. Again they all lay down facing forward. Again the back hatch lifted. Again a dramatic silhouette of a plump, banana-nosed fellow. And again a trained penguin waddled in, expecting to win applause and a fresh fish. What this second penguin thought as it passed the decapitated, dusty football of its colleague I cannot say. "No! No!" cried the little boy to my left. "Fly away!"

I only mention this scene, Mr. Macy, to illustrate the state of the circus by 1922, for I then watched two middle-aged Chinese contortionists twist themselves into the most peculiar shapes, to audience discomfort. I watched a single, spangled trapeze man swing listlessly for a spell before just dropping onto his net and from there to the ground, taking off his costume even as he was walking away. All through it, a visibly disheartened man of sixty played an out-of-tune upright piano. From time to time he murmured with a pained seriousness at the frightened children, "Ah, the circus! It's magical, just magical."

"He is classically trained, you know. He used to conduct our ten-piece orchestra, in Paul's day," Paul Caldwell's chosen next of kin, Emma Hoyt, later told me, her face drooping. Her business was at its very end, of course. I think she held on to it another week, but I'd witnessed the death throes of the Flipping Hoyt Brothers Circus. "In better days," she started most of her sentences, or "When my husband, Boyd, was alive," or most interesting, "Paul would have hated to see things end like this."

A woman of forty-five or so, and not without her charms, she was still dressed like a major in some brightly coloured army, her hair blond and compressed under her red, cylindrical hat. She lit cigarette after cigarette, but didn't smoke them. Her private caravan smelled of perfume, her performing dogs, wild animal dung.

She was eager to talk about Paul Caldwell. I told her she might have inherited some money from him, but she scolded me: "That's impossible. He's only missing." My notes are easily enough compiled for you, more or less as they must've been said. (Do you think we should present polished stories with long speeches, or just the fragments of my notes? The latter is more "real," I suppose, but the reader wants to feel it's happening to him, if you see what I mean, Macy.)

"So many difficult memories are stirred to life by your visit, Mr. Ferrell. Paul was the most wonderful thing ever to happen to this circus, his love of what we did here. I thought of him every day, far away at war, fighting for just this, for the magic of our circus. Oh, don't misunderstand me, I know the Germans have fine circuses, too, but I'm sure the Kaiser was no enthusiast. We free people appreciate things his kind could never tolerate.

"I wrote Paul when Boyd was called to his reward, told him I would do everything to keep his circus ready for him. It was his for the taking, if he wanted, after the War. He could have turned it around. Such devotion.

"Of course, you'll want to be hearing about the beginning. Paul came to us when he was nineteen or twenty. Boyd discovered him, said he had extraordinary natural talent. He had spotted Paul down in the market and followed him a bit, clandestinely, watched him doing it. Then he pretended to walk in front of Paul, unaware, pretended to bend over and tie his shoe, and when he stood up again, he just grabbed Paul's wrist and took back his wallet. Of course, for a while, Boyd pretended to be a copper, you understand, to put a scare up Paul. But then Boyd sat off to the side, pointed to people to see if Paul could do it on demand. Boyd was excited when he brought him back to our camp that day. And what a beautiful boy he was, and intelligent as anyone I had ever known. He had been a librarian, as I am sure you know.

"And that instant when Boyd led him to us! You see a face light up sometimes in surroundings like ours, Mr. Ferrell. Something quite intoxicating washes over certain people. Paul was like a little boy. He wanted to touch all the animals, even the tigers. That was the thing about him that charmed one, you see. He knew so very much about a few things, smart as anything, but he also did not know the simplest things. He wandered around the camp. He walked inside the tent, and I followed him. He gazed up at the tied-back trapezes, at all the seats. 'Haven't you ever seen a circus, Paul Caldwell? Would you like a job with us?' You've never seen such a happy face, and so handsome. 'The circus?' He asked me if I knew of some Italian strongman, some performer he had heard of once. 'The circus,' he kept whispering, like he had landed on the moon. I knew just how he felt."

"And when did he become your lover, Mrs. Hoyt?"

"I was married to Boyd, Mr. Ferrell."

"But I've the impression Mr. Hoyt was much older."

"Boyd was a clown, you know. I mean, professionally, by trade. He could make you laugh so. He would do his 'shame face,' when, for example, he was caught trying to steal a man's necktie, and he would close his eyes in this long blink and shrug like he was a bad, bad, naughty clown, and people just loved it. People loved him. Off the sawdust he was rather colder.

"Boyd had Paul clean out the cages, sell tickets, seat people. That was necessary, of course, seating people. That let him put those who carried their wallets in their trousers on the elevated seats so he could reach up from below during the show. He performed a few times, a shocking magic and drama act for the evening performances. Boyd thought we should try more sophisticated fare, so to open the show after the entr'acte, Paul would come out dressed as a jungle explorer and do a sort of pantomime where he pretended to fight off attackers, five of the bigger fellows done up as jungle blacks. They'd get the better of him, tie him down, and then one of them brought out a snake. Nothing dangerous, just one of the bigger pythons, and they circled round him and danced a bit and waved the snake about and they bent over him, so the audience couldn't see what was happening, but we'd released the power of their imaginations! Then off ran the black villains, one of them hiding the snake in his gown, so the audience couldn't see it, they just saw Paul tied down, writhing in torment, you understand, and he struggles and pulls one of his arms free, and then tears at his chest, he opens his shirt and . . . and his chest bursts open and out comes the head of the snake! Oh, it was a horrible sight, and women would faint, and the lights went out, and when they came up, Paul took his bow. He had to do it then, before the call at the end, so people would know he was alive and well. We used to play for such crowds, before Boyd's stupidity. And Paul brought in so much money. He could put purses back, after they'd been half-emptied, you see, so we rarely had complaints.

"Boyd thought like you, though. He was so certain this little boy was my lover. And so he just spent his days down with the tigers, tossing them their meat with a nasty face. But what did he think would happen? That the police would take

Paul away from me on Boyd's word but not tell the public that, at Flipping Hoyt, thieves prowl under the seats?

"They arrested him during the show, without a fuss, I didn't even know it happened. The first sign was when the native snake-men had to make up some dance with each other, and then just wandered off with the snake while the crowd looked confused and checked their watches, and then Wang and Songchuck were up the pole, twisting on top of each other. 'What do you reckon has become of Paul?' I asked Boyd after the show, and he just smoked and looked at me strangely. And I knew. 'What did you do to him?' I was afraid he had done something horrible with the tigers. 'You vile old man, what did you do?' He wouldn't speak to me, and it was days before I found Paul, but then the police wouldn't let me see him. I kept at them for weeks, knocking every day on the door of this brutish inspector. But they wouldn't let me see him. And then, one day, weeks had passed, they told me he was gone, off to the War to avoid prison."

"You wrote to him when your husband died."

"That was 1917. Also to say I hadn't betrayed him, that it wasn't me who'd turned him in. I was so afraid he blamed me. I didn't know where to send the letter. I just sent it to the Department of Defence. I never heard a thing, until I had the notification he was missing. He put me down as next of kin, you see. At that moment, finally, I knew he was not angry with me, that he loved me still. And at that same moment, I was told I'd lost him.

"Still, I thought I should find his real family. I went to that horrid librarian, Paul had told me all about her. They had been, oh, *intimate*, you see, not his first *love*, more the case of an older woman taking advantage of a poor boy in need. But she at least would know where to find his blood relations. Later, I had a second letter from Defence saying they changed him from Missing to Dead, but they didn't have a body or anything, it seemed just for filing. I so want him to find the circus just as he left it . . . that poor penguin . . ."

Mr. Macy, our story today ends with a circus lady sobbing for her dead lover and her dead circus and a dead bird. I waited for a bit to see if she'd pull herself together, but after a few minutes, the end was nowhere in sight, so I went on my way.

Two or three days later, I had a letter:

Mr. Ferrell. Your visit yesterday was a tonic for a tired woman. You would set my mind at ease with any definitive information you unearth as to Paul's Destiny. I should like to engage you, if that is how these matters are handled. If you should find him alive and if he is staying away from us, amidst the Missing, for reasons of his own, please assure him that I did not Betray him, would never, and that I love him. If he is gone forever, please let me know what became of him. There is little left for me here. I will go anywhere for him—please tell him that. I am soon to become a tiger vendor, at least temporarily, and after that, I cannot say.

With that, Mr. Macy, I had a third client on this same case!

But what did I have of Paul (Caldwell) Davies to present to London? Well, unfortunately, crime. That would probably affect Davies's final settlement negatively. And his volunteer enthusiasm for the War, it now seemed, may have been a product of circumstance, the Australian Imperial Force being more inviting than penal labour.

But I also had two new leads: Inspector Dahlquist, who'd arrested Paul Caldwell and sent him off to die in Egypt rather than rot in prison, and Miss Catherine Barry, the librarian who'd turned up in our tale twice so far, Paul's first lover. The Davies Case was fast becoming a lucrative use of my time.

Which reminds me. I'll send you what I've written so far, so as not to delay your progress speaking to publishers. I will, while awaiting your reply by Air Mail, continue to transcribe my notes and letters.

I am your humble correspondent,
Harold Ferrell,
Private enquiries (retired)

Tuesday, 10 October, 1922. **Hotel of the Sphinx, Cairo**

Journal: Arrival in Cairo via rail from Alexandria. Set to work immediately. Have scheduled five days in Cairo for logistics and background writing prior to heading south to site.

Book notes: To begin at its proper beginning, the completed book must have a frontispiece, protected by a transparent onion-skin overlay. *Frontispiece:* "The Royal Cartouche of King Atum-hadu, final king of Egypt's Middle Kingdom, XIIIth Dynasty, 1660–1630 B.C." Assume only scholarly readership? No—clarify for general readers that a cartouche is the royal seal, one of the king's five names (the Son of Ra name) written in hieroglyphs and enclosed in an oval.

Epigraph after the frontispiece:

"It is the intelligence and resolution of man in overcoming physical difficulty which are to be the source of our pleasure and subject of our praise." John Ruskin, *The Stones of Venice*

Or: "Although we have not yet discovered the tomb of Atum-hadu, we can be fairly certain it is within our reach." Ralph M. Trilipush, *Desire and Deceit in Ancient Egypt* (Collins Amorous Literature, 1920; new edition from Harvard University Press projected for 1923)

Or: "Ralph Trilipush will never convince anyone with a brain that King Atum-hadu ever existed, let alone wrote the so-called Atum-haduan Admonitions." Prof. Lars-Philip Thürm, in the *Journal of Egyptological Studies*, 1921. This epigraph would have an amusing effect when placed next to a photograph of me standing in front of the tomb of King Atum-hadu, holding a complete papyrus of his Admonitions.

Or: perhaps an excerpt from the Admonitions, from the profound mind and naughty reed brush of King Atum-hadu himself. For example, the first line of Quatrain 30 (found in Fragments B & C only): "Atum-hadu smiles upon his brother." Actually, a bit misleading as to its original context, as the complete Quatrain 30 describes the discovery of an impostor claiming kinship to the king:

Atum-hadu smiles upon his brother,
Overjoyed to meet another fallen from the same mother!
Until he learns the claim is but a lie,
And now with fire and asps the liar will die.

> — (From *Desire and Deceit in Ancient Egypt*, Collins Amorous
> Literature, 1920; new edition by Harvard University Press
> projected for 1923)

No, better still, to begin this adventure at its proper beginning, let us open the book with a tantalising glimpse of the discovery to come, and offer as epigraph a thrilling episode not too far off in the future, an

excerpt of events described in the book itself. We shall extract a tri-
umphant moment and place it at the front, a shocking jewel in the
crown, a zesty appetiser to tickle the reader's tongue for the vast feast
to come and to prepare his digestion, lining his stomach for riches for
which his dull daily fare has not prepared him. We shall tentatively use
the events of—to make a conservative guess and present myself on that
date with a nice birthday gift—24 November, six and a half weeks from
now, neither too optimistic nor too stodgy, something like: "page ii:
*24 November, 1922. At the Deir el Bahari site. I cleared away the loose rocks and
descended to my knees, and began slowly—painstakingly slowly, despite my
pounding heart—to widen the hole in the millennia-old heaped rubble. The light
shook in the hands of the irrationally frightened Abdullah. 'It's all right, man.
Just give me the torch,' I whispered, and held my eye to the narrow aperture. 'Yes,
yes . . .' 'Please, what does His Lordship see?' 'Immortality, Abdullah, I see immortality.'* "

   Cover design: photo of RMT standing alongside Atum-hadu's
golden (one safely projects) sarcophagus. Native labourers in work
robes standing off to the side. *Ralph M. Trilipush and the Discovery of the
Tomb of King Atum-hadu by Ralph M. Trilipush.* Subtitle: *Including the archaeologist's private diary, notes, and sketches. Harvard University Press, 1923.*
Dedication page: A discovery of this magnitude simply cannot be
achieved without the tireless help and inspirational example of several
other contributors. To my team of nearly 500 Egyptian workers, whose
diligence was matched only by their devotion to me and our common
effort, who suspended what for them must have been an excruciating
disbelief and instead displayed a simple faith that the objects I unearthed had significance beyond their shiny lustre, I offer my sincerest
gratitude. And, in particular, to my headman, Abdullah, who knew how
to dispense to the men discipline and *baksheesh* in just the right proportions, and whose fierce loyalty to me and quaint efforts to wrestle with
the complexities of English touched and amused me in equal measure
during our weeks of great toil and peril, I offer a hearty *salaam!* Mr.
Chester Crawford Finneran, of Finneran's Finer Finery, is a gentleman
of magnificent depth and parts, a discerning collector of ancient art, a

man of force but also of finesse, not at all what one would have expected to find in an American, let alone a vaunted 'captain of commerce.' But our 'CCF' has proven himself worthy of the noble, ancient Egyptian title of Master of Largesse, that generous and trusted dispenser of wisdom and wealth in times of need, and the title that Atumhadu himself used in his poetic Admonitions to refer to his own trusted prime minister. The tomb of Atum-hadu is known to us thanks to CCF, my Master of Largesse, as well as my other partners in Hand-of-Atum Explorations, Limited. To my beloved fiancée, Margaret Finneran, words are insufficient to express my love, admiration, and gratitude. To my fellow explorers, who labour in the hot sands of our beloved adopted mother, I offer you my thanks for your collective example, your tireless and too often unrewarded dedication. In particular, I wish to mention that paragon of Egyptological exploration, my dear friend, Mr. Howard Carter, who as I set pen to paper here, is deep into his sixth season in an apparently fruitless quest for a chimerical tomb, that of a minor XVIIIth-Dynasty king called Tut-ankh-Amen. I now state publicly in these pages, that—fail or succeed—Mr. Carter's nearly senseless dedication (six years!) is a model to us all, and that for it I have admired him, even before I knew him and called him friend. I salute my elder comrade in dust, my mentor and the dominant figure of the passing generation, reluctantly yielding us the torch. Finally, this book must certainly be dedicated to that great king Atum-hadu, and to his patron-god, the first Creator, Atum. The existence of Atum-hadu's tomb (and of Atum-hadu himself) was long doubted by many, but Atum-hadu's genius, his reign, his poetry: all of these I honour as I greet him across more than 3500 years, I, who never doubted him. Majesty, the world gazes upon you now, in your golden tomb, amidst your vast treasures, in your cracking brown mummy wraps. The world marvels at your life, your words, your brilliance. The world in respectful awe gazes upon your noble organs in their canopic jars. This is the very immortality you pursued and deserved, eternal glory and celebrity.

About the Author: Professor Ralph M. Trilipush was born 24 November, 1892, the only child of the renowned soldier and explorer

Ecgbert Trilipush, and was raised a well-adored, if not positively spoilt, only child in the green, idyllic comfort of Trilipush Hall in Kent, England. Educated at home by tutors, he displayed at a precocious age a staggering aptitude for language and an uncanny absorption in ancient Egypt. By the age of ten, he had mastered the three written forms of ancient Egyptian, and had begun translating ancient documents into English. By twelve, he had recalculated the accepted dates of the Egyptian dynasties and kingly reigns, pinpointing with greater accuracy than any acknowledged scholar the gaps in modern Egyptological understanding. Admired by his peers, remarked upon by his elders, he went early up to Balliol, Oxford, where he was widely viewed as Egyptology's greatest hope, along with his dear friend, Hugo St. John Marlowe. At Oxford, the two students worked under the guidance of the late Professor Clement Wexler, participating in his efforts to prove or disprove definitively the existence of the then-apocryphal XIIIth-Dynasty king and erotic poet Atum-hadu. His master's work complete, Trilipush's doctoral studies were cut short by the Great War, during which both he and Marlowe were stationed in Egypt as officers in counterintelligence. There, under enemy fire, the two explorers managed to unearth Fragment C of Atum-hadu's *Admonitions* from a cliffside path near Deir el Bahari, taking a giant's step towards proving that king's existence and identity as the poet of the previously translated Fragments A and B. Shortly after this discovery, Trilipush was sent along to advise Australian forces invading Gallipoli, in which combat he was wounded and for some time missing and believed dead. Entirely alone, he trekked back to Egypt, arriving after the Armistice, only to learn that his great friend Marlowe had been killed while on expedition in an unsecured part of the Egyptian desert. After demobilisation, Trilipush secured Fragment C, bringing it to the United States of America, where he launched a brilliant academic career. He produced the definitive, if controversial, translation and analysis of all three Atum-haduan fragments, published under the title *Desire and Deceit in Ancient Egypt* (Collins Amorous Literature, 1920). The extraordinary sales of this short masterwork confirmed Trilipush's unique

position as both an impeccable scholar and a popular interpreter of
Egyptian studies.

His full professorship and subsequent quick ascension to Chair of
the Egyptology Department at Harvard University followed his discovery on his thirtieth birthday, 24 November, 1922, of the tomb of
Atum-hadu himself, and the publication of the gripping but academi-
cally flawless work you now hold in your perspiring hands. The discovery of Atum-hadu's tomb was quickly hailed as unprecedented, the
most financially and scientifically rewarding discovery in the history of
Egyptian excavation.

Professor Trilipush was knighted in 1923 and has been honoured by
governments and universities throughout the civilised world.

He is married to the former Margaret Finneran of Boston, Massa-
chusetts, USA, the fantastically wealthy department store heiress.

Wednesday, 11 October, 1922

Journal: Rise late. Luncheon in town. Refresh my warm memories
of splendid Cairo. Explore markets. Purchase maps of Cairo, Luxor,
Theban Valley. Purchase extra dominoes. Incredible fruit stands, the
round fruit stacked in perfect multi-coloured rows like a giant's abacus.
Fresh yellow dates. Nearly black plums whose skins resemble maps of
the night sky, vague clouds and twinkling stars. Discover a shop selling
gramophone styluses which the bizarre bazaar-man claimed would fit
my Victrola 50 suitcase model, but which, in fact, upon my return to
the hotel, did nothing but ruin the first few seconds of "You're a Dream
(and If I Wake I'll Cry)." Return to my writing; continue preparing
documentation and plans, edit yesterday's work.

A Letter to the Reader: The book you now hold is unlike any in
the history of Egyptology, for in order to provide a context for the discovery our team has made, this volume offers both an historical introduction to the reign of King Atum-hadu as well as the actual journal I
kept throughout the expedition, daily—almost hourly—from my arrival

in Cairo until we had cleared, cleaned, and catalogued each breath-stealing treasure from Atum-hadu's tomb.

Reader, as I sit today, at the humming conclusion of this adventure, with my dear friend and colleague, the explorer Howard Carter, both of us guests in the home of our dear friend, Pierre Lacau, the elegant Director-General of the Egyptian Antiquities Service, some three miles from the Hotel of the Sphinx, where I began my journey in October, three months ago, I gaze out on the evening Nile and invite you to join me on the magnificent adventure of a lifetime, 3500 years in the making.

Professor Ralph M. Trilipush
18 January, 1923
Residence of the Director-General of the Antiquities Service
Cairo, Egypt

[RMT—Verify 24 November and 18 January before typesetting.]

Journal: 11 October, and I have just finished composing certain necessary background elements of this work, to be assembled in the proper order later. I can now begin my log from the beginning, welcoming you, Reader, to Egypt.

I reached Cairo yesterday, my first visit to this wondrous city since 1918. I came by rail from Alexandria, after disembarking from the *Cristoforo Colombo,* which vessel bore me here (after a train ride from Boston) from New York, via London and Malta, where I passed a very relaxing week in preparation for my coming work. I have now established my temporary headquarters here in the gold-and-pink Pharaoh Suite of Cairo's veined-marble Hotel of the Sphinx. While I have no taste for luxury, I do need a certain amount of space to perform the myriad tasks I have at hand, and the millions more to come, and the consortium of Boston's wisest and wealthiest Egyptological experts and collectors who are financing this expedition would not wish to have its leader worn down—before he had even moved south to the site—by residence in substandard lodging.

For the extent of an archaeologist's tasks sometimes surprises the layman. By way of example, I shall, when at the site, be the Director of a vast enterprise, commanding an army of workmen, responsible for their salaries, behaviour, honesty, efficiency, and well-being. I shall be measuring, diagramming, cataloguing, and often preserving in some haste several hundred objects, ranging in size from a jewelled earring to the exquisitely carved and painted walls of a massive sepulchre. I shall be negotiating with bureaux of the Egyptian Government, which, for its own protection, is still overseen whenever necessary by the guiding wisdom and financial probity of the French and English Governments. I shall simultaneously be composing a scholarly work, detailing events three and a half millennia old, and likely translating newly found erotic, political, and acerbically witty texts written by a genius in a language that has not been in common use for well over two thousand years. And I shall be preparing detailed reports back to the wise Partnership that is financing all of this frenzied toil. Thus, if I have begun my trip in some style, it is dictated by scientific necessity.

That said, for all its vaunted luxury, the Hotel of the Sphinx displays Egypt's creeping decadence. It is a tourist hotel (in a land that to me has always been an explorer's frontier or a soldier's outpost), and it represents the modern Egyptian's apparently insuperable innate urge to barter his noble patrimony for a shilling. The hotel's emblem—stitched to every conceivable surface—sports a nonsensical group of vulture, sphinx, and cobra, surmounting a motto—an extract of hieroglyphs which warn (to whom I cannot imagine, since who amongst the hotel's guests could be expected to read hieroglyphs?) HORUS CONSUMES THE HEARTS OF THE WICKED.

Horus, ancient Egypt's falcon-headed sky-god embodied by every Egyptian king, would perhaps hesitate to endorse this hotel, and yet, even here amidst the faux-Pharaonic trappings of a fanciful antiquity, through the open patio windows, from out over the Nile, the smell and feel of the real Egypt—*my* Egypt—waft in, and all the modern *luxe* of the suite curls and crumbles under the hot exhalation of the kingdom as it was, sighing to me from across millennia. Atum-hadu, in his power and his glory, summons me even here, as I sip (without the worry one felt, even in Finneran's private barroom, about the American liquor-lawmen) lemonade and gin from cut crystal on the balcony overlooking my Nile, and revolving seventy-eight times per minute on the gorgeous, colossal cabinet-model Victrola XVII I have installed next to the balcony door, is "He's a Fella Who Gets His Way (and Who Can Blame Him?)."

In this respite from my labours, I caress with undiluted joy the recollection of my recent send-off from Boston, though it seems ages ago, a party whose guests included the expedition's financial backers and their ladies, celebrating both our approaching good fortune in Egypt and my engagement to the daughter of the house. The images coalesce into clear memory: crisp evening attire and the new light gowns, glowing paper lanterns, and a Negro jazz orchestra stationed in the garden courtyard, its music drifting in and out of the open doors and windows of Chester Crawford Finneran's Commonwealth Avenue mansion in the unseasonable heat of early September:

> *Canis and man is*
> *A grand combination.*
> *Gee, my dog is swell!*

The already dense Egyptian décor in the Finneran home proliferated for the party: CCF had installed at the head of the ballroom two golden thrones on a faux-brick dais. As the climax of the evening's events, he walked Margaret and me up the three steps to our seats before topping us with outrageous (and structurally inaccurate) Pharaonic crowns, then scowled at the bandleader, told him to "give the jungle noise a rest," and lifted his goblet, bringing an alcoholic tear to an eye or two with the words "Now, desert sands aside, there's no treasure in this whole wide world means a thing to me next to that little girl up there on the throne where she belongs." A flurry of "aww" and "ohhh" and "CC's so sweet" fluttered in the air before the grinning old bear batted his paws at the noise and it retreated. "But that don't mean you're comin' back empty-handed, Pushy!" Vast amusement. "No, folks, folks, serious now, what dad wouldn't just leap at the chance to pick up a son-in-law like this one, hey? English gentleman, well-educated, explorer. Honestly, Margaret and me are of one brain on this: we both feel like the luckiest gal in the world! Now then, you go get our gold, Pushy, my boy, and if you come back with piles of it, ingots and jewels and crowns, well"—wily squint through winding coils of cigar smoke— "that'll just about pay Margaret's dowry!" His splendid oratory extorted its just homage from the gathered party, while my fiancée and I waved from under our tipping toppers, and I squeezed Margaret's hand to keep her awake, as the excitement had not surprisingly exhausted her in her fragile health. She smiled through heavy lids and murmured, "This is really swell, isn't it, love? All this fiesta. I could do with a siesta." Even in her fatigue, she was celestial, grateful to her father and me. The crowd cheered our nuptials and the success of my mission, perhaps not precisely in that order, as CCF had muscled several of the party into becoming partners in Hand-of-Atum Explorations, of which he is President and I am a shareholding Technical Consultant. The band started up again with a peculiar fox-trot, presumably appropriate to Egyptian exploration and an age-old piece of zoological trivia:

> *If you prefer not to hump on just one bump*
> *Then you'd best be wary of the dromedary.*
> *But if you'd like to jump and scrump and pump*
> *Between two big lumps —*

"Not so fast, boys," interrupts CCF, and the music stumbles to silence, one instrument at a time, a sizzling cymbal the last to get the message, "because we've got a little surprise," and CCF calls up Kendall and Hilly Mitchell, Beacon Hill jollies I had met at an investors' meeting and then again when, at CCF's request, I had gone for some very discreet cocktails with Kendall at his exceedingly discreet club, where he interviewed me about my background and Egypt with alarming tenacity and secrecy, an interrogation I simply could not understand until this very moment, when Hilly laughingly tossed her scarcely sheathed hips and bumped the Negro from the piano bench, and Kendall loosened his tie and struck a *boulevardier* pose. While Margaret struggled to prop her heavy eyelids, I listened to our musical tribute, composed by these two party personalities, delirious with cash and inherited real estate, undeterrable donors of personalised song lyrics for gala events on Beacon Hill and in Back Bay. I transcribe here from the drink-ringed dedication copy of the lyrics I was subsequently presented ("To Ralphie! Here's hopin' ya dig up a 'mummy' fer yer new 'daddy'! Lotsa good good luck, from your Yank pals H & K Mitchell!"). Kendall warbled while Hilly jangled up and down the keyboard with clumsy fists:

Pushed early down from Oxford,
With his trousers 'round his ankles,
Came young R. M. Trilipush
And he'll admit the mem'ry rankles.

Well, off he went to Egypt
Where he was meant to fight the Kaiser,
But after several years at war
He left the Kaiser none the wiser.

Instead he sweated in the Orient
Upon his knees and hands.
(Now, try not to be prurient,
I mean that he was digging in the sands!)

He dug and dug with another limey
Until, as Boche guns assailed them,
Those two Brits, they shouted "Blimey!"
For their spades had sure not failed them.

["Unlike ours!" I recall CCF bellowing at this point, referring to, I believe, some waiters who were slow in fetching him another drink. "Oh, Daddy, really," my Margaret gently chided him, her knees pulled up under her chin.]

What they found that day
All of us surely know
It keeps our wives awake at night
And makes our (ahem!) imaginations grow.

They found terrific hieroglyphics,
The writings of some Pharaoh,
Which Pushy published in plain English,
And thrilled the market to its marrow.

[At his club, I had corrected Mitchell several times, explaining with increasing frustration that *hieroglyphic* was an adjective and *hieroglyph* the noun, and that his use of the term *Pharaoh* for an Egyptian king prior to the XVIIIth or XIXth Dynasty was thoroughly anachronistic and, frankly, grated on my ear. The XIIIth-Dynasty Atum-hadu would have been referred to as "King" not by the Hebraicised metonymical device *per-o.* I repeated this easily a dozen times as silver shaker after silver shaker came to the table, filled (the waiter loudly announced each time, for the benefit of whom I cannot say) with "your iced tea, Mr. Mitchell!" That said, his use of *hieroglyphic* when he meant to say *hieroglyph* I now grudgingly acknowledge as a possible debt to rhyming.]

Well, old R. M. Trilipush made some money and his name,
And found across the pond a place to build his worldly fame.
Harvard gave him fresh-faced youths to teach, and then he met a gal,
And now the rest of us know all too well he's CCF's best pal!

So back to the Nile our Pushy goes with Margaret's heart in tow
As well as Chester's cash,

[music stops, Kendall shouts the words]

"And mine, too! And mine, too!"

"And mine, too! And mine, too!"

[pointing to guests who, like him, had invested in Hand-of-Atum]

For he sure came to implore us,
And for an hour or so did bore us,
But now, by Isis, Ra, and Horus,
Ol' Pushy will reward us!

[I should discuss the word *implore* for, if it was not used simply to make the Mitchells' task of rhyming more manageable, it merits clarification. To say the least. I will come back to this point, as to just who was imploring whom.]

By Isis, Ra, and Horus,
Ol' Pushy will reward us!

The crowd soon mastered this couplet and chanted it for some exhilarating minutes while, to my infinitely deeper pleasure, Margaret glowed and glittered under the full moon splashing through the ballroom's glass ceiling, the silver light licking her blue and sparkling eyelids (a Cleopatran effect she and Inge had devised for the evening), and whether she had fallen asleep or was merely savouring the entertainment behind closed eyes, her beauty was then, as always, overwhelming. I felt at that instant as if I had achieved everything I ever dreamt of. A paradox, to be sure, as I had not yet set off on this expedition. I cradled her delicate, pliant hand in mine, each of her long, slender fingers articulated into the graceful arch of riverside narcissi, and she was then, in her drowsy languor, as always, the personification of so many ancient drawings, lounging beauties carved in calcite and lime to line the halls of palaces, the long-fingered serving girls and goddesses painted on tomb walls to beckon, to arouse, to accompany the homesick dead into the next world.

Having carried my exhausted beauty upstairs and kissed her off to slumber, pulling her bedclothes up to her carved ivory chin, I re-descended and danced with Inge and the Partners' wives, some of whom found the close contact of a bona-fide Egyptian explorer rather too heady a draught for their natural Boston modesty, and more than once I felt the firm, caressing need to remind the ladies of the proper hand positions for certain popular dances.

After midnight, the party spilled out of Finneran's ballroom and across Arlington Street. (An image to cherish forever: my future father-in-law, self-described "gentle as a lamb," kicking with grunts of exertion and boyish joy the prone figure of a man who had, as the party crossed into the Public Garden, attempted to grab Finneran's pocket watch on the run. The regretful robber called out for help from the police. "Here we are, son, not to worry," immediately cried four members of the Boston constabulary whom Finneran had at the party to protect himself from any liquor-control inspection. And with a quiet "Thank you, offi-cers," Finneran retreated and allowed the bobbies to deliver their more professional beating to the cutpurse, interrupting them just once, in order to withdraw from his whimpering assailant's pocket enough money to cover "the polishing of my blood-spattered boots, you hooligan.")

CCF had had tents and roasting spits brought out to the Public Garden; the visible aromas of roast suckling pig rose towards the slen-der blue-grey clouds, and guests circled the waitresses in their skimpy Egyptian servant-girl costumes, grabbing—depending on their ruling appetite—at the waitresses' trays or their buttocks, while other, alco-holically calmer revellers wandered down to the duck pond to com-mandeer the public pedal boats shaped as gigantic swans, or—in rolled shirtsleeves and sheer slip dresses—waded into the cool water, falling into each other's slick, goose-pimpled arms.

I stood aside, content in my natural role as an observant explorer, released, for the moment, from my duties as guest of honour, and I was happy, so very happy, when from my left, in the shadow between low-drooping willows that swayed like giant, green jellyfish, I heard my

name gruffly called. Under a dome of willow branches, as fully enclosed as if we were circus dwarves waiting for a cue to emerge from
under the bearded lady's close, musty hoopskirt, I found myself pleas-
antly hypnotised by the perfect, pulsing orange circle of Finneran's
cigar end, illuminating at its brightest a few filaments of blue smoke
(and presumably my own face), but nothing else. "Wanted to wish you
good luck," said my invisible patron, and the orange circle faded to a
coiled spring of dully glowing grey. "We've all taken our measure of
you. Don't let us down." Orange circle swells and recedes, swells and
recedes. "I never will, CC." "I'll always do what's best for my Margaret,
you know, father and mother both to that little girl." "Of course, CC, of
course." "Happy to have you in the family." "Many thanks." "She
picked you and I approved. I picked you and she approved. Doesn't
matter which, you know." "Of course, CC." Orange circle glows bright
and fades. "Don't know about you English gentry, but family in our
country's a serious issue." "Of course, CC." Orange circle. Pause.
"Keep that in mind is all." "Of course, CC." "People counting on you,
Ralph. Lot of people. Lot riding on you. Lot of trust in you." All of
which was CCF's shy preamble to presenting me with this large
wooden humidor inlaid with swirling black ornamentation and filled
with cigars, each chosen specially by Boston's finest tobacconist and
banded with the black label with silver monogram: *CCF.* And the
orange circle of his cigar end fades and grows, fades and grows . . .

. . . just as this morning, this dawn of 12 October, an orange light is
now appearing over the Nile's eastern bank. I have spent the night
working here on my balcony, sustained by gin-lemonades and sweet
mint tea in glass tumblers painted gold, tracing my finger over the inlaid ebony swirls of my humidor, now containing a set of fine brushes
and inks to copy the wall illustrations I hope to find in Atum-hadu's
tomb. (I do not smoke cigars, but they should make fine *baksheesh,* and
the box is lovely.) I sit on the still-warm balcony, watch my sun rise,
and examine the lump of sugar half-dissolved in my tea, for all the
world like the crumbling foundation stone of a temple ruin.

I shall be, in some six weeks, thirty years old, an age I have long hoped to celebrate in this, the country of my dreams, achieving, by that milestone age, the necessary unparalleled victory to justify thirty years of life. And, as I consider the party for my departure from Boston, as I consider the king who has rested undiscovered some 3500 years, I could almost wish that this moment—here on the fast-brightening balcony of my Cairo hotel—might never end.

I mean something more by this than merely blurting out that I do not wish to grow older, that I would prefer to be excused from blundering into corpulent middle age and bleary post-prime. I mean, rather, that here, in the early summer of one's life, with preparatory glory still thrumming behind one and seismic triumph perhaps mere weeks ahead, one desires to hear the soprano of this one particular mosquito singing in one's ear *forever,* to see these precise midges waver forever in their nervous indecision, hypnotised by the very sun which will soon scorch them, to feel the pinprick heat of this glass of mint tea, warming each crevice of three fingertips forever, to see that sugar's disintegration pause *forever.* One's blood roars with the desire that somehow this instant of possibility and potential be seized and held, vibrating and glowing orange in one's softly closed fist. That one might stroke and examine this captured moment, feel its velvety tread in one's palm, that I might remain quivering on the brink rather than tumbling headlong into the future, until I have had my fill of the present. Or, think of it like this, Reader: one climbs a high, steep hill. Then, after years and years of climbing, one sees the crest within reach and one realises that, upon achieving that crest, only two possibilities remain: up and over, to begin an accelerating descent, or . . . to continue moving in the *same* direction one has grown accustomed to and fond of, to *continue* the way one has come, up and up, to ignore the fallible earth that ceases to rise, but to rise oneself nevertheless.

And if you should sit up for a moment from your soft easy chair and wonder, Why? Why Egypt? Why the desire to rummage in the dust? I can only suggest that the kings of Egypt kept climbing. They mastered those frilly, fleeting moments, imprisoned them in soft cages. In their wrapped corpses with their organs bottled in canopic jars, and in their picture-alphabet and in their beast-headed gods, the best Egyptians lived with the certainty that they were owed eternity, that they lived and would live forever in a present of their own choosing, unhaunted by the past, unthreatened by the future, luxuriously entertained in a present they could extend as long as they wished, releasing these savoury moments on their own terms, not at the imperious demand of mere days, nights, suns, moons.

Margaret, may I share with you a darker memory of my shining youth? It is not the sort you prefer, but it makes a point. As a boy, I recall a village vicar berating me (*r* optional) for my obsessive interest in the Egyptians. (This would, of course, happen only when my father was abroad on expedition and unable to protect me from the vile clergyman, and I would wander away from the Hall, roam into the village near our estate. Where the vicar did not realise who I was, so far from my family grounds.) At any rate, time after time, he would appear unannounced. I was easy to surprise, as from a very early age I was generally bent over my labours, wonderfully ignorant of all that happened around me. And he would snatch my work from me, crumple up hard-won hieroglyphs. He would, with a noisy, liquorish menace, uncork the usual cant: "Boy, how can you think it wise to truck with this culture of death?" Even at ten I knew the correct answer to that cataclysmic catechism: "Right you are, Father. Much better to stick with the life-embracing imagery of a cult that worships a bleeding corpse nailed to bits of wood." Of course, I had to be in the mood for a thrashing, or worse, if I chose that path.

But the point, which I understood even at that age: Egypt was not—I must repeat for Readers who still do not know it—a culture of death, for all the mummies and bottled lungs, the jackal-men and cobra-queens. The Egyptians were the inventors of immortality, the first men who saw they could live forever.

Atum-hadu wrote:

The gods and I walk slowly arm in arm
And sometimes we do not walk at all,
But sit upon a rock and watch the charm
Of two goats f——ing behind a peasant's wall.

— (Quatrain 13, Fragment C only, from *Desire*
and Deceit in Ancient Egypt by Ralph M. Trilipush,
Collins Amorous Literature, 1920)

Sunset on the Bayview Nursing Home
Sydney, Australia
December 6, 1954

Mr. Macy,

In my experience of human behaviour (and I've seen all there is to see, it's fair to say), I've concluded there aren't but five motivations for a man to do anything. They're hardly mysterious, you know: money, hunger, lust, power, survival. That's all there is. You hear in the courtrooms and in the cinema all sorts of fancy-dress explanations why someone becomes Prime Minister or kills his neighbours. But if you listen hard, it's all just the same five balls, juggled up in the air, decorated with distracting words. No one ever did a damn thing but for one of those five.

Which brings us to the tale of Paul Caldwell and Catherine Barry, Bolshevik and former librarian, a tale of a power-hungry traitor, a manipulative woman playing on the emotions of a vulnerable young man, leading the weak into corruption. The story of Paul's tragic death in Egypt begins right here, when he's eight or nine years old in Sydney, pushed towards his doom by Catherine Barry, cold, dangerous, terribly beautiful.

I am surrounded by my reconstructions of Miss Barry's words (July 10th, 1922), a typically self-justifying letter from her, an interview I did with her brother (July 11th, 1922), and the summary I wrote for my final report back to London. I also have the letter from Ronald Barry (the brother), engaging me to find any evidence of Paul Caldwell's survival and, if he was alive, to procure his address discreetly. Ronald, I'm sure, meant to kill Caldwell. It obviously never came to that, and it's fair to point out no one'd ever hired me to *protect* Paul Caldwell.

So my memory's feeling well-primed, no matter the shouting coming from some of my housemates, feebly battling for control of a partial set of torn playing cards. When you consider that I took notes, expanded them into full speeches when I got home, rewrote them again for my report to London, and am now fleshing them out further for you here, our readers should get a convincing presentation, but by all means you should add whatever you feel they still need.

Here we are then. Paul's eight or nine or ten. This is before winning the heart of Mrs. Hoyt at age nineteen, before snake acts in the circus, before lightening pockets in the market. This is a little boy going to the state school. He's a quiet, sullen little fellow, no surprise. He absorbs his share of beatings from Eulalie and the men she keeps. But he has no feeling at all for his fellow victims, his half siblings, because when Eulalie's not whacking him about, she's holding him on her lap and telling him that those other filthy kids aren't on his level, since he's the son of the great gentleman Barnabas Davies, lost at sea, drowned on his way back to Australia to take Eulalie and Paul to London. "Paul's mother was so blinded by her respect for the rich, there she was feeding notions of class superiority to the boy, even in the midst of their brutal poverty and oppression," said one of the Barrys, I didn't note which. They were both virulent Reds, you see, Macy, not to shock you, but we have them down under, too. A dark and infectious philosophy the Bolshie Barrys imbibed, and they cherished it, even after it sunk them.

Paul was—except for one quirk—nothing special at school, according to Ronald Barry, his schoolmaster. He kept quiet. Filthy, of course, like most of the very poorest kids, but disciplined enough to sit still and do as he was told. "Mostly we were just trying to move the poor bastards along and keep them out of trouble," said Ronald. "Not permitted to educate them at all, really. Just oppression by other means, pretending to teach them something, to dull them enough to accept the conditions the owning class had in mind for them."

Then one day they do a little lesson on Egypt. Egypt's a place in the desert, very old and pointy buildings, and the pagans in the old days, they didn't know about Our Lord yet, so when their kings died, they wrapped them up in bedsheets and said they lived forever. "I probably added something along the lines of 'The pyramids were built by working folk, forced to labour for their brutal kings,' " says Red Ron. And then they pass around a little picture book, and then on to the day's arithmetic.

Well, end of the day comes and the ragamuffins head out the door, and Ronald Barry is tidying up, and he can't find the picture book about Egypt, too bad, since he'd borrowed it from his sister at the public library. Clearly, one of the scoundrels had swiped it, and next morning, Ronald's thinking about how to conduct his investigations when little Paul Caldwell comes in early. The boy looks worse than usual, but he hands back the missing book. Turns out he hadn't gone home the night before, had stayed out all night long just looking at this book, actually slept outdoors. He doesn't say just what made it such a ripping read, doesn't say much at all, "doesn't even apologise, the little thief," says Mr. No-Private-Property. Then the boy asks, under his breath, might there be other books like this one?

"Mr. Ferrell, there are few moments in my career when I felt real pride in what I was doing. But I remember clearly how I felt that moment. This little child wanted to learn. I forgot at once about the theft: this one was going to be one we could save. Of course, if I knew then what I know now, I would have throttled the viper when I could still get my hands round his neck."

That afternoon, Ronald Barry takes his prized pupil to one of the smaller branches of the public library. And which librarian greets him that day but Catherine Barry, the teacher's lovely sister. "Sis, here's a young fellow with real promise who wants to learn how to get more books about ancient Egypt, of all things." "Hello, Paul Caldwell," Miss Barry says sweetly, a little twinkle in her eye saying, "Don't take me too seriously, I'm a good chum if you want one," all misleading kindness and appropriately *red* curly hair and a sweet face. (Even by '22, even after what she'd been through, I must confess she was a lovely thing. Treacherous, appearances.) The boy has no social graces, can barely speak, looks at the ground, has probably never been in a building as clean and official as our little library, has probably never been spoken to as kindly by anyone, has probably never *seen* anyone as beautiful and apparently friendly as Miss Barry. All because he'd been taken by something in a picture book.

"Well, Mr. Ferrell, we decided to take the little fellow under our wing," Catherine Barry told me with flirtatious pride. "Let's see about making you a member of our library," says the Red agent to the little boy. That first day, Miss Barry showed him all around, and though he barely spoke, she was encouraged to see his eyes widen at the sight of all the books, the neat tables, the lamps and chairs. "This is all yours to use as a citizen, the equal to any rich man," I can hear her saying to the tiny scholar.

"He was heartbreaking," she told me, and I wrote that down and underlined it, noting, "Why no children of her own?" "This boy had been betrayed by everyone—family, state, church. It was all I could do to get the poor fellow to speak to me, and no surprise. Even then, the only thing he would really talk about was Egypt. Something about that book Ronnie had shown him just tickled him. Well, first things first: I found him a different one, *A Boy's Own Book of Egypt*, I re-member the cover. He immediately took one of the chairs in the corner and did not look up again until I came over to tell him the library was closing, but he could come back tomorrow after school, and read some more, if he liked. 'Is no one waiting for you at home, then?' I asked. Poor creature. You could see that home held no meaning for him, even at that tender age.

"He did not want to go home, or say why not. So I asked him, 'Would you eat a piece of kidney pie, then?' and the poor little fellow practically jumped out of his skin." I can imagine that boy, Macy, with her standing behind him, gently placing her hands on his shoulders, looking over his reading, smelling so nice, all false promise. "Mr. Ferrell, it was a class crime, a fine young boy, starved by dev-ilish church and corrupted state. I showed him how to shelve the book, and then I led him back to the office. He was not such a fool as to turn down food, proba-bly more than he saw in a week, more than he could steal in days. Oh, yes, have no illusions, he was already stealing at that age. The rich need thieves, Mr. Ferrell, and they are careful to breed them young. 'It's customary to thank someone,' I told him. He managed to mutter a 'thank you, ma'am,' as he stuffed his face.

"Ronnie and I discussed it next day, and we were of one mind. As charitable people, we would do what we could for this little one God had sent our way. As political people, we owed it to him and to the future to prove that the working class had as much brain and worth as the moneyed. And as educators, well, there could be no question: this one wanted learning as much as he wanted food. We would feed him, Ronnie and I, and split the expense."

(Ronald's words on the matter: "Cassie decided, Cassie dictated. The Pyg-malion Fallacy, if you ask me, but she didn't. Party warns against this.")

Ask me, Paul Caldwell didn't have a chance to escape her lures, Macy. He met Catherine Barry when she was probably twenty-six, and he was a little boy. I met her in 1922, and even at forty-five or so, she was a powerful charmer, smelled nice, smiled sweet. I was a man of the world, had my choice of lady friends, you know, and I knew just how her sort used its wiles for nefarious purposes, but even I found her something potent to sit near, nearly found myself begging her to dis-cuss my questions with me over a supper. Her smile—of course, I could resist it, but a little boy? No hope. It's a very certain smile, the smile of someone who thinks they're so much smarter than you that they think they can see and steer your very thoughts. They toy with you, make you jump to amuse them. Women have it. Reds have it. Red women are the worst.

" 'Home doesn't appeal? Is that why you sit here at all hours reading about pyramids?' I asked him a few days later when he was back, still shy. He had run up to me and asked for the same book without looking me in the eye, as if he'd never met me. I gave him the book, and after he read, I fed him again. And I offered to see him home, it was late, but he said no, and was off.

"After three or four weeks he had come a dozen times and read nearly everything we had on ancient Egypt, which was hardly so very much. Each time he would read until closing, and then I would feed him, and each time he refused to be walked home. He was growing friendlier, but not quickly. Whatever had been done to him was enough to keep him suspicious of people for some time. I asked Ronald to find his address from the school, and I went round to see his home myself. Oh, you've been there recently, Mr. Ferrell? I wonder if it's much changed. When I saw it, it was the scene of a crime, a rape of the worker by the capitalist, and nothing less. That humans were treated like this, and especially a little boy of his quality and promise. Well, the closest I ever come to forgiving him is when I think of how he was raised. Experiences like that make you either very strong or very weak, and in Paul's case, it weakened his moral fibre beyond anything that could be done to repair it. I believe everyone can improve themselves, but the last I heard of him, he was still a selfish sentimentalist.

"He looked up and saw me standing in the doorway of his dreadful home, and I am certain my face revealed what I thought of the scene. I think it was the first time he ever looked me in the eye. Up jumped the little boy, ignoring the chaos and noise around him, and he took my hand. 'Why did you come here?' he asked, pulling me out the door and walking me as fast as he could up the street, while his family stuck their heads out to gawk. 'So I could see if you were all right,' I said, 'because I worry about people I am fond of.' 'I'm fine,' he said, 'but you shouldn't come anymore. That's not my family, not my real family.' He started to talk more than he had the whole time I had known him. 'My father was lost at sea, and *that* woman, she's not my real mother.' I did not know if this was true, but I doubted it.

"Once he asked why Ronnie was not married, and then, very quietly, so I thought my heart would burst, he asked me 'as his sister' if perhaps Ronnie ever wanted a son."

The next day, Macy, I asked Ronald Barry if he recalled Paul Caldwell wanting to be his son. "Didn't last long. By the time he was thirteen or so, he was raging at everything and everyone except Cassie and Egypt. I had done something to offend him. I didn't realise it at the time, but it was only this: I was telling him that I had once wanted to be a University professor, but of course that lofty task was reserved for toffs. I was telling him that brains aren't counted, just your family, and the rich take care of each other. Paul looks up from his reading—a book on Egypt, of course—and he says, 'Your enemies block your advancement? Why don't you slay them?' I thought he was joking. Mr. Ferrell, I tell you this as a fact: he was not joking. That was how Cassie's pet was developing. I should have throttled him right there, saved us all the subsequent trouble. He says to me, 'If you're not strong enough to defeat your enemies, what are you?' A thirteen-year-old boy, Ferrell."

Miss Barry now: "When he read everything we had on Egypt, I tried to lead him into other areas, even other areas of archaeology or history, or just good storybooks, and he would try them, like a little boy trying his vegetables, then he would have no more of it. But the day he learnt I could *order* books for him, nearly anything in the world, you should have seen his face. He asked for titles he had seen in the bibliographies or notes of other Egypt books.

"He was amusing, the little researcher at eleven, twelve, thirteen. He would come into the library, breathing very hard, and I knew he had run all the way from the school building. I used to tease him: 'And what brings you into our humble establishment today, Mr. Caldwell? Something in particular you'd like to read? Perhaps some stories about knights? I have a lovely *Ivanhoe*. No? Maybe a history of Australia's brave pioneers, those raping monsters? How about a guide to sheep and the farming thereof?' I would just talk on and on to see his little face contort itself up, trying to remember what I had taught him about politeness. Finally, he would burst out, 'Please, Miss Barry. Has it come? Has it?' 'And what would that be, Mr. Caldwell? We'll need to comport ourselves like a gentleman in this world, mind our manners.' 'Please, Miss Barry, I am sorry to interrupt you, but I am hoping that *Cults of Ra* by Professors Knutson and Anderson has arrived.' Or some other work, Champollion's work on translating the Rosetta stone. The requests he came up with! The orders I made for him! The time I spent justifying to the Head Librarian these obscure volumes as being part of the local population's bottomless appetite for Egypt." She told me to wait a moment, she went to a drawer next to her bed and came back with a piece of paper: "I used to keep a list," she went on. "Listen: Pásint's work on the judicial records of the necropolis courts. The ex–circus performer Belzoni's exploits with the British consul Henry Salt. Mattison on the use of music in burial rites. Oskar Denninger's pamphlet, *The Chemistry and Function of Feline Mummification in the Shrine to Bastet*. Whatever the latest strange title, he would plead, 'Did it come, Miss Barry? Did it?' 'Well, I certainly do not know offhand,' I would say, biting my lips. 'I should have to examine the New Arrivals department and then the pile from the post, could take me quite a bit of time. I am terribly busy, you know.' 'Please, Miss Barry,' nearly sobbing, he was. 'Well, you have a seat at that table in the corner and I shall go have a look.' 'Thank you, ma'am.' And when he turned the corner to go to that table, he would find the book he had so eagerly awaited already out and ready for him, in a circle of lamplight, next to a pencil and paper, a chair pulled out with a couple of cushions to help him sit high enough, and a plate of digestives. I loved that little boy."

"Did you?"

"Like an aunt, Mr. Ferrell. Or a comrade. I hope that is clear."

"Why Egypt, do you suppose, Miss Barry?"

"I asked myself often, and I asked him often. He would not or could not say. Paul once taught me that in ancient Egypt commoners could become pharaohs in some cases, so that probably appealed to him more than the world we live in, where the king is far off in London and little Paul had no more chance of ruling anyone than you or I. I might add that ancient Egypt was as far as you could get from his wretched life. When he was about eight or nine, not long before he met us, he came home with a stray dog. Bursting with excitement, he shows the dog to his mother, who dithers about expense, hardly enough money to feed the children, how will they feed a mongrel, and so on. Well, the man who was living there at the time took the matter in hand. He congratulated Paul on his usefulness, and he dragged the dog into the courtyard and killed it, and then made her cook it for his starving brood. In Australia. In the twentieth century. And do you wonder that he rarely went home, that he denied those people were his father and mother, and that he wished he were an ancient Egyptian? The day he told me that story, years after the event, he was in my office, sobbing like the little boy he had been when it happened. That was also the time he tried to kiss me. But I am getting ahead of myself.

"When he was fourteen or so, I gave him a job, his first honest employment, quite probably his last. A small salary to tidy up, stack books, order new titles. I would still try to interest him in things other than Egypt, but it was fruitless, so I decided to focus on his political awareness, and leave it at that. He would have two dimensions at least: Egypt and class consciousness. His concentration was remarkable. He was teaching himself to write hieroglyphics, simply by studying books, having me order new ones as they were published. Are you understanding me, Mr. Ferrell, getting every word? At fifteen this boy could write hieroglyphics. But for studying dialectical materialism, which I tried to introduce slowly, relating it to the obvious circumstances of his life, he was hopeless. I told him to look at his home and see it for what it was: a crime committed against him by people who should be made to pay for it. He looked at me blankly. 'Capitalists and monarchists.' Nothing. 'The institutional Church.' He just asked for more paper to practise tracing that silly alphabet."

Ronald Barry recalls Paul at school: "This is, let's see, when he's about thirteen. Apparently he'd learnt something about assertive political tactics from Cassie, because he writes an anonymous letter to the headmaster, denouncing one of the teachers as criminally ignorant, an insult to the proletariat of Australia, a social parasite, a capitalist corrupter of youth. Of course, the letter hardly keeps its anonymity when he lists the teacher's six specific lapses, all of which are confusions of Egypt's Middle and New Kingdoms. He was flogged to within an inch of his life."

Catherine: "His parish priest, God alone knows what the man thought he was doing for his parishioners. Nothing, to be brief. But he certainly scared Paul terribly. This Father Rowley somehow finds out about Paul and the library and Egypt. And only now does he take an interest in the family. One less of his flock taken by drink or sin, you would think, rather a success, this studious boy? No: he informs Paul's mother that her son is learning about Satan and paganism at the library, and must be kept away from these books and this place. I can scarcely believe she knew what the man meant, or even which snivelling, unhealthy son was which. But in front of the priest, she duly forbids Paul to mess around any more with books or libraries. He was fourteen, I think, when he came that very day to me with a bag of his belongings, told me the story about the priest and the one about the dog, wept like a child. I comforted him. He was a boy and I pitied him. But then he was trying to embrace me, as a man embraces a woman.

"I had a difficult task, Mr. Ferrell, and you should judge me fairly. I was shocked, of course. Things had been terribly misunderstood in the heart of a very confused, very lonely boy. He offered up words of love and devotion, most of which were last used for wooing in ancient Egypt. Picture a young man trying to win the heart of a woman a dozen years his senior by telling her that her neck is like a goose's. He told me his loins would burst, that I was his horned sundisk, his turquoise cow, that the colours of my flesh were stolen from Horus and painted by I-can't-remember-which-one. I know, it is laughable. Go ahead and laugh, Mr. Ferrell, it *is* funny, I do understand that. But *then*, oh, it was a strange moment, and I am proud that I did not laugh in his face. Perhaps I should have, but this was only minutes after he had howled about his poor murdered dog, you will recall. So I did the right thing, I would say so even now."

(Ronald: "She killed us both, that very instant. If I'd been there, I'd've whipped the little Romeo black and blue and sent him home to the priest.")

"I told him that if he truly, truly loved me, then he should serve me and the causes that mattered to me. I told him he could keep his job at the library, all the privileges he had there, his books and tracing papers and notebooks. No one could take that away from him. I told him a friend of ours would give him a bed, as long as he needed it, and we would make sure he continued in school. And in return, Paul would serve me by serving the cause. He would study what I gave him, he would come to our meetings, he would do as he was told by his superiors, and his natural talents—which were plentiful—would see him out, would make him a leader and a help to people who needed his help, right here in Australia. And as for what he kept calling his 'love' for me, well, I admit I simply said that when he was twenty-one we would see. I mean, really, it was obviously a little boy's temporary affection towards a substitute mother, and given something else to see of the world, it would pass. I was just using the tools I had for his own good."

Macy, I am doing my best to present this woman's crimes in her own words, as best I can reconstruct them. She admitted openly that she used her uncommon beauty and the boy's natural affections to force him into working for Bolshevism, and then never told his family where he was. And she was proud of what she'd done, remained convinced that the fate that befell her had been a "class crime," rather than precisely what she deserved for manipulating a boy into treachery against a free Australia on behalf of the blood-drunk tyrants of Soviet Russia. And even then, forty-five and disgraced, she looked down her nose at a simple supper invitation.

I hear you ask, not at all unreasonable, why would she talk to me about all this? Well, her tart manner to me wasn't the least of it: she was surprisingly like a lot of upper-class charity ladies, despite her politics. She was a *Lady* saving the poor, not from themselves but from the monstrous capitalists, whoever they are, but still a lovely Lady of salvation, for the poor to admire but never touch. And she had her own little notions of romance, I don't doubt, thought herself a virtuous queen, taking in the poor orphan, letting him serve in the kitchen until he grows up into Lancelot, simply from the guiding light of her chaste example. And, no question, she wanted me to clear her name a bit, would tell the same practised stories to anyone, with the same coy looks and virginal pose, just so she could say she *hadn't* done some of the riper things she was accused of in the scandal sheets.

But, Macy, it's the strangest thing, the strongest feeling I have now, copying over my shorthand and adding my recollections, I realise now: she told me most of this as a proud *mother*. She spoke in her schoolmistress tone about Paul, but saved her harshest words for Eulalie Caldwell, whom she glimpsed only twice. And our Miss Barry had kept diaries, too, she read some of these scenes to me right out of them. And, remember, she had kept and cherished that list of books her little man had requested from her those first months. I'm surprised she didn't have a portrait of her dear Paul to weep over, now that he was dead in a desert somewhere and she was living in a tiny flat, taking employment where she could. Certainly one can say Paul Caldwell destroyed her life (or helped her destroy it for herself, to be more accurate), and that's how Ronald saw it, but for all that, so much of this was pride—in her creation, in her boy.

Well, for some years Paul lives in the bare spare room of a Red agitator, sleeping on a cot. He finishes school. His own family never looks for him, never seems to care that he's run off to join a Bolshevik library. He goes to Bolshie meetings down at the harbour, sets up folding chairs, distributes pamphlets, holds the bags of the leadership while they lie to dockworkers or factory hands. Paul turns sixteen, seventeen, worships Catherine Barry but, so she says, is not encouraged. He reads about Egypt, even sends letters to Egyptian scholars all over the world, asking for positions on excavations. No word is received in return, and Catherine tells him ("though it broke my heart to show him the truth") that he would forever be excluded by the rich classes who indulged in this sort of sport, the noblemen and capitalists and "crypto-colonialists," because he was a working-class boy, and the capitalists wouldn't let him near their elitist games. Not to be dissuaded, Paul read and read, went to look at the few relics they had in the museum in Sydney, and travelled all the way to Melbourne to see the little collection there. By now Miss Barry was heartily sick of Egypt, as any right-thinking person would have been. She no longer asked why it interested him, and he spoke of it to her less and less. From a shy eight-year-old to a nearly friendly eleven-year-old to a lustful fourteen-year-old, Paul was again silent, a diligent seventeen-year-old. He was under her eye most of the time, either at the library working and studying, or at Communist meetings.

The day comes when our healthy young man decides he's done enough to win the heart of the fine lady he wants. That he was confused by her is obvious to men of the world like you and me. But see it from his point of view: he's seventeen, eighteen, a grown man. She's a single woman who knows him, has been kind to him, asked him to serve her. He reaches that age—we've been there, eh, Macy? I remember it, no lie—when he sees what he wants and he reaches out to take it. I don't blame the boy a bit.

He reaches out for her, and (no surprise to me, who spent time with her) he gets an icy response: "Oh, he was so foolish. He'd saved money enough to take me to a restaurant. I should never have accepted, but he said he wanted to talk about socialism, questions only I could answer." Paul had a musician playing at the table, had flowers. "He was making a display, people were looking at us, it was ridiculous. I was so angry, I could have screamed. I was so sure this was all finished, that he'd settled his affections on the Party. 'I thought you wanted to discuss serious matters, Paul.' 'The most serious thing in the world to me is you, Cassie.' I think it was the first time he had ever called me anything besides Miss Barry or Comrade." She stopped him cold, told him he had responsibilities now, commitments to something larger than himself. "I said this to save his dignity. But he insisted: 'I have no interest in it whatsoever without you.' 'Paul, you must work for justice for its own importance, not for me. That is where your marvellous kind heart will find fulfilment.' 'I am a man and you are a woman, Cassie.' Oh, dear. 'We are both people, Paul. We have debts to repay. You owe the cause *everything*, do you realise that? We—Ronald and I—we did what we did for you because of our beliefs.' Mind you, this *was* the correct answer. But he— Some people will not behave according to the logic of what's plainly in their best interests. 'You only helped me for your cause?' I remember him asking, and his face, he looked like that little boy asking for a book, or crying for his dog. 'You don't love me, not a bit?' Now really, Mr. Ferrell, what could I say? If you ask me, I think I made him a real gift at this point: I could have offered him some hogwash. I knew that. This sad young man asking for romance has the honour to work on behalf of the most Romantic movement in human history. All I wanted was to keep him working for justice, and I could have had what I wanted by lying to him. But I didn't, Mr. Ferrell, I would like you to mark that in your notebook now, and I shall wait for you to note it word for word. You shall play your part in setting all the crooked things straight, even twelve years on. I said, 'Paul, you are a debtor to the cause. As a man of honour, as a human with compassion, you have no choice but to continue your good work until the world is brought to democracy and equality. I am certainly not going to entertain your thoughts of other things. You are my comrade. I will walk with you arm in arm, not hand in hand.' And then he was up and gone, left me at the table next to some grinning chimpanzee playing the fiddle." She was confident she'd see him soon, maybe he'd need a week to regain his composure. "I assumed he was taking a difficult but vital step in his development, a transfer of love. Did I make a mistake? Obviously. I should have told him his love was not hopeless, or that I loved him, and perhaps I *should* have loved him, on his terms, just for a bit, until he could grow out of it, become a good man and a good Communist, both of which were certainly in him, and both of which our world desperately needs, Mr. Ferrell.

"I never saw him again, of course, but once. A few years later, Ronnie told me Paul was in a circus, and we went and watched some infantile foolishness, sat far away where he wouldn't see us. Then, in 1916, of course, he did what he did, ruining the lives of a few dozen dedicated heroes. And in 1917, when he could have been at our side, celebrating the greatest event in human history, he was instead off fighting a war of German noblemen against English bankers, and in 1918 he died for it, making the world safe for capital. And that is the sordid story, Mr. Ferrell. Tell anyone who cares to hear it. I never had the opportunity in this little democracy of ours to tell anyone at all, and the police and the newspapers chose to tell their own fairy tales instead."

You can believe, Macy, that there's more to it than that. Ronald explained the events of 1916, as far as he knew them, and which the enclosed newspaper clippings describe fairly, though Red Ron of course called them dishonest. "There was a night of arrests," he told me, stamping out his cigarette. "World events were heating up—the War, the Russians—and we were right in the middle of it, and the authorities were a little overwrought. One of our meetings was broken up, and we were taken to gaol, roughed up a bit. I was worried for Cass, because I lost sight of her right at the beginning and she was taken away by a different route. Now it wasn't a crime to talk about Communism—Australia wasn't as far gone as the USA—but conspiring to overthrow the Government, well, that's something else. Of course we weren't doing any such thing. But the police said they'd found explosives and the addresses of politicians and policemen that we were targetting for assassination, and we had been *corrupting* youth, and Cass and I had a peculiar sort of unmentionable brother-sister relationship." Ronald mildly denies it: "Now I ask you, Ferrell, we weren't madmen. Organising strikes, encouraging resistance, fighting against the proposed War conscription, showing up the corrupt state for what it is—all that was our line. But this police inspector Dahlquist tells the newspapers he's broken up a ring of Communist child-kidnapping assassins. Pictures of us with our names, and pictures of the *very* old explosives he's found under the floorboards under the cot in the room where you-know-who had lived for years. That's when I knew who had done this to us, even if I hadn't heard from him in ages, even if Cassie tried to deny it, telling me I was confused by my emotions. Not a bit of it: the rotter had spun a story for the police, and if you ask me, it was all just a love letter to Cass, just his way of saying he still thought she was the best girl in the whole world, six years after she'd broken what we were supposed to believe was his heart." A dozen of them spent a month in prison, and one of their number lingers there still, the one who actually procured and stored the explosives. "God knows why," claimed Ron. "And of course the damn things were never used, just sat under a floor for a half dozen years. Cassie and I, we weren't even *leaders* in the movement, you know, Ferrell. We were just idealistic people. Cassie still is. I've had my fill of it." So spoke the schoolmaster become barman, talking to me out back behind the pub where he was working in '22, one of the few places that would employ him.

The police had their bomber, but they'd also overreached, taken in a lot of people like the Barrys who hid behind laws saying they could think and say what they liked, and in the end there wasn't much to argue before a jury, and the childnapping charges were rather too risky a thing for public courts, especially when Eulalie Caldwell's meant to be your star witness and silver-tongued, troublesome Catherine Barry's prepared to defend herself with talk of Christian charity. Be that as it may, society had the comfort of seeing the Barrys dispatched from their posts of public trust. A bit of actual proletarian labour no bad thing for such people. In 1922, in her cramped room, she was still singing about Comrade Lenin's immortal accomplishments that would ring through history forever, and from where you and I sit, Macy, it's hard to say she didn't back a winner, even if he was a devilish one.

So we say farewell to the Barrys, July 10 and 11, 1922. Ronald returns to wiping down the bar. Catherine primly shakes my hand as if I'm poison, goes back outside to trim the stems of customers' roses. They curse Paul Caldwell and the upright Inspector Dahlquist when they should curse their own arrogance. (I didn't remind them of that, of course, as Ronald had engaged me to find Paul if he was alive. Looking for an address of a man who's dead, that's an undemanding way to earn one's daily wages, I'll admit.)

I won an audience with Inspector S. George Dahlquist the next day, to understand the relation between the arrest of Caldwell at the circus and the arrests of the Barrys, both of which he had conducted.

Macy, I slept strangely last night, I can tell you. I worked on my tale for you from early yesterday morning until late at night, and even when I wasn't writing, I was rereading the speeches I was re-creating, my old notes, and the newspaper clippings from 1916 I had from Ronald, some of them perhaps a bit strong ("Brother and Sister Reds Imprisoned Our Children," for example, and "Public Library Harbours Bolshie Bombers"). There's one I found oddly moving, to be honest, from the *Herald*, where the head of the library declares the system to be a loyal defender of the Commonwealth and claims it's now completely free of treasonous elements, and Catherine Barry, recently fired, is named by the paper as an example of the malignant virus at work, gnawing at the foundations of democratic society in the most surprising places. It certainly was all true. It was even stirring, a bit, in its defence of our common principles, and yet something seems missing, when I read it now.

I dreamt of Catherine Barry last night, could even smell her in the dream, which smells a sight better than this place at night, Mr. Macy-Up-in-Your-Mansion-in-New-York. She didn't say anything to me, wasn't angry, didn't fly or transmit messages from the beyond. She just sat across from me patiently, smoothed her skirts, smiled, cleared her throat, kept looking at me from her chair, and I knew she was waiting for me to say something, though I'm damned if I can think what it was. She'd raise her eyebrows, laugh a little at my puzzled silence, shrug, lean back in her chair, cross her hands on her lap, and just stare at me, with that wicked little half smile, seemed to say that she had all the time in the world to wait and see if I was going to say the right thing. She sat there forever—*forever*, because in the dream I knew it was never going to stop.

Off this goes to you, then, and I'll set to work on Dahlquist and my trip to England.

Yrs,
Ferrell

Thursday, 12 October, 1922

To Margaret: It is just dawn. You are with me always here. I shall carry you back such gifts from this expedition. You will of course be swimming in ancient gold, you will of course share in my fame, you will of course marry me in circumstances to make your howling, jealous girlfriends scratch out their own eyes immediately after the ceremony.

But I think also you deserve to have your own journal of our long separation, a journal of my love alongside and interwoven with the journal of my work; the two are too tightly bound together to be unwound now, in the heat of action. There will, in a few months, be this long journal-letter to you, to add to the posted letters you will receive (weeks after I send them, unfortunately), and to compare to that letter everyone will have, *Ralph M. Trilipush and the Discovery of the Tomb of Atum-hadu*, by Ralph M. Trilipush. Some of my entry yesterday is destined for you, not for them, I see now. I see, too, that your father deserves some polish in the published version of these journals, and you can trust that I shall perform that service for you.

A discussion of the financing of modern Egyptological expeditions: As for *implore*, per Kendall Mitchell's witty lyrics, I feel it is not inappropriate, nor uninteresting to general readers, to describe something of how archaeological expeditions are financed. *Imploring*, I hope it goes without saying, has nothing to do with it. And while I am as eager as you, dear Reader, to proceed to our exploration itself, I am also hesitant to bring you along with me until you are qualified to understand the context of the events that will befall us out there in the desert.

Join me, therefore, in the first of a series of investor meetings with Boston art connoisseurs and men of finance, June of this year, in the drawing room of Chester Crawford Finneran, who has invited me to his luxurious (and Luxorous) town house, where he has gathered some friends to ask me questions. And though I would have wed his daughter without this money, and I could have financed this expedition elsewhere, still he was offering his money, and if only as a gesture to the woman I love, I gave him and his friends this opportunity to be the financiers of an unprecedented expedition.

CCF's drawing room is decorated—per American fashions just now—in so much Egyptian and faux-Pharaonic décor that Kendall Mitchell claims he is starting to feel "asphinxiated." The joke would normally fall on irritable ears, but CCF has wisely arranged for so much "iced tea" that everyone is beginning to feel very much at their ease. I am addressing CCF, Mitchell, Roger Lathorp, Julius Padraig

O'Toole, and Heinz Kovacs. Lathorp is the owner of an enormously profitable construction firm of some sort. The last two guests have been very vaguely introduced, financial partners of CCF's in other ventures. They say very little, though Kovacs has a ferocious cough loud enough to end all conversation in the room whenever it strikes. When he speaks, on the other hand, his voice is so quiet that everyone (even O'Toole immediately to his left) must lean towards him. Kovacs's eyes run almost constantly, the result of some infection, and he uses several different pocket kerchiefs in the course of our meeting, tossing each saturated, monogrammed silken cloth in turn into the gaping black mouth of CCF's Rameses-colossus rubbish bin. O'Toole, an Irishman of undefined occupation, spends much of the meeting filing his nails and occasionally making notes with a tiny golden pencil in a small leather book. They, all of them, wear their money on their clothes and shoes. Scholars they are not, admittedly, but their passion for art is beyond question. There is a downside in dealing with institutions such as certain leading museums, and often private investment offers unique benefits to the explorer.

"Gentlemen," I begin, "let's for a moment put the question of money to one side so that—"

"I never do that!" japes Kendall Mitchell, to his and Lathorp's explosive glee. Kovacs coughs.

"You sell yourself short, Mr. Mitchell. Let's put the money aside for just a moment and consider what this expedition could bring you on top of financial reward. The history of Egypt carries us back to the very dawn of recorded human history, nearly 5000 years ago."

"Right you are. Back to Jesus Christ Himself."

"That certainly provides a context, Mr. Lathorp, and shows your aptitude for historical method, as it is wise to approach the past through familiar landmarks. But consider that Jesus was born 1922 years ago, and Atum-hadu reigned 1640 years before that, and Egypt in all its glory existed 1500 years before *that*, and one begins to sense the vast stretches of Time we are discussing."

"Of course," agrees Lathorp. "Familiar landmarks."

"Now listen, Pushy," Kendall chimes in, interrupting almost at once the careful presentation I had outlined. "I hear old Egypt's tapped out. Nothing left under the sands. All the other big fellows nabbed the good stuff already. What do you have to say to that?"

I ask them to open their prospecti to the page labelled "Odds of Success." "I think it extremely unlikely. We know the names of several hundred ancient kings, and have found the tombs of only several dozen. There are expeditions uncovering extraordinary treasure right now, even as we speak, though the digging season is mostly ended for Egyptian summer. In the case of Atum-hadu, three fragments of his writings have been found in approximately the same area, yet no relics of his burial have ever appeared on any antiquities market. Which implies that his tomb is intact, luxuriously equipped, and in the Deir el Bahari region shown on this map." I helped them open their prospecti to the map, which matched the larger version I had on an easel teetering in front of a large oil painting of Margaret holding a rabbit or a rabbit-fur muff.

The men peered at the map, which gave me, in the claws of my recurrent personal curse, the opportunity to visit CCF's Pharaonic water closet, where I strained under an untimely attack of explorer's gut, which has tormented me ever since the War, dysentery a nasty little camp follower in Egypt.

Upon my return, CCF was still squinting at the map, indecipherable lines and legends to him, but the others had broken into two distinct groups: Mitchell and Lathorp, giggling to each other over a copy (unsurprisingly open to Quatrain 42, "Atum-hadu Favours Four Acrobatic Sisters") of *Desire and Deceit in Ancient Egypt* (Collins Amorous Literature, 1920; new edition through Harvard University Press expected, 1923); O'Toole and Kovacs sitting aside, saying nothing at all.

"Jesus on fire, why won't Harvard pay your way on this, eh, Pushy?" CCF himself enquired, and I knew he was not truly troubled by the question; he merely did not wish to appear too easily convinced in the eyes of his partners. "Caught screwing a Dean's wife, were you?"

I guided them to the individualised sketches I had included in their booklets on the "Personal Collections" page. "Now, gentlemen, do you want Harvard to own what I find? Do you want this to be the Harvard Collection of the Tomb of Atum-hadu? When the Lathorp Collection, the O'Toole Collection, the Kovacs Collection could fill your own homes with the gold of an Egyptian king and, after you are gone, carry on your name forever in the private wing of the museum of your choice? Know this: every museum in the country will be slavering to house your collection *under your name* in their museum *forever,* as I took the liberty of imagining in these sketches. And here we reach the key issue, gentlemen: the longevity of your names. This is something our friend Atum-hadu understood. If they speak of your name after you are dead, then you are *not* dead. Think hard about this. Your money can buy you precisely what Atum-hadu's bought him, what every king of Egypt knew was the most valuable commodity he could possess: *immortality.* Now when the day comes, what are you going to leave behind? A department store? A construction company? A trust fund? A series of flimsy indictments filed by an envious attorney general? Or are you going to make your *name* live on *forever,* mankind's ultimate prize?"

"Now stop for just a moment, Perfesser." Perhaps I have gone too far; everyone leans in to hear Heinz Kovacs's whisper. "If I may just say. I did a little poking around, see, a little arkie-ology of my own. Like to know what's what before I write whopping big cheques to English fruitcake explorers and pornographers." (I will explain that misconception presently.) "Now my boy goes to Harvard, and his perfesser tells me your pharaoh didn't even exist. So how's that then?"

I will admit that I suffered just then a pang of envy, nothing more, just a single throb, because as I stood amidst the Boston *nouveaux riches* and answered their inexperienced questions, I thought of Howard Carter, leisurely checking his bank balance in Cairo, then simply wiring his placid, noble sponsor back in England, demanding some handsome sum and waiting for his Cairo account to swell accordingly. I thought of Oskar Denninger, nicely outfitted by the plucky Weimar Republic, and of Giancarlo Buoncane pouring into the sands of the Sudan the quarterly profits of Cassini Distillatori, boozily willing to prime the pump as long as necessary until steaming gold geysered back out of that barren Sudanese earth. And I thought of my own "colleagues" at Harvard, taking time out from their busy schedules of miseducating undergraduates and confounding my work and meddling in my financial backing to go spend Harvard's immortal endowment by fouling up the tombs of teensy priestlets.

"Like anyone with vision, ambition, a sense of risk-taking, Mr. Kovacs, you understand what it means to be surrounded by small-minded enemies who hate you not because you hate them, or have wronged them, but because you ignore them, since they are too puny to be of interest to you. As the Internal Revenue Service or the Attorney General must seem to you, so do Professors ter Breuggen and Fleuriman seem to me, for it is they, I assume, who are the criminal befuddlers of your son. Gentlemen, I read Oriental languages and Egyptology at Oxford University. I pulled the writings of this king—this 'imaginary' king as Claes ter Breuggen would have it—with my own hands from out of the Egyptian earth. I believe only in what is real, as you gentlemen do. Now if I were to lay out before you the threads of scholarship, painstakingly gathered over decades and spun to their most tensile resiliency in my own work, if you were to pore over this abundant knowledge as I have, you would, in your simple common sense, laugh at the hairsplitting chatter rising from the sterile offices across the river, and you would say, as I read in the *Boston Mercury* recently that you said of the Attorney General, 'Why don't that boring little man stick with his own beeswax and leave Heinzie Kovacs to Heinzie Kovacs!' and bravo, I thought, as I read that."

"Bravo, indeed," chimed CCF. O'Toole filed his nails. "You see what I'm thinking here, JP?" CCF addressed O'Toole. "Answers everyone's needs, seems to me. Pushy, tell 'em about what the tomb probably looks like."

When asking rich men for their money, be a little standoffish. They want to know that they will get their money back with interest, but they also want to see that you understand there is no guarantee they will. Even as you guarantee they will. They want you to be smarter than they are, but not in everything, and to acknowledge their superiority in matters of finance and "common sense." They would like to display one or two insights into your expertise that have not occurred to you before. Any more than one or two, and they will think you a fool; any fewer, arrogant. They do not want you to ask for their money; they want you to present them with an opportunity and accept less of their investment than they are willing to make. Be dubious of their money, stress the risks even as you underplay the rewards. These, I am afraid, are the lessons any Egyptologist must master. Example:

"Gentlemen. The tomb of Atum-hadu is probably a simple opening into the desert cliff face itself. Attending your walk into this covered arcade are illustrations of the events of Atum-hadu's reign, and hieroglyphs describing his glories and heartbreaks, invocations to the gods. Here, as you walk, the paintings tell a story, as if you were at the moving pictures: on your left, let us speculate, he leads his troops against the Hyksos invaders, or the secessionist would-be kings of the eastern delta, or black armies from the African south. On your right, you watch as he battles conspirators in his own court, impatient nobles who vie for his throne, while he serenely draws close to himself his trusted advisers (as you gentlemen are mine), and his queen, Her Beauty Astonishes the Sun. This much you and I see as we walk down the entry hall. Now through a small aperture we must crawl and we notice a smell unlike anything you have ever smelled before. I will not say it is immediately sweet or pleasant, but that is because it is unfamiliar—no, more than *unfamiliar* (which promises familiarity just ahead): it is permanently unique. You have never smelled this and never will again: it is the first whiff of air that has wafted undisturbed for 3500 years. I do not know if it will make you smile (as it does me) or will make you retch or will arouse you. Our eyes can scarcely open from the sting and the heat and . . . the glare. Yes, the glare, gentlemen: the uncertain light from our electric torches reflects back to us, magnified into blinding rays from gold and glass and ivory and beads and lapis lazuli and gold and gold and gold. Now shall we enter, you and I?"

"I'm sold," says Finneran.

"As well you should be, sir. We know much of our host, Atum-hadu. We know from his writings the external pressures that shaped him, the persona he created to carry him through his career. We know of his overpowering appetites, which he could satisfy only for brief periods and with great difficulty. We know of the family that failed him, the queens and concubines who sustained him, the trusted Master of Largesse who was his greatest adviser, and there, before us, we see all of this. On the wall near the golden sarcophagus of our king we see the most intricate, delicate, erotic drawings of Atum-hadu's amorous adventures, and figurines which, after the tomb was sealed, came to life to warm the king on his voyage to the underworld. And there, on a raised and ornate table, between gigantic statues of the gods Atum and Anubis, there it is: a complete copy of the *Admonitions of Atum-hadu,* the king's writings, undeniably onymous at last, and on the walls, an even fuller description of the king's life, of which it must be admitted — though the confession means we are now dragged kicking out of that entry arcade, past the blur of hieroglyphs, and returned here, to CCF's drawing room — that we know very little for sure, and to feed my famished critics their paltry due: some have said Atum-hadu and his tomb are not only unknown but unknowable, as the king did not technically, literally, exist. Not true, of course, but daunting for the nervous investor or nervous explorer. Which is why neither of those types were invited here today."

And there followed a page-by-page examination of the prospectus booklets: "Odds of Success." "Who Was Atum-hadu?" "The Tomb Paradox, General." "The Tomb Paradox, Atum-hadu's Case." "The Role of Erotic Poetry in Atum-hadu's Court." "Evidence for Tomb Placement and Contents." "Estimated Market Value of Selected Prospective Items." "Maps of Egypt and Deir el Bahari." "Personal Collections." Not all of the Partners were awake for every section of our talk (the dozing J. P. O'Toole's golden pencil, finding itself left to its own devices on its notebook, drew a series of minimalist waterfalls), but at least one of them was attentive for any given topic.

"Let's speak privately later, you and I and Heinzie, CC," brogues

O'Toole as he rises and stretches. Kovacs struggles to his feet, while Lathorp and Mitchell reach, as one man, towards the ottoman supporting the copy of *Desire and Deceit in Ancient Egypt* (Collins Amorous Literature, 1920).

"No need to fight for them, boys." I reach for my briefcase. "I have complimentary copies for everyone."

Sunset on the Bayview Nursing Home
Sydney, Australia
December 8, 1954

Mr. Macy—

I'm working as fast as I can now. You never know what tomorrow's going to bring, if it brings anything at all. That's lesson #1 in this residence. They took a fellow from my room this morning, all covered up nice and neat, with some bored-looking nephew spending a few of his precious minutes to sign for the body.

July 1922. Inspector S. George Dahlquist, an ambitious officer, was more than happy to share his fond recollections, tales of Red bombers and thieving circuses. He was able to answer a few of my remaining questions about Paul Caldwell's Australian life, but not all: from the moment our boy walked out of the restaurant with his heart cracked in pieces by his icy Red lady love until Boyd Hoyt talent-spotted him emptying pockets in a market square, I had nothing on him—two to three years where he was out of my view. And then, 1916, he's tip-toeing on sawdust, reaching up towards the row of tempting wallets above him in the dark when Inspector Dahlquist leaps from the shadows, grabs the boy's wrist, and nearly breaks it.

Paul Caldwell's at least twenty-three, knee-deep in elephant waste, sawdust, and the embraces of Emma Hoyt, when he's arrested for picking the sparsely filled pockets of the audience while they sit in the semidark, their bums dangling over the backs of wooden benches, cheering for or against that evening's penguin. Now, I know enough about how the police manage these things to know that Paul is likely shackled to a desk chair and then hit a bit and then given a large drink of water and then left a long while as the blood dries and then, when he needs a toilet quite badly indeed, in comes beefy Inspector Dahlquist, who says no one will vouch for Paul, Boyd Hoyt's told the police he has no interest in Paul's welfare, they might as well hang Paul high with a snapped neck as far as Hoyt's concerned. "A skinny boy, your Mr. Caldwell, but he didn't scare easy," Dahlquist told me. "Eventually of course they all get frightened, except for the real murderous monsters, but this little bung held out a bit, kept his silence. At the beginning, I just wanted to hear what he could tell me about Hoyt, confirm he was picking those pockets on Hoyt's orders to pay for the circus. I threatened him with long prison terms, which I might have been able to secure, depending on how many people came forward with complaints of larceny. But your Mr. Caldwell still kept quiet. Did Hoyt tell him to steal? Nothing. I described his life in prison to him. Nothing. I say the judge can decide to sentence him to the Army for his role in this lurk, and off he can go to help fight the Kaiser in a far-off field of France, have his head blown open for his trouble, and how did that sound to him? Nothing. 'You been doing it with Hoyt's wife, then? Because Mr. Hoyt, he's a very angry old man. Hates you. Tells me you're the rapist of his wife as well as a thief.' But our Paul's not reacting, not even whingeing, until very slowly, he turns to me and he says, 'Can you send me to the Army if I help you?' and I have to say I didn't see what he meant, but clear as day he wanted something. So now our negotiations begin in earnest, I'm sure you can understand, Mr. Ferrell. We begin to speak in highly removed hypotheticals. What would I be able to arrange for him if he could tell me something extraordinary? Just what would he be able to tell me if I were to know a man who might be able to deliver such a solution? 'So let's see the merchandise, young Mr. Caldwell, and make it ace,' I say. First, Paul says yes, Hoyt trained him to steal, forced him to steal, Paul kept only a small percentage of the take and the rest of the loot paid for the circus, fed the tigers. 'Hoyt told me to do it, Hoyt took all of the money, and Hoyt's the one who taught me how to pick a pocket and Hoyt Hoyt Hoyt.' Interesting, I say, but not enough for the deal you're asking for. All right, then, he says, and thinks silently for a minute. How about this: did I remember the Zipping Zivkovics? Two visiting star acrobats killed in a horrible accident during a performance of Hoyt's circus last year? Well, what if Paul could prove that they had been *murdered* by Hoyt in order to inflate circus attendance, since people always came in droves when there was a chance of seeing accidental death? More interesting, I admitted, but still not enough to secure him the very special package he requested. He sat and looked at his feet for a long while. I wondered if he was asleep, with his head hanging like that, or discouraged, or working up a whopper. But I waited, and I watched. Five minutes, ten minutes, I knew that every minute I kept quiet I was going to get a good one, if it wasn't just fairy tales. I could see his lips moving, he's thinking through something. And then he lifts his head and he looks me in the eye and says, cool as anything, 'Would you do it for a conspiracy of violent Communist plotters in the heart of Sydney?' Well, Mr. Ferrell, now he had my attention.

"The agreement he wanted took some time to guarantee. It was a heavy order, but if what he said was true, it was worth it. I said I'm a man of my word, but this would take some time to explore, and he said, I remember it well, he said, 'Take your time. World revolution and the destruction of all police power certainly isn't worth hurrying for.' And he laughed in my face."

The deal, Macy, was simple in principle, if a little complicated to execute. Paul wanted to be sent to join the Australian Imperial Force in Egypt, and he wanted it guaranteed that he would *stay* in Egypt for as long as the AIF was there. No Gallipoli, thanks, no Luxembourg, thanks. He would do his time in the AIF in Egypt and nowhere else. He told Dahlquist he could read Egyptian and knew the geography of the country as well as any Australian, and he'd learnt to ride a horse at Hoyt's place. In exchange, well, the Barrys and their friends. Of course, he held on to those names a bit longer. He talked very generally of the things Dahlquist would find, until the copper, convinced, pleading national safety, pulled strings at Defence, and arranged it as his star informant desired, while Paul sat in Sydney gaol, kept away from all visitors. When the paperwork was real, only then did Paul speak in specifics. Bombs under floorboards. Lists of assassination targets. Names of conspirators. Child-napping stories. Incestuous librarians corrupting youth. "Of course not all this stuck, but I won't complain," the Inspector told me. "Caldwell kept his word, and so did I. He was on a transport ship within a week of the arrests. That would have been summer, say December 1916."

If some of the newspapers made Dahlquist a hero in '16 and a fool in '17, well, that didn't slow him down any. He stopped an anarchist bomber, and if the price was a cloud of retractions and mumbled official apologies and cancelled trials, that didn't bother him much.

Were you a military man, Macy, hero of Korea or some such? I was a bit too old to spit fire and sign up for this Great War of ours. Down here, most of our boys went off to show Jack the Turk a thing or two, the glory of us Aussies at Gallipoli! To watch your insides stain a turquoise Turkish beach for the good of Serbia, if I understand that one right—not for me, thanks, nor for Paul Caldwell, either, as we now see. If you missed Suez and Jerusalem and Gallipoli, as he did, then Egypt was a pretty safe spot by '17, when he would've arrived, but of course he was going for love, not war. He'd found a way to do the unimaginable for a boy from Sydney's slums: he was going to the land of his dreams. What he thought he'd find there, I can't begin to say, and sure not worth dying for, if you ask me. Better if he took the prison time, my advice with hindsight, at least he'd be alive today.

By this time, July '22, I'd spent a few weeks tracking down Barnabas Davies's long-lost Sydney heir, and I didn't really have much hope I could spin the case out any farther. I'd have a nice, hefty payday for what'd been easy, safe work. I cabled my long report to London, giving the good and the bad of Paul Caldwell. Thanks to this last interview, if you squinted, we did have him working on behalf of the Crown to stop the deadly tide of Communism in the Commonwealth. I mentioned (though admittedly downplayed) that he was likely deceased. There was, however, the option, I wrote, of learning from his regimental mates and officers something about his War record that might be interesting to Barnabas Davies. If he'd been heroic, I advised, perhaps Davies's lawyers could retroactively change the dead boy's name, maybe get him a medal or citation in the new name, if Barnabas Davies felt like bribing the right people. And, for what it was worth, more of a joke than anything, I proposed that my investigations into Caldwell's heroism would most naturally lead me to England, where I should speak with the family and colleagues of Captain Marlowe, with whom our boy had vanished, and who had recommended the boy's promotions.

I expected London HQ would thank me, pay me, and that would be that. I thought it possible they would pay me to write some guidance for some other Tailor detective in England, preparing him to conduct the English interviews I suggested. But four days later, I received a very surprising reply by cable: AUTHORISED IMMEDIATE TRAVEL TO ENGLAND, EXPENSES TO DAVIES CASE. Now this was odd, to say the least. Of course, I was more than happy at the news: see the world, make some more money on a safe and interesting job. But why would such a thing be done? Tailor Worldwide didn't lack for snoops in England. What it cost to pay me and haul me around the globe was far more than any payment Barnabas had authorised in the first place to convince Paul Caldwell into becoming Paul Davies.

I mulled it over for two weeks waiting for the boat to leave Sydney, pondered it hard while I was ill then bored to tears then ill again from Sydney to Melbourne to Adelaide, Fremantle, Port Aden, Alexandria, Malta, and Liverpool, ill and confused the whole trip (though, give old Davies his due, I travelled in the best style available all the way to the end of this tale). I didn't understand it until I reached

England, the 12th of September, 1922, by which point it didn't matter. Turned out to be the simplest thing in the world: Barnabas Davies wanted to meet all of us detectives on his case, anyone who'd met the children or seen the women. I made the trip to England to pursue the case, paid for all the way by Davies Ale, because the old man wanted to know if Eulalie was well and shapely, wanted to see my face when I talked about Paul. Of course by the time I arrived in London, Davies was cold under the ground, and old Miklos Tailor was grinning ear to ear, because the solicitors had just informed him that the Estate of Barnabas Davies was going to pay for this investigation to reach its conclusions. I'd never met Miklos Tailor until the day I walked into that office, but he embraced me, pinched my cheek, welcomed another of his "brothers." He retired at the end of the Davies case, you know, lived high off his inflated billings of the dead man's coffers for the rest of his days.

And obviously, no expense was spared for his detectives on the case. *Davies* took priority over everything else, and whatever we asked for, we got two of. The usual would-be divorcés and adulterous this-and-that and suspected embezzlers had to wait patiently because Tailor was going to make sure every last loose end of this case was pursued, gathered, braided, and dipped in gold paint. The final report he submitted to the solicitors, duly marked up and passed on to the executors of the estate, ran to 2500 pages with photographs, individual biographies of the multi-national bastards, transcripts of interviews with them, maps of their locations, letters of acceptance and name-change certificates, and on and on. You can imagine the proportion of that report dedicated to the late Paul Caldwell.

More on that later. First though is our next interview. Say! What do you think of that idea? *Our* interview, as in yours and mine, Macy! You could write these up with you in a *participatory* role. You could be my Watson on the scene, not just with the pen. Of course, not every scene, that wouldn't be realistic, and we mustn't forget who's the main attraction here, no offence. But still, an assistant, someone to ask me questions, to whom I can explain my reasoning and deductions so the reader can follow along with some of the more twisty turns—this has a nice ring to it. Let's see how it feels.

London had procured a little more information on Captain Marlowe, and they'd arranged for me to pay the late Captain's parents a visit. First you and I examine the information they've dug up, a summary of various available military records and the work of a couple of Tailor's local men snooping around to save me time:

Captain Hugo St. John Marlowe left base camp at Cairo on 12 November, 1918, on four-day pass. Did not return on 16 November. Searches initiated 18 November revealed nothing. Interviews with officers, men, revealed nothing of significance. March 1919, natives appeared asking for reward, having found Capt. Marlowe's identity disks and those of Corporal P. B. Caldwell (AIF), as well as an AIF Lee-Enfield .303 rifle. Natives reported finding these objects near Deir el Bahari. Renewed interviews revealed no knowledge of any relationship between Captain Marlowe and Corporal Caldwell, though AIF records show Capt. Marlowe twice took unusual step of recommending promotions for Caldwell to Capt. T. J. Leahy (AIF), Caldwell's company commander.

"What do you make of that, Macy?" I asked as we sat in the plush offices of Tailor Enquiries Worldwide. (And welcome to the action, Macy!)

"Can't figure it, can't make heads or tails of it, Mr. Ferrell," said my young American assistant. "Most peculiar."

"And so it shall remain, until all at once the truth in its crystal purity will be made manifest to us, Macy, and vile fraud will melt away."

Here's all we had for certain: our Caldwell had some relationship with a British captain who'd poked his nose in Australian affairs enough to get Caldwell promoted twice. And they'd gone on leave together. And disappeared together. And likely died together.

I set off for Kent, and the grim residence of the uneasy, tweedy parents of Captain Marlowe. They sent someone to fetch me at the station, and I was driven to the servants' entrance of their country home and led up the back stairs to a small library, where the Marlowes sat in silence. The thickly moustached but unusually short father did not speak. Having limply shaken my hand without a word of welcome, he sat in front of a writing desk and kept his hands crossed on his lap. He looked only at the floor, but from time to time, as I explained that I was leading a private enquiry to determine events including those surrounding their son's disappearance, he would lift his eyes, as if he was at last prepared to look straight at me, but then his gaze would just continue right past, and he would peer instead at the ceiling. When I asked a question of them, his wife would look to him first, and when his silence was unbroken, she'd turn to me and answer, as fast as possible, addressing only my shins. Certain types of English do this with Aussies, I was learning fast.

The Marlowes had received official correspondence from the British Army, of course, but having no body to bury or story to tell, they'd attempted to learn more; there was another son in the Army still, and a daughter married to a military family, but the Marlowes had found nothing more than I had. Quite a bit less, in fact. Had Captain Marlowe corresponded with them during his time in Egypt? Yes. Had he mentioned a friendship with an Australian soldier, a Corporal Caldwell? The mother looked confused, and the father actually laughed briefly, a short bark, before looking at the ceiling, reminding me of my own accent and the unlikely social allure of Aussie Other Ranks. Had they known that Corporal Caldwell's weapon and identification were found with Captain Marlowe's? Dumbfounded silence and headshakes. Did Deir el Bahari mean anything to them? Nothing. Any idea why Captain Marlowe would have taken a four-day leave so far from base after the Armistice? Well, of course: for the archaeology.

Now that's intriguing, isn't it, Macy? Captain Marlowe had studied archaeology and Egypt at Oxford, I learnt. He'd been quite an advanced student, and had been intending to return to his studies after the War. He'd been quite pleased to be posted to Egypt. Did Captain Marlowe have friends from Oxford who I could speak to? Yes: Beverly Quint, who'd shared rooms with him one or two terms. "And then there was also this rather odd . . ." The mother trailed off and looked at the father. The senior Marlowe shrugged, turned in his seat, and drew a large, brown, opened envelope from the top drawer of the writing desk. He handed it to me with disgust. It was addressed to the Marlowes with a return address care of Harvard University in America, and inside it was a small book: *Desire and Deceit in Ancient Egypt*. It was a dedication copy, and inside the front cover I found this inscription in a blue ink, a fountain pen of eastern American origin, if my lifelong study of inks and nibs did not betray me: "13 August, 1920. To Priapus and Sappho Marlowe, who know well the importance Hugo held for me, my treasured Friend in University and in War, an Inspiration in Life and Death. With fond recollections of happier times in your warm and welcoming home, from your 'other son,' R. M. Trilipush." (Congratulations and thank you, Mr. Macy, for your patience. My promiscuous brewer has led us, as promised, to your aunt's first fiancé.)

"Very kind, I'm sure," I said, solemnly, to the mute Marlowes. "And have you spoken to your friend Mr. Trilipush since Captain Marlowe's disappearance?" The father looked at his hands, the mother shook her head. I stumbled on: "Perhaps he could shed light on your son's life and passing."

"We do not know him," she said.

"Would you like me to speak to him in your place?"

"You misunderstand me, Mr. Ferrell. I mean to say that we have never met him, though Hugo spoke often of him at Oxford."

"I'm confused, madam. What does he mean by 'other son' then?"

"We have no idea," she said.

"Hugo never introduced him to you?"

"Never."

"He hasn't spent happy times 'in your warm and welcoming home'?"

"Certainly not."

"And this book?"

There was a long silence before Mrs. Marlowe spoke in a very subdued voice: "*Filth.*" She swallowed. "And in its foreword he asserts that Hugo assisted him."

"Also"—the noise was unfamiliar and surprising this first time that little Priapus Marlowe spoke. "Also, *those* are *not* our Christian names." The wife nodded in silent agreement.

"I'm inclined to think that perhaps I can be of use to you," I said, and the father chewed slightly on the tapered end of his moustache.

Mysteries upon mysteries, Macy. The Davies Case begins to sprawl all over the globe, and we must ask the crucial question, common at such moments, when the wise detective attempts to frame and limit his field of vision: are we being led astray into unrelated territory? Or are we wise to keep our minds open, perhaps all of this will lead us to a clearer picture of the late Paul Caldwell? And we must find answers, also, for our newest and potentially most lucrative, if dreadfully embarrassed, clients—the mourning parents of Hugo Marlowe, who wish to understand what has become of their dear boy. We've much to do, Macy, so rouse yourself from your pleasure-hunting antics in London, put down the cocktail, say good-bye to the lovelies, and come assist me; the game is afoot! (How old shall you be in this chronicle, given that you weren't actually born yet? I rather like the idea of you being a young pup, a twenty-year-old with no particular expertise but an admiration for my deductions and a weakness for low glamour and Negro jazz.)

So I sober you up, and off you go on my orders to Oxford while I track down and question a few London men who served under arms with Captain Marlowe. What do the good blokes say, as we enjoy our Davies Ale in their locals? Never heard of Trilipush, never heard of Caldwell, Marlowe was a desk wallah interrogating prisoners.

Still waiting for your return from Oxford with the good oil, Macy, I pay a visit on Beverly Quint, and oh yes, despite the name, that's *Mr.* Beverly Quint. What did his parents *think* was going to become of him?

I find Beverly Quint, our Captain Marlowe's Oxford friend, now living in London, by no means gainfully employed but living quite well nonetheless as a gentleman at large. Here's a suggestion, Macy: in your rewriting, perhaps some drama can be added if you're doing crucial research at Oxford (taking my historical place with your more literary presence), at the precise moment I'm in the queer Oriental reception room of Beverly Quint's flat in The Albany. You're asking the ancient, fur-eared keeper of records at Balliol, "Are you quite certain?" at precisely the same moment *I'm* asking the lascivious and supercilious Mr. Quint, "And you're quite certain you knew him?"

"Quite certain, sir, though, it is not impossible that records are lost or removed," says the record keeper under gathering Oxford storm clouds and your mounting excitement. "There is no record of a Ralph Trilipush resident at Balliol in any term between 1909 and 1916."

"Certain? Am I certain? Of course I'm certain, Mr. Ferrell," says queer Mr. Quint at that same instant, leering at me in the lurid sunshine and dust of his rooms, and examining wistfully the Marlowes' inscribed book I showed him. "Ralph Trilipush, Hugo Marlowe, and I were an inseparable trio at Balliol," reminisces squinting Quint. "Though those two were Egypt men and I read Greek, of course, ducks. The closest of friends, we three, shared absolutely everything, quite the three musketeers, or three little maids from school were we, as your tastes dictate." There could be no question what Mr. Quint was implying in this room that dared not speak its name. "Do I make you uneasy, my alluring colonial?" he asked, flipping through Trilipush's book.

"I've seen rather enough of the world, thank you, Mr. Quint, to find nothing takes me unawares."

"Of course, ducks, very man of action of you. Would you happen to have an address for dear old Ralph, you clever man? I've lost all track of him since the War, and I have so much to tell him. Are you going to see him soon? You must tell him that Bevvy sends his very best love."

At my request for photographs of his friends, Quint produced a painting of Hugo Marlowe, a large-scale bust portrait of a very ugly youth, though someone had spilt heaps of pigment to get him on canvas. He was positively reptilian, to my admittedly undiscerning eye. From the base of his neck to the tip of what must have been his chin, there was a nearly straight line, and his curly black hair was stuck at random to his head, here in unstable piles, there just thick enough to cover the scalp. His translucent elephant ears joined his temples at right angles. He had bags and circles under his eyes, and his colouring was as floury as Mr. Quint's manner was flowery. "Handsome devil," I managed.

"Quite, but only the most refined can see it," purred my host with evident pride of ownership.

The odd thing, Macy, is that Quint himself was undeniably handsome, the way we'd all like to be and quite precisely how every pom imagines himself: square jaw, clear eye, cocked eyebrow, and that smirk to make women swoon. If Hugo Marlowe had been Quint's fancy man, it was a lopsided match, beauty and the beast.

And did Quint have a picture of Trilipush? "I think so, I should do." But all he could find was a photograph of some childish theatricals from Oxford, Quint front and center, periwigged and powdered as Marie Antoinette, a very clear (and even uglier) Marlowe as a dour revolutionary, and in the very back, in a crowd of identical blurs, under Quint's manicured fingertip, the blurry peasant third from the left. "There's our Ralph. Just look at that smug expression!" exulted Quint. "Who else could be such an unbearably self-assured French revolutionary peasant? That's just *poetry*. That suited Ralph down to his toes."

"Did Trilipush ever meet your parents? Or Marlowe's?"

"But of course, dear boy. One did introduce one's dearest chums to the old folks. Holidays, dinners, the usual. How do *you* people express friendship down there on the bottom of the earth?"

Meanwhile, Macy, you're reading all the documents you can get from Oxford's old man of records, and while there's absolutely no trace of Ralph Trilipush, there's an extensive trail of the capers of Marlowe and Quint. Marlowe was a student of Egypt under a don, now deceased, named Clement Wexler. Quint read French literature, so his reference to Greek seems to have been a lie, which should cast all his testimony in a certain light. Further interviews that day at the Bodleian and Ashmolean libraries, where they keep the Egyptian stuff, reveal the regular presence of Marlowe but not a whisper of Trilipush, until you're interviewing a librarian in one of these hushed temples of unnecessary education as you're growing convinced that Trilipush was never at Oxford, and an excessively delicate young man behind you says, "Excuse me for interrupting. I couldn't help hearing, did you say *Trilipush*? Are you a friend of Trilipush's? I wouldn't have thought—"

"Do you know him?" you say, much too eagerly, but you're inexperienced, Macy.

"But of course. But, do you? Surely not—"

"No, I haven't had the pleasure." Another mistake, Macy, you should've lied and said you were old friends. "Did you study with him?"

"Oh, yes, Egypt in all its exotic delights, but I really shouldn't tell tales if you don't know him." And the young man walks off, quite unwilling to speak another word but corroborating at least Trilipush's *unofficial* presence at Oxford, so not bad, young Macy. The odd thing, though, is that this undergraduate in 1922, a boy of eighteen or nineteen, wouldn't've been old enough to have attended Oxford with Marlowe, Quint, and Trilipush back in 1914. Mysteries upon mysteries. As you walk into the Oxford rain, puzzled by your discoveries, I'm still sitting in the glowing, dust-freckled drawing room, refusing another plate of Turkish Delight and sipping the thick, strange coffee offered by Mr. Quint, who's smoking a long and peculiar cigarette in a holder and trying to make my interview most difficult, though I see much more than he'd have me see.

"Why didn't you serve in the Army, Mr. Quint?"

"Various weaknesses," claims my strapping interviewee.

"Were you conscripted?"

"Mmmm, I should think I would remember that—it sounds delicious."

"Did you correspond with Captain Marlowe when he was at war?"

"*Bien sûr.* I fretted dreadfully for him, but I knew he had Trilipush there to look after him. Ralph and Hugo were based near those dreadfully grim pyramids they so adored, fighting the Boche or the wogs or whomever merited a sound English thrashing, the lucky devils, until poor Ralph went off to fight in Turkey. We thought we'd lost him, you know, but he's the sort who always pulls through."

All well and good, this tale, but there you sit, Macy, back at Tailor HQ, scratching your head at the official letter, just arrived, saying that His Majesty's War Office, *just like old Oxford*, has no record whatsoever for anyone named Ralph Trilipush.

"And what do you suppose became of Captain Marlowe, Mr. Quint?"

"What do I *suppose*? You Australians are terrible cynics. Just what the Army said is what I suppose. I am not the sort who doubts the official version of anything. He trotted off on leave to look at some dusty queen's tomb or another and was probably set upon by swarthy, bearded bandits or desperately rugged, whiskered Germans who treacherously but manfully refused to accept the Armistice. They devoured him, belching at their good fortune. What do *you* suppose became of him, feral Ferrell?"

"You didn't happen to save any letters from Captain Marlowe, did you?"

"Of course I did, and it would give me a warm and damp pleasure to deliver them to you this very instant if they hadn't been ruined when I had some plumbing problems a few months ago."

"Did Marlowe ever mention a Paul Caldwell in his correspondence?"

"I don't recall the name, no."

"Australian? Possibly involved with Captain Marlowe in archaeological matters? Or personal matters?"

"Speaking as one who knew Hugo's tastes," says this specimen of English manhood, "I should be very surprised if he were too personally involved with an Australian. Pioneer types not at all suited to his palate."

I hurry back to you, Macy, and we meet at Tailor HQ to exchange notes. "What does it all mean?" you ask me, not without frustration. "It's too early to say, Macy. Patience, old fellow, keep your mind open." And I send you off to book our passage to the United States of America, expenses paid by our clients, Hector and Regina Marlowe and Barnabas Davies. Oh, yes, indeed, America: where we must certainly speak to our Mr. Trilipush, professor at Harvard University.

And what *does* it all mean? Trilipush, a man who apparently did not go to Oxford and did not serve in the War, apparently did go to Oxford and did serve in the War. A man who did not know Marlowe's parents pretended or believed that he did know them, and so confidently that he pretended it *to them*. Or he *did* know them, and *they* lied to me to hide their embarrassing nicknames and the scandalous behaviour that must have earned them. Further, Quint, who would know, seemed to say Marlowe and Trilipush shared a shameful variety of intimacy. Meanwhile Quint and the men who served under Marlowe had never heard of Caldwell, but the War Office and Marlowe's soldiers had never heard of Trilipush. What could be clearer?

And with that, Macy, I post the latest chapter of our adventures to you.

Yrs,

Ferrell

(Thursday, 12 October 1922, continued)

<u>Book notes:</u>   To be placed after Author's Introduction and before Journal Entries: *Egypt at the time of Atum-hadu:* King Atum-hadu, to whom I owe my academic reputation and relatively small fortune (dwindling, with ten days still until first financial reinforcements arrive), reigned at

Journal: Visit bank to introduce myself to manager, confirm establishment of account, preparedness to receive credits from abroad. Advise of my whereabouts for immediate notification when first wire, due 22 October, arrives from Hand-of-Atum, Ltd. Explain the need to arrange a smooth transition to the Luxor branch of the bank as soon as I make my move south to the site. The modern explorer, Reader, needs to secure firmly his financial lifeline.

Having been well received at my bank, I then spend the rest of 12 October wrestling not with heavy tomb doors or incalcitrant work crews or fading hieroglyphs suddenly and fearfully exposed to bleaching sunlight, but with Franco-Egyptian bureaucracy. To what they submit an explorer nowadays! It was not always like this; there was once a glorious golden age when men went into the desert with no one's permission and no one's help. Wit and curiosity were the requisites. Once, not even academic degrees were required: Belzoni was an Italian circus strongman, Howard Vyse a demolition expert, but Egypt drew them both into her embrace, and richly rewarded their manly love. Belzoni simply carried off sarcophagi on his own knob-muscled back; Ferlini knocked the tops off virgin pyramids, like a bear batting at a beehive, and descended upon the sweet treasures nestled inside. The tennis professional F. P. Mayer, in a possibly misguided effort to understand how the pyramids were built, hired a team of native workers and closely monitored their work habits, exhaustion, and attrition as they dismantled a small VIth-Dynasty pyramid stone by stone, wheeled the heavy blocks through the desert on primitive rollers, cut the pyramid's perfect blocks into rough, random, "natural" shapes, and buried them in a quarry several miles away. The whole experience proved very little but did reveal at the nearly empty pyramid's central chamber an extremely small gold-flake figurine of Anubis, which I believe was melted down by Mayer's children, after the explorer died quite mad, certain that there was anagrammatic significance to be found in the name of the Vth-Dynasty king Shepseka'are. At any rate, these explorers were men. They came, they dug, they took risks, they walked off with their finds, and their names have entered the pantheon. And while I cannot always endorse the scientific value of their methods or results, they did not wait while an application for an "Archaeological Concession" was pondered by sleepy Frenchmen in a Cairo office, which in exchange for mummifying explorers in red tape, extorts 50 percent of their discoveries to toss into the insatiable maw of the Egyptian state museums.

In short, my visit to the office of the Director-General of the Egyptian Antiquities Service was a grave disappointment. Instead of the ready assistance I could reasonably have expected, I was told that the application letter I had sent several weeks earlier from Boston "wandered, it is possible to say?"

"No," I instructed the secretary, a pale Frenchman who claimed never to have heard of me or my application, "it is not possible to say that my application wandered." He tarried a few minutes behind his boss's evidently soundproofed door, then emerged with the news that my application was once again under consideration and would I please return to the office in eleven days' time. *Eleven days!* 24 October is now my earliest departure date for the site. I had intended to be under way in two days, and budgeted accordingly. This is my error, of course, an error of overestimating the efficiency of others, and now, under this infantilising regime, I have no choice but to postpone. I report to the tourist agency and book first-class passage to Luxor on the *Luxor Princess* for the 24th, return to the hotel and extend my stay in the Pharaoh Suite, an expense I had not foreseen in my planning sessions with the Partners. The wire on the 22nd will be, it seems, more urgent than any of us had intended.

My concession application is cannily modest. Unlike those who would excavate vast stretches of the country on whimsical suspicions, I have applied for the exclusive licence to explore only a very small strip of cliff wall on the Nile's west bank, a secluded stretch of Deir el Bahari. While Professor Winlock burns the New York Metropolitan Museum of Art's money, throwing dust and earth about the open expanses of Deir el Bahari, he has found nothing of significance in more than a year and, predictably, has shown no interest in the spot a few hills away that I intend to explore. I should be absolutely flabbergasted if he or the Antiquities Service hesitate in allotting me my portion of the ground. The Government does collect half of the results, after all.

Visit post to see if any news from Partners/Margaret in the *poste restante*. Assure myself that the postal workers have the correct spelling of my name. Cable CCF to assure my bank information is accurately relayed to the Partnership's bank in Boston, and inform him of my delay.

Begin looking for estate agents for rental of villa near the excavation site in the south, see drawings and photographs of some exquisite and suitable properties. Howard Carter himself used one of these agents, the agent informs me. An impressive credential: the man will know the sort of thing I shall need. Visit bazaar—find a light scarf for Margaret as well as a small boy's hand reaching into my pocket. Nearly snap the little thug in two before a hammy actress playing his weeping mother appears to plead for his life.

Sit at an *ahwa* and have a coffee to calm my nerves. Note the day's frustrating events in journal. Back to the hotel to bathe.

Friday, 13 October, 1922

Evidence pointing to the location of the tomb of Atum-hadu: The dillydallying at Antiquities allows me to address an implied question: how does one know where to look for a tomb? To answer, I must begin some years ago, when I cut my teeth as an Egyptologist alongside and under the heady influence of Hugo St. John Marlowe, who would by now have been one of the most celebrated members of our dusty fraternity had he not been cut down in the mad slaughter of the War.

Before that tragic day, we were both young captains, working for our great cause side by side right here in Egypt (before I headed off in '15 to fight in the Bosporus campaign). We had been at Oxford together, Hugo Marlowe and I, and both of us spoke modern Arabic fluently, as well as knowing our way around ancient Egyptian. Our linguistic gifts were duly noted by His Majesty's Army, our posting to the Near East theatre merely logical. With our linguistic and cultural expertise, we were based in a Cairo suburb, responsible for prisoner interrogations (the occasional suspicious Arab tribesman bearing a German or Turkish weapon or document) and counterintelligence operations (trying to convince Arab tribesmen to carry Turkish weapons but not mean it).

I know it is hardly fashionable to say this about the War, but I had the most marvellous time, until I was asked to advise the ANZACs in that jolly trip to scrap with Johnny Turk and catch bullets at Gallipoli. For in the months before that sad exploit, Marlowe and I took advantage of our happy posting in our beloved Egypt, scouring the sands whenever passes could be acquired and, when the opportunity arose, making ourselves known to some of the old hands of archaeology still trying to do their work, uncovering the past even as the present collapsed around them.

My dearest friend and I spent our free moments (more than you might guess in what was for me, to tell the truth, a theatre of war with a very light repertory schedule) on motorcycles, finding official justifications for visits to the pyramids, the Sphinx, even making excursions of several days to the south in order to see the Valley of the Kings and Hat-shep-sut's temple at Deir el Bahari—all of the fantastical places of my childhood and varsity days, suddenly there before me in the most extraordinary reality. To long for something, from the age at which the very first foundation stones of one's personality are laid and cemented, to long for something from the best part of one's heart simply because it is more beautiful than anything else in one's entire life, to study it, aching to trap it and master it, to spend years in pursuit of it, and then, all at once, through the miraculous intercession of a modern, nonsense war, to have it all delivered up to one's fingertips . . . and then to realise with shock and rapture that all one has learnt in one's years of amorous study are mere surfaces, that the luminous object of one's adoration is so vast that one might spend one's life and every life one may yet receive straining to sound its depths and make oneself as one with it, to make it acknowledge one's love and presence, knowing all along that one will never taste even a fraction of what she hides—all of this I felt

in my first weeks and months serving King and country in my promised land.

When military duties prevented me and Marlowe from leaving our
base to ramble amongst the pyramids and colossi and cliff tombs and
temples, we would instead, from our tents and offices, explore—as we
had done at Oxford—the holes of Egyptian history, those thrilling moments when for all the world's scholarship and speculation, we simply
squint into darkness and we *do not know.* Peering into the shadows
where parenthetical question marks pursue every date and reference
like vengeful cobras unfurled to devour any stray, careless certainties—
as in "Atum-hadu (?) reigned (?) circa 1650 B.C. (?) at the tail end of
the XIIIth Dynasty (?), of which he was (?) the final king (?)"—the
scholar must strain to make out the silhouettes of the kings and queens
whose very *existence* is in doubt. These once-great men and women now
cling to their hard-won immortality by the thinnest of filaments (half
their name on a crumbling papyrus written a thousand years after their
hypothetical death) while, across that chasm of time from them, historians and excavators struggle to build a rickety bridge of educated
guesses for those nearly vanished heroes to cross.

At Oxford, even as Marlowe and I mocked those reckless historians
who too freely plant ancient papyrus in their own fertile imaginations
and chronicle the resulting growths of fantasy with loving care, we
were nevertheless drawn to the halo of uncertainties surrounding the
purported XIIIth-Dynasty hero-poet-king Atum-hadu. Marlowe and I
spent long nights in the Balliol Junior Common Room toiling over the
photographic or sketched reproductions of the first two Atum-haduan
Fragments. We debated the possibilities, charted the chronological im-
plications, interpreted the verses' hidden meanings, and of course
laughed at those first two efforts to translate the Fragments: the skittish
evasions of prim Harriman and the perfumed seductions of Vassal.

Reader, would you know and understand me, as a man and an explorer? Then pay no attention to my childhood; despite my father's influence and our family's ease, it truly does not matter. Rather, if you
would know my passions and understand how I came to be searching

for Atum-hadu's tomb, focus your vision intently on Oxford; these searing sessions of impassioned scholarship formed me, almost literally made me, it seems now. They gave me historical heft, a third and most crucial dimension, while the feeble light of an Oxford winter's dawn crept unnoticed through the leaded glass and we pored over Lepsius and Mariette and the other classic texts of Egyptology. Marlowe and I—nineteen, twenty, twenty-one—fiercely debated the mysteries of ancient Egypt, especially the possibility of Atum-hadu. Our devilish advocacy proceeded with rigour but without rigidity; we debated as a relay, readily passing back and forth the baton of doubt, all in a race to illuminate some shadowed crevice of evidence, an unnoticed nook of possibility. Where, if he existed, might Atum-hadu fit in the chronologies, as his name did not *definitively* appear in the (tantalisingly incomplete) king lists discovered in the preceding decades?

And in these days and nights, you would have witnessed something more: the emergence of a certain voice, the blazing red dawn of vocation, of effortlessness: Marlowe had these without question. More than just memorised knowledge or facility with the language or a hand at drawing the 'glyphs: Marlowe had a manner of mastery that one sees in the *élite* field men, at a deep sepulchral place, far beneath their control or even their consciousness. Even if you draw their attention to their power, such men do not believe it, they do not understand what you mean, they do not seem even to care. For the others, the *strivers*, there is—no matter how much trivia or technique they scrape together— something missing. They lack and can never acquire, no matter how hard they exert themselves, a certain ability to sniff out likelihood, a certain unconscious grace, a lack of doubt or worry, a complete and thoughtless fulfilment of the role. You see lesser men, even acclaimed, accomplished journeymen, shake their heads in admiring frustration when the true masters are at work.

During our time at Oxford, Marlowe and I (under the influence of Clement "I Doubt It" Wexler's trademark scepticism) were still agnostic as to Atum-hadu's existence. It was undeniable that the two Atum-haduan Fragments—Fragment A, translated and published by

F. Wright Harriman as *Athens on the Nile*, and Fragment B, translated
and published by Jean-Michel Vassal as *Le Roi Amant*—were discovered separately but overlapped in content, copies of the same source
text. And it was tempting to agree with Harriman and Vassal that the
"king" mentioned in some of these verses, the narrator-poet-protagonist
"Atum-hadu," was in fact an historical figure rather than a literary fig-
ment. But we were not yet Atum-hadu zealots, Marlowe and I. We
were open to either possibility—that Atum-hadu had been real, or that
he was a vengeful fiction, a creation of the dispossessed of the Second
Intermediate Period, the folkloric hero of exiles or slaves or dissidents
or nostalgics who dreamt that once there had been, if not a conqueror,
at least a man who fought and died for Lost Glory, as Sir Thomas Mal-
ory imagined King Arthur. And he had his appeal, this Atum-hadu, an
intoxicating appeal: he was self-aggrandising, sexually omnivorous,
doomed, bold, violent, beloved, feared, and proud most of all of his
ability to create the world in his image and control it according to his
deific will. The extraordinary, amusing name (Atum-*hadu*!) and the potent final determinative-hieroglyph necessary to produce such a name
(see frontispiece) certainly captured Marlowe's and my imaginations,
but neither of us was (as a limp critic of *Desire and Deceit in Ancient Egypt*
later aroused himself by calling me) "a wishful thinker, a dreamer of
unspeakable dreams, a distraction to scholars, and a corrupter of
amateurs."

The pale and unravelling scrap of papyrus now known as *Atum-hadu
Admonitions Fragment A* came to light in the lily-white hands of F.
Wright Harriman in 1856. A bachelor Scotsman of incomplete religious
training who explored Egypt with his mother in tow, Harriman is invariably portrayed from the waist up, a delicate handling of his
dwarfish stature and the remarkably proportioned posterior that won
him so many unflattering nicknames in Arabic.

Harriman is—as many men are who strain to achieve immortality—
embraced by posterity for something other than what he had intended.
He had dedicated his career to hunting for evidence of Mary, Joseph,
and Jesus' fugitive sojourn in Egypt. And when at home in Glasgow,

he wrote a little verse himself, rugged nuggets of fierce Scotch religion, tinted with a dull pewter irony:

Atheism, too, I suppose, is an act of faith
That demands of its practitioners a sort of devotion.
For they slouch through this world, grey as a wraith
And traipse off to Hell with so little commotion!

But instead Harriman was immortalised by uppity serendipity: chasing the baby Jesus, he stumbled into a lost Sadist, omnisexualist, brutal warrior, symbol of loss and immortality, King Atum-hadu.

When at the site, Harriman insisted that all of his native workers attend Christian education sessions. One afternoon, while he was irritating his dozing Mohammedans with the fish and the loaves, one of his men—having apparently thought his time was better spent working—rushed in from the field cradling in loving, calloused hands a bulky and peculiar item. Harriman stopped his lecture and relieved his man of the scroll he was so excitedly offering, then fired the wretch on the spot for digging instead of praying (thus neatly saving the negligible cost of the *baksheesh*, the cash bonus the worker was due for bringing in his own find). Leaving the relic untouched next to his tea, Harriman finished his hour-long lecture, while his team of Muslim boys and old men nodded off or discreetly faced east and bowed. Finally, they were sent back to the field, duly deterred from hard work by the example of their dismissed colleague.

No great scholar and hopeless at hieroglyphs, Harriman now toiled all night trying to copy down the symbols he found in his fast-crumbling prize, transcribing what he did not understand and was destroying by his ignorance of preservation techniques. (All it would have taken was some damp cloth.)

It is a glorious image to conjure: the midnight return of King Atum-hadu to our world. Harriman bashfully admits in his memoir, *Seven Lean Years*, that the text's prevalent references to certain acts made him stop frequently for cold baths and prayer as his hand was forced to copy, over and over again, my favourite of all the hieroglyphs. And when the overheated archaeo-missionary had finished, he had twenty-six verses or parts of verses, and Atum-hadu's name in a cartouche (the oval drawn around any royal name, see frontispiece). The presence of this entirely new and strange royal name, while fascinating, was nevertheless inconclusive, as it was not clear that the text's author and subject were one and the same. And there was still no other document that referred to this kingly name anywhere in Egyptology. But to give the idiot Harriman his due, he translated the verses (badly) and published them with an essay in which he rashly but correctly identified the author and the king as one and the same Atum-hadu, declaring Atum-hadu a real historical figure, a nervy assertion in 1858, based solely on his shred of scribbled papyrus. Unjustifiably right, but right.

Enter Jean-Michel Vassal, a French amateur off spending his family's money in the sand and in the casbahs, who in 1898 pieced together several shards of limestone into a coherent larger tablet. This find, Fragment B, had been unearthed quite near the site of Fragment A, and it included fourteen of the same verses as well as eighteen "new" verses, but no explicit mention of Atum-hadu as an author, nor of any other author.

Finally, the now-legendary Fragment C, fully forty-eight verses, of which sixteen appeared in neither of the previous Fragments, ten appeared in A but not B, twelve in B but not A, and ten in all three. (Internal evidence implied that at least eighty had existed.) Fragment C more explicitly stated that these verses were written *by* "King Atum-hadu," but still there simmered the historical puzzle: while the verses suggested a king reigning in the chaos that blurred the end of the Middle Kingdom, *none* of the standard chronicles contains any reference to "Atum-hadu," although the first two characters of his five-character hieroglyphic name—the symbols forming the name of the god *Atum* or the first half of the name of the king *Atum-hadu*—*do* appear, beckoning, in one of the king lists, at the very end of a section, immediately before the edge of the papyrus unravels into an oblivion that may represent an inch or a foot.

The story of Fragment C's discovery is one of great personal significance.

Early in 1915, Marlowe and I had requested and received simultaneous six-day passes to make a trip far to the south. Our true aim was to explore the relic-rich Theban west bank. Officially, though, we justified such a long leave with intended intelligence negotiations with some nomadic tribesmen. We never did manage to find them, so instead it was paradise: days of archaeology, pretending there was no War.

The morning of our third day, I cut the motorcycle's engine and Marlowe vaulted out of the sidecar to unload some equipment, and I recall him complaining of the demands one of his many women was making on him. At the time, if I can keep them clear, he was balancing a French singer in Cairo and a Russian countess in Alexandria, and more of the local copper-skinned beauties than can be counted, and one of these alluring women of brushed gold had been demanding that Marlowe read the Koran and convert to Mohammedanism and become her husband, a notion that made him laugh so hard he bit his tongue and then cursed and held a handkerchief to his bleeding mouth. I was, I believe, likely telling him of my plans to refurbish Trilipush Hall after the War.

Soon we were at work, investigating Deir el Bahari, directly (if my map reading was correct) on the opposite side of the thick wall of cliffs from the fabled Valley of the Kings, just a few hills and dales further into the desert from Hat-shep-sut's temple, and quite completely isolated from view from both of those sites. We were scarcely digging, merely scanning the ground and cliff face for glimmers of man-made interference. Were we looking for Atum-hadu? Well, yes, we were in that area (after previous, fruitless efforts wandering in and out of easily breached caves and holes) in the hopes of finding something to corroborate Harriman and Vassal, but we also would have *denied* we were looking for Atum-hadu; we were still not convinced he ever was. We only agreed that, if he had been, it was reasonable that his tomb would be hidden and near his capital (?) at Thebes (?). As the Valley of the Kings, the state-run necropolis, was inaugurated much later with

Thothmes I, and as Harriman and Vassal had made their discoveries
not far from each other, quite near where we stood, Deir el Bahari
seemed the most promising place.

After some hours of slow walking in careful patterns, I spotted what
seemed at first to be a smooth patch of sand to the far left of the path,
as if all the finest grains had huddled together amidst their coarser
brethren. This patch quickly revealed itself to be a smooth stone, and
as Marlowe and I brushed at it, its size grew, as if it were the top of an
emerging head and the very earth our loving, labouring wife. We
brushed until we had a perfect stone circle, approximately two feet in
diameter. The heat was extreme, and Marlowe took a turn in the shade,
sipping at the water, shielding his eyes to keep a keener lookout, for it
is human nature that at a moment such as this, one grows quiet and
suspicious. I began gently probing the area around the stone with the
deliberation that is our art's watchword, dull of course to anyone who
does not understand the potentially catastrophic costs of hurry. It is
precisely this hypnotising rhythm that makes a discovery such a release
of emotion, comparable to only one or two other experiences in a man's
life.

Some time later, after several changes, it was again my turn to dig,
and I brought to the surface a cylindrical jar, the blank top of which I
had noticed some hours earlier. I placed the jar on the earth between
us, and we simply stared at it before Marlowe dared to lift the lid.
Which is when we heard horses' hooves and, a moment later, a shot
ringing out. Marlowe dropped the lid, smashing it beyond repair, and
reached for his Webley. I reached inside the jar and withdrew a bulky
papyrus, cursing that no measure of protection could yet be taken for
it, and I placed it as gently as I could (more gunfire now) under my
shirt, between my belly and my belt. "Get that out of here, my dear
friend. It matters more than our skins," Marlowe said with elegant
calm, and before I could stop him, he was moving up the path, *away*
from the motorcycle, firing haphazardly, making himself occasionally
visible, drawing, in short, the four horsemen (bandits, German agents,
we did not know) towards the west while my exit to the east was freed.

"Go! I'll find my way out of this, old fellow. You can count on it." I ran towards the motorcycle. I carried *Atum-hadu Admonitions Fragment C* snugly at my waist.

I circled the 'cycle around to the northwest as I saw Marlowe break from the rocks. I sped towards him, and as bullets flew overhead, he leapt into the sidecar, head first. I turned us quickly, sand flew, and off we went, both of us laughing until we wept and Marlowe singing an old Balliol song.

We stopped at Luxor. The craving to hurry and open our find was powerful but not as powerful as our discipline. We wrapped the papyrus in damp cloth and talked constantly through an excruciating and sleepless night. When we agreed it was safe, we examined the scroll's first panel and knew at once, within a single line, what we had: three fragments of Atum-hadu's Admonitions had now been found in Deir el Bahari. A day later we returned to base early, only to learn that I had orders to prepare to leave Egypt (for Gallipoli, though I did not know it yet). And so, of necessity, we agreed to leave our treasure in Marlowe's care, to tell no one, and to wait. I think, in both our hearts, we thought we were waiting for my death in battle.

I next saw Fragment C more than three years later, in December 1918, after my unexpected and lucky return from Turkey, alone, practically on foot. I reached our diminished base in Egypt a month after the Armistice, only to learn that my great friend had vanished before my return and was likely dead. Heartbroken, I vowed that I would devote my life to our shared work and discovery. I entered his tent, secured Fragment C, and took it with me when I was demobilised not long after.

That Marlowe died while I survived Gallipoli can hardly be credited to a wise guardian angel. It cannot be accepted at all, except perhaps as the bumblings of a dizzy Destiny who chose *me* to fulfil a crucial task, a task perhaps even Marlowe would not have been qualified to perform. This is the only condolence I can draw from his tragic end.

And in my mingled sorrow and ambition, I decided to wander somewhere new, change everything, cut myself off from all the easy help waiting for me in England. Knowing the reputation of Harvard University, I went to the United States, hoping to put my painful Wartime memories behind me in a strange land. To build a new life. To honour my fallen friend. To continue our joint work where I had only my own talents to support me.

Saturday, 14 October, 1922

An introduction to the Atum-haduan Admonitions: The author of the Admonitions may have been a king, he may have been posing as a king, he may merely have been imagining a king. Hero, fraud, or artist? I have found one's own tendencies dictate one's answer to that question.

Another question: how should one translate poetry written in ancient Egyptian, which has not been used for more than 2000 years, and which we do not entirely know how to pronounce, as in common with Hebrew and Arabic, its vowels were not written? Did its poetry rhyme? Did it move in rhythm? Any answer is unverifiable.

Now, observe: Comparative Translations: Quatrain 73, the same sequence of hieroglyphs purporting to be written by Atum-hadu (purporting to be the king of Egypt) and translated by three different Westerners, two of whom are illegitimately purporting to know what they are doing:

1. (Translated by F. Wright Harriman, 1858): "Perils of Love"

    A beauty's gaze and touch
    Can rain down joy or sorrow
    In equal measure.

2. (Translated into French by Jean-Michel Vassal, 1899, and from French into English by Marie-Claude Wilson, 1903): "Her Dual Nature"

When my Queen examines me
Her gaze is as potent as her touch,
Exciting here the most delicious frissons
There the most excruciating torments.

3. (Finally, translated correctly and published as *Desire and Deceit in Ancient Egypt,* Collins Amorous Literature, 1920): "Pleasure Through Pain"

Atum-hadu's sweet lover
Strokes the royal member first with her eyes
Then with her claws, until they tear
And make bleed the rigid sceptre of his power, and he sighs.

Observe: Harriman bowdlerised, as the preceding extract should make quite clear. Typical of the Victorian moralist, he deemed nothing worth finding that did not bear the lavender scent of uplift. Faced with something decidedly neither pre-Christian, proto-Christian, or even anti-Christian, but simply not-even-slightly-related-to-or-interested-in-Christianity, he was forced to find in Atum-hadu someone other than Atum-hadu. Witness this passage from his Introduction to his *Athens on the Nile,* 1858:

When, having exerted oneself to understand the people of ancient Egypt and the bafflement they expressed in the face of nature and the universe before Christian revelation, Atoom-Hadoo's writings provide a marvellous discovery. For one finds in the king's poems an all-consuming desire for knowledge, and it is this, above all, that made him a worthy ruler in his era and makes him now a worthy subject of study. From this distance, "through a glass, darkly," as Paul wrote to the Corinthians, we can see in this ancient, dusky prince a man struggling in his desire for what in our era we would call Christian enlightenment and divine wisdom. If his topics may sometimes shock us (and I cannot recommend that ladies be exposed to them), let us nevertheless face them boldly, as they are the essential questions of life itself.

Jean-Michel Vassal, the French discoverer of Fragment B, thought little of Harriman, and though he could not recognise his own faults as readily as he could Harriman's, I will allow him to express his opinion of his predecessor in Atum-haduan studies. From the preface of *Le Roi Amant* (1899, Englished as *The Lover-King* in 1903 by Marie-Claude Wilson):

> *As for proving to dubious minds of dubious calibre the existence of Atoumadou, one must also confess that our own side have done us inestimable harm in the form of those bloodless dilettantes I will not name who—choking at the sight of a nude woman, blanching like a virgin schoolgirl at the very mention of man's darker urges, the iniquities of a callous deity, the temptations of power, or the baser motivations of this beast-ape Man—have presented to the world a feeble Atoumadou softened like an old woman's lapdog, castrated, soaped, and fluffed, red and blue ribbons in his fur, fed fat with almond marchpane and numbed by laudanum and lack of open-air exercise, and so as a result, it falls to me (and the scholarship of France, the nation most closely tied by Destiny to the protection and proliferation of the great Pharaoh's thought and writing) to restore to . . .*

(This sentence, incidentally, continues on for more than three pages in my edition of Vassal. Credit is due to Mrs. Wilson for her stamina.)

His protestations of fearless honesty aside, Vassal, too, stopped well short of an accurate translation, preferring instead his mild titillations suitable for murmuring to ladies in the privacy of Parisian boudoirs, but not so forthright as to have the translator prosecuted by the touchy French authorities.

As Harriman hoped to find Queen Victoria in golden tunic and cobra-vulture crown, Vassal was eager to see in Atum-hadu an ancient Casanova, a practical Machiavelli, a prototype Napoleon. Both men mistranslated as necessary to achieve their portraits, leaping far beyond the available evidence to arrive at the conclusions they longed for.

It is vital not to allow one's desires to carry one from observing to creating. Both translators confused what they found with what they wished to find (a disorder perhaps attributable to the influence of the Creator-god Atum himself). They created. The two men fertilised their discoveries themselves. *Fertilise* being the key word here, for let us remind those who, perversely, have not yet read *Desire and Deceit in Ancient Egypt*, in which these issues were most fully explored, the name Atumhadu translates as Atum-Is-Aroused. And, as any schoolboy who has studied the Egyptian pantheon is quick to note, memorise, and then quote in his own defence when interrupted in solitary creativity by a nosy parent, Atum the Creator, the first being (and thus quite, quite alone), made all the other gods and the world, too, by using his own celestial hand to spill his own celestial seed onto fertile ground.

Atum-Is-Aroused: we are on the verge of Creation. Our king was named for that throbbing instant immediately prior to the creation of the universe. And, in a fertile act of Atumic homage not dissimilar, clenched and trembling men like Harriman and Vassal cannot restrain themselves from spilling educated and less educated guesses over barren, tattered evidence, producing great, pregnant speculations, each bearing a book certain to resemble the father. (And, let us take a moment to enjoy the sight of Vassal, with Gallic shamelessness, accusing Harriman of the same paternity claims of which he is equally guilty.)

In one reproduced ancient drawing I found as a boy and spent several hours amazedly pondering (until, from over my shoulder, the village librarian spotted it with a stifled shriek and confiscated the book, securing it in the sepulchral and sealed Patrons' Private Reserve Section), solitary, tirelessly creative, and divinely flexible Atum performs a service on himself that most mortal men's spines will not allow them to execute, though they all know it would be a marvellously convenient knack. (Although in my day, I once saw twin Chinese brothers, acrobats in a travelling circus passing through Kent, who matched the god's feat while hanging quite nude and pale yellow from trapezes, an act of post-performance relaxation they indulged in upside-down and side by side like two eighth notes, late at night in the darkened tent after every show, while outside one could hear the drugged elephant being washed and in the shadowed seats, one unseen audience member secretly watched the meditative display and, probably alone in all of Kent, knew that the two Orientals were, in their twinned self-absorption, unknowingly paying tribute to the god Atum.)

To Margaret: My darling Queen, having spent several hours yesterday and this morning working on scholarly essays, I grew so sad thinking about Marlowe's death and my distance from you that I decided to put work aside for the afternoon and strolled through my Cairo.

My Cairo, it affects me strangely still. Today was no exception: the remnants of religious miseducation drilled into the soft part of one's head, or just dumb superstition embedded in our systems: for whatever reason, I walked through Cairo this afternoon handing out food and some of my remaining money to those who looked most desperate — the convincingly legless, the big-eyed infants innocent of drunkenness. I hope you would have approved, my sweet Queen. Perhaps I did it for you.

I watched the women, those caramelised confections, dark-irised behind long lashes. Some are veiled, nothing but shifting eyes, always downcast or glancing sideways. Others are uncovered, and one can glimpse faces in the distorting heat and the interfering shadows of palm fronds. One of these women was moving quickly from shade to sun, and in that very first instant my eye played tricks: I thought she was covered, forehead to collarbone, with the most intricate tattoo or henna-art, a leering cobra winking at me with every movement of her cheek. But no, that semi-instant was a play of light: as she stepped into the sun I saw the rage and range of her birthmark — no cobra, no shadow, but a purple splash across her face, too intricate not to imply special knowledge and a claim to unique beauty. She looked at me with a haughty sureness of her effect.

And playing off to her left, I saw one of those children dispatched by Atum, Yahweh, Jesus, Allah, the Great Set Decorator, to crack your heart in pieces, his poverty blurring his potential, his tiny face all huge eyes. I called him over and nearly emptied my pockets into his steady hands, laid bill after bill into his palm and watched him watching me. He seemed young enough to have faith still that someone would naturally care for him. I wished I could justify that faith, urge him never to lose it.

I walked in places tourists do not frequent, where lurk the spectacularly freakish, those who slide from poor to deformed to performer with a speed making them difficult to categorise: of course I give money to the blind mothers cradling the blind infants next to the wall-eyed and incontinent dogs, and to the fused-digit flipper children, but what of the man tattooed all over in spider's webs, as if he himself were the trapped fly? What of the man all knobbed joints and slippery-eel limbs whose knees rest comfortably on top of his shoulders?

And everywhere young men glower with rage at everything and everyone, until I wonder if I am even able to understand the facial expression at all; it must be something I do not understand, since no one could be enraged by a tree, a cloud, the glowering friend he embraces.

On the narrower streets, like canals cut through the high, yellow buildings, I press myself against the walls for the barefoot delivery boys to pass with trays on their heads. I overpay them to sample the bread and fruit and chicken legs moving at nose level as I roam. In front of me at a fruit market I find an old father and his grown son. The thin, bearded father selects from the wooden stand, talking to the grey grocer, plainly his old friend. Behind him, though, his son has some sort of palsy; his hands shake and try to fly away from his body while his head snaps back and forth on an uncomfortable axis. His whole body sways like a metronome set to largo. While the father chooses figs, the son's condition worsens, and I have to take a step back not to be struck by flailing limbs. His legs begin vibrating, and then his feet alternate leaving the ground an inch at a time. The father, unhurried by what he must know is happening behind him, pays and at last turns: he gently places a hand on the boy's forearm. With that light touch he absorbs the spasms and shudders, compels the boy to be still again, to take control of himself with the help of his father's patience and presence. The boy calms down and turns his face up in a contorted smile to enjoy the sun and crunch a hard yellow date. His father keeps a hand on him a moment or two longer, grins a wrinkled grin, then turns back to address a few more words to the untroubled grocer, who has no doubt seen this every day for years. On their way past me, I slipped money into their bag.

The money itself is not an issue, as the Partnership's first wired payment is due presently. There is a mist of good luck, I suppose, hanging about the worthy or at least the entertaining poor—as if their one compensation for their lot is to decide upon your future, or as if they are an easy way to impress whichever gods one thinks will be judging one later or clearing one's path sooner. Or, perhaps there is no surer way to prove to yourself that the poor are not you than by giving them your money.

And then to the post, my Margaret, to find *you* waiting for me in the *poste restante*! I sniffed the envelope right there in the Cairo post office. Your precious scent was just discernible still, for all the distance travelled, each jealous, grasping mile snatching an atom of your fragrance. I tore open the envelope with a churning hunger for you and found your letter (?) of 19–21 Sep.

I admit to spending some anxious hours pondering this fragment of correspondence, M., but obviously it was an error of dosage or postage; your sleeping draughts are quite seriously askew, or you lost the other pages. Nevertheless, while I invariably finish your letters wishing for more, in this case my ailment was extreme. I walked very slowly back to the Hotel of the Sphinx, loathing Cairo for being the place where you were not, the place where I could not take care of you as that father took care of his son.

> Sep. 19. Evening
>> *Dearest Ralph,*
>> *Well, it seems you left today.*
>
> Sep. 20. Evening
>> *R, I miss you.*
>
> Sep. 21. Eve's knees
>> *My Ralphie,*
>> *Now you are on a boat, I think, or something like a boat.*
>> *Something afloat.*

Sunset on the Bayview Nursing Home
Sydney, Australia
December 16, 1954

Macy,

I apologise for the lost days. I've been ill, not to bore you with the details, but today's my first day standing in a week. I see on the faces of my keepers a little disappointment at the sight of me not yet dead, but they'll be in my place someday, and that's comfort enough for me.

Writing about my trip to Boston daunts me. I'm just tired, I suppose, from my illness. But even as I recall stepping aboard the *Angel of the Azores,* preparing to cross the Atlantic, thanking heaven that a bloke like myself was going to have the opportunity to see America because of my professional abilities, I sit here in the wretched heat of the games room (two incomplete sets of draughts and one of chess, some playing cards, and a heap of old droolers), and I'm having to overcome something in me that's resisting buckling back to our work. I take no pleasure in re-creating this leg of my adventure. I recall too well the price I paid for my hard work and open heart in Boston. But here's my stack of blank stationery. (Horrible, that emblem of the home, isn't it? Did they think a little drawing of the sea would make it true? Take it from me, you can't see the Bay from this building even if you jump from the roof. Which is tempting.)

I made notes and notes, cataloguing my suspicions and the case's loose ends on that weeklong trip across the Atlantic: Trilipush, Marlowe, and Quint are University mates, except that the University has never heard of Trilipush, though passing students have, years after he was there. Trilipush and Marlowe are friends, War chums, likely something else unspeakable, and Trilipush writes to Marlowe's parents, referring fondly to time spent with the old folks, whose names he doesn't know and who've never met him, though their son spoke often of him at Oxford. Where records indicate he was never a student. And the British Government claims to have no record of him participating in that War, though the unreliable Quint claims Trilipush was at Marlowe's side until Gallipoli. But recall that no one has any recollection of Caldwell, who for his part, has no reason in the world to know Marlowe, a British officer, but Marlowe recommends him for promotions, and they vanish together on a nameless mission, *after* the War is over, while Trilipush is still far off in Turkey, "pulling through." My case diagrams were more question marks than conclusions.

I had a girl at Tailor HQ cable ahead to be sure of Trilipush's presence at Harvard, using a false name as I didn't want to spook him just yet, didn't want to give him time to cover his tracks. No, I wanted this one flustered and bumbling when I got to grips with him. The girl, however, I later learned when I cabled back to London for explanation, had foolishly asked if Trilipush "taught" at Harvard, rather than if he was "at" Harvard.

So, October 13th, 1922, I arrived at ivy-blanketed Harvard University, wandered from building to building looking for Egyptology, where I asked to see Mr. Trilipush, only to learn from a secretary that he'd departed for Egypt not even a month before on an exploration, and would be abroad well into 1923. So be it: I'd find what I could here and then have a holiday in sunny Egypt on the Marlowes' and Davies's shillings. So I asked for Trilipush's chief and was brought to the office of a little round Dutchman named Terbroogan, the head of Harvard's Egypt men. When I told him I was looking for some information about his Mr. Trilipush, he replied with a sort of spittly speech defect and Fritzy accent, "My dear man, vatever elth he may be, by no thtretch of the imathinathon ith he *my* Tchiliputh."

Terbroogan had few gentle (or dry) words for his employee, and the tenor of the conversation was soon fine and candid, quite to my taste when compared to the timid snobberies of the Marlowes and the shadowy half-truths of Quint. "Insubordinate, arrogant, and wrong," chants the fellow. "Insubordinate, arrogant, and wrong. If one is arrogant, one should at least be right. But his book is a tissue of nonsense. I hope he is eaten by crocodiles out there." For a moment I found this violent language suspicious, and wondered how Professor Terbroogan and his rough fantasies might fit into our emerging picture. I wouldn't've been at all surprised to learn he'd been in the same dangerous regiment in the desert or had some other sinister connection, but no, it was a passing cloud: much of this language, Macy, I've come to understand, is quite common talk among University types, and I admit that while I meant to take careful notes of Terbroogan's complaints about Trilipush, I lost interest rapidly and now I'm having some difficulty making out just what I meant by jottings such as "RT's book is about Atoomadoo, who was or was not a king and was or was not a poet and is or is not buried where RT is going and Egyptian poems do or do not rhyme. This is what these men do all day? For work?" Maybe it was the climate or the tucker or the conversation, but I was already finding America rather exhausting and I felt more than just a bit ill. None of Terbroogan's words have stayed with me, until I asked where in Egypt Trilipush had gone. "Deir el Bahari," replied Terbroogan, and I made him spell it for me, to be sure. ("Do you see it, Macy?" I later ask my worthy but dim assistant, back at our hotel, poring over maps, but he shakes his head and chews his lip. You don't mind, do you, Macy? Something of comic relief is how I'm picturing you now.)

"And, because you have such trouble with Professor Trilipush," I asked the turnip-faced chief, who was wiping his mouth with a handkerchief, "you sent him on this excavation? Expensive way to get him out of your hair, no?"

He hadn't. It had been Terbroogan's option, and he'd *refused* Trilipush the money for the trip, precisely because of disagreements over the quality of Trilipush's scholarship. (Honestly, Macy, these people were barking mad.) "Unt I happen to know he vath turned down by the MFA, the Met, and the Carnegie." He's travelling on his own money, then? "Not at all. He sold shares in his misadventure to some local businessmen."

My dear Macy, we now come to some language you may not appreciate. I've been wondering whether to soften certain hard truths as I found them in those days, and perhaps cast things in a more flattering light for you. Well, I will not do that. I'm too old for it, and you've asked me for an honest rendering, and frankly, it isn't my manner to provide any other kind. Slippery slope, that one. I'm a truth man, me, and I think this must be exactly why I was so resistant this morning to getting started on the Boston leg of my tale. Right, then: I'll apologise here, this once, and that will be the end of it: I'm sorry if you read things in this chronicle, Mr. Laurence Macy III, that are painful to you or upset your notion of your family, or your poor, late aunt Margaret.

"Not at all. He sold shares in his misadventure to some local businessmen, unsavoury types, if I may say, with unfortunate reputations." He mentioned your great-uncle Chester Finneran, as well as Heinz Kovacs.

Why didn't he just fire Trilipush, if he was such a thorn in their side? The fellow explained with a certain tone that "the University generally preferred not to do that" (honestly, these people). But "when he comes back from Egypt empty-handed, which he certainly will, that should be enough to shame the man out," he added with a nice shot of venom. Noting how he sounded, the professor then visibly exerted himself to give his bloke a fair go: "Trilipush is a good teacher, he was a heroic soldier in Turkey, and he was educated at Oxford, which does add to our department's credentials, and Atoomadoo is not uninteresting, only not defini- tive, and so when one has problems, one prefers simply to place people where they will quietly do their job, but this one, my Lord." That about exhausted the old man's goodwill. "When he was new here, last year, he was positively fawning towards me, but that did not last."

I think I must have said it something like this, Macy, though of course I made no note of the exact wording: "Would it be useful to you and the University to dis- creetly employ someone who may be able to provide you extra material in 'sham- ing Mr. Trilipush out,' as you put it. If, for example, discrepancies in his Oxford record were discovered—"

"But I saw his credentials, everything stamped and sealed and signed, no question at all."

"Documents, Professor Terbroogan, are only pieces of paper that purport to represent the truth. They're not truth itself. Surely in your field of study, you've seen misleading, even malicious documents."

You've never seen a happier little Dutch professor, Macy, and we had a new client in the Davies-Caldwell-Barry-Hoyt-Marlowe-Trilipush case.

Terbroogan walked me down the hall decorated with sphinx statues and pho- tographs of him in sandy pits, and I asked to see Trilipush's office. This was a small, windowless room in the basement, with shelves of books and pictures of excavators and relics. Trilipush's desk was clean, but for a small stack of post which had arrived for him since his departure to Egypt. And right there on the top? An oversized envelope with a familiar return address, stamped with English postage. Oh, yes, Macy, from our Beverly Quint: he'd asked me for Trilipush's ad- dress and must've set to writing this the minute I left his rooms: a warning or tell- tale reminiscence, certainly some proof of conspiracy in what I was beginning to suspect had been the Marlowe-Caldwell murders at the hands of Trilipush and with the leering knowledge of Quint. This envelope must've come over on my very boat. Quint and I had floated across the Atlantic, one on top of the other, quite unaware, and now we had arrived at our mutual destination, just inches apart. So much might be answered right there, but damn him, my newest client was hovering over me, asking if there was anything else I needed, and looking at me with one of those faces you see from time to time in our profession, Macy, that look of suspicious superiority from someone so removed from the dirty realities of life that he cannot distinguish between the filth of the criminal and the smudge on the fellow who had to wrestle the criminal in order to save the innocent. I could've throttled the professor right there, standing on toff ceremony, pushing me out the door when we might've saved so many middle steps, perhaps even saved two more lives, and your lovely aunt Margaret more suffering. No, we were out the door and into the hall, and the door was locked and Quint's package sat undisturbed on Trilipush's desk, waiting for his return. Professor Terbroogan meaningfully rattled the locked knob and looked at me looking at Quint's package through the glass plate in the door. There it is, Macy: from across the globe a pom poofter could simply address an illicit package and count on the protection of some Dutch University snob he'd never met! Whatever'd happened to poor Paul Caldwell—and I had strong suspicions—was going to be devilish difficult to unravel, because as fast as I was unravelling, these toffs and poms and perverts and professors were going to ravel it up again, maybe to hide something wicked, maybe just because they liked things tidy and that meant not letting a simple Australian working man do his job. "Is there anything else you need, Mr. Ferrell?" Terbroogan asked with an unmistakable tone that meant, "Gentlemen don't read each other's post." No, of course they don't, even if gentlemen are murderers.

I had Chester Finneran's address from Terbroogan. I recall standing outside the gates of Harvard University, hailing a cab. I must've gone to his house across the river, for I've no notes of interviews between those I conducted with Terbroogan and Finneran, dated the same day. But I've no recollection of the cab ride. I feel so ill right now, I don't know if I'll be able to continue. I'll post this at once.

HF

Sunday, 15 October, 1922

<u>*To Margaret:*</u>   It is just after midnight, my love. I sit on my balcony, put the waiters through their paces, relax with a photograph of you before me on the table.

Your abruptly truncated letter troubled me, my darling, not because of the evidence of mis-medication, but because I know that you have been struggling to hide symptoms from me, and when you realised what you had sent me, I am certain you worried and unduly strained your nerves further. And of course, as this was your first letter following my departure for Egypt, your sorrowful emotional state had likely already taken a toll on your still healing body.

You are adorable, Margaret. You have always downplayed your bad days, as if I would not notice the difference between you healthy and ill. When you finally admitted your condition to me, the day after the party, I should have looked more surprised for you. My love, I am sorry if I was unconvincing, but one day last summer, your father had already told me everything. You must not be angry with him. CCF is father to us both now. When I asked him for your hand, he felt himself honour-bound to tell your would-be husband the entire tale. He wanted to tell me the worst and see that my love for you was unshaken. CCF spoke openly and, well before your timid little report, I had heard all about the nerve specialists, the exhaustion caused by the medication, the rarity of your illness. I also heard your excellent prognosis, your imminent and certain cure. And, Margaret, upon my word, I have never had a moment's concern since. I know you are every day stronger, and Inge is but a temporary nurse to administer the last of your medications and nothing more. Whether she joins us for the early days of marriage, or whether you will already be fully restored to health—time will tell. In the meantime, you must not worry, and certainly never about the strength of my love for you, my angel.

Your father is a man of many parts. He presents such a rough exterior to the world, and of course his business milieu allows for no other, but I have seen him speak of you. I have seen him drop his guard and reveal his deep concern and tenderness. I saw his eyes mist when he spoke of the worry your illness had caused him, and his determination when he told me, "Ralph, she's beating this thing. You've got nothing to worry about in her as your hale and healthy, intact wife." He is a father, bless his heart.

I mourn the loss of my own father every day, and you should think of CCF with fondness, as I do, for a father's love is one of the most precious gifts.

I remember the anticipation I would feel, as a boy in Trilipush Hall, when I knew Father was due to return from an expedition soon. He would have been gone for weeks or even months, and I longed for nothing more than to be taken up in his strong arms and popped on his knee in front of the great fire to hear of his adventures. Would today be the day he arrived? How I would pace the vast, echoing chambers of the Hall.

Ah, Trilipush Hall! There were marvels to be found there. The walls cluttered with portraits of wigged and grinning ancestors. The endless suits of armour and forests of halberds, lances, pikes, the walls of unstrung crossbows. The hanging tapestries with scenes of mediaeval hunts and balls. The drawer where Father haphazardly tossed his military honours and medals, and those of our ancestors. The relics Father had brought back from Africa, Malacca, China. The blazing fire in the hearth ten feet tall—a hasp of log the shape of a ham hock, but zebra-striped grey and black and fluttering its long, orange tresses of flame—in front of which I would lie on my stomach in solitude and practise hieroglyphs. On some days, out the east window of the main room, you could see streaming rain and at the same instant, through the west window, sunshine breaking through the clouds, and I would run back and forth from window to window, imagining myself in different countries at Father's side, fighting bandits while he pulled astounding artefacts from the earth. I would look out the window (streaked with rain or sparkling with new sun), and I would watch the birds on the emerald grounds—the omnipresent pheasant and the uncomplaining grouse had grown more plentiful and arrogant in Father's absence, as no hunts took place without him. And I would long for the sound of carriage wheels out front: would today be the day of his return? The great room grew darker and darker until only the fire's orange embers lit my face and the dark wood furnishings carved with scenes of Trilipushian triumphs dating back to the Conquest, and I would fall asleep there, under rugs, ignoring the calls of servants wandering from chamber to chamber, up and down the oaken stairs.

But when it *was* the day! How I sped to the great front door and the gravel drive, how I leapt up to his carriage when it was still moving, and how the door swung open and he pulled me inside, onto his lap, and the tickle of his moustaches smelt of tobacco and faraway lands, and how I relished the laughing surprise in his eyes as he would shout, "What? What? What's this, then? Who are you, young man? I left a small boy behind! Where's my son? What have you done with Ralph, then, you scoundrel?"

"It's me, Papa, it's me!"

"What? Ralph? Is it you, really? Why, I took you for one of the farmhands!"

"It's me, Papa, it's me!"

Monday, 16 October, 1922

Journal: Post. Lunch in town. Post. Antiquities Service, to see if there has been a speedy resolution to my application. Post. Visit a portrait photographer to send my fiancée just the right memento. The afternoon is well-spent: I have a dozen handsome options for her.

Evening, return to hotel to continue writing the surrounding material, the soft, form-fitting packing of this work, as it were, in which its precious treasures shall be carried out of the tomb and into the world at large.

   On immortality and "The Tomb Paradox":   Atum-hadu reigned in a

Tuesday, 17 October, 1922

Journal: Yesterday's work ended prematurely with a boiling, vindictive attack of explorer's gut, the brutal, acidic remnants of dysentery. Lost half a day to treating it, sleeping it off, burning through dozens of styluses on the HMV suitcase model gramophone I have placed in the water closet to make just such afternoons tolerable. Before taking up yesterday's work, I shall set off for town to breakfast, and visit Antiquities and the post.

Sep. 22

Hello, darling!

Who's your good girl? I am, my prince. I set myself the goal of writing to you every day while you are "in the field," and I have kept my solemn promise. I sent you a letter just this morning that I wrote and sealed last night, though I can't remember writing it for the life of me, as Inge had me on some very strong things to help me sleep, because after you left, I was upset, even though I know you will say that I was being simply absurd, but you are absolutely my Hero, and when a girl's Hero leaves town, everything feels a little bleak, now doesn't it? And here I am writing you again, because this morning I had something I wanted to include, but last night's letter was already sealed and ready, so I gave it to Inge just now to run down to Arlington Street while I write you this one, and then I am going to give her this one to run right back down to Arlington Street the minute she gets back, because she is fat and needs the air.

I had an absolutely awful dream last night. Truth is, Inge gave me pain and sleeping things last night, and I didn't remember to tell her that she was giving them to me on top of a drink or two. See, last night, truth is, I hopped out on Inge, completely foxed her. She'd been watching me so close for so many days, it was getting hard to get out of the house, and I was feeling awful bored, which is worse than anything. So I snuck out last night and went over to J. P. O'Toole's place. When I got back, she was waiting for me all angry like she gets when I show her how much smarter I am than she is, so it was sleeping and pain stuff from her (on top of the drink or two), and it can be a plenty deep sleep when they're mixed up like that. When it's just you and me, just the old "man and wife," I'll be so pleased to see Inge get her walking papers. Do you know she had the nerve to tell me the other day that you fell in love with me for Daddy's money? I nearly slapped her, the Swedish hussy, but she had the drop on me.

Of course, even when I'm done with her, don't be surprised if she stays on to "work" for Daddy. I know where she goes when I'm fast asleep. I'm not, after all, a complete ninny. You wouldn't want a complete ninny for a wife, now would you, my Limey?

Are you happy on your Expedition? Where are you now, I wonder? Probably still at sea, consulting with the ship's Captain, showing him your maps and your wicked pharaoh's poems. You're probably surrounded by girls again, just like when I met you. But you know they aren't for you, Ralphie. Only your Devoted Queen-to-be is for you, and you are only for her.

Daddy asked me what you and I were thinking about for our residences after the Expedition and the wedding, and would we live in Boston only or would we move into Trilipush Hall. He looked at me all sentimental like he gets, said he'd always wanted to see me in a big English country house. What do you think? Would you consider going back to England, or would it still be too painful? Will there be enough money to open up the Hall again? Daddy is often an idiot, but on this I think he may be very right: I think I would be very happy as an English Lady.

That reminds me: this dream last night, in the medication-fog. It was just a little bit into the future. You and I were married. I was feeling so strong and healthy. We were so happy, and I never caused you any trouble with my moods or anything. Your digging had made us wonderfully rich, and you were famous, and we were welcomed everywhere with absolutely everyone, and you took me to England to meet the king and queen. And then we came back home and I was going to have our first baby. Ralph Chester Crawford Trilipush was a darling little thing, and just after he was born he was already talking! At first we were all so proud, but then we listened, and he was talking only the most terrible cursing, he just wouldn't stop—the filthiest language you could imagine, and the doctors were shaking their heads and the nurses were *all sobbing, and I didn't know what to think, because they were giving me stronger and stronger things to take, and I was falling back into the special sleep again, but before I could relax into it, I looked up and, Ralph, you, you were just laughing and saying, "Oh, yes, that's my lad, that is."*

Honestly, this letter writing is absolutely exhausting, I have to tell you. It's still God-awful hot here, and I am sleepy just always. Inge will be back soon, which is good, because I want to send you this, but I also need something for the pain, which is bad today. You can't imagine. It's like an itch so bad you'd tear your head off to feel scratched properly. The stuff Inge gives me scratches me for a while, and when I'm asleep it doesn't itch so bad. If it would just stop itching and I didn't always feel so God-awful tired (excuse me for saying it straight), I'd be out having a gay old time on the town with my friends or with fellows. Oh, yes, Ralphie, you'd better come home soon all covered in laurels or I'll find someone else to carry me away! Don't think I won't, Englishman. A good American, stout and strong, could have me in a second.

But I am so tired.

I kiss you, and so do Antony and Cleopatra. They send you licks. Their tails don't wag as much since you've gone. It's true. I really think they miss you just like I do.

Your Margaret

(Tuesday, 17 October 1922, continued)

To Margaret: My darling. Your second letter came today, hard on the heels of your first effort, and my heart steams with gratitude. Your charming Atum-haduan dream was delightful and put me in mind of our first meeting. I have never told you what I was thinking that day last April, but the memory is sweet to me in my isolation here.

My contribution to the Boston Historical Society's Public Improvement Lectures had been promoted as a discussion of ancient Egyptian culture, and though I had promised the organisers I would not do so, I had always intended to read aloud from *Desire and Deceit*. A performer must face facts: the size of the gathered audience left no doubt as to the main attraction on the bills advertising the evening. While I do love my work, I would not be so foolish as to assert that hundreds of Bostonian ladies had gathered for a generic discussion of Egypt. That the speaker would be none other than the dashing and mildly notorious translator of *that scandalous king*, well, it would not have been fair to our followers to deny them a quatrain here and there, and to answer those questions (historical, sociological, anatomical) which naturally arise in a discussion of our king.

Do you know how early in the evening I first noticed you, my Queen? I was explaining the chronic ancient Egyptian tendency to a morbid nostalgia, a trait that paradoxically appeared *early* in the country's development, an illness displaying itself in the Egyptian's persistent political agenda of restoring "debased" religious practise, repeated century after century; in his foolish folk-memory of a lost West that was once rich green pasture, full of mighty bulls; and in his recurring sensation that he was living in corrupted end-times. Usually, such sensations were absurd: nostalgia for things that never existed, restoring something already in perfect condition, paranoia that the end was near or that standards had perilously slipped. However, at certain dramatic, transitional moments, such as the end of the reign of Atum-hadu, these fears were suddenly justified. "At the end of his life, Atum-hadu must certainly have believed that Egypt itself was about to vanish forever," I was saying when I noticed you in the front row: you were dozing off, my beauty, and that would never do, so I noted your position, and a few minutes later I made a point of looking you in the eye when I recited his Quatrain 35 (uniquely in Fragment C):

> She will be mine, she will be mine
> She will be mine, she will be mine
> And her mother and her goats and her sisters nine
> They shall be mine until I tire of them, fine.

This was always an exhilarating moment in my lectures, and I usually selected a young woman at random to feel the savage churn of Atum-hadu's attentions. In this case, my love, I simply did not realise what I had unleashed.

I recognised you later, when you were but one of many pushing to the foot of the stage to ask one last question they were too shy to ask in front of the whole audience, or simply to shake the English explorer's hand. I was answering questions and signing copies of *Desire and Deceit,* so I did not pay you attention, but *you* did not leave the front of the stage, did you? When I looked back, you were still there. I had seen that face before: the woman who has heard the song of the ancient king.

"Professor Trilipush?" murmured a quiet but resonant voice. "Professor Trilipush, I was so interested by your talk."

"Well, to be strictly accurate," I said, stepping down to the floor, "I cannot purport to be a *full* professor, yet. Technical distinctions at Harvard, as in any primitive society, are of the highest importance."

"Well then," you replied with narrowed eyes and upturned mouth, "I cannot purport to have been *fully* interested in your talk. Some of the more technical aspects did leave me a little less attentive."

"Oh, miss, now really," scolded the Nordic beauty to your side, all spheres and half-moons.

"Put a cork in it, Inge," said my future darling. "Why don't you go take a sauna or something?"

You boldly introduced yourself, and I could not resist quoting the advertisements one saw everywhere in Boston: "Life is finer when you find fashion with finesse at Finneran's Finer Finery." But I must remind you, lest you ever believe Inge's Norwegian nastiness, I did not know that the shop was your family's. And recall: you laughed but did not confess your connection, so I assumed the names were coincidental. Atum-hadu was already pulling the strings, my dear, and lucre was never his chief concern.

After the crowd had finally drained out the door, you and I sat and spoke at the foot of the stage, and I decided to trust you, to test you, and I showed you how to write Atum-hadu in hieroglyphs. All the while, your frosty duenna lingered by the front door, talked to the Historical Society workers (delighted at the crowd they had drawn, relieved that the police had not broken up the event on decency charges). What were my impressions of you then? Well, my Miss Finneran was a lively young woman, mildly but not irrevocably spoilt, and clearly a little intoxicated by her first exposure to Atum-hadu. I was not terribly surprised when she said she would be honoured if I would escort her to the Museum of Fine Arts at some later date, where she might have the pleasure of my elucidation of the Egyptian relics on display. Oh yes, do not permit suspicious Inge to rewrite history, my dear. It was *your* suggestion we meet again, my most forward flirt. I have been your creature ever since.

Of course, I did not fool myself that you were taken with *me*, precisely. No, I could see that another twentieth-century woman had found the words of the XIIIth-Dynasty king to be an overwhelming *eau de cologne*.

My darling, I am stuck in Cairo, awaiting my licence to proceed from the Antiquities Service, and I wonder what you are doing this very instant. Here it is 17 October, at 11.36 P.M. How I wish I had a device that allowed me to peer at you right now, a telescope of the most powerful kind. I would watch you ceaselessly, my love.

Wednesday, 18 October, 1922

<u>Journal:</u> Nothing at the post. Four days before my Master of Largesse and the backers will wire and refill my coffers, I set off to continue purchasing supplies in the markets and speciality stores dedicated to men in my position. A full day, and the activity eases the boredom I was feeling from my forced delay. Paints, brushes, pencils, chisels, carving knife, electric torch, camp bed: my list is slowly being filled when, on a quiet side street, I note the storefront of a tailor. I will need several more suits, for working and socialising, and something formal for an official Tomb Opening (an event usually involving high

officials of the English, French, and Egyptians, possibly General Allenby, et cetera).

I pushed through hanging beads and into a well-lit little space where a tall Egyptian was prematurely stooped from spending years under this low ceiling, and I was soon in a padded, wicker armchair, sipping cardamom coffee with the proprietor while two young boys wheeled in gold-painted cart after cart of fabrics. The tailor and I fingered this and that, discussed the merits of certain cloths for resisting the heat while still catching the eye. I was impressed enough by ten of the samples to order suits of them (CCF would have paid ten times as much in Boston) and stood for my measurements. The triple mirrors offered me left- and right-handed versions of myself to play with, profiles in only my undershorts with my bare feet aligned heel to toe, while below me a crouching servant measured my legs and called out the numbers to a scribe cross-legged on a cushion, his sleeves rolled up to reveal hairless arms with embossed veins like relief maps of river deltas, and somewhere behind a curtain out of sight, I heard female whispers and subdued tittering.

A small deposit and the suits will be ready in one week's time, the 25th. Go to tourist agency to postpone departure, booking on the *Cheops*.

And then, as I was strolling along, pleased with my purchase, thinking of my fiancée, I came upon an inspirational sight on a street corner: a wooden easel with two folding stools where tourists could pay to have their likeness painted on a convincingly broken piece of pottery, dressed in Pharaonic garb, surrounded by a hodgepodge of 'glyphs. A fat Egyptian was painting the profile of an American boy while his parents watched, laughing, trading audible asides at the artist's expense.

Well, I certainly shall not pose for a tourist's knickknack, but an official portrait, begun prior to the opening of Atum-hadu's tomb and completed after it, would have a certain timeliness to it, a marker in my career, admired on a wall in Boston or London or Cairo. With a week's

delay still, I have the time. Upon my return to the hotel, I ask the concierge to arrange for the best portraitist he can find to come to my
rooms. I begin my sittings tomorrow.

An evening at the cinema. In the darkened hall, chewing dates and
figs, the natives and I are equally astounded by the moving picture: an
Englishman wrestles a lion, then enters a tent where a beautiful woman
with almond eyes awaits him. Later he battles bandits and enters a
Pharaonic tomb, where he runs his hands through mountains of loose
gold and jewellery. A mummy stands as if alive and attacks the Englishman, but he dispatches the ghoul with a pistol shot.

Thursday, 19 October, 1922

<u>*Journal:*</u> Today's activities included two hours of meditation while
the artist pencilled his rough plans onto the canvas. I also found an excellent craftsman of valises, an unadulterated delight, which I know my
brother Atum-hadu would have savoured in preparing for his travels,
too—the soft scale of the crocodile, the glistening brass of the hasps,
the burnt-black monogram (*A* being only 1/3 the cost of *RMT,* of
course, but that is one of the perquisites of kinghood). Nothing at the
bank today, though of course the wire is not officially due for three
days yet.

Tonight, I toil in the clamour of a little cabaret where the *chicha*
smoke forms jinn who embrace their puff-cheeked masters with massaging fingers. I watch the smoker by the door: a nest slowly coils
around his head, the faint echo of an ancestor's mummy wraps, but
each time the door opens to his right, all at once the smoke rushes out,
away, up into the star-flecked, plum-coloured sky. The door closes and
he begins again, shrouding himself top to bottom with smoke; the door
opens and invisible plunderers again unravel his work.

<u>*On immortality and "The Tomb Paradox":*</u> Immortality is, of course,
the central issue under the sands. The ancient kings, I would remind
my lay readers, all shared a healthy desire to live forever in a well-

equipped eternity. To achieve this personal permanence, two elements were necessary:

- The preservation of their physical remains, eternally secure
- The preservation of their names, spoken forever by the living.

Margaret: M., a memory forms like smoke gathering around my head: that village vicar who would appear when I wandered away from Father and the Hall. "Tell me, child. Do you believe in the immortality of the soul?" Aside from him, I do not remember fear in my childhood, but in the case of this vicar, I can conjure today the varieties and intensities of childish terror I felt at the mention of his name, at the sight of his face across a street (calibrated before and after he caught sight of me), the sound of his voice, the feel of his massive, speckled hand on my shoulder, the smell of his breath, the harsh, changeable weather of his moods, and that tingling dread, most intense, when he would present me with some gift.

"Yes," I mumbled, nearly choking on the proffered sweet.

"And what are the requirements for the soul's immortality in everlasting paradise?" He leaned in close to hear my answer, placed his ear directly before my mouth, where he must have heard the slurping and crunching of the candy, and I saw deep into that bristled conch shell, red and flaking from winter cold.

I was *not* trying to mock him, not at that age, Margaret. No, I was *relieved*, for I knew the answer to his question! I had happened to read it that very day, absorbed until well after dark by Bendix's *Nile Kings* (a work I can no longer endorse for scholars). I was relieved, relieved, and I spoke before I heard a faint stammering voice in my brain telling me to stop: "The survival of your remains and your name. Your name in chronicles, your body in the mummy wrap, and your heart, lungs, intestines, and liver in canopic jars. Figurines of serving girls to arouse you for the act of re-creation . . ." My voice was slowing down at the same speed his ghastly ear withdrew and was replaced by the smoothly shaven face (with a red-brown sliver of dried blood) and the so-blue eyes, and the shards of skin speared and quivering in his eyebrow.

And yet from here the beating that followed seems not to have been administered to me; I can instead (in this Oriental music here that may be scarcely changed from that of 3500 years ago) see that beating delivered to the boy Atum-hadu, still a commoner in the increasing turmoil of his times, realising slowly but with delight that he was endowed with gifts that none around him possessed, that his ascent to the very pinnacle of his world (though that world was crumbling even as he scaled it) seemed inevitable. If in his ascent he offended or was forced to abandon those around him, the cruel vicars of his world, that was to be expected, even enjoyed, enjoyed *even in the beatings themselves* ("What are you laughing at, wretch?" I recall my own clergyman asking, as the ex-boxer-turned-man-of-God's blows rained down harder on the little boy, somehow already the stronger of the two).

But immortality—that is the central issue, and the basis for what I term "The Tomb Paradox," which, I notice now, is as good a title for this book as any other. *The Tomb Paradox: Atum-hadu, Ralph Trilipush, and the Solution to the Puzzle That Has Lasted Three Millennia.*

<u>On immortality and the Tomb Paradox:</u>   The ancient kings required a fair amount of luggage for a successful journey to the afterlife, and as much of that luggage appeared to the average man-on-the-Nile to be gold, jewellery, and luxury furnishings, the temporarily dead king was certain to attract unwanted visitors into his private tomb whilst he was in the awkward middle period between dying and rebirth. The honey of his trappings would draw enough ants to destroy his eternal picnic and perhaps even his corpse. (And potential tomb-robbers significantly outnumbered potential tomb residents, as not even ancient Egypt promised immortality to just any farmer or washerwoman.) Thus, the kings were torn between building, on the one hand, showy but impenetrable tombs and, on the other, completely hidden tombs.

The problem with the former: impenetrability over eternity *does not exist.* Even if the royal tomb architects outthought the wiliest tomb-robbers for 500 years . . . that is only 500 years, a drop in the ocean. The problem with the latter solution: even if the king swallows hard and accepts the humiliation of being buried in an unmarked tomb, far from the temples built to perform the rituals which would speed him into the underworld, even if he would surrender being seen as the sort of king who knows how to throw a funeral and stock a good-looking tomb, all in order to keep his tomb location a secret (surrendering one sort of immortality for another), he then faces a malignant question: just how secret is secret enough?

For, now, observe: your tomb architect certainly knows where your richly appointed temporary resting place is and how to enter it. He in turn will use a few hundred workers and slaves, at least, to build, decorate, and stock it. Well, we can solve that, you and I: use prisoners of war, and then, when the tomb is ready for occupancy, simply slaughter the men who made it. Of course now we have to bury them somewhere far from the tomb site: how to transport them there, dead or alive? Now who else knows, who told their cousins to expect them back from work late tonight, work in Deir el Bahari? And the men who, at your orders, slaughtered the prisoners—do they suspect why they did it? Did one squeal to a brother-in-law who needs money? Loose ends proliferate. As for the architect, the man who knows all your secrets: reward him! Shut his mouth with treasure, pleasure, and immortality of his own! Palaces and gold and a fine tomb just for him, to discourage him from emptying yours the day after you take up residence in it. You breathe easy, for a moment, and then you recall the plundered tombs of your ancestors, all of whom thought they had pulled the wool over the eyes of eternity. Their emptied pits are there for you to consider whenever you feel like taking a walk out from your capital in Thebes, to stroll the bluffs and valleys in the moonlight, to see just where their tombs were ransacked and the authorities, in a panic, dumped the remnants of their bodies and goods into hastily constructed caches, group sites where once powerful men and women now lie on top of each other in crumpled, unravelling heaps, hoping that when the day comes Osiris will figure out whose intestines are whose.

So, making a display of yourself fails. Working in secret fails. The natural next notion is to endow a state-run and protected necropolis, the Valley of the Kings, in which no one attempts secrecy but instead the mummies rely on the well-paid living to protect the crowded, enclosed city of the dead. "We will stick together," say the kings for an optimistic period. "We will build openly, with immortal displays of our wealth and power, and we will lie mummified cheek by mouldering jowl, and make an institution, a governmental ministry of tomb management and protection. The kings who come after us will see that the maintenance of a secure necropolis is in their own future interest; each king will trust his successor, because each king will know that his successor must, in turn, trust *his* successor to return the favour." A golden rule to protect all that underground gold. "You, too, will need the fallible living someday, oh yes you will, so do this for me today and the future will protect us both." Ah, except! Except it does not take long for the present to find the pious claims of the past and the hypothetical necessities of a distant future to be, both, of little weight when pressing, present needs appear. Observe: to a government in need of money for wars or monuments, the immortality insurance glinting under the sand begins to look not unlike a well-located treasury, and the past seems to be volunteering to finance the present, and the future immortality problems of the current spendthrift king seem comfortably far away.

Suddenly, your immortality, which matters more to you than anything else in the entire universe, seems horribly tenuous, as you grow every day older and your enemies approach. How to bring everything that you need for an uncertain future without losing anything or drawing unwanted attention to yourself? Every traveller's dilemma, mine heading south, the king's heading to the underworld: what to pack?

Three days until the wire.

The dancers on the narrow stage here remind one of a verse of Atum-hadu's:

Atum-hadu admires two sisters.
He takes them to his chambers.
Too late they realise the dangers
Of a king whose love produces blisters.

—(Quatrain 9, Fragments A & C, from *Desire and Deceit*
in Ancient Egypt by Ralph M. Trilipush)

The strenuous contortions poor Harriman performed to navigate even that relatively mild passage! "Two sisters' unfortunate behaviour comes to the king's attention," and "Atoom-Hadoo's chamber of justice," and "the heat of royal wrath," and so forth, the injured prude taking shelter in jurisprudence.

19 Oct.
Cairo, a cabaret, late at night

My darling Queen-to-be,

I have just reread your letter of 22 September, as I have done over and over for three days now, and I see your face everywhere I look, even in this Oriental stage show. The women on the stage remove their silken scarves to the sound of the tambourines and moaning violins, and the veils drift down like perfume. They seem practically naked when they step onto the stage, but then even after removing veil after veil after veil for minutes, strewing them in heaps on the stage and my table, they leave not much nuder than they arrived, though the silken skins they have shed form a pile as large as a desert bluff hiding a royal tomb.

Cairo teems with reminders of you. The palm trees at night resemble quite precisely a giant wilted bouquet, like the one I held out for you last spring, as you stepped down from the cab, a distant look in your eye, scarcely recognising me, as I had just spent two hours in the driving rain waiting for you. I was just now recalling the evening in

May you and I rode the swan boats in the Public Garden and I recited Atum-hadu's verse to you and you laughed at us:

Atum-hadu sees his newest queen for the first time.
His heart and body swell and inflame.
He will go mad, will commit some crime,
If she is not brought to him at once, naked, without shame.

There you were, smiling up at me in such calm amusement. You saw *me,* saw past the shock of the poetry and of the king's appetites, and saw the real *me,* as I am. I knew that instant what an extraordinary find I had made, knew it as if I had opened a tomb full of jewels and flashing gold. You looked at *me,* and saw what was valuable and worthy of your love there. There is nothing buried under any sand that compares to last spring with you, finding you, falling in love with you, winning you. You are such a marvellous girl, Margaret. You are everything I have ever wanted in a wire.

And soon nothing will stand in the way of our wedding. I beg of you to wait, be patient, stay strong and healthy, and wait, wait for me, wait. I will be home before you know it, sweeping you away, covering you in treasure, setting you down in a home beyond your wildest dreams, filling your days with entertainments and rest in whatever proportion you desire. In your letter you asked where we shall live. Why, we shall be in a palace, you and I, in a palace, by a river, under palms, wanting for nothing.

> Your king,
> RMT.

P.S. — I hope you will take this expression of my concern in the proper light: it seems to me your father is relying too heavily on Inge to cure you. Whatever the diagnosis, your fatigues and spells should be curable by a proper doctor and medicine that gives you more energy, but judging by the fragment of a letter you posted to me in a medicated delirium, it appears she is administering substances that *exacerbate* your symptoms. Allow me to say that no one knows you better than I, especially when you are fully healthy and vibrant, and when you are my wife, we will spare no expense to have you seen by the best specialists in these matters. You have all my love. You are my Queen.

Sunset on the Bayview Nursing Home
Sydney, Australia
December 24, 1954

Still here, Macy, still here. Though I must've left you wondering. Another week on my back. Christmas upon us. Cheery season, I'm told.

I wonder, Macy, if you're a religious man. I'm not in the slightest, not I, it's patent foolishness. But there's an old woman here, quite out of her mind, like most of them, hasn't spoken in ages, just stares at the radio, but she said to me this morning—first time she's said word one to me—she said people are judged in the next world by all the animals who'd seen them in this one. Not just the cows you ate up or the fish you caught, she isn't a "vegetarian," I don't think, just the nice animals that watch you as you go about your business, if you see what I mean. The cats that watched you when you were otherwise alone. The dogs lying in the heat across the street from you. Birds outside your window. Goldfish in a bowl. They all report on what they've seen you do, she says, they all parliament themselves and then they decide if you fly or if you fry. What do you think of that idea? I think about all those sad-eyed animals I've been alone with, figure they're napping, not understanding anything even when they're awake. Very strange notion, very unsettling. Can't be true, but you ever heard anyone say it before?

Your aunt Margaret, don't suppose you'd know this, back in '22, she used to have these little dogs, although maybe you've seen pictures. Tibetan spaniels, I remember her saying to me when I turned up at your great-uncle's door, October the 13th, 1922. Your aunt opened the door, and these little dogs were yapping at me when I walked in. First thing she says, before I could say a word, she says, "Tibetan spaniels, very pricey, exceedingly *rrrrrrare.*" When she said *rare*, she sort of growled and curled her lip at me. Hello, here's a live one, I thought. She was something to look at, your aunt, and obviously an electric sort of modern girl. I wonder if she mentioned me to you at all, if there's anything you might tell me, not that she would've said anything, I don't fool myself I had that much effect on her, and not that she wasn't above stretching the truth now and again for a story, if there's anything hard to credit in those papers of hers.

Your great-uncle was a no-nonsense kind of man, an admirable man. Tough as a croc, big fellow, hair slicked right back, offered me a very fine cigar. In his great big study, he sat at a large, shiny desk and showed me an advertisement he was examining, turned the board towards me. "For the holiday season," he said. "Trying to decide if I approve or not." A drawing of a woman serving an enormous roast bird of some sort on a huge platter, and the words "Don't serve fine fowl on foul finery! Trust Finneran's Finer Finery for all your holiday needs! (Our goods last an eternity, guaranteed!)" The woman in the drawing was your aunt, you see, she'd modelled for it. "It took such a long time." She sighed. "At least I didn't have to hold the turkey, the artist drew that later. He was a bit of a sissy, I think."

"That's enough language," muttered Finneran. "We have company. What can we do for you today, Mr. Harold Ferrell of Tailor Enquiries Worldwide all the way from Australia?" He examined my business card and rolled his unlit cigar back and forth between his lips. "I don't think I've ever had any business in Australia."

I told him I was working on the inheritance of an Australian fellow and that I thought his business partner Professor Trilipush might be able to help me find this missing heir, as the two of them might've known each other in the War. "Ralphie?" your aunt breaks in. "He's a bit more than a *business* partner, Harry!" I liked how she named me Harry straightaway and never let it go.

"This gentleman has business with me, Maggie, so scram." She raised her eyebrows, made a sarcastic curtsey, collected her dogs, and slammed the door behind her. I understood all about your aunt already, I thought: spoilt, charming when she wants to be, bit of a would-be snob, but she's young and doesn't have anyone to show her how it's done. The money smelled new, no offence, Macy. No butler to answer the door, still a household with real people in it. Understand: I prefer that. I liked the way Finneran spoke, and I liked his home right off. He was a wealthy man (I thought), but still understood what drove real men, understood the limits of his money. I hope I'm describing you as well there in your New York mansion, Macy.

"High-spirited filly," says her father after the door's echo dies away. "But what she meant was, she's engaged to Professor Trilipush." That was intriguing news to me, Macy. "He's a fine fellow," continues Finneran with a certain tone. "Do you know him? No, well, he's a hell of a fine fellow. Old English family, brave as hell soldier, expert in his field. Quite a thing. You don't see many men like him, even in England, I wouldn't figure, and to catch a fellow like that in Boston, and for Margaret to win his heart, we're a pretty happy family here, Mr. Ferrell." I might not have the exact words, but that was the thrust of it. As I was trying to explain just now, your great-uncle wasn't all polished over with lacquer like the Marlowes, but if you'll excuse me for saying it, I knew this was why he was so proud of Trilipush as a son-in-law. No question: this wedding would bump him up a notch or two or three in his Boston social scene.

I started slow, just explained the Davies inheritance case, and asked if Mr. Finneran could tell me where I could find Professor Trilipush. "Of course, of course," and as he's taking his address book out of his desk drawer, I asked, "Just out of curiosity, how'd you come to meet Professor Trilipush here in Boston?" He says Margaret introduced them, brought Trilipush round the house one day like a girl who's bought a fine necklace. She'd seen him give a public lecture, she'd talked to him, become a friend of his, and then had really "taken a shine to the limey." Were they already in love, then, when she introduced Trilipush to her father? "No, no," Finneran says, "she brought him around as a favour to *me*. To have him describe the expedition he was planning, because she knew that a few of my business partners and me are always looking for investment possibilities, and Margaret thought Ralph's project sounded promising. Clever girl, that time." Sure enough, Finneran's "money club" had looked into it and decided to back the Egyptian expedition. (Macy, pay attention: Finneran has bet money, his friends' money, his daughter's heart, and his social standing on Trilipush.) "All the while, I was telling Margaret, that's a fine fellow there, and unless I'm mistaken, he's looking at you with a certain look. She didn't believe me. She's actually quite shy, Mr. Ferrell, but I know these things. Not long after we told Trilipush we wanted in on his expedition, he asked me for Margaret's hand, very gentlemanly, old English.

"I was glad of the opportunity, financially. Just the sort of thing our club likes, a winner, not without risk, but we're protected, built-in protections. Thanks to my little girl, we got the chance to invest ahead of museums and banks and such. Any of them would have jumped at a chance like this, that's sure, but we got first dibs. And, of course, I could see Maggie falling in love, whether she understood enough to put a name to it, and who am I to argue with love? When you have a little girl and a fellow like this comes along, you'll understand, Mr. Ferrell." The wedding would take place as soon as possible after Trilipush's return from his dig.

Did Finneran think an Egyptian excavation was a safe investment? No, ha-ha, of course not, not usually, but there were unique circumstances here, advantages: "Trilipush found something during the War, with a friend of his, and it points right to a very likely tomb. The details of it are complex. I can't say I understand all the scholarly stuff. It's not like a treasure map, precisely, of course, you have to know how to read the historical evidence, what have you, I don't claim to be a scholar, but Trilipush explained it all and he more than convinced the group that, as far as these things go, while there are never guarantees, everything points to a fast and lucrative find."

Now all of this new information placed me in a bit of a predicament, you'll notice if you stop thinking like his great-nephew for a minute and start thinking like my assistant again, Macy. See, I knew enough to stop that wedding right then and there: lies about Oxford, questions about military records, trouble with his Harvard chief. And what would follow from dropping a bomb like that? Well, here's a tip, Macy: it's never quite clear just who'll get blown up in situations like this one. Think for a minute, because you should know how our business operates by now. First, I needed my questions answered, and I can't get answers from an angry, panicked ex-father-in-law-to-be. Second, you and I are in a business that works by the clock; we can't make a living selling *information;* we sell *time.* So, later in this conversation, when we proposed to Mr. Finneran that he become our new client, we set his expectations that a background investigation of his daughter's fiancé would take some weeks. And, finally, information (and the time it takes to collect it) only has value if the buyer will pay for it. If I started telling Finneran the truth that day, he'd've seen me out the door in a rage. It was clear to me from day one that Finneran never wanted to hear anything *true* about his Trilipush, and later events proved me correct in this. No, I saw plain that Finneran would pay for *reassurance.* And a sensitive detective provides his clients what they need and will pay for. Lesson from Ferrell: satisfied clients pay.

Finally, between you and me as men, Macy, I didn't want to cause any pain, and that's the truth. It was clear that I was going to have to head off to Egypt to get to the bottom of the Caldwell and Marlowe deaths anyway, and to interrogate Trilipush about them. So I wanted an address and an itinerary for Trilipush, and that was all. There was nothing to be gained that day by revealing word one about English sodomists or fine young Australian men dead in the desert while English captains who lied about their education turned up safe and sound in Boston winning the hearts of incredibly beautiful young women and spending honest men's money. No, I could be back on a boat, to Alexandria, in six days, and

I'd no interest in bothering your family any more than absolutely necessary to have my information and to soothe your great-uncle's worries for a fee. Finneran gave me Trilipush's address in Cairo, loaned me a copy of the expedition's investor prospectus to read while I was staying at the Parker House, and we shook hands. I said I'd have a preliminary background report for him in a few days, perhaps longer.

Do I wish your family's story ended there, Macy? Part of me does, that's the truth. But it's hard. If I hadn't taken him on as a client, if I'd just walked out the door, read the prospectus at my hotel, had a bellboy return it for me, set off for New York the next day and Egypt five days later, what would've ended different? It's a hard score to tally up for certain, no matter what everyone's recollections say, and I'd sure like to read anything else you might've found after your aunt's death, any letters or journals that'd help me understand what else you know about all this. But one thing *is* certain: if your aunt had married Ralph Trilipush, a lot of lives were going to be built on lies in that household, and that's worse than anything. My actions prevented that. I'm proud of that. The fellow lucky enough to marry your aunt Margaret certainly owes me some gratitude. And I'm sure, after a while, she recalled my services fondly as well. I saved her, at a steep cost to myself.

As it was, I was walking down the main hall, picking up my coat, when Margaret interrupts us at the door, those little dogs weaving in between our ankles, and she says she wants to offer me a lemonade, it's rude of Daddy to shove me out the door without one, so she'll entertain me now and see me out after that. Her father laughs, indulges her as easy as breathing, shakes my hand, and retreats to his study, but leaves the door open.

Now, your aunt had three moods, if I may be honest. I grew to know her pretty well over the nearly two months I stayed in Boston, conducting my investigations. I don't know what she might've told you over the years. I don't compliment myself that I made a permanent impression on her, but at the time, I won't say she was indifferent to me.

Three moods: afternoons, like the day I met her, she was a sharp one. She could make you laugh, she could charm you, she could treat you like you were someone fascinating, and of course, she was a rich young woman (or so it appeared, I didn't yet see the plastered-over cracks in her father's world), and the attentions of rich young women do feel nice; I know enough of human psychology to know that's a pretty unbreakable law. That afternoon, she sat in front of the fire with her little dogs, the three of them all curled up together on a sort of long sofa across from me, and she says, "Now let's have a lemonade, and you can tell me all about Australia, where everyone eats kangaroos, right?" And she gave me such a little look, well, no one could've resisted that invitation. And while you wouldn't've taken her pretended ignorance seriously, you would've taken her very seriously as a woman, even though she was probably only twenty or a bit more. How much could she've known of the world at twenty? Nothing, you'd think. But then how'd she have such charm? The rich, the rich, the rich, even the new ones. They have their ways. Of course, I'm singing to the choir, aren't I, Macy?

She questioned me with a sly look in her eye, that afternoon, about my business in the USA, and I told her very little, just asked if her beloved ever mentioned an Australian soldier named Paul Caldwell. No, she'd never heard the name. I did tell her a bit about poor old Paul the Egypt lover, what life's like when you're not born with every advantage, as she and Trilipush'd been. "Oh, Mr. Ferrell, you are shaming me terribly," she said, pretending to look ashamed. "But Daddy, you know, came over here with almost nothing, so it's not how you think at all. We're really very simple people." She smiled, not simple at all, I'll never forget it. She had a way about her, that one did.

I asked her how she met Trilipush, how they came to be engaged, and did she mind if I took notes.

"Oh, wonderful! Really, I wish *everyone* took notes when I spoke! Well, you don't know Ralph? Oh, he's just *everything*, you know. The fellows I meet around Boston, they're not made of the same stuff, honest. I've had a few of Daddy's managers look at me a certain way, some of the higher-up boys at the store, and there are some jazz men in a few of the places I go now and again, when Daddy and Inge let me, and there are some of Daddy's business associates, J. P. O'Toole and them, but Ralph, well, he's a whole other *world*, like out of storybooks for little *girls*. All my girlfriends say I must be pinching myself. He's an explorer, you know, and from a family of explorers, and practically English nobility, but not the rich kind, and his accent—I mean you have a lovely accent too, Harry, but different. And he's all alone in the world, his parents have died and he was an only child, but he had these wonderful friends at University in England, and one of them, his best friend, got killed at the end of the War, and Ralph was so heartsick, he just wanted to leave it all behind, even his country estate, which costs more money to keep up than he's got, although he can always go back and open it up again if he wants to, and we might end up living there for a bit after the wedding. Anyway, after the War he came here to finish his book, which was a big hit, considering, you know, that it's *history*, and then he started teaching at Harvard, which is the college here, and quite the best one in all of America, and now he'd rather live in America and write and teach, and after this expedition, he's going to have *pots* of money, believe me, if you knew about this Egyptian stuff like Ralph does, you have to know where to look, but gold is just *sitting* under the sand over there."

The fascinating thing about this little speech, Macy, was that while I didn't doubt she thought it was true, she said it with such a tone, this little smile on her lips, as if to say that none of it meant a *thing* to her, not as long as I was there with her—not that I was so impressive, just that a part of her (afternoon) charm was that she'd never make you think her own fiancé mattered to her more than you, whoever you were, sitting with her just then. Maybe it *was* only for me, of course, and I'm sure I liked the idea that it was, at the time. She dazzled a bit, your auntie.

I repeated my question: how'd she meet this hero of our time? In her version, she had them engaged *before* the question of her father's money ever arose, before the investment meeting, but she did know that Trilipush would please her father, and her father strongly supported the engagement, even if she had some doubts at the beginning. *She* had doubts? "Well, sure, I mean he is from a whole other world, maybe a little Boston thing like me . . ." And here, I thought, in her false modesty, she was skirting a hidden truth. I suspected she might've had some hesitations for *good* reason, something she could only sense but not yet say. I don't compliment myself too much to say my presence helped her make comparisons, but it was clear that if she talked enough to a fellow totally unlike Trilipush, she might start realising a few things about how honest men reacted to her, and to women in general. She added: "And I did Daddy a favour by bringing Ralph to his club. I mean, I got to show him Ralph before one of the big museums funded him."

Who was the poor, dead friend from the War? "Oh, yes, another archaeologist, his best friend from Oxford. Get a load of this name, Harry: Captain Hugo St. John Marlowe. Well, during the War, they were always taking leaves to go do their digging, and once he and Marlowe found this thing together—very mysterious name, Fragment C—and they thought they could guess where a tomb would be as a result of it, a tomb just positively *filled* with gold and art. They were going to look for the tomb together the next chance they could, but then Ralph got sent off to fight in Turkey, which was just *awful*, while Marlowe had to stay in Egypt and wait, which he did, of course, because they were best *chums* from Oxford, and blood brothers, but for a while in Turkey, Ralph was separated from his men, and back in

Egypt they actually thought he was *dead*, and Ralph had to make it home practically alone, and when he finally made his way back to Egypt, well just a few days before that, poor *Marlowe* had gone missing, but had left this Fragment C in his tent, and Ralph took it for safekeeping, not knowing if Marlowe was alive or not, and then when he had to accept that Marlowe was dead, Ralph just wanted to put all the pain of the War behind him, so he brought Fragment C with him to Boston, and that's what made his scholarly reputation and got him a job at Harvard, and— oh, just listen to me go on. You can imagine the effect of all these adventure stories on a naïve young Boston girl, Harry."

Indeed I could, but Margaret was simply not a naïve young girl, and so I actually had a bit of trouble imagining the effect they had on her. Did she know she was repeating something absolutely ludicrous? Did it not occur to her that the story was filled with lies and impossibilities and probably hid two corpses in its forged folds? People conveniently missing in Turkey and Egypt? Loyal friends waiting for each other before trying to dig up and share pots of gold? Treasure maps readily available in missing men's tents? Did she think *I* believed it? And, Macy, I must stress that I didn't tell her anything of my suspicions. I was honourable to my clients and to the innocent. Judge me from this: I could've sold out Trilipush a thousand times to your aunt, but I didn't.

But, for the record, here's what I *was* thinking, and pretty canny, if you ask me: if indeed there was a hidden fortune in a hole that Marlowe and Trilipush had found, it was looking more and more that Trilipush—impoverished landed gentry with forged academic records—had killed Marlowe for it and then escaped to America while the heat died down. There he made enough of a showy reputation for himself among the local gullibles to manipulate some money to go back and dig up his treasure. And now, 1922, he plainly would *never* be coming back to Boston from this second expedition. This girl had been used, her family money taken on the strength of his English manner, and now he was done with her. Aside from her money, what else *would* he want with her? He was certainly an invert, like Marlowe and Quint, I knew that even then, before I'd met him. Then it occurred to me: probably he'd been Marlowe's high-class fancy man *before* going off to Egypt; probably Trilipush was Marlowe's discreetly kept amusement all the way back at Oxford, not a student obviously, just living in Marlowe's world, taking Marlowe's money in exchange for illicit affections. That explained witnesses to his presence there but no official record. Then Trilipush joins up for the War with Marlowe in exchange for continued payments, and heads off to Egypt with him, where they gallivant about in the English fashion. But then he gets sent to

Turkey without his rich protector, too bad. Back he comes (or runs, more likely) from the Turkish battles to discover to his horror that in his absence poor, young, Egypt-loving digger Paul Caldwell (*an Australian of all things*, thinks the bankrupt but still snobbish English pansy) has become the innocent object of Marlowe's amorous obsessions. Take it a step further: maybe Trilipush hadn't found the treasure map with Marlowe at all: maybe Marlowe and *Caldwell* had found it while Trilipush was in Turkey. Trilipush, back from Gallipoli, surprises the pair and, motivated by jealousy of his Juliet and greed over their secret find in the desert, kills both Marlowe and Caldwell, hides their bodies, and goes to the USA. Well, I'd some work ahead of me to prove all this, and I still didn't understand why his military records had been suppressed, but this shows how early I'd already understood the main facts of the matter, Macy, as I explained them to you when I met you that evening at the Parker House Hotel after returning from my newest client's home.

The victim of this tragedy, Macy—and this was clear as crystal to me before I'd even finished my first lemonade—was your lovely and hypnotising aunt. A sweet, innocent girl, her head turned by a murderous pervert, used for her family's money. I wanted to help, and that's the God's honest, I saw clearly that she'd been made a fool by a sodomite and was already abandoned, though she didn't know it yet. If I told her, she'd hate me forever. If I waited for events to unfold at their own pace, she'd be the laughingstock of Boston society. I felt, even that first lemonade, my hands being tied, and none of my choices were good.

Your aunt Margaret's second mood, I learnt over the coming weeks, was an early evening specialty. Some days later, I was returning to the hotel, having spoken to more Harvard professors and some students of Trilipush's, and I found, to my great surprise and pleasure, Margaret in the lobby. She hadn't been far from my thoughts since I'd met her. It was about seven in the evening, and she was unaccompanied. "Now tonight you're going to put your notebook away, Harry, and we're going to have some *fun*." She was at her very best like this. She still made you feel like you were the most important person in the world, but she didn't have any of the affectations of the rich hostess at home. No, now she was exuberant and natural, a young girl whose eyes shone, excited to see the next thing life had to offer. She had her jokes, her little smart remarks at your expense, but you liked it, believe me. She put her arm through mine and walked me through parts of Boston it never would've occurred to me to visit. "Don't you be worried there, Harry, I know my way around, we'll be just fine."

She walked me into alleyways that made me wish I had a weapon on me, but she just glowed under the dim lights, smiled at the shady figures lurking here and there, clearly enjoyed herself by shocking her foreign friend, though I did my best to smile throughout it all. "You know, I've *never* taken Ralphie to this place, and I never would. He wouldn't fit in like you will, Harry." I liked the comparison. "Let's keep all this our little secret, Harry." Suited me fine—I didn't want her mentioning me to Trilipush either.

She pushed a button on an unmarked wall in a dark street, I couldn't even tell you where we were. A small hatch at eye level slid aside, black eyes examined us, the hatch slid shut, and the wall opened up to let us into a noisy party, a bar and billiards and dancing to jazz music, men and women comfortable on couches, floor cushions, laps. "Welcome to JP's, Harry," she said, ushering me in. It was one surprise after another with your aunt. That evening she was all charm, and I rather thought it was all for me, and I remember thinking, that evening, that for whatever reason, she'd found something in me she was drawn to. I thought I could see a natural progression unfolding, can't say anyone would've blamed me. Now, of course, I'd say she was just a bit of a flirt. Played with fire a bit, she did, your aunt, didn't know when she'd gone too far, pushed things over a line. Girls like that always look surprised when people turn out not to be toys, when people don't stop what they're doing at the girl's instruction, the second her whim changes.

She brought us cocktails, and we sat on a red velvet couch. I might've been pursuing the case or my own interests, hard to say from this distance, but I asked her about Trilipush again, not sure what I was looking for. "Oh, he's a dream," she said, but looking at the ceiling, hardly paying attention as she murmured, "English noble, explorer. Quite a man . . ." Not the ceiling: she was peering up at the dark balcony that ran around the perimeter of the room before she brought her attention back down to me. "What was I saying, Harry?"

She pulled me up, and we danced to the Negro jazz orchestra. We drank. To be more accurate, I drank one or two, she drank quite a bit more. She patted my hand and let me light cigarettes for her. "Ralph never would go for this sort of thing," she said. "He's very bookish, you know. But Harry, you're quite a dancer!" Now that isn't strictly true, but I didn't argue. My notes are a little unclear here, I'm afraid, Macy. During this period in Boston, I often didn't remember to mark down exactly what was said or on what date, and as I sit here, staring at the green concrete bricks of the games room, memories come back in patches, unchronological rushes of events mixed up with things I recall wanting to happen, but which didn't. I'll do my best to sort this out for you.

She and I sit on a couch at JP's, this private club of hers, and she's stroking my cheek. This is a different evening. She's very drowsy, and I can see myself, a little hangdog-looking. This is a bit surprising, you'll agree, under the circumstances, but I don't take the cheek stroking to heart. You see, she'd left me on the couch for a bit, went upstairs to that balcony—a gigantic Negro guarding the stairs let her by no problem and she pinched his grinning face as she went up. I watched her open a door without knocking and walk into a room at the far corner, turns out to be the office of the J. P. O'Toole who owns the place, the Negro tells me. I return to the couch. Minutes pass. When she comes back down she's odd, laughing too loud. I look at her eyes, and I know straightaway where she's gone. She sat next to me for hours, smiled the whole time, stroked my cheek now and again, but never said a single word. Listen to an old man whinge, Macy: my heart was breaking and healing up again with every beat.

But another night, same red sofa, she's just the opposite, bouncing with a sort of nervous, unhappy energy, explaining to me that she's only marrying Trilipush because her father wants it so much, but she doesn't care a thing about any of them, all she wants "is to be left alone to have some fun once in a rare while. Priorities, Daddy says, good name, good alliance. But Ralph can be a dreadful bore, that much stuff about Egypt makes you fall asleep, you know, and that's just the truth. Nobody could listen to stuff about Egypt as much as he wants to talk about it. Or any topic. A *bore*, Harry, but men usually are after a while. Are you going to turn out to be a *bore*, Harry?"

"You don't want to marry Trilipush?" I asked, amazed at the turn of events, the way this lurking suspicion had suddenly emerged into light, and all at once I was ready to tell her everything I knew about her fiancé, to blow up that bomb and take my chances.

"Oh, I don't know," she said before I could open my mouth. "I didn't say that, did I? Let's not talk about this anymore, how's that sound to you? Just don't be a *bore*, Harry. Can you do that for me? Wouldn't that be the greatest thing if you turned out not to be an unbearable bore? Wouldn't that be swell? Let's shoot for that, Harry, okay? Okay? Okay?" Like this, when she started talking, she didn't stop, she just kept chattering, whatever idea was in her head tumbled out of her mouth, and she'd just repeat herself until she'd something else to say or do or spend her energy on, and sure enough, when she ran out of words, she pulled me up to dance. Maybe this was a week or two later, when she said all this. I don't know what to tell you, Macy. I think I probably fell in love with her, you see, at least that's how I'm remembering it now. And her? Well, I know now she was just a sad, sick girl, too much freedom. I wasn't anything much to her, something, no question, but not much. What could I have been to her? A man from another world, another class, not rich, not posh enough, nothing. That's not a tragedy, hardly, is it?

But what I felt *then*, that's something else. Maybe completely different. Maybe the "clarity of distance" is nothing at all when compared to what's been forgotten. Maybe it wasn't something inexplicable, as it's beginning to look now, but instead was *logical*, and I was acting with clarity that should be respected, clarity of *feeling*, even if I can't reproduce it here on paper, a whole lifetime later. After all, I'm writing to you from notes and recollections, and who knows what's slipped free from those? Maybe I wasn't such a fool as I'm making myself out to be. Maybe I just can't *remember* now what I *knew* then, all the reasons why falling for your aunt wasn't foolish, all the little ways she made me think it was possible. Let's just accept that she wanted me to fall in love with her, was thinking about being with me, too, leaving Trilipush for me, but day after day was passing with me unable to bridge some gap between us.

It seems like a film from this distance. I remember one cold day, I'd stayed on and skipped an Alexandria boat, and the thought was going through my head over and over that there was a terrible crime about to happen in Boston, and only I could stop it. Not just the old crimes I was trying to uncover, but something happening right then and there under my nose: the murder of this girl's soul, forced to marry for her father's social position, father and daughter defrauded by this English invert. I was torn in pieces trying to keep straight what I knew, what I suspected, what I should reveal and what I should hide, how to protect her, how to win her, or both.

That cold day I go to the house to find her, but Finneran's there, and when he answers the door he thinks I've come to see him of course (doesn't know I've been squiring her around), and I can't figure out how to explain otherwise, and so we go to his study and we talk about Trilipush. I tell him more than I intended, but circumstances are different, because Finneran's already suspicious about Trilipush before I open my mouth.

Two days earlier, Finneran says, he'd word that Trilipush was stuck in Cairo, delayed on his trip to the tomb site because of a last-minute bureaucratic snag, and he wanted the Partnership's money sent to Cairo, rather than to the town closer to the excavation. Fine, thinks Finneran, six of one to him, ready to comply, but then Professor Terbroogan from Harvard has just called on Finneran, that very same cold day, came by special to tell Finneran (with Dutch vengeance) that Oxford had just confirmed by cable that no Trilipush was ever educated there, and for what Terbroogan's opinion is worth, Trilipush has a "zero percent" chance of finding what he's promised his backers, the whole expedition is doomed. "He said that, Harry. Doomed." Finneran's keeping a brave face, but he's rolling that cigar back and forth across his mouth pretty speedy-like. He asks if I knew about the Oxford "rumour." Terbroogan hadn't revealed that I helped him find this information (though I reminded myself that I could now send him a bill for services rendered), but I wasn't ashamed of the truth. "Yes, I suspected it," I tell Finneran. "Well, Jesus Christ dancing on the cross!" he shouts, and the cigar falls onto his desk. "What the hell else do you suspect? What did I hire you for? To hear things from professors?" Finneran was worried, understandably: his money, his daughter, his friends' money, the possibility that he'd very publicly backed a fraud. I liked how someone else had brought the bad news, as there was too much at stake for me to be the bearer. But it certainly meant that my "all-clear" background investigation on Trilipush (sitting completed in my hotel room since my first night in Boston) would require a few more days' thought and editing. My position was only getting more complicated. "We'll see, Finneran," I said. "Let's not jump to conclusions yet. Records can be wrong."

"And if they're not? What about poor Margaret's feelings for this man?" he moans pathetically, after sitting in silence for a bit, fighting off his urge to panic. "She loves him, you know, Ferrell. I can't stand in the way of that, Oxford or not." In other words, I still have money riding on this man.

"Where's your daughter now?" I ask. And I swear to you, Macy, this great big man looks like he's going to cry like a girl. He looks away, stands up, turns his back to me, fiddles with a curtain. "Is there something you want to tell me? Confidential enquiries is my line, after all." And then your great-uncle unburdens himself to me, which people always did. He explains he's trying desperately hard to do the right thing for his "little girl," but she drinks and she's had problems with—he moves his mouth a bit before the word finally falls out—opium, and twice he's thought she was cured of it. The last time he'd put her in a sanatorium and paid a fortune to hire away one of their nurses (the buxom Swede I saw around the house from time to time) to monitor her at home, and give her the medications that were supposed to reduce her appetite for "the dragon's breath." But Margaret's started sneaking out again, Finneran says, slumping back into his chair. Inge, the nurse, is supposed to keep an eye on her, not let her out of the house unaccompanied, but she's been slipping free of her guard and is obviously unwell again, and if Trilipush ever found out about it, the engagement would probably be off, and Finneran looks defeated at the thought of it, forgetting for a moment that the blessed fiancé has lied to them about his education and perhaps more.

This display was grotesque, Macy. The strong, rich businessman was on the verge of sobbing because he was unsuccessful in his attempts to imprison his daughter, who suffered, it was plain to me, from nothing more than youthful high spirits and a nasty engagement to a sodomistic murderer, whom the family had desperately been trying to *impress*. *They* had been lying to *him*, telling him Margaret suffered from a rare but curable disorder causing her sleeping spells, mood swings, and so forth (as if Trilipush would even care, since his interest in her extended no further than her father's bank account). It was the sheerest, most sickening lunacy. Finneran didn't want my opinion, which would've been simple enough: save your daughter by letting her be. You're going to kill her in a social-climbing accident. And any pommy idiot who'd refuse to marry her because of a little high-spirited adventure deserved to be shot between the eyes. But I couldn't quite tip my hand that far, and instead I just said I'd try to keep an eye on Margaret, if he wanted, see if she was really in any kind of trouble. He shook my hand. "That's a great relief to me, Ferrell. Thank you, thank you. I didn't know who else to turn to," he says, as if it'd been his idea. "She's my little girl, you know, just want what's best." Right, course you do. Humans, my dear Macy, are one and all champions at claiming they're worried about someone else when they're only worried about themselves. "Count on me, Chester. I'll look after her for you."

"Your father's worried about you," I told her that evening, sitting on a couch at JP's, before she'd gone upstairs. I thought she'd laugh with me, find our new situation funny, not without its charms, and maybe that would lead to a gentle discussion of Trilipush's weaknesses, and that would lead to—

"Harry," she said. "We're having fun, aren't we? It's nice to have a pal to escort me out on the town when my beau's away, right? So now, please, Harry, I'm begging on my hands and knees: don't be a stinking bore." She stood up, her first step towards the stairs. "Why don't you talk to one of those nice girls while I'm gone?" she suggested, pointing to the tarts JP employed to set the male customers at ease. "Do you even *like* girls, Harry? Don't they teach you how to talk to girls down there on the bottom of the world? Just don't bore 'em, Harry, even if these ones here are paid to listen to you."

Friday, 20 October, 1922, Hotel of the Sphinx

Margaret: My love. The first thing this morning, while I was sitting for my portraitist, a boy brought up the oddest cable from your father. Absolutely the oddest thing. I read it without exaggeration a dozen times and then finally, feeling anxiety spread to my gut, I had no choice but to send the painter home. It is a nine-word communication from across an ocean, but apparently across even vaster gulfs of confusion: CLARIFY OXFORD IMMEDIATELY. FERRELL QUESTIONS YOUR ACCURACY. MUCH DEPENDS.

Nine words drawn at random from a hat, some obscure parlour game of the Boston rich? What does your father mean, my love? He is confused about Oxford and needs clarification. Of its existence? Its function? What is a ferrell and in what conceivable manner can it question my accuracy? One point is unquestionable: much does depend. Sunday the 22nd, I shall walk into the bank here to find my account fattened by the prearranged credit which is to be wired from Boston the 22nd of every month as long as the expedition progresses. Oh yes, much depends indeed. This is no time for parlour games.

I am relying—it is this morning clearer than ever—on men far below the calibre I would have hoped for. Not your father, of course, my darling, but his evidently jumpy partners who have prompted this oddity. I accepted his money as a gesture to him, because I love you, M. I will not claim I was blind to the effect I have on him; English snobs and Irish mobs seem to thrill our CCF equally, but I could have found my backers in more respectable, traditional circles. You knew that, and that is why you suggested this as a gift to your father. I sincerely hope our favour to him—mine to you—will not be one I live to regret.

Enough. If I am anxious now, it is because I find myself running out of funds, expecting your father's help to arrive in forty-eight hours, and instead he sends me riddles. I shall not show you any of this. It will resolve itself.

But I will someday be able to hold you, in our own home, and remind you of the moment I knew I would marry you: May, only three or four weeks after my talk at the Historical Society. You are in excellent health, and as lovely as anything imaginable in this life. We walk along the banks of the Charles, with giant Inge gliding a constant ten yards behind us, first to our left and then to our right, as if she were a dinghy. The sky rolls and the clouds wring their knotted fingers, nervous to rain on your beauty. You float forward away from me as I bend to tie my shoe (and Inge stops the same respectable margin behind me, pretending to sniff a spray of blue flowers), and one ray of sun emerges and paints a patch of river and your white dress with a single brushstroke, and while I fumble with my bootlace, I watch you bend to pat the head of a small tan-and-white hound with a wonderfully wrinkled, smiling face. He has just run through a picnic, collecting a string of sausage without breaking stride, dodging all avengers, leaving chaos in his wake, but at the sight of *Margaret*, he stops, drops his prize at your feet, and allows you to scratch his chin, while he tips back his head and stretches his neck to savour the affection. That was it, my love: I decide at that instant to make you my consort in this world and the next (for you will be mentioned in my every written work, assuring your immortality, too). And at that instant, I imagined you sculpted by the great artist Thothmes, bent over the banks of the Nile, placing a long-fingered hand upon the soft head of a canine envoy of Anubis. "I have something urgent to ask you," I shouted as I stood. "What did you say?" you cried, the rising wind bringing your voice to me. "I have something urgent to ask you!" and I began to run towards you. My excitement agitated the little dog, who began to run in circles, howling the most melodious song, leaving his sausage in the grass as if he had stolen it not from any hunger but from sheer joy of mischief. "You must be my queen, you must, you must."

"You will be the one to rescue me?" you asked as I took you in my arms.

"Of course I will. That is why I'm here with you."

It was days later when you suggested your father's investment club, eroded my doubts and arguments, and some weeks after that when I asked him for your hand. And yet today I am forced to sit as a python squeezes my belly, and I scratch my head and puzzle over his cryptic cable, running through a dozen styluses for the WC gramophone, and in short losing a day to worry. I suppose all of this agony is somehow a tribute to your beauty and love, my troublesome darling who brought us all to this point, but I trust you are already setting your father straight.

Journal: Find, with much trouble, an open cable office, and cable Boston to confirm certain details necessary for the Partnership's first scheduled wire, as preliminary resources are dwindling, and we are only beginning.

Bank closed. No one responds to knocking.

Call for portraitist to return; nothing else to be done on a Friday in a Mohammedan city.

CABLE. CAIRO TO C. C. FINNERAN,
BOSTON, 20 OCT. 1922, 3.18 P.M.
OXFORD UNIVERSITY IS IN ENGLAND. NO FURTHER
CLARIFICATION OF MY ACCURACY NEEDED. KNOW NO FERRELL.
22ND APPROACHES. MUCH DEPENDS. Q3: IN ALL ATUM-HADU'S
REALM, THERE IS NO MAN MORE TRUSTED/THAN HIS MASTER OF
LARGESSE, WHOSE EVERY MOVEMENT IS DIVINE./I SHALL
REPLACE WITH GOLD ANYTHING OF HIS WHICH IS RUSTED/AND I
SHALL ASSURE HE CAN AT HIS WHIM SWIM IN WINE. DADIAE,
CAL, 1920. RMT.

Saturday, 21 October, 1922

Journal: Today, with time nipping at my heels and still no word from the Antiquities Service, I paid them a call. For last night, in troubled pre-sleep clarity, it occurred to me that I have been fooled into worshipping a slip of paper. Such fragile fetishes, an archaeologist knows better than anyone, are not carved in stone. There is no use

making a god of before-the-fact permission, as Marlowe used to say in
the matter of applying for leaves. A man-to-man chat with the Director-
General, perhaps a gift and a candid negotiation over terms, even an
expression of willingness on behalf of Hand-of-Atum, Ltd, to offer him
an honourary share in our discovery, and with that, we should at last
be under way.

I presented the D-G's secretary with a signed first edition of *Desire
and Deceit in Ancient Egypt.* He was duly impressed, grateful, muttered
some French. I requested an urgent audience with the D-G himself, to
share my latest thinking about the tomb of Atum-hadu.

"You are wanting to make change of your application?" asks dubious DuBois.

"No, I am wanting to *enhance* my application, ducks." Which is true:
I am willing to make one last goodwill gesture to their rules.

As DuBois apparently could not blink without clearance, he duly
retreated into the D-G's chambers and left me standing at his desk. The
trappings these office-officers feel they need! "From the desk of the
Director-General of the Antiquities Service." "From the Desk of the
Chief Secretary to the Director-General of the Antiquities Service."
Wax and seals, presigned, prepaid blank telegraph forms. Frippery.

I waited my turn in one of the overstuffed leather chairs, withdrew
my papers from my bulging briefcase, and have now updated my Journal to the present moment. And I wait, hopeful that my visible willingness to submit myself to their corrupt rules will unclog the constipated
system.

And now it is later this same evening and I am back in the hotel,
and it is with pride and excitement that I write these words: today I
met and befriended one of my great heroes, a man whose professional-
ism and dedication I respect above all others, even though he is now reduced to chasing shifting shadows in the Valley of the Kings.

Sitting, waiting the word of the D-G, and having finished my up-
dating of the Journal, and still with no sight of the toadying Frog, I felt
the shaking-jelly preamble of a medium-grade gut attack, and so I retreated to the gilded facilities of the Antiquities Service's gentlemen's

lounge. Though it may strike you as indelicate, I must invite you, Reader, to join me there, as I wash my hands and watch in the mirror as the colour returns slowly to my damp, exhausted face.

I had recognised—from the sounds of unhappiness in harmony with my own that had risen from the next closet over—a fellow member of the digestively damned, a brother of the beastly bowel. And then at the sinks and mirror, as I rose from the basin with my face dripping luke-warm water and cursed the native towel-boy who took his sweet time drying me before my shirt collar was soaked, I examined next to my blinking reflection that of a moustachioed older man studiously soaping his hands. I recognised him at once: my indigestive colleague had been none other than the great Howard Carter, former Inspector of Antiquities, discoverer of countless tombs and treasures, including Thothmes IV and Mentuhotep I, currently the well-endowed beneficiary of the Earl of Carnarvon's aristocratic interest in Egypt, painter, authority, and great genius of digging, now on the verge of (it is hardly credible even as I write it), his *sixth* long season seeking and failing to find a minor XVIIIth-Dynasty king's tomb on the scantiest evidence. Six years, wasting Milord's money! One could hardly be surprised that the poor fellow's stomach was in open rebellion.

I studied him in the mirror, the grace with which he moved, the bearing, the air of masterful indifference. He wore a light twill suit. I was fascinated to see, even in his dotage, the obvious relationship be-tween his manner and his expertise. Like Marlowe, he is one of those for whom his work is his destined calling, and so it is visible even in how he washes his hands, how he bears up under the banal but omni-present burdens of his body. I introduced myself.

"Trilipush?" he repeated. "Trilipush?" He washed his hands and peered into my reflected eyes, all of Egyptology nestled in his memory, organised and comfortably accessible. " 'The pornographer'? "

His sympathy at the pain I have suffered at that idiotic epithet ap-plied by small minds to my work was evident in his compassionately humorous "quoting" tone of voice; we both knew that even one more word on the topic would be lending the ignorant too much of our time.

His ironic question was a welcome "how-d'ye-do" from a peer who knew all too well what sort of envy and stupidity we sometimes meet in this treacherous world.

"Ah, yes, quite so! And a fellow slave to wicked Intestinus the Large, if I may be so bold. Local food doesn't agree with you, old boy? Or are you a chronic victim, diet aside? This is no continent for the in-continent."

As the towel-boy dried my hands, I noted with interest that Carter chose to take his towel himself. As if he knew that an explorer, accustomed to the rough ways of the site, cannot allow himself to grow used to the city's soft luxuries.

We sat and smoked in the D-G's waiting room (even the great Carter has to wait his turn for the attentions of the desk-wallahs), and he accepted and placed in his portfolio my gift to him, *Desire and Deceit in Ancient Egypt*, which I inscribed, "To my dear friend, a fellow sufferer of both imbeciles and irritable innards, and a great archaeologist, truly the passing generation's greatest Egypt-man. With fondness on 21 October, 1922, in the waiting annex of the D-G's office at the Antiquities Service, Cairo. Ralph M. Trilipush."

Carter's renowned quietness, combined with—let us just imagine—some exhaustion at the prospect of pursuing his minor but elusive prey for another season, having burdened himself with the concession for the obviously drained Valley of the Kings, was remarkably stylish. His manner was of the insightful monosyllable, the expressive eyebrow, the breath that could be tuned to the most precise gradations of meaning, practically the sculpting of exhaled cigarette smoke into hieroglyphs which, translated into English, would fill pages. His repose (especially after those internal barrages that would have reduced lesser men than us to outright sobbing) spoke volumes.

We conversed for several minutes about explorer's gut, my discovery of Fragment C, my prospects for finding Atum-hadu's tomb, his own prospects for success in the Valley. We discussed Oxford, my childhood in Kent, my military career, Atum-hadu. "Gardiner had some rather choice words about your rhyming translations," Carter teased, shaking his head at the dishonest and dim-witted philologist who had reviewed *Desire and Deceit* in *Chronicles of Egyptology* as "embarrassing for laymen and painful for scholars."

"Amusing, wasn't it? That reminds me: I must ask you, Howard, what you make of those who even at this late date still harbour doubts that Atum-hadu—"

"Oh! Meestair Cartair! We are apologising for your waiting with all of our most sincere hearts!" And out of the D-G's office rolls the little secretary, burbling over with admiration and excuses. "You are back from your villa in Gurna? You were not expected, but what complete happiness to be seeing you!" And similar sycophancy, at which Carter and I rolled our eyes at each other.

"What! Is Carter out there, too? Send him right in!" booms a voice from the D-G's office, neatly illustrating the bureaucrat's typical preference for dealing with the unthreatening embers of past success rather than the burning fire of present-day promise. Carter's bearing, even in the few steps from his chair to the D-G's door, was highly impressive. Were I still young and malleable, I would have sought to emulate him: his unspoken but unmistakable conviction that everything important was somehow more complicated than the layman could understand, but that the only necessity was a clear intention, and that a relaxed simplicity would always yield results. Although perhaps even *results* are not the point (sixth season, after all) and to conduct oneself as if results *were* the point is to strive for something illegitimate or grubby. Rather, his bearing implies that one should conduct oneself as if acknowledging that success is often out of one's control, and—I seem to be having trouble pinpointing the exact effect Carter has—he made one feel smallish, I have heard others say, as if he knew more than you but felt neither superior nor apologetic for that, only wanted, as long as you were in his presence, that you would feel neither inferior nor sorry, but strive, as he did, not for petty things, but only for some unnameable greatness, and to do that with precisely his same sort of unexcitable but stylish calm. And never to mention any of this aloud.

Nodding to me to acknowledge the unfairness of his welcome over my own, Carter took his leave. Before he entered the D-G's office we made plans to dine often, later, upriver at Thebes during the digging season, and he complimented *Desire and Deceit* again.

DuBois informed me that the D-G was busy for the rest of the day and to make my "retour in other weather."

Sunday, 22 October, 1922

Journal. Logistical planning: Visit bank, which is open, but Sunday, of course, is a bank holiday in America. So, tomorrow, as soon as credit is established, first task will be to settle rental of villa in the south, ideally near Gurna. Make appointment for lunch tomorrow with agent. Prepare schedules, begin packing. Hard to know which gramophones to bring south for the villa, and for on-site at the excavation. On the one hand, the Victrola XVII is an excellent salon unit and fills a room well. The Edison Audiogram 3 is very small, fine in a bedroom to help one sleep. Depending on the ease of transport between the villa and Atum-hadu's tomb, I could bring the Columbia Favorite. But the XVII's power and volume would be ideal for inspirational music for the men and myself. Popular songs. Old Army favourites.

But, as Carter reminded me yesterday, the great delight on excavation is hearing the men's work songs, the simple melodies these simple people chant to keep their minds occupied as they burrow away, uninterested in the search itself, and the sweetest sound of all is the sudden silence that falls magically everywhere and all at once when one of them unearths something. Carter spoke of that silence with nostalgic rapture in his eyes.

Monday, 23 October, 1922

Journal: Bank first thing, but there is a delay of some sort. Bank manager asks me if I am "quite certain about the details of my financial arrangements?" I am ready to strike him as he peers up at me from behind his ludicrous spectacles, one of those Englishmen who in the heat of the tropics does not bronze or blossom, does not sweat through with passion, but instead shrivels, a sun-dried little fruit, desiccated and clinging to his figures and protocols, the only things that can save him from total disintegration.

No matter. The delays of the modern financial system are one of the unavoidable obstacles thrown in our path. Were our task easy, anyone could accomplish it, and immortality would be a cheap honour.

Lunched at the Explorers' Club in Cairo, and I must admit I found it rather overwhelming to see the company I hope one day to keep. The building was an officers' club in the War. I had heard of its transformation and I had vaguely expected some rather crass or amusing tribute to the fathers of Egyptology and excavation, perhaps something to lure American tourists, or more practically, a well-decorated house of assignation wherein impoverished archaeologists could discreetly pair off with cash-heavy would-be patrons, whether the representatives of skimpily stocked but well-endowed American museums or bored and daffy English lords, ideally shell-shocked and narcoleptic, fanning themselves with signed cheques.

But no, I found something else entirely, a little vanity of the French and British Consuls-General perhaps, but one which had quite an effect on me, as if a panorama of my future were laid out glistening before me. In the pillared, sandstone building—a bank at first glance—one entered a dark wood hall on bloodred carpets as gaslights cobra-hissed behind globes of lapis and crystal. Floating fezzes unburdened me of my things, and then I stood quite alone, straightening my cuffs and tie in the dim light under the watchful eyes of a portrait gallery of the men who came before me, each leaving his large, ineffaceable footprints in the sand. To the left of the mirror where I examined my own face hung old Henry Salt, whose memoirs I devoured as a boy. Next was Salt's muscleman, Belzoni, the former circus strongman who opened Abu Simbel's temple. Then, the half-mad, hypnotic gaze of Fouéré, who was reputed to have kept a harem with the full blessing of the French Government, as it kept him more productive in the accepted Golden Age pursuit of unwrapping mummies for their golden rings. Next in oils was Champollion, white-collared, stiff-necked, and a bit cross-eyed, as if the effort of decoding the Rosetta stone had twisted his eyesight and reason into a coiled snake. And a dozen others hung there, too, nearly all of them retiring or dying with the warning to the world that there was nothing left under the sands of Egypt; they had found the very last of it themselves. And each being proven wrong by the bold fellow who followed him, who in turn said he had been the last, who in turn . . . and so on.

I stood amidst these pictures, my own mirrored face hanging equal amongst them. I could see the reflection of Carter's face over my shoulder. "Hullo, Trilipush," said the painting, so audibly that if I had not been alone I would have asked a companion if he had not heard it, too. A foolish phantasm, but I understood at once the meaning of this mad vision, this excess of imagination too long trapped in the city and the corruptions of hotels and clubs: I could hear the pantheon welcoming me into its ranks.

Exhilarated, I retreated into the dining room to look for my lunch engagement amidst the tables drooping with mouldy consular staff. The vicious *maître d'hôtel* would have dispatched me to the membership office before seating me, but my companion arrived in the nick of time and we were soon seated, examining his photographs of Nile-front villas.

A few moments later, the living Carter entered the restaurant and passed close to my table, dressed, as in his portrait, in a light gabardine, and peering strangely at me, nodding as he does. "Ah, feeling better, are you, Trilipush?"

"So far, so good, old man. Avoiding the more *recherché* dairy inventions and anything hailing from our friend the goat, but otherwise nothing should keep me out of the sand, thanks." He looked at a few of the estate agent's photographs on the table. "We shall be near neighbours," I told my colleague, and he expressed his pleasure at the news.

In the end, confident in CCF and the Partnership, I settled on a large house in a secluded suburb of Luxor on the eastern bank of the

Nile instead, close to the ferry crossing to the west bank and the path to Deir el Bahari. I signed a five-week lease with an option to renew month by month after that. By then, purchasing a place may be more logical, but for now we are cautious as we approach our prey. I paid the deposit from my own resources. Subsequent rental payments will have to await the coming wire.

Nothing at bank, post.

Return to hotel. Considering the Explorers' Club, a long session with the portraitist is an urgent necessity before my departure south on Thursday.

Tuesday, 24 October, 1922

No news at bank. Why has M. not made sure that precisely this did not happen? Surely it is not unreasonable to assume she would take responsibility for what she began, the wealth she waved at me like so many veils.

Door still impenetrable at Antiquities.

Nothing at post. Cable CCF to express urgency.

I won't deny I was in some confusion, pain even. Your aunt teased me mercilessly. Some days (my wise ones, I'd say now) I decided the best thing to do was just to leave Boston quick, but when I told her I'd booked my passage, she'd pout and say, "No, how could you leave me alone with no one to have fun with?" I'd change my plans to stay, and next time I saw her, a bouquet for her in my shaking hands, she'd ask me with a sneer why on earth I hadn't left for Egypt yet. When I couldn't find her, I'd find myself wandering about Boston (a city far, far from home), unable to see how to move forward my stalled investigations or what to write for Finneran, and I'd go book another New York–Alexandria ticket package, which of course I wouldn't use. I convinced myself that my numerous clients and the twists and turns of the case required my presence in Boston. And maybe she didn't want Trilipush, she'd almost said, nearly. Are you laughing at me too, Macy? Go right ahead and laugh.

I'd call on Finneran, tell him I was keeping an eye on Margaret (never talking about our evenings at JP's, of course, that's why I never took a shilling from him to look after her, wouldn't've been right). I'd try to get him to see the situation clearly without me having to spell it out, but he wasn't going to see or set things straight on his own. Really I went to the house just hoping she'd be there. Sometimes she was, and the charming hostess offered me lemonades in the parlour and patted her dogs, and we sat quietly, and she'd mock me because I didn't know what to say anymore without disclosing some secret—hers to her father, Trilipush's to her, her father's to her, or of course, mine, which was the most painful for me to hold tight. And she'd look at me in my afternoon anguish and say, "Harry, you're getting quieter and quieter. Do try to be fun, can't you? Didn't you once promise not to bore me? I can't *bear* men who break promises." But still she'd turn up at my hotel (where she'd be sure to find me waiting and hoping) and lead me off to evenings at JP's.

Then one afternoon, Finneran called me at the hotel, invited me over for my "advice, as a fellow who understands complex situations." He'd just had a cable from Trilipush: the brave explorer was moving from Cairo to the digging site in the southern desert, and he needed the investors' money wired to the bank in Egypt immediately. It seems Finneran, while he considered the Oxford business, had delayed sending the money they'd agreed upon, but now I could see the shock of Oxford had worn off. No question: Finneran was softening. He plainly wanted me to tell him that Trilipush was trustworthy after all. He hadn't wanted my advice, not a bit of it. No, he wanted me to lie, plain as day, and hold his hand while I did it. "Margaret really loves this fellow," he said, as if that, even if it were true, argued for anything at all, other than adjusting her medication. "And the investors are counting on him. And on me." One minute he's chomping his cigar, and he's all croc hide covering shark cartilage, proper captain of business issuing orders, the next minute he's pathetically asking *me* (hardly a close mate or impartial player) what he should do. He rages one minute, looks confused the next, argues with himself: "A lot is riding on this investment," he mutters. "Now's not the best time for money to go the wrong way. But if you want the payoff, you can't hesitate in the breach. If you commit, you can't tie a man's hands for want of a few dollars." The thought crossed my mind: Trilipush had the entire Finneran family in his pocket. There didn't even need to *be* a buried treasure!

The madness of this family (no offence there, Macy) made me feel like an old clucking maid: I thought of his daughter out there in the parlour, her disgrace when Trilipush never came back, when all of Boston society would learn she'd been engaged to a confidence trickster and a murderer, and *he* had abandoned *her*. The longer Finneran paid Trilipush, the farther off that day of reckoning, until finally Trilipush would simply vanish without a word, probably having taken enough of Finneran's cash to refurbish the Trilipush estates back in Kent, Finneran's new money coupling with Trilipush's old name nicely. And when that day came, who'd have Margaret after something like that? I would, I saw, clear as a bell. I would.

I was gentle with Finneran. I said I thought Trilipush "*might* not be a wise investment, the evidence was certainly mixed." He took that all right. So I tiptoed forward: perhaps, if Finneran was truly concerned about Margaret's health and happiness, there were other men who could care for her better than this Englishman. There were too many risks attendant to a man already shown to be of dubious character, considering the Oxford news. I said my background investigation would take more time still, but perhaps better for him to find her a proven honest man, even if he weren't an impoverished English toff. Finneran looked at me close, calmer now, seemed, I thought, to understand me. He nodded, thanked me for my time, said he would consider my words. But would she?

Her use of opium was a bit worrisome, I could see that. I wasn't as blinded by her as all that, and I'm writing to you, as I said I would, Macy, without apology or softening of the truth. I assume, by the time she wed your uncle, that she'd freed herself of these youthful indulgences. But in October and November '22, she was indulging. I don't know how she administered it, but she was procuring it from the shady J. P. O'Toole up there on the catwalk. And when she'd come back down to the couch where we sat side by side, her eyes wide and her pupils tiny, I knew she'd gone far away. "Harry, darling, how queer you look. Why don't you ever come with me? Would you, darling?" I never did. "I live a million years while you live just this one night," she told me once as she drifted away, something she read in a book, I think. "A million years, Harry. Don't you want to be interesting, and join me for a million years? Can you imagine the two of us going into eternity together, man and woman, two bodies entwined for a million years?" I'm proud, Macy, of what I used to do for your aunt in this condition. I protected her, just as her father would've wanted. The record should show who the gentleman was, between the poor Aussie working man and the toff Englishman. We'd stay in O'Toole's establishment as long as necessary, and I'd wait for your aunt to return from her million-year voyages, hold her hand as she fell asleep, or stroke her hair and forehead. When she rejoined us mere mortals, I made sure she reached home safely and secretly. Yes, I repeat, I was worried about the opium, but to me it was only a part of her, and when she told me in her other, daytime, moods that it was just a toy she played with at her whim, certainly not worth mentioning to her overtaxed father, well, I had no strength to doubt her. And, looking back, obviously she was right. How else did she marry your uncle and live a happy life?

Wednesday, 25 October, 1922

Journal: Today the bellboy delivers me a souvenir worthy of some paste in my journal, a little programme note from our depraved era's bureaucratic farce, in which we must all accept our roles, though we are quite randomly cast.

> Mr. Trilipush,
>
>   I wish to clarify that under the current circumstances, the entirety of the Deir el Bahari area, as outlined on the enclosed map, is to be considered as Professor Winlock and the Metropolitan Museum's exclusive concession. Your application has been duly noted and reviewed. As soon as there is any change in the status of the Metropolitan's concession, we will contact you. Should you move from the Hotel of the Sphinx, please inform us where in the United States you can be reached. Also, I regret to inform you that last week I cabled Professor ter Breuggen at Harvard University to confirm his position as a co-applicant for your request and he has— I am certain this is a misunderstanding—declined to attach his or Harvard's name to your application, though he does ask that I send you his "good wish" [*sic*]. I am your humble correspondent,
>   P. Lacau, Director-General, Antiquities Service

As for Claes ter Breuggen, no surprise whatsoever from my dear Chair. This merits "Sup with the Devil, but Use a Long Spoon" on the Victrola XVII.

Ter Breuggen. Claes ter Breuggen, the Walloon Buffoon, the Belgian Waffle, putting the phlegm in Flemish, catastrophically chairs (for

the time being, just for a few more months) Harvard's Department of
Egyptology, curating the University's teensy collection and miseducating the sons of the Boston wealthy, which poor boys stumble out of ter
Breuggen's bumbling and often inaudible lectures to stagger into my
office for some much needed tutoring. "Say there, Pushy," began one
rosy-cheeked moron befuddled by a classic ter Breuggen lecture, all
damp throat clearing and nasal clatter in which the first row can certainly count on having their faces moistened if not their curiosity whet-
ted, "what's all this about Pharaonic seal-bearers? Surely it was hot and
sandy there, desert and everything, am I right? Not the right climate at
all, you'd think."

Ter Breuggen's last days as Harvard Egyptology's high priest have a
certain doomed, end-of-an-interlude, a-conquering-hero-is-coming-
soon feel to them, as he schemes by written message to thwart his rivals
in a period of instability. One will surely rise from within his court, win
great victories abroad, return to the troubled kingdom to restore order.

This greasepaint devil bared his rounded teeth at my most recent
appeal before Harvard's interdepartmental tenure review committee, in
which ter Breuggen fired his latest soggy charges at me and manned
his crumbling defences for the last time. Several of the committee members—shocked by ter Breuggen's outrageous accusations and willingness to forsake any semblance of personal dignity in his fearful
campaign against me—told me after the hearing that I had been the
committee's darling, but ter Breuggen had threatened, wheedled, and
outright sobbed to keep me in my lowly place. Even Dean Warren,
who chaired the raucous hearing, took me aside afterward to encourage
me, wishing me luck on my expedition, practically guaranteeing me
tenure should I make a find contributing to Harvard's eternal glory.

Ter Breuggen's loathsome manner can be explained simply: his re-
sentment that when I joined the faculty, I refused to hand over Fragment C to any collection under his curatorship, even as he goggled and
drooled over my papyrus. No matter. Now, blackballed by the corrupt
priest, I bide my time, I do battle for the kingdom abroad, win renown,
and will return.

Bank. Nothing.
Post. Nothing.
Bank. Nothing.

Thursday, 26 October, 1922

Journal: Noon, final day of Phase One. Expedition HQ moves south. A new start, and I can feel the strength and inspiration pour back into me. I was going quite mad waiting in this hotel, my enthusiasm curdled by the city and luxury. And now, a busy day, improvisations necessary. Letter to Lacau at Antiquities, thanking him for his correspondence, and giving my address at the villa where I will be vacationing and awaiting "any fortuitous change in Mr. Winlock's status *vis-à-vis* Deir el Bahari." Visit to bank to be under way at last in the matter of the first payment.

No word there, however, which is professionally and personally disappointing, but clearly there is a problem with the system, and these are the rough obstacles that will bruise us on any travel. Confirm they have the address and wiring information for my corresponding bank in the south. Deliver also a sharp word to the little clerk who has made me so uneasy these past weeks. There were, unfortunately, black-painted iron bars between my flexing fist and his smug little face (no doubt for this very reason, middle-class English bankers being not entirely insensible to the effect they have on other people).

Go to collect my new suits of clothes, but find that, the international money transfer system being the shambles it is, I can, after a damned difficult selection, approve only two of them—an Egyptian twill and a light gabardine. I reassured the poor tailor he would be paid for the remainder when I send for them.

The portrait artist is not yet done with his work. In its current condition, I am in full colour from the top of my head to my upper lip, at which point I fade into sketched brown lines. He has me looking directly outward, but with my head turned slightly to one side. Handsomely done. However, he has imagined a certain sagging under my

right eye that no mirror can confirm and no gallery tolerate. So I in-
struct him that the painting is to be delivered upon repair and comple-
tion to the Explorers' Club, from whom he may collect payment.

And back to the hotel, where the morning manager—an Egyptian—
wants to know how much longer they should expect the pleasure of my
stay, as I have extended my original reservation. The international system of money wiring is infuriating: these native fellows are doing their
best, running a not-at-all-bad hotel to the best of their ability, and it is
quite disheartening that they should be so much at the mercy of a bank.
But I shall need a base of operations in Cairo, of course, even when I
am working down south—mail forwarding, my suite on short notice, a
place to store some items, a *pied-à-terre* for my fiancée or my business
partners as they come through town, a central facility for certain Government celebrations projected for early December. And so, excellent
news for the manager: his most expensive suite of rooms will be occupied well into the winter. I hold it until January 1, for now, and perhaps longer, I will wire from Luxor with final dates. I pay a small
portion of my balance to hold the suite until then. I distribute copies of
Desire and Deceit in Ancient Egypt to the concierge, the bellboys, the
African chambermaids, et cetera. Supplies to be left in the suite: the
Victrola XVII, largest of my gramophones. Supplies to take for the trip
south: more letterhead for the journal, convenient towels and bedding
sets: the hotel's absurd emblem and motto should be highly amusing to
everyone at the site. Have my bags taken to the dock, and enjoy one
last drink on my veranda while I update this log. I shall miss the
padded bed. I shall miss the Sekhmet Bar in the lobby, decorated with
paintings of that ancient lion-headed goddess who would, were she
ever allowed to sober up, destroy humanity. I shall miss the service. I
am older now than when I was in the Army, you know, and cannot say
these creature comforts mean nothing. Oh, make no mistake, I shall be
delighted to lie again on a camp bed under the stars, guarding my find,
coping with heat and cold in rapid alternation, singing and chatting
with the native men who treat me both as one of their own and as their
natural leader. But I am not as devotedly rugged as all that, not any-

more. Sixteen nights in the splendour of the Hotel of the Sphinx, on my smooth bedsheets printed with the vulture, sphinx, cobra, and HORUS CONSUMES THE HEARTS OF THE WICKED—well, I shall warm myself with them (and the memories they carry) on cold desert nights.

One last visit to the bank: nothing.

And at last, at last, my great voyage has begun: I write now from the deck of the steamer *Cheops*. Ahead of me, a journey 500 miles to the south, 500 miles up the Nile to where my king awaits me, to where Marlowe and I found Fragment C, and where he later lost his life.

My departure and the setting of the sun coincide, and from the white deck under the purpling sky and over the boiling, blackening Nile, I see Cairo recede, the crowd on the dock, the lights of the square, the smoke rising from the houses and the *ahwas* and shops, mingling with the smoke from the boat. One can almost see from this distance the smiling faces of the luggage porters as they sit down on the dock to begin without delay their study of *Desire and Deceit in Ancient Egypt* (Collins Amorous Literature, 1920). One wears one's twill suit, tailored by one of Egypt's greatest men of the needle. One leans on the polished wooden parapet on the port side of a fine vessel. One watches in anticipation and relaxation as one chugs past narcissistic palms and nearly naked peasants, virtually unchanged from their portraits on ancient papyri. One admires the ladies onboard—almost all American, one notes—and one thinks of home (so far) and of destiny (so near), and one remarks with frustration the premonition of thundering stomach pain to come. Descend to my cabin.

Later, calmer, below. I was soon able to rise to the saloon level, the god of belly disorder granting a respite after only an hour or so of enforced worship. Soothing drinks above and belowdecks. And a jazz trio in the saloon, Egyptians, in fact, tootling competently enough. While I danced with tourist ladies rapt by tales of exploration, the native bandleader, in red smoking jacket and fez, slapped a banjo while another honked a dented cornet and a third crooned, with a wonderful accent, songs such as "You're a Lucky Fellah" and "I Love That Man and I'll Keep Him, Just Aziz" and:

In old Pharaoh's Egypt,
The Hebrews came to stay,
Until old Moses rose up
To lead his folks away.

"Let my people go," said Moses.
And Pharaoh said, "No, sir!"
And then gave baby Jesus
Gold, frankincense, and myrrh.

Quite so. That and the oily churn behind the boat do give one a
sense of peculiar disorientation that the gin cannot quite overcome.

Margaret: Tonight on the boat to Luxor, my dinner companions at
the small table set for three were an old American couple, who I assumed were on their first travels abroad, the spicy reward for a life of
bland savings, children and grandchildren seeing them off for their
whirling adventure, their last but one. But, no, they turned out to be
something much more substantial, difficult to explain as I lie now in my
cabin, trying to capture their charms as sleep gnaws at me and the recollections of what they showed me tonight fog my thinking. They were
not like anyone I have ever known. Such a *softness* to them.

They hail from Minneapolis, or some such outlandish hamlet in the
corn-blanketed depths of your America. There, Len and Sonia
Nordquist are pillars of society, such as it is. He is an executive in a
grain-milling concern of some sort and is fascinated by how the Egyptians harvest and process their flax and millet. She is on the board of
the little city's museum, its theatre, its school for deaf-mutes, all manner
of thing. Of course they did not appear as grandees. In their travel kit
(he in light Scotch hunting tweeds, she in a stylised pith helmet with
some symbolic mosquito netting tied under her chin), the two grey
birds were peculiarly American in their friendliness. They sat hand in
hand whenever possible, but she would often take my hand in her old
fingers, or Len would pat me on the back paternally. When one of them
irritated the other, they would snap with much rolling of eyes and

headshaking wonder at their mate's stupidity, and then, a moment later, they were holding hands again, or stroking their partner's sagging cheek. Len suffers terribly from the climate or the dust; he was an almost constant source of noise, but Sonia would hand him a handkerchief without even looking up or dropping a line of conversation. Taking care of him seemed to have become like breathing for her. It was quite a sight, M., quite magnetic, and I thought of you and me as old folk.

They asked about Oxford and you, and my explorations and hypotheses. They bubbled with enthusiasm to hear about Atum-hadu, even asked me to recite a quatrain or two. "Oh, you must give us absolutely the most scandalous one," Sonia pleaded, and Len concurred, sneezing. "Yes please. Don't spare our sensibilities." I started them on something mild, your favourite, Quatrain 35 ("She will be mine"), but when I reached the end, the dear little lady looked rather blank: "Is that it? Really? I can hardly see what the fuss is about. Surely they get spicier than that?" "Positively Scandinavian," Len concurred. "Was your Atum-hadu a Lutheran?" "Very well, then," I said, "let's try 57: Roused from sleep, the hooded cobra." After this quieter recitation (the jazz band was resting and some of the younger ladies in the dining room seemed to be looking our way, leaning towards earshot), the ancients only stuck out their lower lips and wagged their heads from side to side, the identical gesture in them both. "Yessss," said Len, dubiously, "I suppose some might find that a little off-colour, the snake image, but from your description of the man, I imagined something more." "Right then, folks, we'll have 48." I leaned far in and whispered, as the room's other diners had stopped talking entirely. Now Sonia was convinced, her hand over her mouth, and Len was nodding quietly. "Oh, my, oh, yes," sighs Sonia. "You must find this fellow's tomb! He's enchanting!" "I'll have to recite that at the next meeting of my lodge," says the old man, and Sonia agrees: "Please do write it down. I belong to a poetry club in Minneapolis, and the other ladies will think me quite clever to have found this." I promised them copies of *Desire and Deceit* before they disembarked; their pleasure and gratitude at the gift was quite overwhelming. Soon there were endearing invitations to explore Thebes and the Valley of the Kings together, and to visit them in Minneapolis, spend a summer at their house on some lake with an enormous Red Indian name.

We ate lamb and couscous and drank quite a good claret, and over dessert (a sticky native pastry of honey and sesame and orange flower water), Sonia passed Len a clean handkerchief, waited until he had honked his nose again, then asked him, "Well, shall we propose it to our new friend?" and Len said, "By all means. I think Ralph will jump at the chance. Besides, I want to meet the old lech." And Sonia turned to me and petted the back of my hand and stared into my eyes with a mischievous little grin and sweetly asked if I would like to know anything more about my Atum-hadu, or my prospects of finding him, perhaps even to learn where he was that very instant?

Oh, what a pity, I thought with real sadness to have so quickly lost something of value, the old things are daft. "You have access to such information?" I asked, masking my horror as best I could.

"Perhaps, yes," said Sonia, and she smiled with such broad joy and excitement, while Len nodded sternly and repeated, "Oh, yes, that we do, dear friend." Could they have some scholarly background? One of the younger Nordquists perhaps an Egyptologist at Minneapolis's agricultural university? "Patience, Ralphie, patience," Sonia said slyly as I followed them, spry for their aggregate centuries, out of the dining room, down the hall, up the main stairs, and along a vibrating passage to their door.

They had taken a cabin easily six times the size of my own, and I had splurged (still confident in your father and the Partnership, as I still am, no question at all). Near an upright piano, on a round table with a fringed green baize cloth reaching nearly to the floor, sat a silver candelabra with three intertwining arms, each with a zebra-striped taper, which Len lit before extinguishing the overhead electric lights and covering the porthole. "Sit, dear boy," said Sonia, wheeling three small chairs to the table.

Len joined us, and my hands were taken by my neighbours. "Oh, it feels lovely tonight, doesn't it, bear?" she asked, and Len replied, "It does, dearest, the air quite hums."

"Please state your name and your purpose, dear heart," she said and squeezed my fingers with surprising strength. "For all to hear."

"My name is Ralph M. Trilipush, associate adjunct instructor of Egyptology, Harvard University, author of *Desire and Deceit in Ancient Egypt,* Collins Amorous Literature, 1920, new edition projected from Harvard's press next year. I am the leading scholar of King Atum-hadu of Egypt's XIIIth Dynasty. I have come—"

And with that the candles extinguished themselves. Neither Len nor Sonia blew them out. And, Margaret, they did not snuff out as if blown, the flame leaning first to the side opposite the source of the wind. No, they turned themselves off, darkened from the top down, with no scent of smoke. I was stunned, as anyone would have been, and assumed some trick, though I cannot say what or how.

"Oh, that's remarkably good!" said Sonia, pinching off the circulation in my fingers. "You've been heard very fast indeed!"

"Is that Your Majesty, great King Atoom-hadoo?" intoned the chief salesman of Minnesota's largest food manufacturer. And, Margaret, the table jumped slightly off the floor. A trick, of course, Margaret, of course, and yet, the effect, then, was really astonishing. And they are very old to be lifting tables with their knees.

"Do you have a message for our dear friend the professor?" she asked, and the table bumped the floor again.

"Do you wish to be found by the professor?" Bump.

"Do you wish to tell him where he can find you?" Bump.

"Will he succeed in finding you?" Bump.

"Will anyone help him?" Bump.

"Someone on this boat?" Bump.

"Do you wish to speak through the board?" Bump.

"Your wish is our command, great king," said Len, very much the polished courtier.

"Please just wait one second there," said Sonia, asking His Majesty King Atum-hadu the Engorged to hold the line while she fetched a piece of paper to take a message. She released my hand and stepped away from the vibrating table, rummaged in the dark of the room for a moment or two. She relit one of the candles and laid on the table a board of some sort, I can hardly describe it, this oddity. It was a folding piece of wood painted with an ornate alphabet and numbers. On top of the board she placed a kind of lens with crosshairs in its centre, large enough to point at one of the painted letters at a time. The glass was set into an ivory disk on tiny rolling wheels, with delicate indentations to hold in velvet-lined luxury the tips of your fingers. Sonia placed my hands on the disk, and in the dim light of the one black-and-white-striped candle, their four ancient hands seemed very pale and soft on the peculiar device, as if made of the same ivory.

"So ask, ask, dear boy. He's waiting for your question." I did not understand what I was meant to do.

"Oh, I'll get the ball rolling," says Len. "Great King Atoom-hadoo, who will be of the greatest help to our friend Ralph in his quest for you?" And the glass and ivory absolutely begins to skitter across the table under our hands, stopping here and there, very precisely centring its crosshairs over the letters A H A H R T N W.

"Ah, well," chided Len. "His Majesty seems to be having a bit of fun at our expense."

"Majesty, we're not here for your amusement. Perhaps you don't know just how we view kings in our day (no offence intended to you and yours, Ralphie). If you don't wish to speak to us, so be it, but we won't stand for any—" and Sonia positively scolded the spirit of the last king of the XIIIth Dynasty for engaging in "immature shenanigans." There was a moment of silence and calm, and then the disk flew again, nearly throwing my fingers from it in its haste: A H A H R T N W.

"Maybe he just wants to stay with yes and no," suggested Len.

"No, no," I finally found my voice. "Let me try. Lord of the Nile, Master of Two Kingdoms, where shall I find you?"

R X K S T.

"Oh, this is really too much," exclaimed Sonia, removing her hands from the ivory, which then tipped onto its side under the unbalanced weight of my and Len's fingers. "I really must apologise, dear Ralph," she said as she switched on the electric light and we all squinted in the glare of the 1920s. "I had hoped, you know."

"Please, I found it all fascinating," I said. "I am rather more scientific on these matters, so I cannot say that I sat with you as much of a believer."

"Of course not, dear, of course not," said Sonia, and she smiled precisely as one wants one's mother to smile when she allows your lie to traipse by unharassed.

I bade them good night, left them waving to me from their doorway, hand in hand, made plans for breakfast tomorrow, and I lie now in my vibrating cabin (irritatingly Spartan after what I now know is available on the ship—I have half a mind to go back to Cairo to take it up with the man at the ticketing agency).

I do not wish to encourage quackery, Margaret, but these lovely, lovely people must have been rather well-practised, well-synchronised confidence artists and helpful amateur Egyptologists both, and eager to see me succeed, for how else to explain that A H A H R T N W, plus a few spaces, yields "aHA Hr Tnw," which means "a fighter for honour" in the standard Roman-alphabet transliteration of hieroglyphs, and "rx-k st" translates, to the letter, as a very encouraging "you know the place"? What can I write here, Margaret? I saw what I saw. I do not believe it any more than you. It cannot have happened. It happened.

I have just awoken, 4.15 in the morning by my watch. In my dream just now, the engine-buzz of my wooden walls became the murmur of an impatient audience in a full lecture hall, like the room where I met you, but infinitely larger. Thousands of people are awaiting my remarks. I sit at a table on the stage with my lecture in front of me, several sheets in a hand I recognise as my own boyhood efforts to write demotic script. I am a little uncomfortable due to the weight of my headpiece, burdened as it is with golden figurines on the brow representing a vulture, a sphinx, a cobra, you, your father, Inge, and the Nordquists. Next to me on the dais sits Carter, very chatty, though in the rising ululating coming from the far, far back of the Boston audience, it is increasingly difficult to concentrate on his flattery: "Of the utmost importance, of course, we must always maintain, the manner in which we proceed from chamber to chamber within the tomb, my admiration extends far beyond your discoveries and encompasses also your heart." The ululating grows louder and sweeps forward over the crowd, row after row of Boston ladies suddenly standing to shriek with contorted faces, flinging their arms and programmes towards me in pleading. "How do you maintain your calm in the face of such pressures?" asks a visibly nervous Carter. Half the crowd is ululating now, tearing at their collars and belts, the throaty howling, a noise as old as Egypt, echoing from the Boston ladies, Dean Warren, Professor ter Breuggen, all of Finneran's flunky and criminal partners. Inge has torn her dress away from her magnificent body, and even you stand now, shaking off the groggy murk of painkillers to wail as everyone is wailing, and I stand up from the table and stride forward, naked and powerfully tripodal, holding my lecture in one hand and Carter's still beating heart in my other.

I am tired. My eyes are heavy but I feel so very strong, strangely strong.

Friday, 27 October, 1922

I awoke late this morning and heard the news from one of the native pursers that last night a brawl erupted between two members of the kitchen staff and that one of the devils cut the other with a bread knife before two waiters could restrain him. I learnt also that the combat had begun over an insult by one of the blacks to an American tourist, and that the other Egyptian was moved to fight because he could not bear rudeness to Westerners. He defended the insulted American against his own countryman. A fighter for honour.

I finally convinced the purser to take me to where the poor fellow was lying, bandaged up, recuperating from the slashes to his arms and back. His English was not bad, but we spoke mostly in Arabic. I introduced myself, explained a fraction of my plans, presented him with a copy of *Desire and Deceit in Ancient Egypt* (inscribed to a "fighter for honour"), and described the merest sliver of what I expected to find in my king's tomb. I asked him a few questions, and the answers were highly satisfying: a native of Luxor, he knew the paths and byways of the areas west of the Nile like the back of his hairy hand. Did he have strong friends that he trusted? He did. Did he wish to make more money than he had ever seen? He did. Did he wish to participate in a venture more important than emptying ashtrays on a riverboat? Not much of a talker or a smiler, for all his fire to defend insulted Westerners, Ahmed looked me up and down and insolently agreed (for all the world like a sergeant-major I once knew, short-cropped hair and snarling silences). Either way, my expedition now has a headman, though it took some negotiating to convince him he would work for salary and *baksheesh*, not for "a share of the treasure." And while he did not leap to his feet, bow down, take my salt, pledge his lifeblood, well, he was wounded only a few hours earlier.

I gave him the address of my villa and instructions for preliminary purchases and hiring. Discretion was stressed. He nodded his replies. He asked for and received two days to recover, attend to personal affairs onshore. And our meeting was over. I waited a bit for a burst of gratitude or childish pleasure, but received only that unblinking stare.

Breakfast with the Nordquists, fond farewells, give them address of my villa, invite them to come often, visit my site when we are up and running with a public operation. They are justifiably thrilled.

Journal: Alight in Luxor! Rental agent's representative awaits with cart and donkeys to carry my luggage to the villa, takes payment through November 30. Banking concerns a matter of some urgency now. Banks closed until Sunday.

My luggage installed and key in hand, I take the ferry across the Nile, hire a donkey, and ride out to walk the sacred land I have not seen in seven years, since 1915, soil holy to the ancients and myself in equal measure. The emotion is difficult to express as I trot past unimaginable changes, tourists filing past sights that, in 1915, had been nothing at all, mere sand dunes still sheltering hidden mysteries; Antiquities Service guards making their scheduled rounds; the complex of Hat-shep-sut's temple at Deir el Bahari; and the roped-off land where Winlock of the Metropolitan Museum will be digging again in a few days' time. I passed all of this, trotted up and on behind Winlock's site, over hill after hill, one after another, the gentle rising and falling land along the cliff face, until at last I recognised the landmarks Marlowe and I left behind seven years ago, the day we discovered Fragment C and fled with it in such a swashbuckling hurry.

This preliminary tour of the ground gives the experienced eye an idea of the challenge ahead, the scope of the problem: how many possible places to break ground, how many men will be needed, how long we can expect to work, what sort of specialised equipment we shall need. I draw a pen-and-ink survey of the cliff face, noting every possible cleft on its façade, plotting a strategy, ranking by likelihood of success all the areas I can cover, setting priorities, as time and money demand.

Assuming my financial backing is secure, I think a team of ten men will suffice for early explorations, this number quickly growing as the digging becomes more intense. I do not think, if Marlowe's and my guesses are correct, that this will become a case of several hundred men moving vast amounts of earth. I know where my king should be, at least I think I do. Assuming the financial backing is secure. Sunday's issue.

Tonight, I sleep in my villa on the secluded banks of the Nile, closer and closer to my king and my destiny.

Saturday, 28 October, 1922

On "guessing" where to find a tomb: The Reader, not unreasonably, asks how one loses a tomb for 3500 years and how one knows where to look for it again.

Even if a tomb were publicly acknowledged, over 3500 years things do get misplaced. Even a pyramid, while not easy to lose, has now and again been found where no one recalled leaving it. One hypothesis of Atum-hadu's invisibility: we are looking too low; his tomb (like Hat-shep-sut's first try) was built into a cleft halfway down a cliff face, then covered with rubble, all too easy to forget. Weather and erosion may conspire to cover a tomb with rocks and mud. Slaves building another tomb nearby may dump the dirt they excavate onto an older tomb, hiding its front. Or they may build their own working huts right over an older tomb's entryway. Clumsy archaeologists today might dig and dump *their* dirt on a tomb without noticing. Or the tomb front might resemble something else, a bland façade not worth peeking behind.

And, recall, the tomb was perhaps never meant to be noticed from the outside, as was clearly the case with our Atum-hadu. For, consider the last days of his life: invasion from the Hyksos to the north and Africans to the south. Betrayed by his nobles. Rival kings setting themselves up elsewhere on the Nile. The end of the world, in short, and no exaggeration: the end of all tradition, culture, daily life, rightful authority. In well-lit retrospect, we or some XVIIIth-Dynasty Johnny-come-lately, silver-spoon-sucking princeling can always come along and say, "Tosh, it was only an Intermediate Period, and lo, a mere ninety to one hundred years later the garish princes Ahmose and Kamose wrapped up the business of driving out the invaders and reinstating proper rule." But as you watch your world collapsing, that future is just a faint hope among a crowd of likelier dooms, and you can see only an eternity of despair stretched out before you.

Atum-hadu watches with furious eye
As the foreigners rape his land.
And he will take with him into the sand
All the gold and gods and wives and [fragment].

> — (Quatrain 17, A only, *Desire and Deceit in Ancient Egypt,* Collins
> Amorous Literature, 1920; Harvard University, 1923, if they
> are not absolutely poisoned by ter Breuggen)

Now, observe. Atum-hadu clearly intended to be discreet with his tomb. He was forced to be, unlike previous and subsequent kings, for it was not only *his* immortality he was taking with him; he was carrying into his hole the entirety of an Egypt he thought was finished. It was not mere tomb-robbers and spendthrift successors from whom he needed to defend his resting place; an entire alien race, the so-called Hyksos (a later Greek term), were belching their way through the land of Horus and Isis and Ra. Therefore his tomb would be (will be) both hidden and overflowing with wealth, artistic and otherwise.

Ma'at has forsaken me; I tear my hair.
When I need her, must have her, would splay her,
She proves herself a fickle slut,
Suitable only for taking from behind.

> — (Quatrain 72, ABC, *Desire and Deceit in Ancient Egypt,* Collins
> Amorous Literature, 1920; Harvard University, 1923)

Atum-hadu's harsh words for Ma'at, goddess of truth and justice, while all of his world was disintegrating, provide us some insight into the temper of the times and of the man.

But perhaps a less literal reading of this earthy verse is in order (though we need not go as far as Harriman: "Order collapses and I am lost/Justice turns from me, unfaithful and cruel/Showing me only her receding back." Vassal and Wilson: "Ah, but she is a sly one, that Ma'at/Tripping me up, taunting, *une vraie coquette*/Flaunting at me her shape/When affairs of state are pressing").

The brilliance of Atum-hadu is nowhere clearer than in this complex verse: hear this king, raging, crying out not for cowardly escape (bartering kingdoms for a horse, a horse) but instead, in futile combat with Fate herself, his eternal life against her amoral machinations, our bold hero spits his disgust at the pointlessness of relying on truth and justice, as if to say, "Such ideals merit only a backdoor visit."

All Egypt dies with me
And I will leave nothing for the accursed.
Cowards and invaders pursue me
But I will quench my thirst.

— (Quatrain 74, C only)

We may safely assume the following about Atum-hadu:

- He is buried.
- He is buried with as much wealth and art as could fit in his tomb, since the act of burying this last king coincided with a need to preserve as much of a vanishing kingdom as possible. A complete copy of his Admonitions will likely be found with him, ending all question of his authorship and my scholarship.
- He is buried near the sites of Fragments A, B, and C of his Admonitions, all found within a half a mile of each other.
- He is buried near Thebes, where his capital was.
- Since he died prior to the earliest use of the Valley of the Kings as a necropolis, he is not buried there.
- His tomb is unmarked, well-hidden, and perhaps high off the ground, not unlike the empty cleft tomb prepared for Hat-shep-sut that Carter stumbled into back in '16.
- As none of his relics have ever turned up for sale (keeping his reign and existence in doubt for the debating-club pleasure of idiots), one can logically conclude that he was never found by tomb-robbers. His tomb is gloriously intact, safe for his dear friend, Ralph.

- Therefore, he is in Deir el Bahari, in or against the cliffs near where Marlowe and I found Fragment C, where Marlowe and I conjectured and mapped and intended to return, before I was sent off to Turkey.

I shall be in Isis's bed
My tongue swimming in her Nile delta,
E'er any intruder find my head
Wrapped and resting upon a lion's pelt.

— (Quatrain 52, B & C)

And yet, how did he do it? It is a maddening puzzle. How did he arrange, in the chaos of the end of days, to have a tomb built and stocked, and to know that after his death (in battle? in bed? in battle in bed?) his body would be transported there, mummified, sealed in, and then promptly forgotten? Tomb architects, decorators, workmen, Overseers of the Secrets (the priestly specialists who would disembowel, preserve, and wrap him), and strong men to seal the tomb: none of whom would reveal to a living soul what they knew? How did he know that his authority would endure to the last crucial minute, and that his world would then disappear a moment later, under the onslaught, before anyone who knew enough thought to disturb his peace? Somehow he did it, setting for us the most brilliant Tomb Paradox in the history of Egyptian immortality and preparing, for only the most brilliant and deserving, a discovery like no other.

Sunday, 29 October, 1922

Journal: Up early, hours before the bank will open, and I find . . . Cats! Wonderful family of cats appears outside the villa this morning, and as the rising sun gilds our Nile, I happily share water and the food I bought yesterday in town, all adorably lapped up from the villa's dishes decorated with romanticised pictures of Arab horsemen.

There are three of them, two toms and the most endearing orange girl. Name the toms Rameses and Rameses (II and VI, of course), but a creature as rare as an orange girl can only be Maggie. She has a fine appetite, and after finishing off her breakfast she immediately reports to my lap for an affectionate round of petting and purring. The ancients were wise to see in these charmers the wiles of goddesses: they know more than they let on. When Maggie turns her gold-and-green eyes on me, with their slim, sharpened ovals of anthracite, I am clearly in the presence of an eternal force occupying this body for just a spell. And they know who their friends are, with neither hesitation nor misstep; they recognised at once my lap as that of a cat-worshipper.

My father kept hounds, of course, kennels full of them, maintaining at all times five to six hundred English and American foxhounds, harriers, beagles, beagle-harriers, and anglo-français. The kennel masters (a team of twenty-five, dressed in my father's unconventional livery) were some of my keenest childhood friends, especially when Father was on expedition. In such numbers, of course, the hounds lived very much as a dog community, rather than as domesticated house pets, though there were two merry beagles I took as my own companions in the Hall. I spent many years at the kennel masters' sides observing that crowded, well-governed dog world with the purest respect and fascination. The dogs' baying, which the masters in their flared harlequin trousers and winged helmets could start and stop at will, enthralled me, and I would beg the houndsmen to set the dogs to singing. When, with laughing eyes, the masters had all of the beasts *roo-roo-roo*ing at once, the countryside echoed with the sweet choir, and as far away as the village, house windows rattled and bells clanked in sympathy and the children were all happy, crying out, "The Trilipush hounds! The Trilipush hounds!" It was, of course, a sound the animals produced unprompted when Father returned from expeditions, even when he was still several miles away, farther, one would think, than his scent could carry, but no farther than his love for them and theirs for him could stretch.

There is no peace in a world of fighting men,
And no woman feels right without soon feeling wrong.
There is no lasting comfort in [fragment].
To know the gods, only scratch to make the neck long.

It is at the very least anachronistic if not positively insane to see in Quatrain 16 (Fragment A only), as Harriman did, "a primitive's first, tentative desire for God's grace (the sinner-king-poet stretching *long* his *neck* heavenward to *scratch* the itch for God's love)." And, while I admit that in *Desire and Deceit* I not illogically interpreted this puzzling verse as a reference to the primal Atumic act ("scratching" to lengthen a "neck"), I believe now that the verse refers to something quite different, and it is a case where the illustrative hieroglyph expresses meaning better than the cryptic Roman alphabet. The stretching neck belongs to none other than a dog being scratched under the chin or a cat being stroked from shoulder to tail.

And so, should the Press someday enquire in its raucous, childishly fleeting clamour for knowledge, "Mr. Trilipush, what drew you to Atum-hadu? Why not Rameses or Akh-en-Aten or this unlikely Tut-ankh-Amen?" I might answer that we are both lovers of animals, my king and I, and see in their dark eyes a wisdom and sympathy too often bleached from the whites of men's eyes.

Margaret: Your spaniels, the little picnic-pirate dog that day we were engaged, my father's hounds and horses, Atum-hadu's menagerie, the pictures found on so many tomb walls of salukis or greyhounds: they have been with us from the very beginning. My three cats here ran off again after our morning's petting. I hope they will be back tomorrow, and as long as I am here. The moment I was looking into Maggie's golden eyes I could imagine you lying awake in Boston, stroking the bellies of Antony and Cleopatra until their back left legs shook uncontrollably, so that at that very instant you and I were meeting halfway, and our hands were somehow touching through the soft bellies of these beasts. I hope you are keeping a journal while I am away. At just after midnight your time on 29 October, were you petting your dogs and thinking of me?

Journal: I set off to explore Luxor. Not in a position to buy much just now, but I examine its markets and bazaars, its hidden streets and public squares, try to get my bearings as, though it is much smaller than Cairo, I do not claim to know it well. Try again, and futilely, not to think of the fate of this expedition if my financiers fail now.

I take the opportunity to visit the bank, introduce myself, provide them my address, ask for notification as soon as the credit is settled. Which it is not, as of this morning. Remind myself that Sunday in Boston the banks are closed.

Ferry across the Nile again to walk to Deir el Bahari, time the trip on foot, try to plot a route that leads me to the site of Fragment C without passing in view of Winlock's cordoned-off areas or the touristic centres around Hat-shep-sut's temple. Cannot quite see how to do it efficiently. I remember Marlowe leading the way, sensing just the place to begin, hill after hill: "A bit farther on, I should say, old boy, just a bit farther on."

Return to villa. Organise my drafting table, desks, notebooks, journals. Shelve research texts, translating dictionaries, gramophone records. Prepare daily work packs with canteens, chisels, rope, et cetera.

After sundown here on the banks of the Nile, with my back to Villa Trilipush, it is no lighter than it was 3500 years ago, and one can imagine the great king himself, walking perhaps this very ground, gazing, as I just have, into the darkness across the river, wondering, when the inevitable end can be held at bay no longer, how he will cross that river and hide his earthly remains with none to bear witness.

Monday, 30 October, 1922

Journal: I am established in Villa Trilipush, the (returned!) cats are fed and thoroughly petted, and I admit this morning I awoke actually worried about the expenses ahead, but I have vowed not to waste another minute doubting my backers. Instead I cabled CCF and encouraged him once more with a promising picture of the coming weeks' labours.

A busy day follows. In the few hours before Ahmed is due to meet me, I collect portable and nonperishable foods, a cooker, matches, cells for the electric torch, et cetera.

When I return to the villa for lunch and my meeting with Ahmed, the Nordquists are there, the good people. I have Ahmed wait while I show the dears my preparations, maps, library, tour them around Villa Trilipush with pride, and they are kind and complimentary, a pleasure. Over lunch, I help them plan their itinerary, advise which tombs are worth the trouble and which are derivative. They set off, waving farewell to me and my silent headman, the very image of one's sweet, doddering parents.

Ahmed is going to be an excellent foreman, and I must congratulate myself again on discovering him. He is all business, no smiles or chitchat. I explain to him that our temporary but essential challenge will be to hire and move enough men to our site and have them moving earth, while maintaining discretion as the concession politics untangle themselves. (Success will certainly produce a concession, but in the awkward meanwhile, one must be outwardly respectful of how things are done.)

Winlock and Carter have not started yet; Ahmed and I were first on the scene, and so there was no shortage of poor, strong, uncurious men looking for work. We hired some for now, and engaged plenty for later. To be sure, Ahmed's few choice mentions of a curse on any who attempt to dig for King Tut-ankh-Amen, and his remark here about Carter's bankruptcy and there about Winlock's criminal record, and a nonchalant but audible comment that both Carter and Winlock have used flogging to keep their natives in line should keep the labour market nicely softened up for the coming season. I hardly endorse such methods, but I did not wish to chastise him on our first day, and his inappropriate behaviour was on my account. As it is, we shall begin our expedition with a small, mobile core of six stout men, including Ahmed and myself. He will report at dawn tomorrow with donkeys and harnesses, heavy shovels and picks, canvas sacks, and a wooden cart, and we will begin, though the route still troubles me.

Margaret: In the bazaar today, I found two items you will appreciate. The first is a little toy, a fine gift someday for some clever little boy, my sweet Queen, some rugged little fellow with a taste for Egypt and his father's company (unknowingly receiving a lifelong training as a future biographer!). It is a jack-in-the-box, painted like a brickwork tomb. One cranks the handle, and a faint ghostly screech emerges, like gas escaping from a nearly sealed bottle of fizzy drink. The noise grows louder until the top of the tomb opens and up rises a fake-stone sarcophagus, a kingly face painted on its head. Keep winding and the top of the sarcophagus opens with a pop, and a golden mummy case rises. Crank more and the mummy case slowly opens to reveal a lily-white mummy, a childish smile and lovely blue eyes peeping through its linens as it sits up.

Even better, my love, is a little painted figurine made of dried mud, a striding fellow in tunic, sandals, and crown, a competent reproduction of some anonymous Middle Kingdom work. The winning feature, though, was the sly little grin on his face, completely unacceptable in such pieces, not the usual calm smile but an absolutely inappropriate and charming expression of knowing mischief. It is the perfect companion piece to the other statuette I travel with, the one I received at an intimate luncheon *à deux* at Locke-Ober (as Inge lingered at a café table outside).

You were glowing; love had quite illuminated you, even if I did not yet realise it. You were adorable, quoting from the book I had told you to read. "Is it true," you asked, sly kitten, "that when the tomb was closed and sealed, they believed everything inside it came to life?"

"That's right," I said, proud of your progress.

"And paintings of feasts became feasts, and statues of beautiful serving girls became beautiful serving girls?"

"Yes, my dear, you have it." I looked up, and you were handing me that perfect little statue: you, nude but for a modest blanket. "Daddy found out this Frenchman was coming through Boston, so he paid him to sculpt me. I was thinking, maybe if you put it in your room, when you close the door and switch off your light, well, you never know, do you?"

Tomorrow I go to the site, but tonight you are here with me in my villa, M., quite come to life at my side. Good night, my love.

Tuesday, 31 October, 1922, Excavation Day One

At last, into the fight! Now evening, and I am back at Villa Trili-push, the end of our first day. We are moving with a fine speed at last.

Ahmed arrived this morning when it was still dark, and he had the heavy gear and animals ready on the far bank. More importantly, Ahmed had solved my geographical issue. Last night he succeeded in the reconnoitre task I assigned him, stout fellow, and this morning he bent over the giant map on my main worktable and pencilled in a better route than I could find, leading from the river to the path where Marlowe and I found Fragment C, but never passing within sight of anyone who would find our progress threatening. (In the event of a proven Atum-haduan find dangling in front of their faces, Lacau will happily cut Winlock's concession down to make room for me.)

Thanks to our early start, Ahmed tells me we had the pick of the mules and equipment. It is for precisely this luxury, Ahmed explained, that he presented me with receipts for significantly more than I had budgeted, but such is the price of doing the job right, he reminds me. I was at a loss, actually, staring at the figures in my leather accounts book and the pile of scrawled slips my man dropped on the table. "Why are you looking like this? I can bring you to every one of these merchants to verify." A bit of a child, Ahmed is. "Mistrust makes figs of men," he informed me with Koranic intensity, and I suspect I may have misunderstood him, but I can scarcely allow him to think my Arabic is lacking, or he will attempt all manner of mischief with the workers.

Across the river, our first four team members awaited us on donkeys. Dawn on the Nile's west bank, and we followed Ahmed in a wide

loop to a path behind Deir el Bahari. The entire hike took no more
than ninety or a hundred minutes, up and down the rocky hills. "There
is a faster route here," muttered one of the anonymous quartet, but
Ahmed quieted him with a hard look, bless his black heart.

And then we were there, where Marlowe and I had had our great
victory, and where I was now returned with my own team to consum-
mate the work my partner and I had begun seven years before. We
were there! Under the high cliffs, on the sand which sunrise was flattering as orange-rust, I called a halt, which Ahmed seconded. I ordered
two of the men to begin a preliminary inspection of the lowest part of
the cliff face, walking along the terraced paths which abut and twist a
ways up the cliff wall, examining it for jarring unevenness or excessive
smoothness, symmetrical markings, anything at all that seemed man-
made. My other three men hiked some hundred yards out from the
cliff, looking upward while the sun was still low, to examine the higher
reaches of the cliff wall for likely clefts, marking off anything I missed
in my first sketch. Meanwhile, beginning at the landmarks Marlowe
and I had made to help us find our way back here, I continued farther
to the north and west, simply trying to get a sense of what if anything
had been trampled over by Winlock. While the men marched along in
their gowns and head wraps, covering their eyes, touching the cliff
wall, I found the two boulders leaning against each other that Marlowe
and I had noticed when we parked the motorcycle, and the pile of
smaller stones we had placed atop one of them when we realised we
had discovered something.

"It will be near here," I called to Ahmed in Arabic.

"Was he a rich king?" Ahmed asked, and to the point. I would have
to keep an eye on this one, and no mistake.

Ahmed led me up a path he knew to the top of the cliff wall, some
300 feet above the valley bed. It took us an hour to ascend to this high
position, from which my four workers below seemed the merest mice in
a vast field searching for one particular twig. Unfortunately, standing
on this point, we would be visible to parts of the Valley of the Kings on
one side of the wall, and Winlock down in the main basin of Deir el Ba-

hari on the other. So, if there were discoveries to be made from the top down, I would have to work quickly. Clearly, the high clefts would have to be our first priority.

The trouble with these clefts, and their appeal as secret tombs, is that they are invisible from the cliff path above and inaccessible from the ground below. I sent Ahmed back down to the base and then out far enough onto the main valley floor so that he could signal to me with waving arms when I stood directly above the clefts in my drawing, which procedure we repeated until I had placed markers on the cliff-top path, a dozen positions from which ropes would be hung for my close inventory of the cliff face. By this time, our day was nearly complete. We trooped back to the riverbank following our wide safety loop and bid each other *salaam* until first light tomorrow.

On the gramophone: "No Man's Land Belongs to Me, Otto."

Dominoes: A snake up and then back down the stairs ending in a spiral formation under my main worktable. The clicking sound brings the cats!

Wednesday, 1 November, 1922

Ahmed and I disagreed for some time (he with a restrained menace in his voice) as to how best to secure a rope 300 feet above a rocky death. Even as he asserted an expertise with knots (not without some thin-skinned pride), he was praising my upper-body strength (accurately), and claiming a Mohammedan contravention (new to me, but he was adamant) against undertaking any action that would show a hubristic desire to fly in the manner of the Prophet's ascension to Paradise. Doctrine is doctrine, so with my heart pounding in my ears, I flung myself down 100 feet of cliff while my four labourers wasted valuable time gawking at my bumping, yelping descent until I reached Cleft 1. I alit on a smooth ledge, still in sunlight, but found it was the front porch of nothing at all; the sun easily lit the far back wall of the aperture, no more than four or five feet deep. No inscription, pottery shard, sealed or secret door. I spent an hour assuring myself of this, brushing at every available surface, jabbing with a long metal rod to see if any wall resisted more or less than any other, but I was exploring a water-worn cleft in a cliff face and nothing else. I may have been the first man ever to set foot on it, or I may have been preceded by medi-aeval hermits (though I would well understand if they found the perch too isolated and depressing), or perhaps by ancient tomb architects, scouting out possibilities, tetchily shaking their heads at another poor-quality cleft. And another morning vanishes, quite mortal indeed.

I hauled myself up to the summit, an exhausting business, resting whenever I could find a notch to place a foot, and my arms were twitching and I was spitting dust when I scrambled to the top, where Ahmed was lying down, having a smoke under a makeshift sunscreen: a Hotel of the Sphinx bedsheet (with that mad emblem of vulture, sphinx, and cobra) spread out and supported on sticks. I cursed his laziness and had him prepare me lunch, which we shared in the pale yellow shade. The sun hit the sheet and cast its emblazoned seal in a slightly darker shadow between us. "Hotel of the Sphinx," says unsmil-ing Ahmed in English. "A-One, Jack. You are a happy digger, eh?"

"Where did you learn English?"

"I don't speak English," he replied in English.

"*Digger* is a term for Australian soldiers," I explained. "I am English, so the term is inappropriate."

"I hate the Australians," he replied calmly, in English. "They were the worst men here during the War. Worse than any of the others, even the Turks. They made whores of everyone. You English, yes, you are trouble, and the French, *pah*." Ahmed spat. "The Americans, I do not know them. But the Australians. These were a disgrace, these men." All of this he said with a strangely toneless voice, his hand rubbing the short fringe of hair around his temples. It is an odd thing, to hear the grievances and passions of a native people, the misunderstandings or petty concerns that animate them but that are inexplicable to Western-ers. I can understand Ahmed's ancient ancestors better than I can un-derstand Ahmed himself, but then his ancestors were their own masters, not Protected by foreign Powers. To cheer him up, I described something of Atum-hadu and his times. He nodded, seemed to understand the significance of what I was telling him, seemed to grasp towards a sort of pride that these were *his* people, *his* history.

After our meal, I hopped over the edge again, my last reassuring sight on the surface being Ahmed's glowering face as he double-checked the knots gripping the rocks and posts.

This time I descended approximately ten feet further to the next smooth outcropped ledge, but found something far more promising. This shelf was indubitably the porch of a chamber cut into the cliff face, approximately twenty-five feet into the cool dark after a slight turn to the right, so that even a bird hovering directly in front of the cleft would not see the depth of the chamber, and my heart began to pound. Untying myself, I looked over the edge and noted with a thrill that I was nearly directly above the spot where I had found Fragment C, seven years before. This chamber was absolutely man-made (or at least man-enhanced), just like Hat-shep-sut's unfinished tomb. In this case, however, despite nearly four hours of my massaging the walls from top to bottom, poking with the testing rod like a drunken fencer, scraping my electric torchlight over every inch of shadow, I could conclude only that I had a *dry hole*: an ancient tomb architect had started on this first room but then found something not to his liking, or a king changed his mind and opted at the last minute for a nice, opulent pyramid instead. There are many such disappointments lurking out here to devour the hopes of the overeager.

The sun, though still cruelly hot, was lowering quickly when I had tied my rope again and called up to Ahmed to lend some muscle, a request I made again and again as I pulled myself, squeaking and wheezing with peeling palms, up to the top, finding it to be quite unoccupied. I collected the gear, folded the sheet, gathered the dirty cooking equipment, and wove my way down the hill alone to find harnessed donkeys, but not a single workman.

I sit now, at the end of day two, in the lamplight of Villa Trilipush, holding this inadvertently comic cable from Finneran (predictably confused by the Gregorian calendar: MONEY? TOO SOON TO SEND MONEY.

WHAT HAVE YOU DONE WITH ALL YOUR MONEY SO FAR? BEST LUCK, CCF). I can imagine Atum-hadu pondering the Tomb Paradox that he would most surely face. I can imagine him sending a scout to examine the cliff face of Deir el Bahari and report on likely locations, a scout who perhaps swung into the very same clefts I saw today. Or, as I think more of Atum-hadu's unique position, perhaps there was no scout at all, for we must remember:

I am the lord of all Egypt, the son of Ra, Horus's essence,
Master of the Nile, host of every feast.
Lover of every woman, lord of every man,
Every hill, every cliff, every beast.

— (Quatrain 23, A & B only)

Given such pride and his need for secrecy, would he have trusted even a single scout? Or did his majestic kingship himself wander these stones, alone or with an expendable companion? Did he gaze up to those secluded clefts, dispatch disposable, de-tongued slaves to crawl into them and gauge their suitability?

To continue my day. The team found me packed and waiting at the donkeys, prepared to think the worst of them. But Ahmed, with characteristic effusiveness, informed me in Arabic that, having found nothing in their continued investigations of the cliff walls, the men had scouted further afield and witnessed activity at both Carter's site and Winlock's, which was why Ahmed had descended from the heights, leaving me hanging. "To keep His Lordship's trespassing a secret," he added in English with no more facial expression than ever, the troublesome man.

We followed the usual route back to the river. Having said farewell to the men, leaving Ahmed to return the donkeys and store the heavy gear, I was heading back to the ferry pier, when on the path I came upon none other than Howard Carter. He was leading a train of carts overflowing with shovels and levers and filters and other toys, an orgy of Carnarvonian excess, biting out orders to his parading dozens, his

Arabic slightly accented but transmitting the same dignified manner of command as he displays in English.

Eager as I was to head off for my evening's tasks, I found myself drawn into conversation with Carter, strolling alongside him at his rapid clip. He was on his last trip of the day, hauling equipment into the Valley to begin his *sixth* season's work on that same pointless quest—an act of defiance, almost of madness. "Well, good for you, despite it all," I encouraged. "Don't lose hope, old boy." Bit of a cold fish, really, that one, but I learnt from one of his natives that his scheme this year is to trench out a long strip of earth starting from Rameses VI's tomb. A droll plan, but if nothing else Carter was doing an excellent job of rotating the sand, giving each grain a chance to see the sun for a bit, digging up no end of *sebakh* fertiliser for the peasants.

Egypt at the time of Atum-hadu's rise: Atum-hadu rose to power in a time of dire trouble. The kingship was failing, flailing, dying for new blood and leadership. Long-lived kings had left behind uncertain, distant heirs, weak grandnieces whose shaky hands in marriage offered the keys to a shaky kingdom. Royal wealth had simmered away; too often the future had been mortgaged to pay for present needs or recreations. External enemies and internal pretenders gnawed at the dynasty's foundations. And in this troublesome era a leader appeared, one final hero. But what do we know of him with certainty?

We know from the more autobiographical verses of his Admonitions that he was the last king and that he felt that his death would be the death of all Egypt. We know that he trusted only a particular adviser, whom he calls his Master of Largesse. We know that his appetites for love and violence were equally unappeasable. We know little else with certainty.

And yet, standing here, where he stood, facing his Nile, imagining the approaching end of his kingdom as the Hyksos invaders closed in on his capital at Thebes, it is not difficult to know what he was feeling, this mortal man planning for immortality, this king of a doomed kingdom, heir to nothing, the recipient of a valueless present, which his ancestors had viewed only as an infinitely mortgagable future. But the future was not infinite; one specific day, on a given date, the future shimmered away in the desert heat and Atum-hadu was left alone whilst from nothing one, two, four, ten, fifty, a hundred, a thousand, ten thousand spear tips pricked the wavering air over the next bluff.

Thursday, 2 November, 1922

  Journal: Morning: we have cleared three more clefts, for a total now of five, though the process is slowed by remaining hunched out of sight when on the cliff top. The men again retrace the path 200 yards in either direction from where I found Fragment C, this time moving even slower, testing the cliff-face surface. Twice they find smooth patches of possible interest, and per my standing order, they call me down from my work above, but both times slow clearing of the rock face reveals only wind- or water-buffed ancient stone. Lunch with Ahmed, discuss Oxford, about which he is charmingly curious. Afternoon: two more clefts, one more false alarm of smooth rock.

  These are the days of mounting excitement, of false leads, of second guessing. In retrospect they will seem like steps in the right direction, inevitable and unalterable, but when you are taking those steps, when they are still the present and not yet the sanctified past, they are all possible wrong steps in the muck, sloshing with doubt, confidence, despair.

  I bid my men farewell until tomorrow, and head to town to check my new *poste restante*, where I find this paste-worthy relic of a crumbling dynasty:

```
October 19, Cambridge

My dear Mr. Trilipush,


   A happy day for me here in Cambridge! After my
visit with the  trusty  Mr. Ferrell last week, I
```

contacted Oxford, and today, having heard from them, I spent a happy hour with your fiancée's father, a fine, rough fellow who learns quickly and understands at once what an expert has to tell him.

If you are surprised to learn that Oxford says you were never there, and that you did not study under Professor Wexler, then your surprise pales in comparison with my own when I learned this news. I shared my surprise with your Mr. Finneran, as well as my opinion that your expedition will produce nothing of value. You will not be surprised to hear this doubt from me, as your speculative specialization in the putative Atoumadou has hardly impressed me. And, continuing your lack of surprise, I would be surprised if you were much surprised to learn that, given this clarifying news, the Egyptology Department and, in truth, Harvard University, esteemed and immortal, will be able to survive most adequately into the future without your continued presence on the faculty in even the most menial role. Please accept my gratitude for the amusement you have provided us with your indelicate translations of apocryphal erotica and with your spurious background. With every good wish, I remain your superior in every way,

Claes ter Breuggen

The gibbering indiscretion of the mad shocks the sane man's mind: did ter Breuggen think I would not publish this letter? But, my dear professor of falsehoods, corrupter of youth, of course I will publish it.

I will publish it on page 1, reproduce it over your infantile, wobbly signature and print the letter alongside a photo of me holding my Oxford
degrees in front of Atum-hadu's mummy.

Ter Breuggen is an object lesson to us all: a man who purports to be
a scientist, trained in weighing evidence carefully, has apparently fallen
credulously in love with a random liar, this Ferrell, a man of mist, fallen
from the clouds like bad weather. And this lie that he so eagerly gulps
makes no sense; that Ralph Trilipush did not go to Oxford makes no
sense whatsoever. A missing file, a misspelled name—whatever the corruption that has seeped into some text in a damp basement in Oxford is
merely that: a corruption. Corrupted texts do not change reality, they
merely confuse the feebleminded.

Ter Breuggen grasped at this to fire me, no surprise there, I wa-
gered my job on Atum-hadu so on my shoulders be it, and if that know-
nothing wishes to cling to some criminal's lies to justify his ignorance,
I cannot care. But, honestly, what a flimsy reed! A file is lost, therefore
I did not attend Oxford? Brilliant. And so? So I do not know my field?
So I did not translate Atum-hadu's verses? So I did not hold Fragment
C in my hands? But I *did*, I did all that, and I *did* attend Oxford, and no
file's errancy can make it otherwise. If Oxford burnt to the ground
today and left no trace of *anyone's* records, did therefore *no one* ever
walk its gracious ivied halls, luncheon in its open-air rooftop restau-
rants amid the spires, sail on its stormy saltwater lakes, attend its Sunday night bullfights in the company of dons and proctors, wrestle nude
on its green quads while the young women of town cheered and threw
potatoes? With a single cleansing blaze, would the world be at once
filled with Oxford impostors and false graduates?

These mad assertions of insidious, invisible Ferrell produce an absurd retroactive unwinding of the truth. If I was not at Oxford, how
did I meet Marlowe? How did we come to find ourselves unearthing a
pot containing Fragment C? If I was not his school chum, how did we
come to be in the same unit in Egypt? If we did not enlist together, how
did I find my way into the Army? Told this way the story makes no
sense at all. Ferrell is a madman.

Reconstructing the order of events with these slow letters is maddening. Obviously, whatever poison ter Breuggen spilt into Finneran's
ear on the 19th would explain CCF's financial delays and enigmatic
cables. Whoever *Ferrell* is, he is on an incomprehensible quest to dis-
credit me. He succeeded in ter Breuggen's office, but the fear and in-
competence there made for fertile ground. CCF is of sterner stuff. Oh
God, M.

CABLE. LUXOR TO MARGARET FINNERAN,

BOSTON, 2 NOV. 1922, 5.47 P.M.

MY DARLING. HAVE LEARNT A LIAR LURKS, A STRANGER CALLED

FERRELL. DO NOT KNOW HIM, DO NOT BELIEVE HIM. IGNORE AT

ALL COSTS. YOUR CONQUERING LOVE. RMT.

CABLE. LUXOR TO C. C. FINNERAN,

BOSTON, 2 NOV. 1922, 5.49 P.M.

MASTER OF LARGESSE. HAVE LEARNT MORE OF FERRELL, A LIAR

OF MYSTERIOUS MOTIVATION. YOU MAY SAFELY DISREGARD HIM

AND INSTEAD COMFORTABLY AND QUICKLY PROCEED

ACCORDING TO OUR ORIGINAL PLANS. RMT.

Margaret:　　I just sprinted back into town and cabled you to ignore
this Ferrell. I am sure you will if you have not already. He is a mythical
nemesis dispatched to harass me, by I cannot imagine what forces for I
cannot imagine what reason. Even so, he is a clownish, flabby nemesis.
And yet, also necessary! Great men, my darling, are often troubled by
just such petty thugs and anaemic ill-wishers. These troubled, rodential
men are driven by a need to tear down because they cannot create, they
have been denied Atum's spark, the bit of godness that great men desire—the power to create. And, sulphur-veined, they cling instead with
ragged claws, driven by the satanic urge to destroy.

If you have heard his nonsense already—and I suppose you must
have, since it appears he was in your home two weeks ago—then my

heart breaks for you, because his hissing words no doubt sizzled away at the very idea you have of me. What must you have thought to hear the mad, impossible notion that Ralph was not at Oxford? If you believed for even a single, shocking moment, then I am so very sorry.

I know, Margaret—I am not such a fool as all that—I know that what first drew you to me was my manner and my history: an English explorer, sculpted from old gentry, Oxford education, War heroism. I know these were our foundation stones. But now, my love, Ferrell provides us an opportunity to grow stronger, to forge a deeper love and understanding. We both know that my *curriculum vitae* is not the best of me, nor the most of me. And if Oxford were not real—as Ferrell would have it—what would that change between us? Nothing. My accomplishments were the means to bring us together, not the sustenance off of which our love will last forever. If foiled Ferrell has helped us to see that, then our magnanimous thanks to him!

After a ghastly evening, I am finally feeling myself again. Is this what "court intrigue" actually felt like, when it was a daily reality and not an historian's dry phrase? When Atum-hadu's courtiers could not be trusted, when conspirators crept and pretenders to his throne bribed the cooks in the heat of the palace kitchen and priests whispered obscene lies and promises in the shadows of torchlights, did his stomach churn as mine does? Did he grapple with slippery destroyers when he would rather have honoured his name and patron-god by creating?

Friday, 3 November, 1922

Journal: Extend the men's wall searches nearly half a mile into the desert. Clear another four clefts, the most promising of which shows some evidence of human contact, but nothing definitive. Twice the men find something in the wall face worth my hurried descent from the path above, but both times it is a false alarm. I must soon face the possibility that ground will have to be cleared, earth moved. If all of the clefts prove valueless, and the cliff face reveals nothing, then we are left with the inescapable conclusion that Atum-hadu's tomb is in the flat valley basin, which will mean trenching operations, similar to Carter's antworks on the other side of the cliff wall. Efficiency will demand several score men if not more. An impossibility without a complete and unequivocal concession from the Antiquities Service.

Saturday, 4 November, 1922

Journal: Clear five more clefts, and have the men begin physically scraping the cliff face to a height of seven feet, 250 yards in either direction from the Fragment C site. It is a necessary next step, and I hope it will reward us, but I fear that the vast, flat desert floor now seems a more likely hiding place for Atum-hadu. This possibility stretches out our likely time commitment significantly. Will the Partnership's nerve hold for another year if necessary? Perhaps I should introduce myself to Professor Winlock, discuss with him man-to-man a partition of the Metropolitan Museum's land. He has no interest or expertise in Atum-hadu, and can cover only so much land in a season, even with his museum's obscene resources. And he may welcome some complimentary shares in Hand-of-Atum, Ltd., considering his ltd. success in recent months.

Late afternoon: I descend to find I am missing Ahmed and one of the men. They return an hour later with this tale: while I was above, one of my workmen's cousins came to visit him at our site and bore interesting news (gossip-bearing cousins being this country's chief industry): Carter had found something, and my men's afternoon absence (much *salaam*ing and "thousand pardons, Lord Trilipush") was due to their infiltration of Carter's site, where it appears that Carter had found . . . a stair. Good Lord, a cause for jubilation to the poor old-timer, I am quite sure. Six years later and a stair! Ah well, he deserved to find something, and the Earl of Carnarvon can now feel his money was not entirely wasted.

Home to relax with the cats, some music.

The Nordquists stop for a cheering visit and we share supper. I recount my days, and they detail their touristic adventures. Their kind questions and interest in my every word warm me, a welcome surprise and marvellous tonic for my confidence.

Sunday, 5 November, 1922

Journal: Visit bazaar, dressed in native garb (it wins me better prices). Buy a few souvenirs—scarabs done by an excellent forger, aged brilliantly. The merchant gamely claims they are authentic Thothmes III. Nonsense, but it should amuse Carter, a congratulatory token from a sand-spitting brother.

Venture on donkey out to the Valley to see Carter's stair. I feel queer, hot and cold in turns. How wonderful for him if he has made a find, of course.

His encampment is a ludicrously large presence squatting practically on top of Rameses VI. Finding Carter himself was rather tricky, as he moves in the centre of a crowd of workmen. Only calling his name loudly caught his attention. He emerged from his throng to greet me, dusting off his hands and usual frosty manner, an easy affectation to maintain with Carnarvon's cash and a supporting cast of hundreds. He should try surviving on charm alone.

"Yes, Trilipush," he says, pocketing my proffered gift of one of the rare first editions of *Desire and Deceit in Ancient Egypt*. "What brings you round?"

"I hear you've tripped over a stair, Howard. Mind if I have a look, professional courtesy, peer review, all that?"

"Word's already out, is it?"

"You know the native love of sharing a secret."

"Yes, well, I'd rather not have visitors at this point."

"Of course not, old man, too early for a bunch of tourists and grandees to muck up the works." And he is right, the old professional: the thought of civilians tramping away on a new find—unspeakable. I set off towards the spot where his workmen were kneeling, a row of a dozen men with screens, sifting through all of the lifted sand, rebagging the confirmed dirt, calling for a supervisor if any shard of anything turned up. What a production! It was a factory, a capitalist's "sweat-shop" more than a scientific expedition. Massive archaeological waste. No wonder Carter has burnt years at this. I finally penetrated to the centre of the fuss and found that his one stair had been hard at it, *à la* Atum, and had multiplied with showy fertility: now a whole staircase burrowed down into the earth, ending with a wall of stones and rub-bish. My God, what a sight, an incredible discovery, no question, of what I cannot say.

"Cache of plundered junk?" I asked him when he caught up with me. "Ancient storage facility? Granary?"

"Probably," he agreed. "Well, if you will excuse me, dearest Ralph, we have days ahead of us to clear this rubbish and gently open any doors we might find." As I rode off, I looked over my shoulder, and he was all energy in all directions, a remarkable sight for an old fellow, es-pecially if his bowels were in a state anything like mine. The expres-sions on his workers' faces were quite unlike anything my discount team can manufacture. Of course, even in his dotage, Carter has such an ability to make one feel completely invisible, weightless. He does not seem to know he does it; it is precisely as if he constantly, from birth, had given off a blinding light from his face that made everyone he spoke to cover their eyes—how would he ever know that people were not dazzled when he was not looking at them? Even if someone told him, he would likely disbelieve them. "What?" he would say, looking incredulously at yet another squinting face. "What do you mean? How am I different?"

I need to take some air, check *poste restante*.

Letter from my fiancée, dated 13 October, twenty-three days ago. What has happened since?

A long, vindictive session of enforced closet time. Gramophone not helpful. Fever.

Oct. 13

My Ralphie—

 Strange adventures to relate, my Egyptian Lord.

 A snooping nosy parker named Harold Ferrell came to our house today. He's looking for a friend of yours. Get a load of this, Ralphie: he says your friend is a poor Australian boy named Paul Caldwell, an amateur Egyptologist who has lived what sounds like a positively dreary and horrible little life. "A friend of Ralph's?" I asked in a tone to get the point across, and then, to be quite sure he got it, I told him that even though you were forced to mix with all sorts of odd types in the War, this Paul Caldwell didn't sound like your sort of friend at all. He's Australian, too. The snooper, I mean. He also spent time behind closed doors with Daddy, and I tried to put my ear to the door for you, but it was very tiring.

 You've been gone forever, it seems like. It's hard to imagine what you do all day there in the sand. It's hard to remember having you around. The weather is turning cold here, and Inge has me under such careful watch it's an absolute bore. J. P. O'Toole comes around with an invitation or a present from time to time. He sends his best to you. Oh, yes: I nearly forgot to tell you, he asked me a favor. He said I should ask you to send him "any and all news" of the excavation too, don't just send reports to Daddy, because JP doesn't want to feel left out. Isn't that sweet? He's a very sweet man, you know, and so generous.

 That reminds me: I hope you are having success and that it is fast. I think you are a wonderful, heroic man, Ralphie, you know I do, but I don't like having you gone all this long time. I don't like it at all, and I think that if there are any more of these expeditions after we are married, I will come with you, or I will wait only at Trilipush Hall with crowds of friends and servants, or at a hotel in

*Paris. Boston is a horrible bore. You are beastly to have left me
alone this long. Daddy is a bore. Inge is a fat bore. What am I supposed to be doing here with my time while you are off having
grand adventures? I know that "it is all for us," and when you
come back it is our future you are going to carry home, I know. But
still. Being here under Daddy and Inge's thumbs makes me feel
like a little girl. I know that they only want what's* best for me,
but that also seems to mean boring me to tears.

m.

Monday, 6 November, 1922

Pay men for one week, send them home. I am not in fit condition to
work.

Wednesday, 8 November, 1922

Night. Three days lost to fever, et cetera. By nightfall, I am able to
rise. The cats were a comfort in my illness, especially dear Maggie. I
eat dinner for the first time since Sunday. After days of nauseous, anxious sleep, I am, tonight, of course, unable to sleep. I am curious what
ancient, desiccated wine cellar Carter's found at the bottom of his
stairs. I shall climb aboard a nocturnal donkey, trot into the Valley, and
find my heartbroken colleague atop his stairway to ancient rubbish
bins, and I shall succour him in his despair at six years of wasting
Carnarvon's good, easy money.

Later: I dressed in native garb. I paid a boy with a boat to ferry
me across, and made the moonlit Valley in not much time. Hiked up a
side path, behind Rameses VI's tomb, to look again at the precious
stairwell. But instead I found a few of Carter's workers, standing watch
and sleeping, no sign of the great man himself. And there was a pile of
boulders *atop where the staircase had been.* Nothing else. If there ever was
a staircase, if heat and solitude and frustration and fever have not tick-

led me into meaningless hallucination, then Carter has apparently *reburied his find*. Exchange a few *salaams* and chitchat with his workers. My disguise is flawless. From what they told me, Carter has set his team to work in the *other* direction, trenching around the ancient huts of the workmen who built Rameses VI's tomb. What a man, this Carter! What style! Faced with a black eye unlike anything in Egyptological history (six years and a staircase to a dry hole), and with his noble moneybags sitting in Haw-haw House back in green England, Carter's simply buried his folly and turned his back on it. Never happened! A trickster, our Mr. Carter, it now seems. Makes one wonder what else he has covered up in his glorious past.

I set off, back to the river by way of his villa in Gurna. The windows were unshuttered, the moonlight silvering one side of the house. A little corner of England deposited here in Egypt, his easels and books sitting in tidy order in what must be a sitting room and study. The easel's back was to the window, so I cannot comment on his skill as a painter. He did not clear away his tea things, no doubt he was drinking something potent to erase the dreadful memory of burying rather than digging, covering up his staircase from the 1890s. Who else besides me heard, too early, of his "triumph"? How many souls did his workmen tell? "Ah, yes, Lord Carter has found King Tut-ankh-Amen's tomb today! He found the staircase today, and tomorrow the treasure room! Tell all the cousins!" Poor Carter. No wonder the tea things sit unwashed.

The back of the house revealed an interesting tableau, framed by the green-painted window sashes. He was sleeping like a man at peace, which is odd, unless one considers the sleeping draught he likely gulped to beat back his roiling worries. His thin eyeglasses were folded on the bedside table, over a pre-slumber read, the cover of which was the same colour as *Desire and Deceit in Ancient Egypt*, which would not surprise me, but I could not quite make out the title. Carter himself lay under white sheets and a tent of mesh. He held his old, wrinkled hands up near his neck like some rodent burrowed down for a long, hard winter. I do not envy the questions coming the poor man's way.

Thursday, 9 November, 1922

Journal: After losing three days to fever and sublimated, unnecessary worry, I awake early today, refreshed and ready to work. I feel absolutely tip-top. Set out food for Maggie and the Rameses.

Ahmed and the men are waiting, loyal and relieved to see me
healthy at last. They have come every morning and left only after hours
of waiting. Today their eagerness to work is palpable and infectious.
They look at me with enthusiasm and respect.

I have the men continue their careful scraping of the cliff face abut-
ting the rising path. Our progress is heartening, though progress without discovery can also be viewed as a shrinking field of prospect, but I
do not indulge such thinking. I clear three more clefts. Not many remain, and more difficult work will be required, I fear.

Maggie and the toms take their supper with me in my dining room
and spend the evening peering curiously at the gramophone.

Friday, 10 November, 1922

Journal: Distribute two dozen of CCF's monogrammed cigars to
the men as *baksheesh*. Tokens of my faith in my workers. It is often and
boringly repeated that Carter "inspires loyalty in his men." But "inspir-
ing loyalty," as I learnt in the Army, is a caveman's trick. Anyone can
do it with gifts or fear.

Today I acknowledge the need to begin planning for next steps. I
send two of the men out into the flat basin of this section of valley, to
mark with stakes a square, 100 yards out from the cliff wall and 100
yards long, centring on the site of Fragment C's discovery. If it comes
to excavating trenches, we will be ready. I ask Ahmed's opinion how
easily we could hire a team of 100 men and equip them all with digging
tools. The timing is certainly possible, but the cost will require waiting
for the Partnership to act. And the Partnership will need to be prepared for a full-team budget. With nothing to show yet, I am unwilling

to go back to Lacau or to Winlock, but it is simply not feasible to tramp in a full excavation team unseen.

Saturday, 11 November, 1922

Book notes: Change the epigraph to 11 November, 1922! The 24th was too generous by a full thirteen days!

Journal: And today we were smiled upon. Just as I was about to change strategy, the world reveals itself to us in a new light, and we see more than anyone else has ever seen before. It is late at night now, and I write from my cot under the stars, outside the tomb of King Atumhadu. I have sent Ahmed to cable CCF and feed the cats.

My heart still beats with the knowledge of our victory, the strenuous and delicious effort to taste every instant—where do I begin? I cast aside the moon and haul back to the sky the solar chariot and replay our day from its glorious dawn:

The morning was spent swinging in and out of two of my very last clefts. I was practically forced to crawl when atop the cliff wall so as not to be seen from the Valley below, now a hive of wasteful, aimless trenching. I had left Ahmed to secure the ropes above and had two men out in the basin beginning to poke at the soft ground, leaving the two other men still scouring with slow diligence the cliff wall alongside the path. My instincts were infallible.

After lunch I was halfway down to the third cleft of the day, sensing that my nearly complete inventory was doomed to futility. Worse, I had misjudged the length of rope I would need to reach the floor of the crack for which I was aiming, and I realised in frustration that I would need to climb to the top and buy longer rope for tomorrow to reach this last array of lowest ridges. I was halfway back up the cliff face, cursing my ill-preparedness, when I heard shouting from below, my idiots who had been told to keep quiet at all costs. At the same moment, two blisters opened up on my hands, making climbing viciously painful. I called up to Ahmed for assistance, with predictable results. I looked down and saw the four men all gathered in the same place, perhaps

200 feet below me. It took me twenty minutes more to reach the top, flaying the skin off my palms as I rose, looking up for the persistently invisible Ahmed, looking down at the shrinking cluster of my men, doing apparently nothing. I rested and swung. I climbed and stung. At last I reached the top, found no Ahmed, and crawled along the path. Ahmed, it turns out, was already on his way down to look into the men's excitement, and by the time I reached the bottom, at least three-quarters of an hour had passed.

Which is to say, no time at all, considering how long my friend has been waiting for me under the earth! What had we found? By God, what had we *not*? One of the men—name escapes me, cannot regularly tell two of them apart, perhaps brothers—had in his scraping noticed on the cliff wall at eye level a very small patch of smooth, whitish rock, sunk a few inches back into the dirt and stone of the cliff face, not 100 feet from where Marlowe and I found Fragment C. The aberration was, when they found it, the size and shape of a thumb, an oblong and perfectly flat rock where all around it was irregular brown dust and stone, packed hard, crumbling only when hit with force. It was exactly the sort of thing that had led to a dozen false alarms in our work so far, and by the time I arrived they had taken it upon themselves to try to confirm their discovery, hacking at the brown wall, levering against the white stone with a metal bar, managing to scratch its surface, triple its size, and enrage me for violating my instructions to touch nothing in my absence.

I told Ahmed to explain the rules to the men again; there would be no *baksheesh* for damaged finds. I examined the stone under a magnifying glass and found on it what appeared to be regular patterns, though it was hard to be sure, considering the scraping the men's levers had caused. The white rock was without question an entirely different surface than the stone even a foot above it, so if it was large it extended downward only, but it did not display the texture of erosion. I sent the men to fetch shovels and brushes from the donkeys, and I set to work myself with painstaking care. "This is it, then? We are close?" says Ahmed, his first sign of real enthusiasm yet.

Neither supper nor nightfall slowed me in my cautious work. And, to their credit, Ahmed and the men showed no interest in leaving the site even as the sun set, though it was hard to know for sure, as their Arabic has grown increasingly incomprehensible over the past week; private slang and slurring seem to be replacing proper diction. Using a variety of specially crafted small chisels and brushes, ranging in size from a half-inch to more than a foot, I worked steadily, a surgeon conducting the most delicate of operations. Tempting as it was to use battering rams and dynamite (as the early fellows did decades ago), our responsibility is not only to preserve the item inside (rushing it off to a museum or private collector) but to see everything in its original context, and to map and re-create that context for posterity. For observe: we never know the range of our ignorance. We do not know what significance we fail to see by hurriedly smashing a wall that seems blank and meaningless. Preserve every stone and fragment, note each brick's relation to every other brick before removing anything: this is the care that separates the professional from the tomb-plunderer. And so, if I delay in the description of this unsurpassed day, it is only to give you, eager Reader, a sense of both the building excitement and the strange passage of Time.

For at the moment of discovery, Time goes all agog, flows in every direction at once and at every imaginable speed until the sun flies through the sky even as you feel you have just begun; your work will never end; you can count your every breath; you can imagine what you are going to see, behind this door, in the greatest detail (for it was a door, oh yes, I will reveal that much); you can picture every golden bracelet, majestic throne, jewel-studded garment, alabaster sarcophagus, calcite head atop a canopic jar of royal organs. And, more: one can see the change that will overtake one's life in that instant, the dress your beloved will wear at your wedding, the glimmer of gold on the sash around your sovereign's neck as he asks you to rise. One knows, too, what one will feel a mere foot farther on, though how long it will require to penetrate that single foot one does not know: which shall be *the* instant? The shard of shattering crystal time that will embed itself into eternity, bridging now and the soon-to-be-clarified past and the fixed, inevitable future? Will 12 November at 10.14 A.M. be the moment? Will it delay until 4.16 P.M., that instant when one's friends shout with joy and love?

Who will peer after me into this gold-reflecting murk? What poets, scribes, tourists? Let the schoolboys practise Atum-hadu's pretty cartouche on their drawing tablets, and begin the school day in compulsory recitation of our king's inspirational Quatrain 7 (Fragment C only):

> *When we triumph over our enemies or fate, we call for a dozen girls*
> *Who come to us in haste, and Atum-hadu's robe unfurls.*
> *And they dance and bare themselves for us, their breasts so high*
> *That Atum-hadu's hooded cobra leaps as if to fly.*

While I would happily celebrate with my king tonight in his preferred manner, I cannot, as my queen-to-be awaits me in her pure beauty far away, and my jealous mistress, Science, demands that I recline on this service cot, under sheets emblazoned with cobra, vulture, and sphinx, and guard my discovery from the bandits and jealous peers certain to arrive when word escapes, as it surely will, or I do not know the modern Egyptian labourer's natural threshold of discretion. But when they come, they will find me with my service Webley (for bandits) or a smiling silence (for Carter). Ah, that will be tasty. The Carter way is not the only way; my hale and hearty nature served ten thousand times as well as his *hauteur.*

I have got ahead of the story. Time, as I said, will play its tricks.

So, the first glimpse by the men was thus:

(FIG. A: VIEW OF ATUM-HADU TOMB DOOR A AS FIRST
SEEN BY ANONYMOUS WORKMAN, 11 NOVEMBER, 1922,
AS WORK SONGS ARE REPLACED WITH A SUDDEN,
HAUNTING, AND BEAUTIFUL SILENCE)

The covering earth was at some places a foot thick or more, often rock hard. But at the end of several hours of chiselling, brushing, and sifting, we had a door, approximately five and a half feet high and three feet across (must send Ahmed to buy a ruler). It was found approximately two-thirds above the level of the cliffside path, and one-third below it. After spadework, we had revealed:

(FIG. B: RALPH M. TRILIPUSH NEXT TO
ATUM-HADU TOMB DOOR A, 11 NOVEMBER, 1922)

Must arrange for photographic equipment after the wire.

The portal is absolutely intact, absolutely unpenetrated. No robbers ever broke through it and no later authorities ever replaced an inch of it. It has not been seen in 3500 years. Further and significantly, it was not "sealed." That is to say, there were no impressions on the stone door of any royal cartouches or symbols, no marking of any kind implying the presence of a professional tomb guardian. This would be somewhat strange in times of peace, but given what we know of Atum-hadu's last days, the door's pristine purity is further evidence of its identity. Whoever closed this door had been instructed not to mark its exterior with anything to identify its occupant (thus identifying him to me, with unmistakable clarity).

Of course, if (as I am absolutely certain) I write tonight outside the tomb of Atum-hadu, he was laid to rest at the end of the XIIIth Dynasty, at the end of all culture, religion, life, Egypt, hope, time. For though a mere hundred years later, the XVIIIth Dynasty would rise from the XIIIth's ashes and restore Egypt in a glossy, refurbished glory (a bourgeois restoration, the kitsch New Kingdom, imitative, luxurious but false, the prancing ground of pudgy-bellied androgynes and the research pool of equally soft scholars), at the time of Atum-hadu's death, with Hyksos invaders declaring themselves the kings of a country they could never hope to understand, barbarians playing dress-up games, defiling the temples with their efforts to worship gods who despised them, there was no reason to stamp official seals onto the tomb of Atum-hadu, the last of Egypt's kings, no reason to boast of his presence. While Carter's tomb, should he find it, will be stamped liberally with the hieroglyphic equivalent of "Tut Slept Here," Atum-hadu's door was left blank, covered in fast-drying mud, and off the king hurried to the underworld with not a moment to waste.

I probed the perimeter of the door, found it securely wedged into the rock of the cliff. The door seems to be at least a foot thick and should come out as a solid block, a task for tomorrow, or as long as necessary to do it correctly, as Carter would do it, to give the old, unlucky fellow his due.

Meantime, Ahmed and the men have been sent home to perform a series of crucial tasks while I sleep guard under Atum-hadu's sky. I wish I could imitate the ancient kings and cut out the men's tongues, then count on their likely illiteracy, but tasks do need to be performed, and I cannot do them all. Tomorrow they will return with ropes and harnesses, metal cylinders to roll the door out, a cart with padding, and a canvas to get it back to my villa unseen.

Under traditional protocol, I would now contact the Antiquities Service for an Inspector of Antiquities to be sent out to participate in and oversee a correct opening, excavation, clearance, and cataloguing of the tomb located within the area specified by my concession. However, due to my continued gavotte with Lacau, I am at a bit of a loss, and see no other way than to continue for the time being on my own, until I know what help I will actually need from them. When that time comes, I will return to Cairo and tell them in person what treasures I have found. I will complete their paperwork, pay gentle fines, play along as they snicker and delicately slap my wrist, watch them lick their lips to hear where the tomb is, and listen closely to the slicing sound of Winlock's concession being trimmed to accommodate the hauling and laboratory needs of the Trilipush Expedition.

Tomorrow we open our tomb!

CABLE. LUXOR TO C. C. FINNERAN, BOSTON, 11 NOV. 1922, 5.58 P.M. MASTER OF LARGESSE. VICTORY! THE GLITTER OF DISCOVERY IS MINE AND YOURS. ASSURE CREDIT FOR THE 22ND. DELAYS OVER PENNIES RISK MOUNTAINS OF GOLD. RMT.

I'd been buying gifts for your aunt, truth to tell. The usual sort of thing. Billable, of course, since she was a key source of information. And she accepted all my gifts, you know, no hesitation at all; I wasn't a fool. And the day came when I decided to tip my hand, declare myself a little. That same morning, before I could even decide on my technique, I was summoned to the royal court, for Finneran had news from Egypt. "Look at this, Ferrell," he says to me, pushing me into a chair. "Looks like we were both wrong about my boy, and that's good news." He showed me a cable from Trilipush: the devil had found his tomb, or so he claimed, and his team was opening it up, glitter and mountains of gold. "You should've seen Maggie's face when I showed her this," Finneran said, waving the cable about, too excited to sit down, capering about his study, offering me a drink from beneath his desk. He'd never shared any of his concerns with Margaret—no mention of Oxford—and he begged me—no, he commanded me, and you could see what a tough old bastard he really was when he felt strong about something—commanded me to follow his lead, now that his decision was "vindicated."

Finneran was so delighted, he was going to restart the money supply that he'd halted when the Oxford news had come in. "Are you sure that's wise?" I asked. "If Trilipush is a liar, and we do have some reason to think so, surely this cable doesn't prove anything." Do you blame me, Macy? He'd asked me to look after his daughter. And I really spoke not out of any self-interest, but just because that was my honest advice. My mistake. I proved my very first opinion of Finneran's appetite: honest advice was not what he hungered for. He stopped in the middle of lighting his cigar and he turned on me. It came absolutely from out of a clear blue sky: Finneran displayed a temper I hadn't yet seen, though I should've guessed it was there, and I fled his study and the house, delighted never to see him or his opium-gobbling daughter again. This client was a lost cause. I was for Egypt at once.

Such are the resolutions of foolish men in love, Macy, even detectives who should know better. When she appeared at my hotel that same evening, laughing at her effortless escape from the house and her Great Dane guard dog, I eagerly escorted her to jazz club after jazz club, into quarters of Boston where we were the only white faces to be seen in a sea of dark ones, then into a district with no one but Chinamen for street after street, and finally back to JP's, where she raised every glass to her fiancé's triumph. Oh, yes, she was cheerful that night, and didn't touch the opium, never stopped singing her Trilipush's praises. Clear as clear water I hadn't made the slightest impression on her despite it all. She drank and I paid (or the immortal estate of Mr. Davies paid, to be fair). A necklace sat bunched up in my pocket.

That was also the night I met the mysterious J. P. O'Toole, if I recall right. I'm sure you've heard O'Toole's name, Macy, rather infamous after the gangland shootings at the end of the '20s. Back then, he operated this club among other lurks, fed opium to your aunt, and was one of the investors in the Egypt expedition. When he descended to our couch (probably to see why Margaret wasn't coming up for her drug that evening), he gave me two fingers of his hand to shake, affected a sort of French royalty attitude to anyone who dared speak to him, though he took Margaret on his lap and bounced her on his knee, calling her his wicked goddaughter, a freedom that made my blood boil. Still, I won't say he was a bad fellow, since he does turn up again as one of our clients just a ways down the road, Macy.

I helped her home that morning, just before dawn. We stopped in the public gardens near her home, and I was ready to tell her everything. I was going to tell her that Trilipush had used her for her money, that he'd never been to Oxford, though plenty of his perverted friends had and had forged his diplomas for him. I was only deciding where to start the whole tale: the dissipated English gent, sodomist, murderer of his male lover and an innocent Aussie digger. I was going to tell her for her own good, you see. And I hoped—I *knew*—that when I told her the truth, she'd be grateful, would thank me, would finally see me in a new light, a light I hadn't been able to turn on by myself because she was blinded by Trilipush's lies. She said, "Good night, Harry." I didn't speak. She turned towards the gate of her home, not caring if she was caught coming in or not. Then she looked back at me and said, "Can you even believe it? My hero found his treasure! Ain't it grand?" And off she went. And now I called her name, but too quietly, and then the gate clinked shut. I can hear it still, that sound. There's a gate here at the nursing home, between the so-called garden and where the rubbish bins stand in a sort of shed outside, waiting for collection, and when the orderlies carry things out there and the window is open in certain weather and when there's a certain smell in the air, that gate latch makes its little clinking sound, and I remember your aunt so clear I could cry. Surely she told you about it.

Sunday, 12 November, 1922

Book notes: Yesterday was Armistice Day, a moment to recall our brothers fallen in the Great War, and to be thankful for the blessings of peace that the rest of us now enjoy, eternally, one hopes. Include something here about Marlowe and me saying farewell before my departure to Turkey, Marlowe promising to hold Fragment C until my return, recalling in that moment our green and happy days at Oxford, him blessing me before battle, my optimism for our eternal partnership when I left, my sorrow upon my return from Turkey, et cetera.

Journal: It is a new Ahmed today, smiles and bowing, and the men follow his lead. Most gratifying. They arrived at dawn, cables sent and cats fed, and with an impressive train of new gear, though before this adventure is done I will have to go to Cairo myself for some of the more critical scientific equipment. Also, tonight I must send him for mosquito netting if I am to sleep outdoors again—my arms resemble one of my father's relief maps of the Himalayas.

We began at once, driving wedges under the door, digging as we went along its top and sides. The work is painstaking, and by lunch we have dug a space around the door's perimeter about a foot deep but still have not loosened it. We have concluded our only choice is to run ropes behind and around it and then with all twelve of our arms control its descent onto its outside face, onto padding to protect any microscopic inscriptions invisible to my lenses, on top of rollers we can tie directly to the donkeys' harnesses. Back to it.

5.00—I am now able to discern a seam where the top surface of the door abuts something, probably the ceiling enclosing the space behind the door. I am able to place the first wedges into this seam, hammering bars into the slim resulting space, and gently prying the block of the door away from its frame until one of the first wedges falls out of view, behind the seam, and we all hold our breath as we hear it click against stone. We are nearly there. I insert a testing rod into the space where the wedge fell (a space we would already be in, curse the Metropolitan Museum of New York, if we had enough men and were not forced to lurk in the shadows like criminals). I perform a candle test to assure no poisonous gases leak from the crevice. There is not enough space to see into or to insert a torch so, eager as I am for a look, I call a break for the men to rest. They chew jujubes, say nothing, grin at me whenever they catch my eye.

7.30—An hour of backbreaking pulling before the first motion of the door is achieved and I am able to lower a small candle inside the tomb and press my eye to the space. At first my vision cannot adjust to the dark, to the haloed, wick-speared cone of the light, unstirred by any moving air, nor can I yet see what I hope to see (shadows, winking metals), and for a long moment for all of us, there is only breathless anticipation. "What do you see, curse you?" mutters Ahmed in English. "Immortality!" I say (change the epigraph from Abdullah to Ahmed, though the bugger hardly deserves his name mentioned at all).

Finally, a space clarifies itself, walls of a dusty white, a section of a similar floor, but little else. By nightfall we have succeeded only in clearing the door far enough from its frame that we will be able tomorrow, with fresh muscles and a night's sleep, to succeed in lowering it. I authorise Ahmed to return with extra hands and I send the men home.

Monday, 13 November, 1922

11.00 A.M. — Ahmed, late but with six men today, arrived at 8.30. Paid five salaries to date, and the two new men for today only. We have just now lowered the door onto its padded transport, crushing flat the transport cylinders almost at once. It must weigh, we agree, nearly 2000 pounds, and the men strained to lower it safely, and the two new men hobbled off doubled over, clutching their backs, but the job is done and I was immediately down a single step and into my chamber with an electric torch. The air — hot, thick, immobile for 3500 years — was delicious. The door had stood at the centre of one wall of a square chamber, approximately fifteen feet to a side, perhaps seven feet tall. Every surface was a uniform, smooth, yellow-white stone. Of objects, wall decoration, statuary, footprints, guardian gods, wall inscriptions, a later inventory will perhaps be able to reveal what I have been unable to see so far, alone and with my one torch. But I would say, tentatively, that of these, for the time being, I would have to say it appears probably that there is very little and conceivably none at all to speak of so far.

I stand and write in what I am for now forced to call "the Empty Chamber" of the tomb of Atum-hadu. A map would appear thus:

(FIG. C: THE EMPTY CHAMBER)

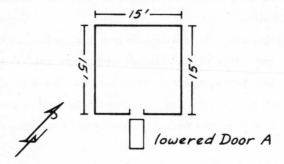

lowered Door A

Despite my explicit orders, I found Ahmed stepping into the Empty Chamber. "Out!" I cried. "This space cannot tolerate amateurs." He did not move or acknowledge me, just swept his torch around the walls, and I watched misinterpretations infect his tiny mind. He sighed and stalked out. What difference can it make to him? He is paid for his time, surely the slower the better for salaried men. "Send the men home for the day," I called after him. "You and four men at first light tomorrow." For I needed the rest of today to consider and to perform careful analysis of this room.

Now it is nightfall. I do not judge Ahmed's reaction with harshness. I, too, might despair and write the word *disappointment* rather than *success* here, were I not better informed. Now, observe: it is precisely Ahmed's ignorance and childishly predictable frustration that are the key issues here, the best defence that the architect of Atum-hadu's tomb could conceive. By the flickering lamplight here in the Empty Chamber, I lay on my cot and I understand precisely what such a room means. Imagine a tomb-robber in ancient days. Though we know now that there never were robbers in this tomb, definitively none, the architects did have to plan for them. So, imagine the architect preparing for the thief. For the thief, imagine a man like Ahmed, who has with some scoundrelly mates exerted vast effort to get past the massive door they found by chance or guile. At last, skulking around so as not to be seen by whatever authorities took an interest at the time, they stumble into

the transit point of the final Lord of the Nile and they find in the form
of this empty room a smiling apology: "Nothing to be found here, old
chum, off you go to plunder elsewhere." For none but a keen-eyed soul
mate will notice the faint outline at the back wall, nothing less than another door, nearly invisible by clear intention but indubitably there.
And even R. M. Trilipush, the king's rightful discoverer, did not notice
it until nearly 8.00 P.M., his men having gone, and his own spirits a little troubled.

(FIG. D: THE EMPTY CHAMBER, CORRECTED)

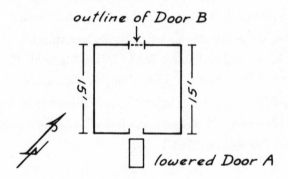

A gentle chiselling and dusting, a few hammered wedges, and there
is no question about it at all. Tomorrow we proceed deeper into this remarkable labyrinth laid out for us by our lord Atum-hadu, this puzzle
which is also in its turn a solution to the different puzzle presented to
the king himself, the most brilliant solution to the most horrifically
complex Tomb Paradox in the history of this extraordinary land.

Consider Quatrain 78 (ABC, from *Desire and Deceit in Ancient Egypt,*
Harvard University Press, 1923):

No falcon will spy on us, no saluki hound renowned for sight
Will see as I take Isis roughly, her mouth and her rear.
When Ma'at's wet kiss is to my left and Sekhmet's breast to my right
Mortal enemies, thieves, traitors will all wander above us,
    blind in a desert sere.

As pretty a synopsis of both the Tomb Paradox and the delights of the underworld as one could hope to find. And for any ancient lucky enough to find Atum-hadu's entry, inside it there was only a discouraging room, apparently already plundered. Let us form an hypothesis as to how the Tomb Paradox could be honoured here: we can imagine that Atum-hadu arranged that the man who would seal the second, inside door (Door B) would be killed by the man who later sealed Door A, who in turn was marked for subsequent murder by a third man, who knew nothing of the tomb location at all, or of the purpose behind his lethal contract. Atum-hadu's death is followed by two others, unrelated, inexplicable even to their perpetrators and hardly noticed at all in the permanent nightfall which had overtaken Egypt by the end.

Tomorrow, we penetrate our king's tomb, interrupt his avid intercourse with his eternal bedmates. Tonight, sleeping in his Empty Chamber, I can almost hear him, breathing steadily, sated, knowing that his camouflaging murders have been carried out to his instructions, that his women will pleasure him forever, that he was more clever than our resentful mother, Time herself.

Tuesday, 14 November, 1922

Ahmed returns, shamefaced, delighted with Door B. "Milord Trilipush, your falcon's eye and bloodhound's nose and unfailing heart are a model to us all and a symbol of all the gifts the Englishman offers Egypt."

We begin the same painstaking process again, but now in flickering torchlight and shirt-drenching heat, as we outline the placement of the second door. We double-check and triple-check it for seals, inscriptions, markings of any sort, and I am pleased to find none, confirming beyond any question my hypothesis as to the function of the Empty Chamber. I give each of the men a turn with the magnifying glass, and the six of us agree: blank.

Now, two of them stand guard outside, two serve as runners to fetch water and tools as requested, while I chisel with care and precision, and Ahmed holds the torch, mostly to stop him pacing like an old woman.

The outline of the door deepened and clarified itself quickly, as if the white-yellow wall was a very superficial camouflage and we were now into the darker dirt of complicity with our waiting king. It is clear that several crowbars will be necessary, and as there is a slight incline to the Empty Chamber—descending from the cliff path down to the second door—it will likely require a wheeled stretcher and a strong one at that to move the second door out of the tomb, and it will have to be secured on such a transport precariously on its side to fit through the space left by Door A, unless the Antiquities Service decides to leave Door B ajar, *in situ*, for a purist *frisson* in tourist season.

Given all these complexities and the impossibility of thieves making any headway with such a barrier, I left the men to stand guard and sleep in the Empty Chamber under their vulture-cobra-sphinx-Horus-consumes bedsheets, and I returned to town. I wonder what family lives the men have that they are not expected home and can sleep in the desert on a moment's notice.

At the post, there is a letter from my fiancée, dated twenty-four days ago (a lifetime ago, before our find), and there is a cable from my Master of Largesse, proving himself the worthy equal of any who ever held that title: WELL DONE! SEND DETAILS. CREDIT COMING. Purchase crowbars, food, et cetera.

And now, from this distance, dusk on my terrace at Villa Trilipush, an anti-malarial cocktail in hand, Maggie purring on my lap, the gramophone singing, I imagine what awaits me behind Door B, the shadows cast against the white walls by the torchlight, the door behind us, the crowbars dropped in wonder. Tomorrow.

Oct. 21

Hey-ho, Ralphie!

> *While you're off chasing black girls around the casbah (oh, yes, sir, I went to the moving pictures the other night and now I*

know exactly what drew you to Egypt and Arabia, my wicked Sheik), I won't just sit on my behind listening to Inge talk about the hard winters of Iceland, mister.

I've been able to spend some very happy evenings at JP's place, of which, I know, you simply do not approve. I wonder which it is that you do not approve: JP's place, or me having happy evenings. Honestly, you'd think I was a convicted criminal or something the way I'm treated around here.

It might interest you to know that JP introduced me to a friend of his, now let's see, what was his name, tip of my tongue, yes, now I have it: Cornelius Macy. Well, I'd say Cornelius has taken quite a shine to me, and quite a dancer. Four nights in a row he's been there, since he met me on Tuesday. JP was saying that this Corny fellow is worth absolute barrels of cash. He certainly dresses like a tycoon. I could do with barrels of cash, oh yes I could, Mister Trilipush!

Settle down, Limey. He don't mean anything to me, you're my only true explorer Hero.

That snoop is being friendly to me too. I don't know what I think of it. He's nothing to look at, I'll tell you that for free. A couple of days after we first met him, I was going out to a little party I'd heard about with some girlfriends, just like the old days, but when I left the house, there he was waiting, the snoop, and he said, "Come on, I'll take you for a drink." A girl doesn't need to hear that twice.

What will you bring your Queen from over there? I know, I know: the tomb will be filled with jewelry a million years old. And it's true that Egyptian stuff is very fashionable right now, so that will be nice. But won't that stuff be musty and used? A girl doesn't really like wearing a museum piece around her neck, you know, Ralphie.

No, he's nothing to look at, the snoop. Carrot-topped and all bumpy. He's shy, though, around me, can't look me in the eye.

That's a sure sign they're getting weak in the knees. You were the exception to that, my Hero, looking at me bold as anything, reciting your dirty poems. But this one, he takes me to JP's when I feel like it, when I'm bored and need a night out, and he's like a little puppy dog. But I can tell you something, he says he's looking for the poor Australian kid, but he's real curious about you. I think part of it is he wants to know if I have room in my heart for a new fellow. Oh, don't you worry, Ralphie, just come home soon! I'm teasing you terribly, aren't I? But see it from my place. You're having the adventures. I'm treated like a convict all because I'm a little tiny bit unwell right now.

Have you found the treasure yet, I wonder? What do you suppose the walls of Atum-hadu's tomb look like? When I think about his poetry, boy oh boy, you have to think that his tomb is going to be quite a show. Don't get any ideas, mister, or at least nothing you can't hold on to until you get back. I am waiting, you know, pure as snow for you, Hero.

Of course, you're an awfully long way away, aren't you? And I haven't heard a peep out of you since you jumped on that boat, waving your hat at me. I keep your book next to my bed, and your picture, too, the one of you in your explorer's duds. I fall asleep imagining you reading me your wicked, hungry king's poems. Sometimes I wake up and see Inge reading your book. No surprise there.

How much longer do you think you'll be? It's a bore here and I blame you. I was never ever bored with you, even when we were doing boring things like staring at another pharaoh's old, broken chair in a museum. But now do let's get on with it, Ralphie. I want to be married. I deserve better than this, don't I? I deserve what you promised me. I don't like being here anymore, I don't like Inge or even Daddy right now.

So there!

m.

Wednesday, 15 November, 1922, Villa Trilipush

Rise before dawn.

Back at the site just after sunrise, bringing food, water, two more electric torches. Roused with gentle kicks my men huddled in the Empty Chamber.

And again, into the breach! Placing wedges, using crowbars, attempting to drive hooks, straining backs, kicking stronger cylinders back into place, while the men in increasing volume voice complaints of palms blistering on slipping ropes (forgot to buy them gloves), pushing on the left, pulling on the right.

Lunch. Need heavy equipment which I cannot yet afford or openly bring to my site. It is a question of overcoming this difficult angle, which makes the door seem even heavier. Or, I need to behave with less responsibility to my find and simply smash my door to pieces. That I will not do, despite the excitement. We dig to preserve.

Our progress is excruciating, almost imperceptible in our aches and bruises and sticky, fiery burst blisters. At dusk I send the men home and I collapse on a cot in the odd draughts and patchy warmth of the Empty Chamber.

Thursday, 16 November, 1922

<u>*Margaret:*</u> 3.30 in the morning and I write by lamp, sleep prematurely finished with my aching body. I can no longer sleep for more than four hours a night, and fitfully at that. I think of you, horribly far just now, my sweet and trusting thing, despite all your hardships, the odd world your father's money has built around you, the fog of medications, the troublesome mood swings, this odd duck Ferrell attempting to yank you out of my affections, the tedious company of Inge, whom I agree, it is possible, may have slid into your father's grasp.

<u>*Journal:*</u> Afternoon. With more hours of labour, the door has slid slightly out towards us, creeping a grain of sand at a time, and by early

afternoon, I am able to peer through a crack: gold, no question, practically my own startled eye reflected back at me. Give the men a short rest to prepare for the final heave. "Why not a sledgehammer?" asks Ahmed in English, and I am astounded to see he is serious. It is incredible to me how little these people understand what we are trying to do for them. I begin to explain the foundations of archaeology, but I must preserve my strength and I can see he is not terribly interested.

Thursday, Friday, Saturday, 16, 17, 18 November,
written Saturday, 18 November, 1922

Journal: Victories and temporary, minor setbacks. Excruciating pain.

On the 16th, another hour of heavy work with crowbars and ropes resulted in a pyrrhic victory: we had achieved the position described above, and Ahmed was a stern and helpful foreman; he saw a certain sureness in my face, and I had his attention now. After the break, we set to our work with a fury. I drove us too hard, I see now, my own fault. Two men on each side of the door, throwing their full strength against the bars, and Ahmed and I in the front with ropes, pulling until our gloves were as hot as fire—and then, to my shame, it happened: first it was a sound, a horrible sound, the rush of events overtaking scientific control. To a superstitious ear (as some of those in the chamber certainly were), a booming cry from the past accompanied by a rush of hot air (perhaps they thought it was Atum-hadu's angry breath upon us) and the shouts in English of my frustration, and then the shattering of the massive door as it pitched forward and burst against the hard floor, a million grey marbles skittering in all directions like shrapnel, then the screaming—of one of the men, cut very slightly over the eye by flung stone—and only then the pain, the excruciating pain as I realised my own foot was inside the perimeter where the door had crashed and exploded. Hobbling, bleeding, the toes crushed, the side of my boot burst, so be it and no matter—I was into the next chamber in a flash, my electric torch lighting a path here, there, up and down each

wall, invading each corner as the electric pain from my foot flashed behind my eyes.

The curses in Arabic were extreme, those that I could understand,
and I thought at first they must be coming from the wounded man, but
they were falling from the mouth of Ahmed, cursing fate and the West
and Egypt (for in his blindness, he saw only another empty room). His
greed for gold feeds his frustrations; he lacks the temperament for science. What Carter and Marlowe and I share is simply not an Egyptian
trait.

I ordered Ahmed and two others to take the injured man back to
town to see to his wound, and to return in twenty-four hours, and I
kept one man with me for the painstaking work ahead and to assist
with my own injuries.

My man pulled off my boot, and I nearly bit through my cheek at
the pain. Some of the hotel's sheets and the water were sacrificed to
washing and wrapping my hideous, bloodied foot. By late in the afternoon on the 16th, I was finally able to hobble about and place lanterns
in the new second chamber. Unfortunate Door B is a particularly terrible loss considering its inscription, which read in excellent hieroglyphs:

ATUM-HADU, LORD OF THE NILE, SPITS UPON HIS PURSUERS,
WHO TOO LATE DISTURB HIM, AND WHO WILL PAY A HORRIBLE
PRICE FOR THE INTRUSION.

The inscription was a splendid proof, should there remain anyone at
this late date who questions our premises or accomplishments. I hope
we will be able to reconstruct it from the pieces of the shattered door,
but I fear it is lost. I blame myself, and the fools at the Antiquities Service who bound me in this position and have now extracted from my
foot their pound of flesh.

My fast-swelling foot forced me to put off exploration of the new
chamber and I spent the evening changing again and again the sopping
dressing—an ugly wound indeed, though of course, a small price for

our discovery. I sent the man away for his own rest, some more water, and a cane, but I could not in good conscience return to my villa or see a doctor until I had mapped the tomb's new chamber. Sleep was nearly impossible.

17 November came, a flicker of light, and as my man was not yet back, I again washed and wrapped my foot with another strip of bedsheet and the last of my drinking water. A fair problem I found in the murky dawn light: the two outside toes were certainly broken, as were, judging by the purple swelling, a bone or two or three in the foot itself. The cuts were mostly superficial, my boot having served as armour, but the skin was split in a few places and the sheet was brown. I finished my nursing and stumbled off to explore what we will temporarily refer to as the "Chamber of Confusion."

This second chamber is as superficially empty as the Empty Chamber. And so one must conclude that Atum-hadu and his anonymous tomb architect decided that any robber who breached the Empty Chamber, discovered the ominous curse written on Door B, and yet was strong enough to forge on could be dissuaded only by total frustration, as neither fear nor obstacles had so far stopped him, and so the king and his builder likely decided not to bother with further curses or obstruction but merely attempted to convince a potential burglar that he was absolutely wasting his time. Thus, another bare room. Of course, no observer ever made it so far, so while I admire Atum-hadu's craftiness, it was, in retrospect, quite superfluous.

At any rate, my tomb is now laid out thus:

(FIG. E: MAP OF ATUM-HADU'S TOMB AS OF 17 NOV., '22)

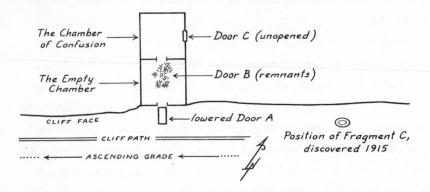

The Chamber of Confusion → Door C (unopened)

The Empty Chamber → Door B (remnants)

CLIFF FACE ← lowered Door A

CLIFF PATH

ASCENDING GRADE ←

Position of Fragment C, discovered 1915

Were it not for the (lost) inscription on Door B and the seductress's song of Door C, my own confusion and despair might at this point have matched those of the hypothetical ancient robber.

It was late in the morning of the 17th before my man was back with bandages, water, food, and a cane, curved at the top like a royal sceptre and crafted of a strong, dark wood. "Do you know he smashed a foot on the dig and then, cool as you like, merely sent for a cane while he carried on? The cane's on display at the Explorers' in Cairo."

The cane was a help, as with every step my foot throbbed out a perpetual echo to the fallen door's impact. I ate, drank, and finished my magnifying glass inspection of the Chamber of Confusion, confirming its brilliant "possum" design, but for the very faint but unmistakable outline of Door C, quite blank.

With my one man's help (Ahmed and the other three were late in returning), I commenced dusting and chiselling around Door C, the same slow work of chisel, brush, mallet, wedge, brush, chisel, brush, mallet, wedge, brush. I was feeling terribly weak, perhaps even a bit feverish, no doubt from excitement at what was behind this last remarkable door. And, two or three times, I hobbled back outside, where I was slightly ill. Twice also, at least, I was so exhausted that I slept uneasily on one of the cots in the Empty Chamber, trying to make up for many lost hours. Night fell on the 17th with me having slept most of the day away, and I awoke—as was my unfortunate habit, and Atum-hadu's as well—in the earliest, dark hours. The 18th. I could hear but not see my one loyal man asleep in a dark corner, but the others had still not returned. I went outside to consider the stars above Deir el Bahari.

I will not say I was cheerful in this night watch.

Dawn of the 18th finally arrived, and the pale light revealed that I was alone; I had evidently misconstrued the echoes of my own breath as that of a loyal worker who was not there. I noted that Ahmed and the others were now eighteen hours late. The possibility of betrayal occurred to me, the cowardice and avarice of the local workforce a constant threat. With no immediate gratification to astound their eyes, abandonment was a likely explanation. So be it. I decided that I would continue alone to prepare Door C, despite my wound, thirst, hunger, and justifiable rage. Then I would cover up the front of the tomb with stacked rocks and mud, return to Luxor, present my discovery to the local Antiquities Service Inspector, and accept my scolding as well as the men and technical support they would issue me as a result of my discovery. In particular, wiring electric lights into the tomb would be of great assistance, ridding the space of torch and lantern smoke and greatly increasing the number of hours in a row that work can be conducted without being forced outside for fresh air.

Late in the afternoon of the 18th, today, Ahmed returned with three of the men. Their apologies were profuse, and they were delighted to see the outline of Door C. The injured man had required care, Ahmed had stayed at the villa until the cats had arrived and taken nourishment, and then Ahmed and the men had obtained, on their own inspiration, tools they thought would be helpful in "our shared task." To wit: two massive sledgehammers. I was touched by their efforts, but I could not help but laugh at their expressions when I asked them the elementary question: what would happen to the treasures just on the *other* side of Door C, if we were to use their door-smashing technique?

And so I left Ahmed and one other man to stand watch for the night while I relied on the other two to help me back to Villa Trilipush, hoping, with every jarring, bone-shredding step of the cruel donkey, that I would soon travel to my site with easy candour in full daylight, blessed by the buffoons in charge, the Hyksos of modern times, who drive men to such necessary deception.

Villa Trilipush, at least, did not disappoint: a hot bath, a drink or two, new bandages on a foot which is now far too large to fit into a boot, and I bring this journal up to date.

Later now. My man has returned from the post, where a letter and cable awaited me. Cable: CCF congratulating me and alerting me that he has authorised credit transfer and requesting I send him immediately a catalogue of the finds, "esp. items of private, personal interest." The letter was from the Luxor bank, confirming CCF's cable: a credit to my account from the USA had been made two days ago, on Thursday the 16th—an amount only one-eighth, to the disastrous piastre, of the expected and painstakingly agreed-upon monthly payment under a Preliminary Team Budget, and twenty-five days late for good measure. After my recent expenses and extended promises, CCF's octro-deposit registers as scarcely more than the faint aroma of funds.

It is a staggering betrayal. I would like to credit him with some sort of logic, some reason, but of course he has none. Does he mean to make up the difference at the next scheduled wire, 22 November? I spend an anxious time trying to untangle his thoughts, which were perhaps—it must be at least considered—corrupted by the sinister Ferrell. CCF is obviously under the sway of a dark influence. I have means to force his cooperation, of course, but that is not at all how I would wish for this partnership to function. Why is he doing this to me? I search in vain for a reason to explain why my wretched, skinflint Master of Largesse has not lived up to his limited requirements, and has instead probably slithered off to some Boston gin palace to burn Atum-hadu's necessary finances on bootleg alcohol and flappers in the company of his hoodlum chums and Scandinavian concubine.

My loyal man is still outside waiting for my orders. I send him back to the post with my considered reply to CCF: HAVE OPENED SECOND

GLORIOUS CHAMBER DESPITE SHAMEFUL PENURY. NOW IS NOT THE
TIME FOR PETTINESS, WITH YOUR SPECIALISED COLLECTION AT STAKE.
Much needed rest. I will sleep like the dead, and tomorrow charge
back into battle, with whatever weapons remain. I will not be deterred.

Sunday, 19 November, 1922

3.55 A.M.—Wrote too soon. No sleep, but the foot is positively
numb, a welcome blessing.

The night is black. Atum-hadu's solution to the Tomb Paradox—
the solution that has so far choked me with dust and claimed a foot—
is so elegant and yet still out of my grasp. Hidden doors. False dead
ends to throw off robbers. There is more, something I cannot see.
What did he decide under these stars? One must put oneself in his
place.

He walks the illuminated, nearly abandoned halls of his Theban
palace, throws himself in restless agitation from golden throne to
carved couch. Does His Lordship wish to see acrobats? I do not. Does
the incarnation of Osiris seek company? I do not. Does the celestial
lover of Ma'at wish to ride a camel, feed a tiger, flay a prisoner, swing
from the hanging bars, play on an elephant's trunk, caress the giraffe? I
do not. My royal concerns tonight overwhelm me and deny me my
sleep. Tonight, after only a few minutes considering my predicament,
Horus extracts his tribute with more cruelty than usual. It is an ana-
gram in the language of my future friend: Horus demands hours, hours
spent clutching my aching belly, burning in shame and fiery solitude,
unapproachable, precious hours of my dwindling mortal span, for
which my falcon-headed protector will repay me how? How can my
final journey be made? It is coming soon, no question, seen off either
by Hyksos arrows or by the poisoned blade of one of my crumbling
court's proliferating traitors or by this crocodile growing every day inside my belly, who will at last eat my stomach if I have not secured it in
an underground jar in time.

—

Now I have awoken to the setting sun; I have lost another whole day to my injury and exhaustion. My foot weighs one hundred pounds. My head is pinched between a giant's fists. My stomach roars in fury, and several minutes doing its bidding do not suffice in placating its rage.

It is dark before one of my loyal idiots thinks to check on me. They have spent the day sitting in the Empty Chamber gossiping. A day has passed, they were paid and did not find my absence strange. I send the man back to assure a guard is kept on Atum-hadu's tomb all night, and to have the men ready at dawn tomorrow for a final push into the last chamber and our just reward. He also has a letter he collected from my *poste restante*. From my fiancée, dated 2 November. The crossing of letters in the post is a particularly cruel game.

Nov. 2

My dear Ralph,

I will be brief. I need a letter from you very soon. I'm worried by things here, and I need to hear you telling me everything will be fine and explaining everything.

The snoop is still here. For a while I thought he was harmless and even some fun. He's not a bad dancer and he kept me company. And I know he's taken a shine to me, and that's some fun in this gray weather. I can manage fellows like him. But there's a problem. He's told Daddy things that I've heard, and he's told me things. He makes it sound like he's just talking, but I know he's trying to tell me something about you. He asked me about Oxford, and I told him easily a hundred times that you were there with Marlowe and you left to go fight for Democracy after your M.A. but before your Ph.D., and Oxford said that was OK. Ferrell asked for a picture of you and Marlowe together, and I showed him the one you gave me, of you boys in your digging duds, with your arm around his shoulder, you grinning and Marlowe pretending to look all serious and above-it-all, but this Ferrell just says, "Of course." He's a little ratty, if you ask me. I hope you're not cross about the picture.

I don't feel very well lately, Ralphie. I don't want you to worry, it's just that I don't feel very well, like things are getting the better of me again. I always think of you as the one who makes me feel healthy, and that's true, it's just that you've been away a long time, so it's hard. I miss you a lot, but some days you feel so far away, like you can't help me, so I might as well be sick. So don't worry, it's nothing, it's just that, that's all, that I miss you.

Ferrell's gone in to talk to Daddy in Daddy's study once or twice, and I try to listen for you but I'm not much of a snoop. And when I've asked Daddy what it was all about, all he said was "We'll see." And when we go to JP's, Ferrell doesn't drink much so he doesn't talk, and then I get bored being your girl detective because after all that's not fair to make me do, is it? It's a bore.

Can you tell Daddy again that you went to Oxford? And this snoop, Harry, keeps looking at me with a wolf-face, and saying things like "Well you never know" and "Things ain't always what they seem, especially with poms." Poms he calls the English. He's jealous. I hate him for not respecting you like I do. I love you, Ralph, because everything about you is real even though it's exciting, and everything about him is a lie even though it's boring, and that's why he hates you and makes out to Daddy like there are things about you that aren't true.

Don't worry. Inge is going to cure me of my little things and I'm getting better every day and it will be just as I promised by our wedding day, all cured. But I need you around to help me do that, OK? You're my best doctor. I can get better with you around to keep me busy and happy, so come home now, please. Bored is bad for me, really bad for me.

If there's something you want to tell me, I would listen, you know. Anything you told me would be OK. Just like you'd still love me no matter what you learned about me, right? I don't want to *know anything more about it, just put everything back the way it was. As soon as you can.*

I'll be healthy and so very good to you, just for you. But you have to come home now.

Your girl.

m.

(Sunday, 19 November, 1922, continued)

What is all this? Did I already know of all this? Did my cable telling you he was a liar and a stranger reassure you after this? If this is nothing but misunderstandings exacerbated by crossed letters, then more letters will only distort things further, each one passing the next, curdling it into nonsense as they float blindly past each other. What is going on there now, right this moment? I am reading of events of long ago, of extinguished stars. I cannot understand who Ferrell is, or how he has crept into my family's bosom.

You will be well, you will be well, you will be well. I will it. I have never doubted it, never worried. Once, only. At the museum that rainy day in June, I worried. I have never told you.

I escorted you to the Museum of Fine Arts, Inge still a silent, hovering valkyrie, though by now I had noticed in her face the expressions of an incurable debauchery, particularly as we passed the magnificent Maiherpri loincloth (and I tried in vain to interest you in how Carter had stumbled upon it way back in '02).

As we gazed at the statue of the ram-headed god Herishef, I told you how as a boy I had dreamt of opening tombs even before I knew what the dreams meant, even before I knew the word *tomb* or had ever read of excavations. Before I even had the vocabulary to explain it, my imagination produced the most wonderful things in my sleep: comforting caves filled with lights and warmth and sleeping bodies in soft beds, animals and friends and food and happiness, always in a safe, enclosed place, far from danger. I was probably three or four at the most, and my claustrophilia had begun.

And I explained to you the displays we were passing, even as I noticed you were needing to rest more often. I described Harvard and its conservative faith in old excavators using old methods. As recently as 1915, I was telling you, Lyman Story still wanted to use TNT for his expedition for this very museum! "Harvard is not ready for Atum-hadu or for me," I said, "but they will be." I turned to you, and you were shaking: out of sympathy for my trials, or from the beauty of the relics? "Nothing to worry, sir," says businesslike Inge, already leading you off to the ladies' lounge. Twenty minutes limped by, but then out you came, fresh as anything, lovely, ready for a day of shopping and eating. You had never looked so lovely and fresh, but you did not seem to recall *anything* of the last hour, including the stories of my childhood. Oh, my love, your father told me you will be well. The doctors have told him you will be well. I know you will be well. You must have faith in that, and you must have faith in me. At night, alone, it is difficult to have faith, I know. But you must. Ferrell is smoke.

And I will make what you so endearingly call my "Find," no matter the obstacles, no matter the misunderstandings or outright treachery, the yellow fog of crisscrossed letters. Your father is confused about me, or he was, but this will pass, if it has not already, and not another word need be spoken. On 19 November, your Ralph was thinking about you with love, no matter your father's passing worries, no matter the curse of Ferrell you are suffering on my account. You will read this when I come home, and we will compare notes, and laugh at the distortions of time and distance and postage.

Since Trilipush's find, I found Boston suddenly chilly. There was neither money nor love here. I had only that tongue-lashing I took from Finneran and Margaret's refreshed insistence that Trilipush and only Trilipush was everything to her. Days passed and I didn't hear from Margaret and I no longer went to their home. I was ready to wash my hands of the cursed Finnerans. If Trilipush had found his dirty gold, either he'd come home or he wouldn't, and you know what my bet was. It made no difference to me, because if he'd killed Paul Caldwell, I'd go to Egypt to prove it, to shout it loud enough for even the stubborn Finnerans to hear round the world.

I spent slow, empty days checking my transcripts, redrafting notes, submitting my reports and expenses to London, interviewing another of Trilipush's students, or explaining to HQ why my pursuit of Paul Davies had required so much time in Boston. I hardly think they cared. I wrote my other clients, telling Tommy Caldwell, Emma Hoyt, Ronald Barry, and the Marlowes of my progress.

I would sit in my hotel, doing this busywork, waiting for the day to head to New York, hoping Margaret would come looking for me one last time, or if, in some anger, I finally saw that that was unlikely, I was just waiting for news, for anything. I felt that something clear and clarifying would happen; there'd come a moment when it would be obvious that the time had come for me to move on to Egypt or, instead, to stay close to Margaret's side, to protect her, to catch her in the storm that was sure to come. I was a young man, Macy. Something could've changed with her. Life could've taken any number of turns, you know. And so if I sometimes stood outside her home, raging in the dark, I know you can understand that, as a man of the world.

And I did see her a few more evenings: once she turned up, and all evening didn't mention his name even once, just fell asleep on JP's sofa with her head on my lap and her hand in mine, abusing me cruelly, and I watched her breathe for hours and hours. She'd appear at my hotel these last nights, and each time I had my little speech ready; maybe this was the night she would fall into my arms and I would save her. But the time was never right. She'd be vicious, call me a crybaby or a bore if I ever stopped making her laugh or refused to dance. On the way to the club she'd be telling me about Trilipush's latest news (always good, always vague), and no sooner were we inside JP's than she was climbing the stairs looking for the man himself and her drug. I'd sit there stroking her head, and then, when she was able, I'd walk her home, struggle, in the grey dawn light, for the words, for even the opportunity of words. I vowed again to end this.

Monday, 20 November, 1922

Withdraw pay for the men, though the account audibly creaks at the disbursement. It hardly matters. I will go without before they will; I will never abandon my men. And I am off to the site.

I arrived at just the right moment to prevent a cataclysm: I found the dark bastards setting at Door C with a sledgehammer. I was as affected as if they were striking me. Ahmed was sitting there, smoking one of CCF's cigars, looking on at the mauling. I shouted for them to stop, but at least one more slamming crunch was heard before the noise ended. We stared at each other in mutual incomprehension.

I have clearly left them alone too long, counted at least on their ability to follow orders if not respect the precision and passion of my work. My disciplinary financial penalties were understood at last. I distributed their pay accordingly reduced. Now I noticed the injured man has never returned. And Ahmed was a silent, glowering beast.

Only then did I hobble over and examine the damage they had done to my Door C. My own fault. I should never have left them on guard so long near the hypnotising wealth hidden behind this last foot of rock. The loss of the inscription on Door C is nothing less than tragic, and the Antiquities Service will be right to chastise me for not having brought in an Inspector, though I can hardly do so now, with the evidence that this is Atum-hadu's tomb again lying in a fine dust at my feet. I should have marked down the inscription back on the 17th, but my injury prevented me at the time. How could I have known this would have happened? I should have known. Now I must re-create the inscription from memory:

ATUM-HADU, LAST KING OF THE BLACK LAND, AUTHOR OF THE
GLORIOUS ADMONITIONS, SAILS TO THE UNDERWORLD,
ACCOMPANIED ONLY BY THE WEALTH OF HIS MUCH-RAPED LAND.

I explain to the men that their brutality has delayed our discovery, not hastened it, and that the mountains of gold on the other side of this door must now wait, as I cannot risk opening Door C without first stabilising the fissures caused by their savage pounding, or I will lose the artwork I am sure to find on the door's opposite side. Which means plastering will be necessary. (This will also give me the curatorial opportunity of reinscribing onto the restored door a facsimile of the hieroglyphs lost to the idiot hammers, simply to give a sense of the original inscription's size and placement.) I send two men for plaster, water, trowels; Ahmed to Carter's site to see how he is now filling his days; and a third man to Winlock's end of Deir el Bahari. Reports of inaction there will be useful for renegotiating a concession.

The report from Winlock's camp: nothing of interest, random digging, brushing things they have had out of the ground since last year. At Carter's camp, they are clearing land desperately to the south and west, digging feverishly in search of their buried reputations, though Carter himself has fled to Cairo. Six hours later, they are definitively idiots: the plaster is all wrong. Despite hours of different mixtures trying to make do with what they brought me, all I do is splash Door C with white water. Send them back to town for proper plaster.

It is early evening before I get another try. Fill the main fissures and allow it to dry, which it does. Slowly.

Tuesday, 21 November, 1922

This morning I find that the first coat of plaster dried well in the door's fissures, but also in the bucket. When my men finally deign to appear, I send them back to town for more plaster and a new bucket. It is evening before they arrive, this time without water, which one of them finally brings after nightfall, nearly ten o'clock. Time is haemorrhaging and probably my support in Boston as well. I am tempted to sleep in Villa Trilipush tonight, but the foot is on fire and I no longer trust these hammering apes to be left on guard.

Margaret: You will ignore Ferrell and keep your father on track, won't you? You already are, I am sure. You are my protectress and inspiration, as I stare at your photograph by lamplight and desert starlight outside His Majesty's tomb. I can see you across a desert continent and a sea as you prepare for bed high above the moon-frosted snow of the Garden.

In this photo, the light was behind you, making you a silhouette against white, a near perfect profile, bending forward to look at something on the table (if I recall, it was the necklace with the cameo of your profile I had made), and your beauty reproduces itself in the smallest detail: your eyelashes just protruding over the profile of your nose, making a bird's wing of black, the thinnest of fine lines.

I remember the night you were gently crying in my arms, troubled by your illness and your anxiety for my departure, and I touched my finger to the corner of your eye, caught a fugitive tear under the tip of my finger, and pulled it and your streaking eye makeup to your temple, just to dry your tears, but I produced in that gesture the perfect face of a pharaoh's queen, the malachite stripe of the eye of Horus.

The twenty-three-year-old daughter of the department store pharaoh is stately in profile, alluring in three-quarters, overwhelming head-on. The thin nose with its expressive nostrils, as if controlled by a dozen dedicated strings at the hands of a thousand-fingered puppeteer of unsurpassed sensitivity and haughty pride. The slightest upward motion of her eyebrow and we commoners know her will and shall serve it. The pouting, heavy lower lip, under the cresting wave of the upper, carved from smoothest yellow stone, the single, loving chisel stroke that cleft the heavenly valley below her nose. The arching neck, a bit of swan, a bit of swelled sail on a Nile *felucca*. The majestic curve of her fine figure, her treasures, her mysteries of line and texture, that dress slit directly in the centre-back, as if merely the continuation of her magnificent crevice, and she turns from the throne to consider the slave who kneels at her sandalled, beaded feet, and she raises her hand to strike with naked blade the miscreant who brought her the wrong drinking vessel, when her king appears behind her and stills her tensed hand.

Wednesday, 22 November, 1922

The men return early, and I am finally equipped to plaster the damaged door, while Ahmed sits, cobra-silent, smoking another of CCF's cigars and crunching fresh dates. But by late afternoon, the door is still damp. Time is killing me. I have no choice but to leave them on guard with Ahmed's solemn word he will watch them and enforce my will, so that I can go to the bank for news of the letter of credit due today, the wire of the 16th being too small to consider as anything but a bonus from CCF personally.

The bank clerk shows solicitude for my injury but regrets to inform me that as of yet, et cetera. Return to the site.

It is early evening before I am able to recarve the lost inscription into the plaster, and then give the go-ahead to start placing wedges. The men set to the work with all the pent-up energy of young boys recovered from a long illness, and their enthusiasm is catching. Ropes, wedges, cylinders are in place by midnight, and everyone readily agrees to stay the night if necessary.

Their childish moods ought not to surprise me. I blame myself for any problems we have encountered, for the men do not stand to gain what I do, nor do they have my passion. They need a firm hand and a guiding voice. I explain myself to them, and we understand each other again. We renew a brotherhood that forms in only a few experiences in a man's life.

Thursday, 23 November, 1922

Earliest hours after midnight. I write by lantern light now as the men share a meal, and stretch their legs and aching backs before we return to this final door, this Door C. Behind it lie a tomb, a treasury, a history, a genius now black and crumbling under his linen wraps. The explorer must pause here, to acknowledge the responsibility, the vast expanse of time about to be breached.

The men are ready. It is now . . .

Later. Dawn rises on Deir el Bahari, but the sun is too faint to illuminate a mystery unlike anything in this mystery-wrapped land. The Pillar Chamber joins our map, and Atum-hadu's humour is unmistakably in play:

(FIG. F: THE FIRST SIX CHAMBERS, 23 NOVEMBER, 1922)

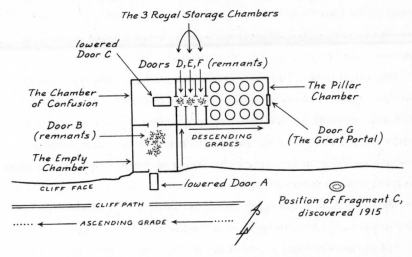

How my map has sprouted in the sleepy sunlight of 23 November! The new team will arrive with Ahmed tomorrow, and now I have the day to myself at the site to rest, make measurements, take notes, clean up our debris, and prepare for our assault on Door G, "the Great Portal." Carter's face at this discovery, I can scarcely imagine. He would cross his arms, keep his silence, reveal nothing.

But first, I must relate the events of the past eight hours, the horrible and the wonderful, the betrayals and the triumphs. I must remember to sleep today.

Door C required our muscles and our hearts, but she finally yielded to us more easily than her violent predecessor. We were able to lower her until such time as I can manage her trip out of the tomb to a laboratory for careful preservation and examination, before her final journey to a permanent home in a central gallery at the Cairo Museum. By our electric torches, the inside face of Door C (its top surface now) seemed disappointingly blank, and I had to block the new opening and shout at the men to stop their griping about how I had wasted their time when the sledgehammer would have served. I ordered them all outside. I entered the next room alone, my heart pounding, my foot and ankle nicely numb. What I found, I must admit, baffled me: a narrow niche, quite empty at first glance (a more thorough investigation will have to wait—first I must commit to paper my accurate recollection of the order of events). And no more than three feet in front of me, directly across from Door C, another of Atum-hadu's maddening doors (Door D). A bare, thin room—perhaps a granary, I thought, though without grain. A room for statues to guard the tomb? But then where were the statues? I heard the men back in the Chamber of Confusion, debating something in their private dialect. I continued examining Door D and the walls of this niche, trying to comprehend Atum-hadu's bizarre sense of mortuary security, trying to unravel his Tomb Paradox alongside him. A burial place for wives? Servants? Animals? Storage for weaponry? Or clothing since turned to dust? Food? I stood still in my deep consideration, I cannot say for how long. I felt a tug on my sleeve. "Lord Trilipush," said Ahmed. "Please, sir, come outside. Let us break bread, take some air. Let me tend to His Lordship's unfortunate foot while His Lordship determines our next step." Ahmed's kindness, all the more impressive for being so damned rare, moved me. I hobbled out of the baffling tomb, leaning on my cane. He led me down the cliff path in the purple darkness and set me on a rock, brought me a meal and hot coffee, asked me what we had found and what it meant. He changed my bandage with a nurse's touch, though he need not have bothered being gentle, as the reeking, blue-black injury is entirely without sensation. We chatted for half an hour, perhaps longer, and the first streaks of pearl appeared in the east. It was something of a college tutorial for him, and a chance for me to expose my cramped thoughts to the air. I tried several hypotheses, explained to him the complexity of every Tomb Paradox, and the fiendish complications of this one in particular. He understood, and I was pleased to see an intelligence in his eyes. After this respite, though, I was eager to work. But Ahmed was hungry for learning, and his questions about excavation and preservation, about my attempt to restore the inscription on the front of Door C for curatorial purposes, about the likely wealth of an end-of-dynasty tomb were all insightful. We chatted on.

It was only when they reappeared that I realised I had not seen the three other men for some time. They came down the path towards us, shimmering out of the murky light, white with dust, spitting, and they hurled their beastly hammers to the ground. "Nothing!" they shouted to Ahmed in suddenly distinct Arabic. "Nothing. Pillars and nothing at all." And they mounted three of the donkeys and trotted off into the rising sun, not caring what path they took.

"What have those swine done?" I cried and hopped back to the tomb. Oh, what had they not done? The dust and rubble bore grim, stony witness: my men had been overwhelmed with greed. They had destroyed Door D, revealing a second narrow room and Door E, which they destroyed, revealing a third narrow room and Door F, which they destroyed, revealing the haunting Pillar Chamber.

The rage I felt is difficult to describe here. I have nothing in my life to compare it to. Even as I write now, hours later, my eyes fill with tears, my pen shakes. I can only ask myself, and not without scorn, Why was I surprised? When in my life have people not proven themselves to be precisely like this? No one can be trusted, except those rare ones we love, the wives and fathers.

The betrayal of me, of science, of their own heritage, of Ahmed, the man who had honoured them with this work! He stood next to me, shaking his head, and his anger was plain. For observe: I cannot say what information had been pounded to dust. I cannot say what small treasures were lifted off the floor and wound in the criminals' head wraps or in their gowns as they left, protesting too loudly in clear Arabic that they had found "nothing." When the time comes, I see now, I will have no choice but to tell the Antiquities Inspector that there never were Doors D, E, and F. My hands are tied. Their crime has forced me.

I sent Ahmed away, though the loyal man wished to stay by my side, explore the damage and the new rooms right with me. But his orders were clear: fire those men, hire honest replacements who will be paid at the end of every three weeks, rather than weekly. Off he went, muttering in our shared dismay.

I turned back to my tomb, howling at her violation, but still a triumph. The three "Royal Storage Chambers"—identical, symmetrical, of the most brilliant design in their simplicity and solidity, their elegant proportions and mystical purity—were undoubtedly designed to hold paraphernalia specifically necessary for the king's voyage to the underworld. And, with no question at all, the three chambers held, in this order: food (long since decomposed); incense (lit at the time of burial and now vaporised, though the 3500-year-old, sealed-in smell of it was still faintly but unmistakably present and astoundingly like one of Margaret's perfumes, the one in the little beaded carafe shaped like an ancient amphora); and gold coins or small jewellery, something shiny, of medium value, but just small enough to be grabbed by donkey-thieving ingrates whose names I do not even know.

But, ah! The Pillar Chamber! Here Atum-hadu has left us an enigma to tickle us a bit longer before all is revealed behind Door G (which the vandals apparently did not see in their dust clouds, too eager to stomp off with their burgled baubles and showy protests of disappointment).

I have just spent several hours of the afternoon and evening thirstily measuring and conducting an inch-by-inch survey of each and every surface of the Pillar Chamber. The Pillar Chamber is approximately twenty-five feet long and contains twelve identical floor-to-ceiling stone pillars, round, brilliantly white and unmarked, their perfect cylindrical shape a mathematical accomplishment of such internal significance that any further ornamentation to the room would have been vulgar or perhaps even counterproductive to Atum-hadu's pious requirements. The spacing of the pillars is regular, four rows of three—each pillar is about twelve feet in circumference—never very good at maths—so that means about three feet in diameter—their placement makes it difficult to walk across the room quickly, so any ancient tomb-robber would have had difficulty making a speedy entrance or escape—their proportions are almost certainly mathematically precise and significant,

and if one takes the proportion of the total space in the room, as in
25×15 feet $= 375$ square feet, of which 12 pillars $\times \pi r^2$ where $r = 1.5$

1.5
<u>1.5</u>
 75
<u>150</u>
2.25
<u>3.14</u>
 900
2250
<u>67500</u>
7.0650
<u>   12</u>
141300
<u>706500</u>
84.7800

so then 84.78 square feet of the room are pillars, meaning a proportion
of 84.78/375, or precisely the proportion used in— There were, of
course, twelve dynasties preceding Atum-hadu's own, so the pillars
represent without question the twelve previous dynasties, which he
viewed himself as protecting, symbolically, in his burial—zodiacally,
the placement of the pillars represents the placement astronomically of
the constellation we call Sirius, which the Egyptians took as the celestial incarnation of Isis, and to thank her for her assistance guiding
Atum-hadu to—we must seriously consider the likelihood that the pillars contain valuable material cached within their hollow forms, and
must somehow be stabilised and opened—the ancient robbers whom
Atum-hadu feared more than anything would have found their
progress through the tomb stymied by fine threads running between all
twelve pillars, making the Pillar Chamber nothing less than a deadly
spider's web entrapping the fat flies in filaments laced with a lethal poison known only to the ancient magicians of— Twelve tribes of israel

twelve months in the year twelve provinces of canada twelve days of christmas—what would Carter do faced with such a room? He would look and measure and say little, just nod, hold his cards close to his chest. "It is too soon to say," he would say, but his manner would imply that he knew far more, that glimmer of arrogance shrouded in humble quiet.

Friday, 24 November, 1922

Noon. I worked myself to mental exhaustion last night. Strain of the men's betrayal, excitement at the new chambers. And today is my birthday and my original target date for success. My early hopes for this day have surely been exceeded.

The Pillar Chamber's significance is elusive at this point, though of course an expert can easily produce myriad hypotheses, one of which may well be true. We must simply keep our counsel for now, and await further data. We may, however, reasonably expect that whatever awaits us behind Door G (the sepulchre, the treasury) will also explain the geometry and function of the Pillar Chamber, placing this majestic example of ancient Egyptian tomb architecture and mystical thought in its proper context. [RMT—Door G must now be Door D. Go back, redraw affected maps and edit references. Door B admittedly destroyed, Door C stabilised with canny plastering, no doors until D (formerly G).]

(FIG. F: THE FIRST SIX CHAMBERS, 23 NOVEMBER, 1922)

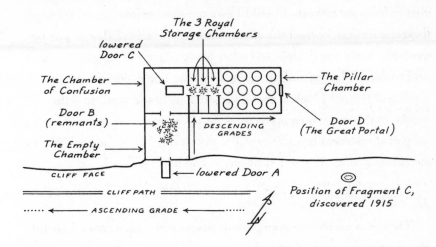

Painstaking work, and no sign of Ahmed and the new team. Clear debris from the Empty Chamber and the three Royal Storage Chambers, scooping it into canvas bags, carrying it out to the cliff path. I have become Atum-hadu's limping charlady. Leave the bags just outside the tomb, as I suspect I will need to seal my discovery for a return to town.

Work takes until nightfall. No Ahmed. Finish the food. Prepare to sleep again in the Pillar Chamber, where I collapsed last night. Might it have been designed as some sort of game? The simulation of a chamber in Atum-hadu's Theban palace? Too soon to tell, must keep my counsel on this point, fruitless speculation is the wine stomping of unconfident dilettantes. I have pins and needles up past the ankle. Will need to go back to Villa Trilipush for bandages, as fluid seems to be an issue again.

I realise here tonight, rereading letters from home and a tattered copy of *Desire and Deceit* by the flickering light of my smoking lantern in the Pillar Chamber: I know more about Atum-hadu, his impulses and purposes, than I do about my fiancée or my patron. This despite kissing the former and engaging in equally intimate business with the latter. There is more clarity in Atum-hadu, distilled by the millennia down to

the essential: sixty verses. Each verse brings to light another crys-
talline, objective facet of his immutable self. But she whom I love?
Each of her changeable moods dictates an entirely new view of her and
new futures for us both. Should I pity the sick, or love the endearing?
Fear the furious, correct the spoilt, ignore the teasing? Rescue the op-
pressed? Scold the fickle? And what of my Master of Largesse, brutal
and cowardly, loving and perverse: what can one make of such an
equivocal figure? I look at them, yet can hardly see them, as if the
smoke in this very room is too thick, as if my eyes were covered with a
strip of translucent linen.

Saturday, 25 November, 1922

Odd dreams, as can be expected, sleeping in such a room. I spend
the morning covering the tomb opening with wooden boards, then
stacking rocks in front of them, spreading the remaining plaster to hold
it in place. Frustrating work, but necessary camouflage. By noon a pre-
carious screen covers the hole that once held Door A, and while it will
not stop a dedicated intruder, at least it will draw less attention than an
open cave mouth.

At which point Ahmed returns, begging my forgiveness for having
hired such untrustworthy dogs and also sons of dogs, hoping in the
name of Allah and my own God that they did no serious harm to my
great work, and did I discover any treasure in my further progress? I
decline to respond and withhold my forgiveness. Does His Lordship
hold out hope for the remainder of the tomb? Was it, in His Lordship's
opinion, common for the old kings to put all their gold in the last room
and leave the tomb empty in the front? Should loyal Ahmed bring
many, many more men, who will work for nearly nothing, he has
cousins eager to participate, men who love the English?

I confess to a moment's hesitation. For nonscientists, the tomb to
date probably lacks a surface glare that would help them see the success still wafting, no question, from behind Door D, and Ahmed's enthusiasm (though its source is obvious) is not discouraging: he too

suspects there is something grand lurking still. I merely nod at him, encourage his patience and faith in my knowledge. "We will all be justly rewarded, as your Koran promises," I tell him. "You are sure?" he asks. "I am sure, Ahmed." And I am.

He helps me onto the donkey he has brought, and I order him to hire a carpenter to build a gate to cover the tomb entrance, buy a padlock for said gate, hire two of his most trusted cousins, and meet back here with gate, carpenter, and men (all by the discreet route) in three days' time. I need the interlude to give CCF a chance to return my expedition to full power.

Ferry back across Nile. Bank. Post: urgently cable CCF: SIX ROOMS, MAJESTIC FIND. WHERE IS MY SUPPORT FROM YOU? THINK ABOUT YOUR COLLECTION. Return slowly and painfully to Villa Trilipush. Rebandage foot.

But there is still loyalty in this world. Maggie and the Rameses await me. They take pleasure in their dinner, but more in my company.

Sunday, 26 November, 1922

Ahmed wakes me. "Is it Tuesday already?" I ask, groggy. "No," he says. "What day is it?" He says, "Be quiet. You have found nothing, yes?" "Not at all, on Tuesday we will return to install the gate you'll arrange and begin work on the next door." "No," says Ahmed. "No?" "No." He says that all of his cousins have gone to work for Carter, who is now hiring as many men as he can find, and paying well. Ahmed, too, is going to work for Carter, and has come today only to collect the money he and his cousins are owed. "I do not understand. Carter has found nothing, returned to Cairo," I say. Ahmed corrects me as the cats flee (smarter than I, sensing danger before me): Carter has only been waiting for the arrival of Carnarvon from England before proceeding with his find. Carnarvon has arrived now, and they have reopened the staircase. They have found a door with Tut-ankh-Amen's seals. They found boxes and pots, and *baksheesh* is plentiful. It is in all the newspapers. They are paying well. They will find riches. There is no shortage of money. And now Ahmed demands to be paid by me at once. "You are a bounder and a thief," I tell him, but still lying down, practically nude, my bad foot up on pillows, my position is poor.

"I am a thief? I dig in the ground to steal the gold of buried ancients and do not inform the authorities? I hide in the desert like a criminal?"

"I am not going to enlighten you in your childish misconceptions, Ahmed. You are dismissed. Leave my sight."

Ahmed empties my wallet, counts out my money but says he is owed still more. "I will come tomorrow for my money. And you will repay me and my cousins. And I will expect a payment as well to prevent me from informing the Inspectors that you dig without permission."

"You are an unspeakable swine," I tell him, refusing to explain the errors upon which he has based his hopeless blackmail. But by then he is squeezing my exposed and wounded foot with a surprising force.

It occurs to me I may have made a mistake in Ahmed, perhaps misunderstood that purser's slovenly Arabic on the boat, approached the wrong man from the brawl, left a fighter for honour behind me.

My predicament: I need men for Door D and I need to pay Ahmed for his work last week, and I am not in a position to call in authorities at this time, though his crimes will be avenged when I am stronger.

My foot is numb, but now my shin and calf burn.

Can Carter really have found something? Buried his find for weeks while patiently awaiting the return of his patron? Difficult to imagine. And now he lures away my men? Of course: my men are trained, hardened. Carter would naturally seek such men out, indifferent to leaving me in the lurch.

I dress in native garb and limp to the ferry, then hire a donkey to ride into the Valley. I ask one of the workers in Arabic if it is true they are hiring here, and he replies in English—I cannot say why, perhaps it is policy on the site (a damned good policy, now that I think of it). Ask him what news, and his response is reassuring: yes, at the bottom of the stairs they found a door covered with Tut-ankh-Amen seals, but now that door is down, and behind it there is only a blocked passageway, entirely filled with rubbish. The tomb was plundered a few thousand years ago.

One simply must sympathise with Carter, even in his aggression and provocations. He has found a tunnel of rocks, with the whole world watching and his patron called back specially from England for the sight.

Monday, 27 November, 1922

Cable from CCF: NEWSPAPERS FULL OF EGYPTIAN DISCOVERIES! MARVELOUS. NEVER DOUBTED YOU. PARTNERSHIP WILL WIRE NEXT SUM SHORTLY — SEND DETAILS.

I have trouble believing this. American newspaper coverage? The Nordquists, I suppose, may have said something to a reporter, or perhaps Margaret and J. P. O'Toole. Smart girl. More likely, it is a result of Carter's noisy error, the Press taking the opportunity to write up all the current excavations. I hope this does not bring too many unwanted observers up here, but publicity protects me as well: the Antiquities Service can hardly shut down an expedition that has already attracted the world's notice, no matter how unintentionally.

I am alternately a victim and a beneficiary of distance. I cannot control from here what CCF hears or thinks, and so now, thanks to the Press, he has decided that all is well again. I cable my reassurance to my nervous Master of Largesse: GLAD TO HAVE YOU BACK. OUR DISCOVERY WILL DWARF CARTER'S, WINLOCK'S, OTHERS. SEND MONEY AT ONCE.

Either way, the return of his enthusiasm renews my confidence; I can put Ahmed behind me. I find my makeshift wall in good condition, untouched. I replace a few of the fallen rocks, balance them in the corners, but it is a frustrating game of spillikins. I am tempted to knock it all down, rush right in and continue my work, but without a new team, without better tools, before the money arrives, it is still too soon. Patience wins out.

Evening, back at Villa T. It turned out to be quite hard to reach Carter's staircase today. Said one of his men, "The electricity is being installed through the whole place." The whole place? Yes, indeed: yesterday Carter, Lord Carnarvon, and Milord's daughter, Lady Something, and some Inspector from Antiquities burrowed to the end of their rubbish tunnel and found another door, behind which (damn their speed—they must be recklessly hammering the things down) is quite a scene, evidently, though the natives are much too pleased with knowing something to reveal it easily. If the blacks are to be trusted, little King Tut-ankh-Amen, missing these 3200 years, has turned up bearing statues, gold, chariots, jewels, vases, thrones, couches, clothing, manikins—no end of treasures, says one of the chattier workers. Imagine, I say to him, taking him by the shoulders, what a truly *significant* king at the *end* of a dynasty carrying *everything* with him into his tomb might reveal! He is understandably astounded at the prospect, as the whole world will be.

Of course with a Lord Carnarvon bankrolling you, rather than the idiot prince of American shopkeepers, events oil themselves, but as an unhappy fellow I once knew used to say *ad nauseam,* "The rich will always make it easy for the rich; the working man who wants to do it on his own has to fight."

By the time I found Carter in this carnival, he was locking a wooden grille at the base of his stairs and he was escorting his guests— rich and malleable father and daughter—up the sixteen sacred steps. His tie and jacket, his moustaches trimmed—always dapper, our Carter. Look how he carries himself at this moment, as he closes and locks the tomb which has so far—*so far*—outshone my own. Look at his style as he guides his dim-witted patrons up and away from what they scarcely comprehend. He lets them glimpse their winnings, but not muck up the works. Look at his trouble-free, effortless mastery of his site, his men, his patrons, even his own excitement. Surely he has discovered more than most men do in a career, and even as he greets me, he neither gloats nor hides, seems not to imply anything at all. "Ah, Trilipush," he says as he steps to the top of the staircase. "Trilipush, yes, of course."

"Carter! What news, old boy?"

"Lord Carnarvon, Lady Evelyn, allow me to present Professor Trili-push. He is the translator of the putative [*sic*] king Atum-hadu, some-thing of an Egyptian scholar, and currently visiting the country, seeing the sights of Thebes."

Two soggy handshakes follow. The Earl is a fop of the lanky, good-natured, imbecilic variety, too big to be a lapdog, too stupid to be a gar-den ornament. He walks and talks with a limp and a lisp, products of a motoring accident. "Excellent, excellent," he says, "must read up on your work. Fascinating, those apocryphal ones."

"Not quite suitable for Lady Evelyn," interjects Carter.

Carter wears a homburg and carries a walking stick, not unlike my own. The moustaches must take effort: trimming, wax, whatnot. "So, great marvels underground?" I ask. "Might one get a professional look-see?"

"Oh, you are a colleague. You can well imagine how unstable things are down there right now."

"Curse talk," mutters His Gimpiness, out of the blue, as Carter marches us to the perimeter of the site. "The natives are all buzzing with rumours of spells and curses, wonderful stuff. All agog with talk of Tut protected by evil magic. Marvellous, don't you agree, to live with such potent belief? Makes one think we lack something—" But by then someone was calling for Carter and he was unable to chat, which I well understood, a fellow in that first moment of excitement, far be it from me to get in his way.

The bank is not yet aware of a new letter of credit.

Poste restante is overflowing with letters. Rent due on Villa Trilipush 1 December. Invoices from the Hotel of the Sphinx for suite during November as well as for the sheets, towels, robes that they lent me.

I returned to the villa for tedious but necessary task of examining the accounts books and budgets, perhaps cutting some expenses. Strange, but Finneran's fumbling of a simple task (and Margaret's fail-ure to apply pressure to him) have resulted in *me* resembling *him*, ob-sessed with money, which the gentleman of course knows to ignore as an element of life's background, like plumbing. But this, as my father used to say, is invariably what results when good blood marries bad: a counteraction.

Rent, men's salaries for last week that Ahmed was so eloquent about. I will need also to hire a new team. I work late, planning, rechecking the accounts, redrafting budgets. The money is not there. It is extraordinary that Carter has had such luck *now*, after all those years wandering about.

He comes to my villa just before I go to sleep. He apologises for intruding, all smiles and excuses, seems a bit embarrassed, declines a drink. "Simply came to tell you how much I admire your work," he says. "Your brilliant translations, analysis. Couldn't be prouder than to call you brother. My little tomb is something of a tribute to you and your persistence. Easy pickings, really, a target like Tut, nothing but road signs all the way, tomb practically uncovered itself, but, Ralph — may I call you Ralph? — you are in *terra* very *incognita*, very *mysterioso* and profound, can't quite say I'd be able to do it myself, wouldn't know how. Also, oh, yes, also wanted to tell you Lady Evelyn asked after you in a very curious manner when we parted this evening. Told her you were engaged to be married in America to an heiress, and her face just fell, old boy, just fell, sad to see. Pity, too — the girl's worth about all the tea in China, and her dad, well, he's good to have on your side, the Earl is, holds about 36,000 acres. You should fall in love with Lady Evelyn, if you want my opinion."

"If only love were so easy," I call after him as he disappears into the night.

Tuesday, 28 November, 1922

Cable from CCF: CARTER NOT ON YOUR TEAM? PAPERS ARE FULL OF HIM — HE IS NOT YOURS? CATALOG OUR FIND AT ONCE. IS CARTER ACCEPTING INVESTMENT? ADVISE.

There is a disturbing moment when you hand the boy the cable reply slip and instinctively expect him to answer it, when of course he is only a mute conduit. It is like shouting into a deaf and deafening wind. And yet one can hear a distant echo, read something in the boy's blank face: CCF is done with me. In the end, trusting others always leads to this, always. Yet you are always surprised by those who snort after grubby self-interest and will spend anything for it, will spend love, will abandon you to any risk if it saves them even an instant's trouble.

On the difficulty of trusting one's financial backers: "Professor Trilipush," I remember him saying, just after the other investors had left our June meeting, "if you would have one more moment for me, it would be much appreciated." I remarked his sudden politeness, as no matter what you think of Chester Crawford Finneran, *gentlemanly* does not usually jump to mind. "I'm wonderin' if you could gimme yer opinion of my personal collection." His tiny, agate eyes wandered just over my shoulder, and his cigar tip flared and faded. "I know there'll be piles of gold in our Pharaoh's grave, mummies and everything, as you described so elegantly just now to the fellows. But I'd like to show you other aspects, those fine arts, plastic arts, sculptural and graphical, although maybe less likely to show up in museum collections due to debate over interpretation. More of interest to a private collector. As I know you know. More functional." On and on dithered this monologue, and I nodded noncommittally. "You of all men, of any scholar, will surely understand." Finneran picked at an invisible thread near his waist.

He led me into his study and stood at the bookshelf behind his desk, from which he repeatedly half-withdrew and then replaced one volume, rocking it on the bottom edge of its spine as if he were unable to decide whether he wanted to remove it. Leaving it, sighing in his increasing discomfort, he turned to me and crossed his arms. "It's simply a question, see, of your, your, uh . . ." He reached up to stroke his thick moustaches and mutton chops, but those still existed only in the portrait of him hanging on his study wall. He followed my eyes to the picture. "You always been clean-shaven? I can't get used to it." He put his smouldering cigar, glowing and askew like a lightning-startled tree trunk, in an ashtray and returned to pushing and pulling that same book halfway off the shelf. He called on Jesus to perform a specific action on a particular Boston-Irish carpenter. He pushed and pulled the book with frantic energy, over and over again, cursing.

"What's the book, CCF?"

"Milking mother of Christ, I will roast him alive," he mumbled, rocking it madly back and forth.

"Hello, Daddy. Is your meeting over?" She had appeared unheard behind us. "Hello, Ralphie. How'd you make out with Boston's plutocrats?"

"My lovely darling," I say. "You are a sight of unimaginable beauty."

"We're busy. Scram," snarls the ever-engaging master of the house, crouching now and rounding his gorilla rear for our delectation, for when I turned back from her I found CCF on his knees, tipping his head, browsing a lower shelf, well below the book he had been massaging when she interrupted.

"A rose of the finest colour," I continued, "the walking fragrance of springtime." And she was that day, damn everything, and healthy, too. I should have turned on my heel, ignored my monstrous patron and his driving urges, and simply swept her up there and then. I could have taken her off right then, ended all this right where it mattered most, forgotten all the rest of this and just won her as my wife. No, no, she would never have had me, not then, not without a victory. But she was clean and clear that day. She will be still, if I can somehow win the chance to be back with her, successful somehow.

"I'm sorry for the interruption, Perfesser," says Finneran and summons Inge to pull Margaret out of the room and haul her around the Garden for some fresh air. The moment the oak door shut on his den he was back on his feet, furiously tipping that first book up and down again. An instant later there was a scratching at the locked door that provoked in Finneran a sort of spasm in his back and cheek. "Christ's kidneys and spleen!" he shouted, or some such Celto-Catholic nonsense, and vaulted past me to open the door, but it was only one of Margaret's spaniels, who paid dearly for the interruption.

"Finally!" he bellowed, after returning to his hypnotic task, as the

bookshelf emitted an audible click and moved a fraction of an inch, dis-
lodged by some spring mechanism under that sluggish book. Finneran
put his shoulder to one edge of the bookcase and turned the whole six-
shelf structure on its centre axis, opening it enough for him to squeeze
his girth through. He beckoned me to follow. With the portal closed
again behind us (apparently relying on that same untrustworthy spring
to release us someday), he switched on a row of electric lights.

"Perfesser, the Finneran Collection of Fine Art," he intoned, waving
grandly at the glass cases and racks of portfolios in the brick-lined en-
closure in which we stood. "Perfesser, great civilisations have, as I'm
sure yer aware . . ." And on and on wheezed the justifying drone, the
text of which I need not write here, since it varies so little from one to
another member of his pitiful community. Finneran's loot was not bad,
of type, and quite varied, though he had miscalculated embarrassingly
when he assumed my work with Atum-hadu had any relationship to
this hodgepodge. He adjusted the focus of the small electric lamps that
lit from above the six or eight glass cases, each holding eight or ten
pieces: stone Incan crocodiles grinning as they unfurled themselves
over Guatemalan virgins; Ming dynasty urns, blue on white, the un-
robed emperor squatting on concubines, ortolans performing nonculi-
nary stuffing functions; multi-limbed bronze Hindu goddesses
engorged, engaged, entwined; a slab of what appeared to be ivory or
bleached wood crowded every which way with carved pictures of
huskie dogs, seal flippers, fur-ringed faces grinning in closed-eye rapture. "Inuit. The Eskimo people of Greenland," commented the mad
curator. "On whalebone." And then we were examining the leather
portfolios, each embossed, bless his knotted heart, with the words THE
FINNERAN COLLECTION. "Works on paper," he declared as he delicately revealed his treasures: first a series of Georgian engravings of
roast-beef-cheeked, periwigged scowlers examining the scullery staff
for personal ailments; then: "Japanese. Woodcuts," and his inkspot
eyes examined me as he flipped slowly through a series of ornate prints
that told the story of a samurai and the village women who served him,
much sheathing and unsheathing of swords, grasping of topknots, et

cetera. "And contemporary artworks, too, of course," he whispered, picking up speed and confidence. "I'm not, you know, a stick-in-the-mud conservative, not a, not a . . ." But he could not think of the thing that he was not, too eager to untie the portfolios of photography: nothing so surprising, nothing you could not see in the Army or in backroom bazaars the world over, even in Boston. Nothing so uncommon, but for the predominance of his daughter's nurse as a model. "Inge has a rare understanding of the art of the human form."

"Very impressive, Chester."

"Thank you, Ralph. I knew that you would understand, as a scholar. As you can see, though, I lack, sadly, anything of Egyptian providence. And, from what I read and hear from other collectors, there are items kept in the basement of the Louvre and your own British Museum that make the case for your ancient Egypt as a very mature artistic society." Finneran peeped through a hole into his office, then pushed open the door and guided me quickly back through his bookshelf. He sat at his desk, mopped his head with a kerchief, crossed his arms, and arrived at the predictable point. "It seems to me, Ralph, that—" And all at once a perfect symphony of church bells and chiming clocks started to cascade, beginning from his desk to his wall clock, to pendulums all over the house, and then to the twelve o'clock performances of steeples from one side of Boston Common to the other. It must have been some sort of feast day for the locals, because at least two minutes passed while drunken belfry men and savant hunchbacks up and down the city vied for our ears with tinkling and crashing compositions, each ending with twelve booming cannon shots, but staggered (as if each church was just slightly in its own time zone) so that at least sixty closely spaced explosions thundered by before Finneran could muster the nerve to whisper his conclusion. "—your particular specialisation and my artistic and cultural tastes intersect here." Another one of these sad men who cannot see the distinction (vast, elemental) between what I study and respect, and what they consume, thirst for, consume, thirst for. "And so, if you were to find, as you certainly will, any examples of . . ." I wondered if his secret was known to his daughter. "Of course," he interrupted himself to answer my unspoken thought, "a single word of this side transaction to anyone would mean an instant end to our little financial arrangements, make no mistake."

This is the man who for mysterious reasons—for *no* reason—has abandoned me in midexpedition. That he would do this to me, leave me in this fix, fall under the sway of some itinerant liar. A *nouveau riche* pornographer who would have made of his daughter's fiancé a smut procurer. He and his hoodlum chums. Silent O'Toole, the kleptomaniac who pocketed one of CCF's silver coasters in front of him at the investors' meeting. Kovacs with his perpetually wet eyes, as if his conscience is so sodden with his crimes that he weeps the tears of his victims on their behalf.

The whole town is jabbering of Carter's find. The rumours were deliriously implausible, and rightly so, since only the imagination of the underemployed, *chicha*-puffing Egyptian could conceive of such marvels as the fairy stories I heard today. And the rumours moved with great velocity. For example, I mentioned in passing to a fruit vendor that if I were Carnarvon, I should simply land a small 'plane in the Valley and fly my loot back to the British Museum, not give the Egyptians one bit of it. Sure enough, by the time I was in another district, where I finally found a haberdasher with a homburg my size, a finely coifed, trim-bearded Egyptian customer was telling *me* that Lord Carnarvon had last night landed three aeroplanes in the Valley and was running a series of flights every night, carrying Egyptian treasure out of the country to his estate in England, where (I informed the bearded ass) His Lordship kept slaves, a perquisite of the British peerage. He nodded, unsurprised.

Finally find a moustache trimmer. I purchased this last item from a barber, a muscleman-Mussulman of such massive strength, it is by Allah's grace that he has not yet inadvertently crushed the heads of any of his clientele. I asked him, considering his strength, if he would be interested in working on an excavation of one of the most famous of the ancient kings. He declined: "I am very sorry, Mr. Carter, sir." A laughable and not entirely complimentary error. He continued: "But I have heard of the marvels you have found and if I might send to you my cousin?" Agreed, address given, and I can begin at last rebuilding my team.

I headed back to Carter's site, as I was now prepared to execute a rather brilliant plan to settle my expedition's financial crisis. There in the sand I found the Earl of Carnarvon and two natives standing over Lady Evelyn, who was having a go with a brush and a small, ladylike shovel. With a titter of surprise, she stood up holding a shard of pottery. Honestly, you just have to bend over and kick at the dirt around there to find something.

I left them to their fun. Carter's command tent was an interesting, if gaudy, sight, a nice effect, I suppose, if you have confused yourself with Caesar. The handsome Lett's #46 diary seems to be his calendar/log of choice, and tomorrow seems to be the official opening of Tut's tomb. Quite a guest list, including me, of course.

Back outside, I fell into conversation with one of the many journalists lingering about the site, confused. I stood with him at the balustrade directly above the pit (such vanities! Tourist-restraining balustrades!), and I was helping him understand what he was seeing, the procedures, and helping him place Carter's discovery in historical context for his newspaper article — those excavations that outshone it in the past, those that were still expected, Tut's relative obscurity and unimportance in Egyptian history. His affected manner of journalistic integrity was to treat everything he was told as if it were a lie. Helping the illiterate with his spelling, I overheard directly below me a conversation between Carter, Carnarvon, and some other Englishman. Carter was saying: "In light of the discovery and its magnitude, and in light of His Lordship's selfless commitment and that of his family over the years, I believe the Government should consider recompensing His Lordship for —"

"Tut's a minor king? Why all the gold and treasure then?" demands the infantile journalist, snatching at my attention.

But the gist was clear: repaid for his six years' wager on Carter's slow work, His Lordship will be looking to reinvest in a new expedition. I had confirmation of my plan's premises. I shall haul my expedition's finances out of their dreary state, and at the same time—not wishing to burn any bridges with my father-in-law-to-be—push CCF to see the value of the work he is endangering with his jackal-hearted miserdom.

On the necessity of human emotion in scientific research: This is a simple story, and if I choose to include it in the finished book, it will be with Lord Carnarvon's kind, condescending approval and CCF's sheepish, after-the-fact amusement, no question. Everyone will look good, except perhaps Carter, who is becoming insufferable since his little stroke of luck.

When Carnarvon was left with a cup of tea trying to look involved or educated, vacantly examining the lintel at the bottom of the stairs, I made my excuses to the ink-stained pressboy and called His Lordship's name. He climbed up to the viewers' gallery in his halting fashion. "I really shouldn't grant interviews, this is Mr. Carter's accomplishment, pure and simple," he began amiably, mugging like a circus clown.

I reminded His Daffiness that we had met yesterday. He is really a marvellous example of the English peerage.

"Of course, of course, the fellow with the dirty king. Well, I do like the hat, sir," he says. "Rather more casual in my day, when I did a spot of this. All you digging chaps do dress to the nines nowadays."

"Yes, the old homburg. Sets an example of composure for the natives."

"Are you the banker, sir?" interrupts the journalist I had left behind, jabbing his pen at Carnarvon.

"Well that's a new one, I must say," laughs the jolly lord, and after he repeats his little caveat that it is all Carter's show, he nevertheless gives a lengthy interview while I wait as patiently as I can.

At last the reporter, all bowing and scraping to an English peer—no more put-on air of doubt for Carnarvon, oh no—rambles off to misunderstand or exaggerate something else.

"Lord Carnarvon, if I might still have a word. I have a small token of my esteem." I presented him with one of the rare 1920 first editions of *Desire and Deceit*, inscribed, "To the Earl of Carnarvon—Patron, Explorer, Friend of Egypt, a true Master of Largesse, from his admiring colleague R. M. Trilipush."

"Lovely gift, very kind," says the gawky millionaire.

"Well, Your Lordship—"

"Please, call me Porchy."

"Very well. Porchy, you may not know, but I am quite close to an—"

"Where are you from, old boy?"

"Kent, Your Lordship. Military and explorer family, small family holdings there, modest manor house."

"Really? Must stop and see the place. Adore that part of the country."

"Well, Porchy, we should be delighted to host you. Now, as Carter may have told you, I am quite, quite close to an astounding find, the tomb of King Atum-hadu, a discovery which, with all due respect, might well outshine whatever Howard is dusting off underground just now. With your support, and my reputation—well, I am not talking about six years here. I would be able to give our friend Carter a run for his money—by which I mean your money, of course. I am talking about perhaps a month from start to finish, and I see us achieving—"

"My God, man, what have you done to that peg of yours?"

"Oh nothing at all. Hardly aches."

"Better watch something like that in this climate." (Very solicitous, the Earl, but almost pathologically distractible.)

"Thanks, but Atum-hadu, you see, was likely the last Theban king of the XIIIth Dynasty, when Hyksos invaders were rampaging throughout the—"

"Real king, was he? Historical? Carter says he was a fantasy figure, apocryphal, bit of a King Arthur imagined by de Sade. Product of later poets, or some such, the old Egyptian nostalgia, artistic mischief."

"Arthur and de Sade? Very droll, our Carter."

"Am I?" And sure enough the jealous man had snuck up on our private conversation, had somewhere learnt to approach in total silence like an assassin. And before I could say another word, he led Carnarvon off to inspect some Tutty relic or other. "We should speak again soon, Porchy," I called, assuming the poor man could untangle himself from his clinging nursemaid. In fact, Carter seemed conspiratorially intent on keeping me away from Lord Cashbags, even as he glided with that usual Carter superciliousness, effortlessly exclusive, but now rather exposed for what it is: an act covering fear and envy. I stood in the dust and heat in my hat and jacket and tie, my trimmed moustache and walking stick, and off padded Carter, dressed like me but still clutching my next patron, as if Carter had never gone and asked for money himself, as if he merely nodded when the Earl came to him on bended knee and pleaded for permission to stuff Carter's pockets with cash. Perhaps that is how it happened.

Interesting, too, how assiduously Carter had sought to belittle my work behind my back, not just my work, but history itself. How quickly he would lie to Porchy that Atum-hadu was not. Restrained, silent, nasty, and now dishonest.

His type, how they make you feel, like you are incapable of counting the fingers in front of your face, or even being certain that they are fingers. Even now, as I sit here on the bluff noting the day's events, it is as if I am not holding a pen. As if I did not publish a work of Egyptology. As if all I have accomplished was accomplished in a darkened room, alone. As if Carter and Carnarvon and ter Breuggen know something they do not speak aloud but know that I do not know and never will. As if theirs is a silent, expressionless laughter transmitted invisibly from one to another and only for an instant, before they turn away to focus on their celestial tasks, tasks I only *believe* I understand. As I only *believe* this to be a pen making notes on a Lett's #46. As I only believe I exist and do my relevant work. As I only believe I can judge what goes on around me or in me. "But no." They smile without moving their lips. "You cannot." Lars Philip-Thürm's smug critique of *Desire and Deceit*, right here in my wallet: "Trilipush digs, but I will not call him an archaeologist. He writes, but I cannot call it scholarship. I do not know what to call this, but it is not of the field I serve."

Reader, Reader, the point of my discussion with Porchy is only this: this is all a necessary application of psychology and human emotion to the problem. I know that CCF is susceptible to pressure because he uses pressure in his daily dealings, and he understands, as a business-man, that value clarifies in the heat of competition. I will tell him the truth, not because I wish to replace him with Carnarvon (I certainly do not want any such thing; I prefer a financier far off in Boston to one stumbling about the site), but because he should know that I do not need to scrounge American pennies when I could be tossing Milord's pounds all about. Especially now, when my work is halted for my reor-ganisation of men and money. Finneran forced me to accept his money, which I did as a gesture to my fiancée, so I will do him the kindness of continuing to accept it before accepting Carnarvon's instead. These are human complications, which, Reader, invariably intrude on what should be pure science. I cable CCF accordingly, and return to Villa Trilipush.

Back from the post just now, and my barber being as good as his word, I found squatting outside my front door his cousin, Amr, my new second-in-command. A boy of sixteen, Amr will be an excellent head-man, though he has much to learn. "Lord Carter," he says to me, "I hope I am worthy." We shall see, young Amr. [Correct opening epi-graph and dedication to "Amr."] I told him not to call me that, and I told him that the ancient Egyptians valued discretion highly, as would I, but that the ancient kings also dealt with indiscretion with the most unspeakable rigour. Arrange to meet tomorrow, and as a symbolic pre-liminary *baksheesh*, I give him a charming jack-in-the-box mummy.

The 29th of November, before I set off for Egypt to catch Paul Caldwell's mur-derer, I practised my best speech and went to the house to say my farewells to the woman who was breaking my heart for sport. But Finneran answered the door. "Good," he said to my great surprise. "I could use an ear." Margaret was nowhere to be seen as her father walked me down the hall. He pushed me into his study and apologised gruffly for our previous meeting, when he'd shrieked at me in his nervousness.

"Now give me your advice, Ferrell. I wonder if you've seen more than I have," he said, cracking his fingers, a sort of admission and apology and invitation to tell all, you'll admit. Four days before, it seemed, Finneran had received a cable from Trilipush: the finds in the tomb were extraordinary, beyond wildest dreams, rooms and rooms, and Trilipush needed money to complete his work and pay his team, but otherwise victory was theirs. Up until this cable, Finneran had *still* been withholding payments except, he admitted, for one small sum he'd sent in a burst of hopefulness. But with this cable on the 25th he'd been ready to renew the money definitively and in full. And, sure enough, Finneran said, on the 26th, the newspapers were shouting of an incredible find in Egypt. Now, you can look that up yourself, Macy: the Press was bashing on and on about King Tutankhamun and an Englishman named Howard Carter, who was the chief of that expedition; it had *nothing* at all to do with Trilipush, but the coincidence was so strong (Trilipush's cable had just come the day before), and Finneran (I later learnt) was in so much danger, that he just pathetically assumed and hoped that Tutankhamun was somehow related to his investment and Howard Carter was one of Trilipush's men, some subforeman. "Honestly," Finneran said, "all those pharaohs' names sound alike, don't they?" Finneran cabled on the 26th congratulating Trilipush and informing him that the wires of money were going to start up again. He also informed the other investors that everything was on track, and they'd made a spectacular investment. He was decided: Trilipush was on the up and up, Oxford was a misunderstanding, not worth talking about, Margaret was pleased, and so Finneran was planning to release the investors' monthly payments, funds he'd been holding in his own accounts. But on the 27th, he realised his mistake— Carter and Trilipush were working on different projects—and Finneran hesitated again. On the 28th, he received another cable from his man. Finneran threw it at me. It read, SEND ME NO MORE MONEY. HAVE FOUND NEW, RELIABLE SUPPORT. CARTER'S BACKERS HAVE PLEADED WITH ME TO ACCEPT THEIR INVESTMENT. I can't say I was surprised by this: Trilipush had used Finneran to find his desert hole full of gold, and now, having found it, why would he need the Finnerans ever again? He'd moved up in the world to a better sort of people, cutting off his Boston crowd. I told Finneran this in no uncertain terms. He goggled at me. "You think he's not coming back? But I needed that money," he stammered. How much had he sent? Not so much, just that one small credit, because the original protection for the investors had been that Trilipush agreed to spend his own money in the opening weeks, as a proof of his confidence. "So what's the problem?" I asked. "You've lost hardly a penny." No, he wasn't upset about the money he'd *spent*, Macy, he was actually worried about his share of the purported *treasure*, if I understood him correctly, which he was now going to lose. "What am I going to tell—" he began, but I interrupted him, told him to relax, said I'd tell Margaret, not to worry. He looked at me amazed. "You idiot. O'Toole and Kovacs, O'Toole and Kovacs— what am I going to tell *them*?"

I looked at Finneran's face, and now, Macy, now I finally understood. I'd seen that face before and I've seen it since, the twisted mouth of the man who realises he won't be able to pay his dangerous creditors.

"That I don't know, Finneran, but I know this. Cable Trilipush over Margaret's signature, breaking the engagement. Trilipush is washing his hands of you fast, so save Margaret first. Do that for her good name as soon as possible: she has to break with him before he does it to her. You owe her that. And *if* he has any feeling for her, which I doubt, she's your only hope to keep any control over him, now that he doesn't need your purse."

The doorbell rang. Julius Padraig O'Toole entered and nodded to me coldly. I was dismissed while Finneran welcomed O'Toole into the study with an expert display of boot licking. I waited in the parlour. There was no shouting, no guns went off. The study door opened a quarter of an hour later, and O'Toole strode calmly down the hall and out of the house. Finneran sat at his desk, thumping his humidor with his fingertips. I asked him what O'Toole had wanted. "Shut the goddamn door," he replied. I left. Margaret was nowhere to be found then or that night.

Mr. Trilish. I am needing rent money for the next six months, right this moment, yes surely a necessity minor on you. Quick quick! And here also an issue of bony contention. For if it is different, yes, than we discussed through the agent, this is necessary now to increase times 5× the amount for each month of renting the house. And this is obvious, yes, because of the interest in the Tut things. So many people all influxing! Happy circumstances! Thank you heroic Mr. Carter! And with a house beautiful like this one! Ho boy! So at least ten people have asked the agent if my house is available and it is unless rent is paid by you now for six months more at once, on this new price. Yours very seriously, Mr. Gamil.

Wednesday, 29 November, 1922

Journal: A message was slipped under my door during the night that puts the expedition's finances under new strain. Heroic concentration on the issues at hand is now the key. Feed the cats and set off into the rising dawn, to *work*.

Amr meets me on the Nile's west bank with plaster, and with the sun rising behind us I show him the correct route to the site. He has his own donkey, which is excellent. He follows me to my tomb and says not a word. I order him to clear the makeshift screen away from the opening of the tomb, and I allow him to walk in behind me. He is duly awed. I owe this boy an education in exchange for his muscles, and I mean to do it well. "Archaeology, Amr, is not only digging, but an approach to our surroundings and our labourers (you, for now) that expresses our unselfish, unself-conscious appreciation of the historical surroundings to which we are the heirs."

He is a brave boy, a proud example of the modern Egyptian, fast to understand. I have him begin hammering boards together and plastering them a uniform white to make a better screen for the tomb's opening.

In the meantime, I reenter my tomb and reorient myself to the work left to be done in this vast and extraordinary space, which maps for now as

(FIG. F: THE FIRST SIX CHAMBERS, 29 NOVEMBER, 1922)

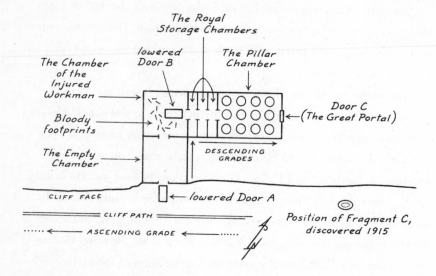

Plainly, the treasures to date are not so much material as historical, the clues that we are on the right track, tauntingly leading us to the more palpable findings, which are soon to appear and soon to outdazzle by a wide margin this season's other finds. As an example of the historical prizes I mean, the unmistakable bloody footprints all over the Chamber of the Injured Workman should be noted briefly, as they are quite unique in the history of Egyptology. The likely explanation—and one readily admits that it is for now merely a hypothesis—is that a workman was injured, perhaps closing and sealing Door B.

I mallet in wedges and chisel away at the outline of the Great Portal. I begin trying to fit a crowbar in the spaces, but it is absurd to think that the boy and I can do this by ourselves. I could wait until Lord Carnarvon's decision opens this and any number of other doors for me. I could hope that Margaret will finally exert herself to tease her father and his flunkies back into line. I could go ask my barber to lend some muscle. Carter shoved through his tomb very fast, and if hammering is the method down there, I can hardly be expected to preserve every blank rock stuck in my path. *What might be behind Door C?* I keep asking myself. Yet more definitive proof of Atum-hadu, as well as, at last, the treasury? How close I am and how abandoned, how completely left to my own wits.

I have much work to do at the site, and time is running out, if CCF's will has withered as badly as I fear. But Carter's site is magnetic, and I do not wish to offend the old-timer by skipping his big moment with the crowds and Press today, so at noon I order Amr to finish his carpentry and stand guard until later this afternoon, while I set off on his donkey to the Valley and Howard Carter's celebration in the sands.

Margaret: My darling. I am sitting above the Valley of the Kings, about to attend a luncheon and the official opening of one of my colleague's tombs. I am in a fix here, your father's stubbornness having glued my hands together. I am reassured at least to know that there is no stronger solvent than your love. I know you are, even as I write this, pushing your father back to the correct path.

My love, it is a bit later now and I have returned to this same secluded spot to jot down my thoughts of what I just saw, before I head back to Deir el Bahari and my own pressing work, though I do move slowly on my injury. It is worth noting these events simply to show you, one day, when all of this is cleared up, the sort of people that so confused your father's loyalty and judgement. Nothing! There is nothing in this find of Carter's that should give a man even a minute's envy or confusion. Your father's bumbling is positively comical now that I have seen the "splendour" of Tut-ankh-Amen.

Besides Merton of the *Times* and other journalists grubbing for a free luncheon, there was Carter, the Earl and his daughter, a passel of pashas, Lady Allenby, Engelbach from Antiquities, the Commandant of the local police, Effendi the Antiquities Inspector for Luxor, and a veritable Burke's of English fops and their women, one of whom, a Lady Prattlemuddle, as far as I could hear, brought her Yorkshire terrier with her to the event (a sweet but unmanned, silky thing with a black leather collar) and then bleated like a birthing cow when the dog inevitably pranced off somewhere, no doubt to find a lunch more appetising than what we were offered on the long tables out at the head of the Valley.

The chatter at lunch was unbearable as the ladies all challenged each other for touristic dominance. Behind their scarab brooches of diamond and onyx and under their straw headpieces, they spat pit names at each other, waging battle for supremacy with tales of authentic sights of unspoilt beauty, witnessed in only the most privileged circumstances.

"Well of *course* you've seen Rameses VI's hole, and not bad accommodations if you must die in Egypt," one lady scolds another who dared admit she was impressed by R6's tomb, "but the Rameses II colossi down at Abu Simbel are vastly superior, if you can be bothered to make the trek to see real art."

"Not bad, true," sighs a third. "I cast an eye over them. Cheeky fellow he was, having himself done up in that gaudy dimension. And the sculptor a regular Michael Angelo. But there is something about seeing only the expert-acknowledged masterpieces, you must agree, that deadens one's palate. Surely the *discovery* of a new piece with your own eyes and taste is as important as mere passive appreciation? Surely that is why we are here, the very first to see this Tut chappy, though I doubt we can expect anything as magical as the first time I *stumbled*, really, into the work at Tuna el-Gebel, the glasswork carvings . . ."

"Done by an overeager student. The hidden masterpieces are down at Nuri and El-Kurru."

"*Maestrosities*, I'd call those. Really, you must get to the Sudan, though you'll have to know the right people to be allowed in, I could drop them a line for you . . ."

". . . that site where King What's-His-Name just up and slapped his cartouche on the previous chap's monuments? Hardly fair play . . ."

". . . a six-day trip to reach it, but the sunrise there is unlike anything . . ."

". . . sunrise? Astronomy is not *art*, dear girl."

"You should see what they are finding up at Atum-hadu's tomb," someone added, and everyone was quite curious, as they always are when the great king's name is mentioned.

Finally Carter muttered his remarks, and then we were all paraded, three at a time, down the sixteen magic stairs and into little Tut's hole for a hunched walk down a bare corridor and our precious glimpse of a haphazard storage room with this and that tossed any which way inside it. I heard it compared to the property room of an ancient opera, and for a moment the thought occurred to me that perhaps wee King Tut had ransacked a preexisting tomb, erased Atum-hadu's name and written his own on it. It was often done.

"What's that dreadful aroma?" asks some civil servant's wife, and Carter tries to explain that the tomb's air is 3200 years old, but I also realise that my bandages need changing and I can do without this display anyhow. I stride out.

Margaret, poor Carter has foolishly made his discoveries in full public eye and now must pay the price: a carnival of twits twittering around him while he works. He spends his days hauling amateurs through a tomb where every single placement of your foot must be carefully considered, where every breath you exhale adds deadly humidity to the air, pollutes the delicate gesso of a painted box or the inscription on a wall, where some great lady's stray sleeve might brush against an item which, until preservatives are applied, can literally disintegrate at the touch, and one of these ladies today was even wearing a dangling silver and sapphire necklace, which could have fallen or brushed something when she bent over to look closely at an item in this storage room of Tut's. Tours of clumsy, uninformed, admiring fans! Poor Carter!

This storage chamber, this Tut's tomb, one does grow tired of hearing about it. Seeing it, after all the chatter of the natives and the papers, was none too impressive. Yes, the Press have told the truth in *nouns* but not in *adjectives*. I heard the *Times* called the chariot wheels "haunting" and the gold "blinding" and the statues "magnificent" and the tomb itself "unlike anything ever seen in this land." It is not true, it is simply *not true*, Margaret, it is just a room stuffed without logic or story, just a room of eye-catching mishmash, and of course, the untrained tourist *ooh*s and *aah*s and practically drops her own jewels at the sight of these semiprecious relics, but for an expert eye, I really feel a certain amount of pity for Carter and a general sense of *disgust*, as if I had just been forced to eat sweets and sweets and sweets in the most sweltering weather. There was one piece in particular, this huge bed with carved lion-head footboards, and I could just hear dear Hugo Marlowe's voice crackling with laughter at the gaudiness of the thing. The throne with a backrest in gold bas-relief, these jars of carved calcite and alabaster in this grotesque XVIIIth-Dynasty, decadent, sagging belly, overwrought, neurotic androgyny. Of course I was kind to poor Carter, complimenting him, but I saw in his eye a bashfulness that was new to him: my friend was a little ashamed of the whole production, that he had the public's attention but for all the wrong reasons.

I am off to my own site now, Margaret, my work, my puzzle, my glorious discovery. All for you, my love.

Journal: To achieve *despite* your conditions, not *thanks* to your conditions, you see. That is something Atum-hadu understood, and there comes a point where it is comic, more than tragic, where the indelible character of the self-powered man is so much stronger than any challenge Fate can fling at him, that it becomes exhilarating and humorous to see him overcome all that.

To wit: Amr was gone when I returned from the Carter show, though the boy had done a fair job on my temporary door. I called for him, but out of the tomb emerged instead an angry Ahmed. He had sent Amr home, told me not to expect his return, so I can only imagine the threats this brute made to the poor boy. There remained this issue of back salary for Ahmed, for which I do have a certain amount of sympathy, and so I spent my valuable working time trying to explain the situation, gently reminding him of his failures in our bargain, and of the difficulty in handing him all of his cash today.

Ahmed boasted of his patience. Ahmed raged. Ahmed threatened. But there was no cash, so threats did not avail. So then Ahmed offered another solution: he handed me a sledgehammer. I would have done anything to escape this, would have paid him anything, but I had no choice. At his forceful insistence, I opened Door C, and every stinging blow vibrated mercilessly down my leg and up to my head by way of my breaking heart. Ahmed ran in ahead of me — I cannot believe I am even writing down this sorry fact. He emerged shaking his head. I will never forget: "My disappointment is keen, Englishman." Unsatisfied, he expressed his rage in the primitive's usual fashion. Most of his assault consisted of kicks to my wounded leg, but also blows to the face, and kicks to my back when I was prone. But he did not proceed any farther in his destruction, thank God, than the one door. Greed blinds, you see, so he could not be bothered to open the Great Portal, which still awaits my care and love, and which will reward my sacrifices.

So be it. I wash my injuries as best I can, bandage where necessary. The swine stole Amr's donkey and one of my gramophones as he left— the Columbia Favorite.

Circumstances aside, I have today opened the seventh chamber of the tomb of Atum-hadu.

(FIG. G: THE FIRST SEVEN CHAMBERS, 29 NOVEMBER, 1922)

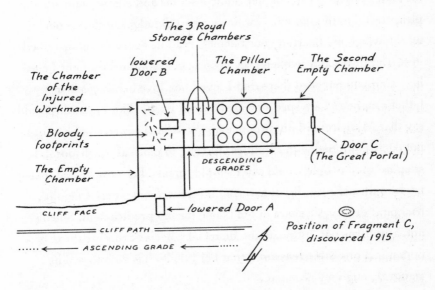

The rest must wait until tomorrow, the description of this new chamber, which is remarkable in a dozen different ways. Wedge Amr's door in the front hole.

Bank is disappointing. Post yields an incomprehensible cable, like a joke. It is a joke, or at least some fool's game.

CABLE. BOSTON TO RALPH TRILIPUSH, LUXOR, 11/29/22, 10:27
A.M. ENGAGEMENT OFF. YOUR LIES REVEALED. DO NOT CONTACT
ME EVER AGAIN. M.

I could reply, but to whom am I replying, the author of this "cable from Margaret"? The mind reels at his crimes and betrayal. He merits a punishment worthy of the great king's imagination.

My cats lick the wounds administered by Ahmed and Finneran alike. Why does Fate insist on casting us in such unoriginal, flat roles, when so much more is possible? My own self-casting would have been—could be still—far more interesting, but no, I must be taken for whatever flinty Finneran can paint in stick figures and garish colours. He cannot afford to cover an Egyptian expedition that does not instantaneously produce treasures and barrels of smut for his needs, and so he must betray me and dream up stories about me to poison the love of his poor daughter, keeping her semiconscious and stupid while he pleasures himself with her Nordic warden. O judges of the Underworld, weigh my heart in your balance, read its every secret inscribed in scarlet fibres and swollen grey vessels, every hidden thought I ever had. Can you not read there that I loved her, love her, *despite* her father's money? I am sure a cynical user of people like Finneran would say that Margaret did not produce for me what I expected of her, did not come equipped with a limitless fortune to place at my disposal. I suppose such people would say I should forsake her now, reveal that my love for her was all a sham. And it is true, from where I lie, that Margaret deserves a share of the blame for my predicament. She did not, as it turns out, lubricate the financial wheels of this great excavation, nor is one quite reassured that her fidelity has maintained its vigour through my absence.

Was I "slumming" when I swooned for her, or was she? I will not deny my first thought was of her wealth. No, I *must* deny it: that could not have been my first thought, since I did not know of the fortune to which she was heiress until much later. And so my first thought was of her beauty. No, that was not true either, for by many standards, Inge is more lovely. My first thought, knowing me, was one of pity—a young woman burdened with some sort of physical weakness, ashamed of her condition, at a public lecture on a notorious subject, failing to hide her infirmity, sidling to the stage to introduce herself and compliment the lecturer, claiming she was an amateur of Egypt and— No. No, I cannot say that I even noticed her infirmity. I did not desire her money, nor her beauty, nor her weakness. She made me laugh.

I would sail to her this very day, prove my feelings, but I cannot leave this place until my work is done, my discovery complete and acknowledged. She certainly will not return to me if I arrive broken and empty-handed; if I am not her English explorer then I am nothing to her. Nothing and no one waits for me in Boston without Atum-hadu wrapped and stately in golden bedding, the last chambers of the tomb.

They were gods for good reason, these cats who repay loyalty and understanding. Maggie the orange beauty is all kindness, like her namesake, who did not mean what that cable says. She did not write that cable, she did not even *see* that cable.

Nov. 15

My own, sweet Ralph,

Yesterday I got your letter of October 19th. And it made me so sad. I miss you very much. And of course just four days ago was the cable bearing the grand news of your Find, Daddy showed it to me and I was so very proud of you. We both were, of course.

I read your letter again just now. I don't know what to write I am so sad. I'm crying as I read your lovely letter, full of concern for me, which I fear I do not deserve. That's being very absurd of me, isn't it, now that everything is going well?

Daddy finally lost his temper and showed the snoop the door the other day. I didn't hear the whole thing, and when I asked Daddy what had happened, he just told me to go away, and not very nicely. Daddy's under terrible pressure, you see. He never tells me a word of it, doesn't want me to worry, but you must forgive him if he gets angry sometimes or listens to liars like the snoop or that professor, your boss, the German. He came to the house last month to talk to Daddy about dynasties and fragments and you and Oxford and whatnot. (And besides, are we supposed to trust Germans now? Not me, darling, not after everything you went through in the War.) Ralph, you know I never listen to these people. I know just who you are, and I love you from the top of your head down to your dusty boots and I always will. Do you know that? You simply must believe me, you must. Without you, I would be so lost. I keep your cable telling me Ferrell is a liar under my pillow.

But you have probably already been told that Finneran's Finer Finery is having certain problems. I can see it, and Daddy looks worried often, and J. P. O'Toole tells me this and that. So your wonderful Success is even more important to everyone here, and they are even more proud of you, almost as proud of you as your Queen. I hope this news is not alarming to you, or changes anything about how you view Daddy, or us. But I know you are not like that. And it is not so serious as all that.

You are so good and kind to be so worried about Inge and my medicine and seeing me healthy for our wedding day. Please don't worry. It will all be fine. Just knowing how much I mean to you and how important it is that I be healthy for you is enough to make me healthy and keep me healthy. I will simply get myself well out of love for you, and so you won't worry another moment for me. I can feel it happening already. I can do this for you. Anybody could for a man like you.

You are coming home, and then I won't be so bored and that's usually what gets me thinking about going out on the town. This is it: I will not go out even one more time.

I think of you whenever I am awake and able. You always said that you are guided by science and deduction, not passion. Do you remember saying that when we walked on the river? But all the evidence says you shouldn't love me, archaeologist. But you do. So I swear I will be better for you and will deserve you and will make you feel rewarded. I will make myself better right now. Done!

Write me again soon, and about our wedding, tell me about our wedding and all the gold rings and crowns you're finding in the sands, tell me of the Hall in Kent and when we will meet the King of England—a live king, you know, is better than a mummi-fied one when it comes right down to it.

I am your eternal Queen.

m.

Thursday, 30 November, 1922

<u>Margaret:</u>   Margaret, my love, you will want to know all about this someday, the order of events as precisely as we can reconstruct it. So, first thing this morning, the day after your "split" with me, I hob-bled off to the post. And of course, today's post brings a letter from you, dated 15 November, and it makes me laugh, the sweet thing. I cabled you right away, my darling, thank God for cables to clear up misunderstandings completely and at once from far across the sea. Now all is clear. Our love is unshaken. Of course: your father is in fi-nancial strife and cannot bear to admit it to me, the poor man! Of course! Of course that would make him feel ashamed and worried about the integrity of those around him, and he would test me by sending me that false cable. And what have we learnt? I love you no matter, no matter.

That explains all, and I feel nothing but pity for your father today. It is for the best, my love, that my relationship with your father be de-tached from the issue of financing the expedition, especially now, when he is under pressure. I have been presented with a likely new backer here, so it is all for the best. You did your father a good turn when you introduced us, and I will do him another by releasing him from his debts to me. We will find a solution to it all, as long as you and I are together. I am so relieved, my love. Last night was unbearable.

I will return to the site tomorrow, but today I must reflect on all I have discovered so far. Carnarvon will need to understand my success before we can proceed as partners. I must concentrate my battered energies on making my work to date as clear and tidy as possible for my potential new financier. Margaret, I can offer no greater proof of my love than this: Lord Carnarvon will assume the responsibility of financing the expedition for the tomb of Atum-hadu, and still *you* will be my wife. You and CCF cannot possibly still nurse doubts after hearing that. It is 30 November, 1922, at 11.15 in the morning, and my love for you is an indestructible stone.

Journal: A few hours' consideration and planning, out of the sun, taking sweet tea. After lunch, I now feel able to consider again the state of Atum-hadu's puzzling legacy. A stage performance has begun, a small-town imitation of the cabaret I saw in Cairo so long ago. The girls nod as coins fall at their slippered feet, the drums throb and odd fiddles keen, and the veils drift down like leaves shaken loose by a light autumn breeze.

Historiography lesson: Understanding the relationship between a (complicated) life and a later (simplified) account of that life, using the case of Atum-hadu: One can imagine one's own future archaeologist making a terrible mess of it. Trying to explain you, he fills and fudges where he must, and all of your nuance and detail—which is precisely what makes you you—is lost or imagined, replaced by the nuance of your chronicler instead. Your virtuous behaviour, your generosity or bravery or acts of humble gratitude—if there is no record of it, it did not happen. And if there is instead a record of something else—a momentary lapse, a persistent rival's well-recorded lies, an angry lover's obsessive, unilateral collection of correspondence, a detective's confident miscomprehension of a smudged dossier—what will your hapless excavator say of you?

And this is why one must be careful to leave one's own truth behind oneself, honest but unambiguous, loose ends snipped off: the *Admoni-*

tions of Atum-hadu, for example, or this very notebook, whatever the
result of my work.

When our excavator, our clarifying biographer, comes for us — as
we all certainly hope he will — when he chronicles our life and simpli-
fies it enough for the dimmest reader to grasp and remember forever,
how can we have helped him ahead of time? How can we help him
know when to stop digging and start writing? Where is the centre of
our life, the core of our character, with all extraneous detail eroded?
Under one layer is another and another, under each silk veil more silk,
under dust more dust, behind one door another and then a sepulchre
and an outer sarcophagus and an inner and the cartonnage and the
golden head mask and the linen wraps and then . . . a black skeleton in
tight, crispy skin, intact but with no brain, liver, lungs, intestine, stomach. Is *this* the truth? Or did we, in our rush to get to this "answer,"
pass right by the humble truth, knock it down, cover it with the dust of
our hurried burrowing?

I think before further excavation, which is slow and expensive, the
tomb as it stands now deserves a more careful examination, a detailed
inventory of my hurried progress to date.

I have underestimated the amount of ink, paper, and paint I will
need to copy down the tomb's extensive illustrations, the ladder I will
need to read and copy out the highest rows of hieroglyphic inscriptions.
So, off now for last supplies, with nearly the end of my funds, and then
to bed with the regal cats.

This is my last night in a soft bed for a spell because, with this next
phase of the excavation, it only makes sense that I sleep at the site. Tomorrow I move out of the villa; it is a burden for now. Must think of a
plan to care for the cats.

The next day, the 30th, things had gone from bad to horrible in no time at all.
He wasn't well, your great-uncle, swinging from screaming rages to periods of
quiet that were anything but calm. I'd rarely seen him drink before, but now he

was on the nose. Obvious he hadn't slept. I've seen men in his predicament before, Macy, and it's interesting how alike they are. Pressure does predictable things to men, that's what I've learnt. There are really only two or perhaps three human responses to high pressure. I've seen them all.

The evening before, Finneran did as I'd advised and sent the cable breaking off Margaret and Trilipush's engagement. Today, Trilipush had responded, and with some heat. That did puzzle me, I have to say, as I didn't think Trilipush would've cared one way or the other at this point, since he'd taken what he wanted from the family and Margaret could therefore hold no further interest for him, and I was ready to catch her in her fall, but Trilipush's plans were evidently deeper than I could see, and he didn't seem to like losing his fiancée one bit. No, in response, he'd cabled not Finneran or Margaret but *O'Toole*, and the Irishman had ominously sent that cable round for Finneran to read and sweat over. Trilipush's cable read: O'TOOLE. CONGRATULATIONS ON OUR MUTUAL GOOD FORTUNE. I ASSUME FINNERAN HAS SHARED WITH YOU ESTIMATES OF THE FINAL FINANCIAL PAYOFF. HANDSOME RETURNS FOR US ALL. O'Toole had scribbled at the bottom of the cable in pencil: "Good news indeed, CC. Do come around with an accounting."

Trilipush knew just where to shoot. "He's trying to get me killed," moaned Finneran, showing me the ominous cable. "I just broke the news to O'Toole yesterday that the expedition was a bust." Trilipush wasn't finished: an hour earlier, a reporter from one of the scandal sheets had rung Finneran's doorbell. "Can you imagine?" Finneran shouted as he told me the story. "A scribbler from the *Boston Mercury* came by because they got an *anonymous cable* saying I'm a collector of filthy art and I want to talk about it to the Press. He's playing games with my reputation in my city. I am gonna crush his neck," he roared, spilling his liquor on his desk. "And the cardinal's office telephoned. The cardinal. Of Boston. My cardinal. A prince of the Church. His office had received a *disturbing cable*, they said, probably a vicious joke, they said!"

I listened politely; displays like this are nothing to me, Macy. I'm a professional and I'd seen it all before. But in this case, I was also involved. "Has anyone told Margaret yet?" I asked, getting back to the important issues. Finneran's anger melted away, and he slumped into his chair. "She's a wreck. I told her he used her, us, been playing her for my money. She was out all night. Inge has her upstairs now. What am I going to do?" he muttered, running his hands through his hair, picking at his collar. I didn't pity him much, Macy. He'd been warned often enough, but he hadn't wanted to hear it. He'd wanted social standing and easy gold to pay off his debts to very bad men, but he got himself a confidence trickster instead, lost his reputation and his daughter's happiness in the bargain. Nothing I could do for him.

He looked at his watch, took up pen and paper to write, waved me out of the room. I left him chewing on the nib, shaking his head, still in the stage where a doomed man hopes he might only be dreaming.

I walked upstairs in the Finneran mansion for the first time. Talking to Margaret was impossible; Inge had her quite asleep. "She was hysterical," said the Viking. "She is adjusting to some new medications." Inge allowed me into the room to see her, but there was no budging Margaret. I can't even imagine what Inge'd given her. The ministering devils of Sunset on the Bayview give some of the rowdy ones here something strong, too, a horse tranquillizer, I think, when the old fools realise too clearly that they've been parked here to die and they raise a stink about it, or when the nutters start screaming like they're invading Turkey again. It must have been something strong like that in your poor aunt's case, because it was all she could do to push the air out her nose.

I sat next to her bed, waiting for her to come around, her *rrrrrare* Tibetan spaniels snoozing in a heap on a little white-and-green sofa across from the bed. Hours passed, and the last November sun set early. I went downstairs to check on the man of the house, but amazing: he was gone, hadn't thought anything of leaving me in his girl's boudoir, you see, when *his* hide was in trouble. So much for the doting father charade. He'd left letters and other papers on his desk, including a letter to Margaret I found, in which he apologised for everything, not very clear what that meant, said he was going to fix everything and would be gone for a while, would contact her soon, don't worry, trust Inge for everything in the meanwhile. I had my suspicions where he'd gone, and I was right: as it turned out he was on his way to New York on the sleeper that very night. An Alexandria boat left the next day, see, December 1st. I knew the timetable well: I'd reserved a place on that boat several times in my long, hesitating sojourn in Boston. I wandered the Finneran house, and Inge left an hour or so later, perhaps assuming I was on to watch Sleeping Beauty (or guard the prisoner, depending on point of view).

A few hours later, your aunt was sitting up awake, as if she'd just had a quick nap, not a drugged sleep of the dead. "Oh, it's you," she said sullenly and turned away to face the window. She asked me for her coat but didn't look at me when I gave it to her. She searched it, alternately furious and dazed, scratching at the pockets but then falling asleep for a few seconds at a time. "Can I help you find something?" I asked. "Shut up," she said and finally found what she'd been looking for, something small enough to hold in her fist. "Bless you, JP," she said.

Macy, I just reread this long, long letter. It's taken me the entire damn day to write about my time in Boston, which suits me fine, rather write down this diffi-cult tale than play along with the forced Christmas cheer the rough bastards try to push on us this time of year. Especially since, tonight, it's not even the usual crew of thugs who run this place but the rare monsters who are pleased to work Christmas, with nothing better to do than clean up after the old and the ill and the batty and slap us around a bit for fun.

I think I mentioned somewhere in here your aunt's three moods. Well, what to call the third? Maybe it was a real part of her, or maybe just a product of the opium, or maybe it was something about me, something only I brought out of her. Either way, it was ugly. "Get away from me, you," she shouted, when I tried to hand her a glass of water. "What did you do, Harry? What did you do? Get away from me, you horrible— Just leave me alone. I'm going to JP's." But she didn't move. She wouldn't look at me.

"There are things you don't understand, that I have to tell you."

"Aw, can it. Nothing's that important. You've done your dirty work."

"That's not fair." I desperately tried to get her to listen, to see that I was the unwilling messenger, not the cause of her trouble. I told her Trilipush had be-trayed her family, had only pretended to love her, had spent her father's money to get other people's money, and now he was running off with the ancient gold he'd dug up, without a thought for her. "He used you, he's not coming back here. I know you don't truly care about him and your father forced him on you, so it doesn't matter."

She didn't take this how I'd expected. I'd started to think—I don't know what I'd started to think. "You don't know anything! You don't know anything! I hate you, you make me sick." And then she was screaming for her father and her nurse, but I knew we were alone in the house, and no one was going to interrupt. She felt she needed to humiliate me. She was calling me some rather horrible names, pushing at the bedcovers like they were choking her, insulting anything about me that caught her anger. I tried to get her quiet is all, for her health, tried to prevent her from hurting herself and throwing things at me, tried to tell her how I felt, that I loved her and she'd be safe with me, that she'd escaped a close call with Trilipush, and I was an honest man who could offer her proper happiness.

Well, some of us aren't built for love, I know after a long life, Macy, and she didn't—it pains me to admit even years on—she didn't stop and look at me with wonder and gratitude, dawning affection, all that. No, she laughed at me, and it was a nasty little sound. She mocked me, and I looked away, looked at the two little dogs sitting on the white sofa with the green painted design of French country scenes: the milkmaid and her lover hand in hand in the woods. I looked at those dogs looking me in the eye curiously, while she just did not stop: I was nothing next to Ralph, I didn't know anything, I was a fool and a monster and a bastard, a joke next to a man like Ralph, I wasn't fit to say Ralph's name, didn't understand anything, I was less than a joke, I was pathetic and disgusting, and on and on. "A stupid Australian is what you are, Harry, you horrible ass. You spread these lies. You made Daddy do this. But your lies can't ever touch a man like Ralph." And on and on, crying and yelling, throwing pillows and dolls and glass things at me, repeating what a wonderful man her English murderer was, how loyal and true and English and noble, while I was a red-haired pygmy from the bush who deserved to be spit on by everyone. "And *you* love me? You make me sick, Harry."

After a spell, I'd had my fill, and I walked out the door and I never saw your family again, Mr. Macy. Those dogs were still sitting on that painted sofa, still looking right at me when I left, never took their beady judge's eyes off me the whole time. They say every hero has his weak heel, so there you are then. I only did what any man in my position would've done, trying to win her heart, you see, a girl like that. I was foolish, but that's no crime.

I'll drop this in the box to you now and hope for some sleep. You're getting these, yes? I think I'd give up the ghost if they were lost in the mails, or sitting in an unread heap on your desk. I'd throw myself off the roof of this place, if I thought you weren't hearing me.

Merry Christmas, Macy.

HF

Friday, 1 December, 1922

<u>Journal:</u> Spend morning moving my base from villa to Atumhadu's tomb, as intensive work approaches. Rental agent assists me in storing certain items in a shed. Hate to part from Maggie and the toms, but I will attempt to feed them as often as I can conveniently come back across the river. It is tempting to bring them with me to the west bank, but they have their hunting grounds here, I am certain, and I would not wish to disorient them.

Work to improve the door Amr made. I use adhesives to cover its front with rocks and sand, and cut it until it fits snugly and invisibly, flush into the tomb's opening. Efficient, inexpensive protection! Also, the former Door A, lying on its crushed cylinders, was unfortunately likely to attract tomb-robbers, tourists, other unwanted attention, so it had to be sacrificed, not a significant loss.

Summation of our finds in the History Chamber: The ornamentation covering from floor to ceiling the walls and pillars of the History Chamber is preserved in astounding condition. Every imaginable surface is covered with text and illustration. The text is the highest quality hieroglyphs, all written — to my trained eye — by the same hand. If I may speculate further, I would say that this hand belonged to a scribe of impeccable intelligence, but perhaps not one who came through the recognised academic training of the day.

The walls' hieroglyphs include passages from the Admonitions, extinguishing any smouldering doubt that (a) Atum-hadu existed and reigned; (b) he is the author of the Admonitions; (c) this is his tomb, or was intended as such. A triple crown, certain to move Carnarvon to a quick decision to finance further explorations at this site, or other likely sites nearby.

And, if the accompanying illustrations are not of the highest artistic accomplishment, if their composition is unwieldy, if the faces are not as iconic as one would expect from ancient Egyptian tomb-painting, if the animals are not easily distinguishable from furniture, if here and there the paint seems to have smeared or dribbled down the unforgiving tomb walls, if the artist was not apparently even trained as an artist, well, one can only say that the rough last days of the dynamic XIIIth Dynasty were not the soft, easy days of the flaccid XVIIIth, and perhaps Atum-hadu's court had more vital attributes than the dainty painterly facility of the peace-drugged faux-raonic dynasties that served as epilogue to my king's grand drama.

For now, I expect it will take me several days at least to complete a full copy and translation of the hieroglyphs, and make descriptive notes of the paintings. After the chamber is fully catalogued, I will invite

Lord Carnarvon to examine our discoveries to date before proceeding through Door C, the so-called Great Portal, and into the tomb's likely treasury, sepulchre, and other chambers. Or perhaps Carnarvon and I shall continue excavations in other locations instead, if in the end we find this tomb unoccupied, with only the History Chamber to identify it (as if such a find alone were not remarkable enough).

(FIG. H: CHAMBER 6, THE HISTORY CHAMBER,
OPENED 23.11.22, SHOWING THE PLACEMENT OF THE
ILLUSTRATIONS AND TEXTS)

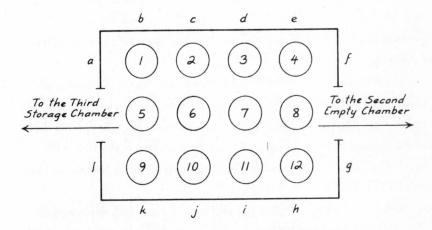

Each of the twelve pillars depicts one key event from each year of Atum-hadu's twelve-year reign, a span concretely determined now, thanks to these twelve pillars, and likely having occurred 1642–1630 B.C. More comprehensive than the pillars, each of the twelve wall panels tells, with text and image, a portion of the life of Atum-hadu, from his conception through his reign to the end of his earthly life.

WALL PANEL A: "THE BIRTH OF ATUM-HADU,
FINAL KING OF THE BLACK LAND"

Hieroglyphic Text: The great king's titulary has been composed and will forever be Horus—Son of Osiris and Seth; He of the Two Ladies—Restorer of the Lost Kingdom; Horus of Gold—Ma'at's Ferocious Lover; He of the Sedge and Bee—Hand of a Scribe, Victorious Bull, Fish of a God; Son of Ra—Atum-Is-Aroused. But the king was born with his name hidden.

He is born far from the capital, near the waters. [His] mother is chosen for her especial grace and beauty and intelligence to receive the seed of Seth [god of confusion and disorder—RMT]. The summer at its zenith, Seth disguised himself as a fisherman and lay with this woman. At the moment he delivered his seed, Seth revealed his truth, and the woman saw his donkey head and was frightened. Seth departed, and she would kill the life in her womb. Seth stayed her hand. Seth made her fingers like an animal's paw. Seth took from the ungrateful her beauty, and she became dull and her name is everywhere forgotten.

The woman washed clothes and drank beer. She was heavy with child by as many men as stars in a sky. Her first son asked her who his father was. She pointed to a fisherman who resembled Seth when he had disguised himself. "This son of a whore's vulva is the father of you." The fisherman said no, she had copulated with a donkey and her children were all donkey-children.

Seth saw the boy grow strong and visited him. Seth explained all, and the boy understood. The boy was made not by people but by gods and himself. He created himself. The god whom he most resembled was not Seth but Atum, the great creator of everything, at the moment when the god strained towards creation. He named himself Atum-Is-Aroused, and Seth came to Atum-Is-Aroused and praised him. With a blinding flash of the sundisk, Seth made the boy forget his false birth name all at once and forever.

At this time, the priest of the temple of Amen was jealous. The priest's hungers ruled him, and he often skewered the boy like a veal to be sacrificed, and the boy was forced to burn brightly and the boy vowed that the priest would see his own heart beat in a fire fuelled by camel dung while Atum-Is-Aroused would lay with the priest's sisters and nieces before the priest's bleeding eyes.

Illustration: Extraordinary illustrations: here we see Seth copulating with a beautiful woman under a midsummer sun, his head in mid-transformation—half-donkey, half-man—the very instant of impregnating Atum-hadu's mother. And here we see her with a golden child in her transparent belly. Here we see her attempt to beat her belly with fists, and Seth's punishment for that crime, transforming her into an ugly, charmless washerwoman. Here we see the boy—golden-skinned and beautiful—surrounded by countless other children—squat and dark—while his mother lies drunk. Here we see the boy taken brutally ("made to burn brightly") by the temple priest. Here we see the boy visited by Seth. Here we see the boy teaching himself to read and write, to hunt and fish. Here we see him standing aside from the fishing village and his family, and the boy gazes towards the sundisk, where Horus and Ra admire him in return.

The illustrations are not of an impressive accuracy, by Western art-critical standards, nor are they quite typical of Egyptian art, yet still how affecting!

Analysis: Despite my easy childhood, the men whom I admire most in this world are self-made men, a description which seems to fit the king.

By *self-made* I do not mean poor men who have become rich. I mean, rather, those men who gathered the fragments made available to them as abandoned or downtrodden children and then, with the boiling, creative force of their own minds, forged a self marked by strength and, more importantly, by style. Such men create selves that bear no trace whatsoever of their dark inheritances, no trace of foolish parents or dusty childhood towns or the crimes committed against them, no trace of the deprivations (money, affection, nourishment, friendship), no trace of any source material at all, but instead an aesthetic and practical creation, godlike in its simplicity and in its completeness. Simplicity: everything is from within this one head, no parental influence, no village tradition, nothing that did not hail from the self-creating mind itself. Completeness: everything must be created, every attitude, every mannerism, every belief and value and stylish gesture. Nothing inherited can be tolerated from an intolerable past.

And yet, great irony that is our world, such men are often not honoured, while men like *me*—born with love, guidance, every advantage—are. I admire, perhaps most of all the verses, his Quatrain 24 (Fragments B & C):

> *Atum-hadu looks behind him and marvels at the height.*
> *Atum-hadu looks at all he has surpassed with great delight.*
> *Atum-hadu owes nothing, is in debt to no man,*
> *And will therefore act as no other man can.*

One can easily imagine the young man composing this verse not long after he found he had become the king of Egypt.

On Atum-hadu's Name: Underneath the story's typically Egyptian mythology, we find two details of crucial historical importance: Atum-hadu came from nothing, and Atum-hadu named himself. The legend allows for no other explanation. He was not of royal birth but of peasant birth; in the chaos marking the end of the dynasty, a climb like his was possible. The king's full five-name titulary—which opens the text and ends with the "Son of Ra" name Atum-hadu (Atum-Is-Aroused)—is given here for the first time. Usually, the "Son of Ra" name was the king's birth name and was unsurprisingly royal in tone, given to a royal newborn. But it appears that, in this case, this extraordinary mind risen from humble beginnings had some other name at birth.

One pities him as a boy, of course, telling himself stories to fall asleep, creating this dream of a celestial parent. An analysis of Atum-hadu obviously benefits from modern sociology: in these terrible modern cases one hears of, research reveals that there is typically a critical moment, the age at which the child first realises his predicament, finally understands his relationship to his mother, for example, and thus with the entire world. This moment is too easily bathed in retrospective bathos, as I fell victim to just now, above, but in truth, one need not pity such children. On the contrary, see the beautiful and heroic aspects: a boy of eight runs for the very last time into his ramshackle home (for there must have been a *last* time, whether he knew it or not just then), and he shouts with pride about some accomplishment, still expecting (with the dregs of his childish instincts for love) to receive praise from the lady of the house. He shouts with pride that he has learnt to do this or that, something academic or athletic. And he receives as a mark of her definitive indifference to him either a blow or a fruity curse marinated in liquor or mere runny-nosed, vomiting silence, while new semi-siblings mewl and squat all over the room. As if such a moment is, in the child's blossoming mind, necessarily tragic! Not at all: why assume such a moment represents a door closing, rather than the equally creaky sound of a door opening? How can the untrained ear tell the difference? Close your eyes, and if, after that tooth-grinding squeal, one feels a breeze of insight or opportunity, then you know. As Atum-hadu apparently knew. Something had opened for him, which he chose to recall as a nocturnal visit from Seth.

Modern sociology shows that the brightest children understand the significance of this moment, and their adaptation to it can only be termed a *second birth:* a birth into total independence, free of any ties to illusions, free of any illusions of ties. A birth in which the child becomes both his own parents. He alone will make himself from this day on. There can be no question what passed through the great king's mind when he chose the name by which the world later knew him: *the greatest act of creation will now begin, the creation of myself.*

And, of course, it is only by this superficially torturous second birth that one is able even to aspire towards the *third birth,* which eludes most men, even men who have made themselves (let there be no doubt of the monstrous odds at play here). The third birth is that of *immortality,* in which, after a productive life guided solely by one's own auto-parental instincts, one's name is remembered and loved forever, in an underworld or merely in celebrated glory. But, if you are unable to realise your way out of childish delusions, if you blunder on, relying on the love of a mother, the trustworthy interest of the priest or the teacher or the employer or the lover or the officer, the benevolent concern of the rich for the poor, the jolly companionship and foul-weather loyalty of trusted pals, well, then you are doomed to a life of childhood. You will have no real adulthood, and no hope of making an achievement worthy of permanent note.

All of this makes Atum-hadu a worthy model for study. For if one thing is clear in Quatrain 80 (Fragment C only), it is how closely the great king's life illustrates the principles I have just outlined:

The mother's heart seals itself shut to her child.
No greater gift can she bestow, though he weeps and wails,
As we weep on our deathbed like a maiden defiled,
But it is when our tomb door is sealed that our soul prevails.

The donkey-headed god Seth—sexually aggressive, mischievous, power-hungry—is depicted on these walls also as sympathetic and caretaking, almost a family dog rather than a donkey. The nameless mother, the priest, the neighbours are all—even in the restrained profiles and formal requirements of Egyptian art, even when they are little more than dribbling stick figures—clearly depraved and vicious.

Sunset on the Bayview Nursing Home
Sydney, Australia
January 5, 1955

Macy,

I've been unwell again, not to be a bore about it, old men do fall ill, and who cares. Also, I rather hoped to have heard from you by now, a response to my first letter, but now I look at the new calendar they've tacked up here, pictures of the bloody ocean, and I see I'm being impatient. Even in the fastest circumstances, I couldn't hope to hear from you for some days yet, I suppose. Still, a word from you that you've had some luck with publishers or motion picture people, well, that would go a long way in helping me feel fit again, mate. Tired more than ill is how I feel, didn't much enjoy mucking about in all those memories of Boston, had quite put them out of my mind for some years, bit of a splash of cold water on the face and heart after all that time. When I think of your poor aunt, finding happiness again after this misadventure, well, that gladdens the heart, it does. But that she's passed on already, at a young age, makes one feel old. Haven't had many close chums in my life, a risk of the trade, you see, something for you to be wary of before jumping into the detection game, Macy, little free advice from me to you. She was a fine woman, your aunt. I do still hope to see a copy of your family history when it's done.

Let's see. I went downstairs. I'd a job to do, for her as much as for anyone. On Finneran's desk were the notes for her and the nurse I already described, I think, as well as a stack of other incoming and outgoing correspondences, and a cable from Trilipush to Margaret, still trying to patch things up, just to buy himself some time. I left everything undisturbed.

Finneran's note to Margaret mentioned being out of town for a spell, and it took me only half a day (the 1st of December) to confirm that he was on the steamer leaving that very day from New York, due in Alexandria the 14th. There was nothing to keep me in Boston another day now, so I spent the rest of the 1st making my own travel arrangements, returned to my hotel to pack. I was a bit low, rather like I feel now, hoping I'd feel back on track when I was clear and away from the gathering Boston winter, pursuing the case in the homier, more Australian warmth of Egypt. The end was in sight.

Well, comes a knock on my hotel door: J. P. O'Toole looking down his nose at me, and next to him a perfectly round little man I recognised from newspaper photographs as Heinz Kovacs, though O'Toole never introduced him, and he barely spoke throughout our meeting. (You remember what happened to Kovacs, I think in the late 1930s? It even made the newspapers in Australia. Jesus, that was ghastly.) In they strode like they owned the place, sat in the chairs by the window, and O'Toole talked at me in his Irish brogue: "You're a detective, yes. Then haven't we got a wee spot o' detecting for you to do."

We had new clients, Macy, and the first thing I learnt from them was what would drive Finneran to play Holy Family and vanish off to Egypt in the dark of night. In the previous eighteen months, the man had gone well past bankrupt, I can tell you now, seeing as the news certainly comes thirty years too late to prevent your uncle from marrying my Margaret! Yes, Finneran was quite out of money, his shops were in danger, and as I'd deduced, he'd gone to O'Toole and company for sizable sums on several occasions, with quite harsh terms. The last time, he'd sold them on Trilipush and his no-fail Egyptian excavation as a way for him to raise money to pay back his debt. O'Toole and Kovacs had played along, even loaned him *more* money to buy his share of the expedition, when his credit should've been long exhausted. What's more: "We put money of our own into this venture," O'Toole said. But now, to their "vast disappointment," Mr. Finneran had departed for points unknown, leaving only a very vague word that he would repay everything as soon as he'd returned, a very vague date. This far I understood everything, and I was expecting a simple tracking job for us, Macy: they were going to ask us to find an address for their frightened and empty-handed Mr. Finneran-in-Hiding. Off the angry debtor had run in desperate hope of finding his wretched son-in-law-to-be, somehow squeezing money out of the rocks, and now after him would follow the irritable creditors, in the person of Tailor Enquiries Worldwide, Sydney Branch. Not a new story, a case I'd handled a hundred times before, though the details of this edition certainly intrigued. A simple enough task, and not inconvenient, since my itinerary was bound for Egypt anyhow, and one did like to have multiple clients paying expenses.

All correct, but I'd missed one wrinkle. "The man abandons his own home and daughter," warbles O'Toole, "to run off and spend his ill-gotten gains all alone. Quite a wretched thing to do, you'll be quick to agree."

"Ill-gotten gains?" I must've sounded a bit thick.

"Quite. We're owed most of what the professor found, that's all square and legal, in writing, nothing mysterious about it."

"It's in god damned legal writing!" bellows Kovacs, flecking saliva everywhere, the only six words he spoke the whole meeting.

"First, Mr. Ferrell," continues O'Toole, unaffected, "you'll discover with precision what amount our friend Mr. Finneran has already received by way of proceeds from the professor's digging and you'll report it to me discreetly. You'll let me know by cable where Mr. Finneran is, and where the gold is, and you'll await my instructions, which will be explicit."

This I hadn't seen coming, had almost forgotten the possibility: O'Toole and Kovacs were entirely convinced by Trilipush's cables reporting great finds and their share in them. They were sure there *was* treasure all right, and Finneran had already pocketed his dividends from it, which he should've used to pay back his debts, not to mention O'Toole's and Kovacs's dividends as well. But instead Finneran had run off to steal it all for himself, they thought. Until this moment, I'd been rather undecided on the question of an actual treasure: either Trilipush had found it and was planning to run off with it, or he'd never found it and had just taken Finneran's money to burnish his appearance to find some new victim to steal *more* money from in turn, to pay for his deprivations and his English estates. The question of *actual* treasure hardly mattered to my murder case, but O'Toole and Kovacs were believers. Did they think Trilipush was in on it with Finneran, the two of them were off stealing the gold together? "Don't be daft," O'Toole said. "Why would Trilipush wire us the news if he means to cheat us? No, the professor's on the up and up." O'Toole and Kovacs feared worse than that: either Finneran had already received money he'd no right to and now had sailed off with it never to be seen again, or he'd gone to Egypt to steal even more of O'Toole and Kovacs's winnings by ambushing Trilipush and lifting the whole load. "We don't care one way or the other what becomes of the Englishman," admitted O'Toole. "However, if as a result of anything untoward happening to him, then the number of partners is reduced by one, and our percentage of the final haul grows accordingly. But, to give our Chester the benefit of the doubt, he may be going over to secure the entire pie in some fashion that should not offend us silent partners. I could certainly understand this in his situation, and so be it, since this would mean he could acquit more of his responsibilities to us. And if that's the man's honourable intent, then that's cheering and fine with us, and he can come home in perfect confidence. Tell him that from me, detective."

We'd a peculiar brief, Macy, and things unsaid hovered, thick-like.

I set off to New York on the 3rd and caught the steamer for Alexandria on the 12th. I felt refreshed and daily stronger. Leaving America was just the ticket, and I remember standing on the deck, despite the swirling snow in New York Harbour, looking out to sea and knowing that we were coming to the end now, the end of ambiguity, the end of lies and hidden truths, of wealth protecting evil.

Finneran had taken his partners' money into his own accounts to send to Egypt. What had happened to it? He told me he never sent it. Did he lie? Either he'd wired that money to Trilipush or he hadn't. Meanwhile, either Trilipush had found his treasure or he hadn't. If he had, either Finneran was going to steal it or Trilipush already had and Finneran was trying to stop him. Either way, Trilipush was in immediate lethal danger from none other than Finneran, and ironically, *I* was Trilipush's best hope for protection. I hoped I wouldn't be too late. Finneran wanted revenge or treasure or both—I'd seen that clear enough. But I didn't want any more death in the desert, Macy, not I. Your aunt deserved better, and besides, the murders of Hugo Marlowe and Paul Caldwell, murders of which I no longer had the slightest doubt, were still to be accounted for, and I would not be thwarted. Justice and truth in the person of an Australian detective and his young American assistant were closing in on the malefactor. Would they arrive before petty vengeance and greed (in the person of a Boston businessman) reared their ancient and immortal heads?

Saturday, 2 December, 1922

WALL PANEL B: "THE MAGNIFICENT RISE TO POWER OF
ATUM-HADU, FINAL LORD OF THE TWO KINGDOMS"

Text: Atum-hadu—may he live mingled with the body of the god and in the company of Isis for one million years—was strong and brave. He made himself a soldier in the army of the old king Djedne-ferre Dudimose, who had seen the Lower Kingdom consumed by ene-mies as the young of a turtle are consumed by even an extremely lazy crocodile. Foreigners from the north and east plundered. Little men near the mouth of the Nile dressed themselves as kings just as children do but killed those who would not play with them. The few victories in these days came from the bite of Atum-hadu's arrows. All who saw him knew that Montu [the god of war—RMT] favoured him.

When at last General Atum-hadu seemed to have stopped the mil-lion enemies, the old king called for this son of Seth. Atum-hadu came to Thebes. The court was full of animals and acrobats, but there was not food. The people had their heads upon their knees, and had no de-sires. There was fear.

Atum-hadu [entered] the palace. He was beautiful and strong and bloodied from battle. He was rubbed with oils, given food and drink, and he took a young woman whose limbs pleased him, and no one knew if they should tell him that she was the old king's newest queen. Behind a curtain she showed Atum-hadu the colour of her limbs, and he was pleased. A messenger brought Atum-hadu to the king.

Illustration: The animals are not bad, it must be admitted, and show a certain improvement in style over Wall Panel A. The vast illustrations must have taken hours if not days to complete, and the artist's skills progress over the course of the wall; he controls his materials better, with less dripping. I would draw the tourist's eye to the depiction of the young Atum-hadu, embracing a woman with a warrior's hunger, then feeding dates to a giraffe. I would point out the tenderness displayed in his obvious love for the animals of the dying king's menagerie. The court of Djedneferre Dudimose is depicted with great care, and the array of statuary, furnishings, flower-garlanded pillars, and other trappings of royal power is elegantly achieved. The couch with the carved lion-head footboards, upon which Atum-hadu takes the reigning queen (with her remarkable birthmark), is a marvel of decorative arts, both as a painting and as it must have once appeared (and perhaps still does in an unopened chamber, or a nearby tomb annex elsewhere in Deir el Bahari). The broad lapis necklaces on the court's women are jewellery depictions of the first order.

Analysis: We have confirmation of Atum-hadu's historical context, as he comes after Djedneferre Dudimose, until now recognised as the last king of the XIIIth Dynasty.

Journal: Tired from my translation and transcription. Wedge my door into place and hobble down to the ferry. No post. Bank closed—a pity, as I am hoping that O'Toole and the other partners might take up the responsibilities CCF has so far fumbled. Feed the cats, though now I must approach the villa with as much discretion as I do the tomb. Return to my work after a sad and prolonged farewell to Maggie and the Rameses.

WALL PANEL C: "ATUM-HADU IS CHOSEN BY
THE DYING KING DJEDNEFERRE DUDIMOSE"

Text: The old king, Horus resident in the palace, could not rise. He said, "General Atum-hadu, I have lived 110 years. All around me are those that hunger to be king, though I cannot say why, as there will never again be joy in the black land. I do not fear death, Atum-hadu, but I fear that all that we have received will be lost. Guidance must be preserved for those who might someday restore our land. I pray there is time for scribes to write the glory of our past and hide the texts. This is all one can hope the next king might achieve, and even for this strength will be necessary. No man who is clever would wish to be king, but only a man who is clever can succeed. My ministers are not clever, and so they scheme for the throne. Atum-hadu, will you take my grand-daughter's daughter? Take that girl and our two kingdoms and our palace and our land and all the people of the land." And Atum-hadu said, "I will have them, King, though long will you still rule in health and life." And Djedneferre Dudimose said, "Oh, yes, of course, and crocodiles will fly. But now in seriousness, will you vanquish the priests and ministers who would see you fail?" "I will." "And will you, with your strength, preserve what can be preserved of the story of our land before night falls?" "I will." "And will you forsake all other tasks and pleasures to preserve and hide our glories?" "I will. I will do all that and more, King. I will drive out the invaders. I will defeat the rebels in the Delta. I will make the two kingdoms whole and strong to the sea. I will see the gods worshipped correctly as they have not been for many years. I will give to you many descendants, and I will assure your name is sung by all." And Djedneferre Dudimose said, "Do not exhaust yourself before you have taught my pet monkeys to shoot bows and arrows. Now stop talking. You have been surrounded by enemies from the moment you entered my chamber. Except for your queen-to-be and my Master of Largesse, who will support you. Forsake glory, it is too late. Only strive to preserve the memory of our great land." And the king was seized in the doom of death.

Atum-hadu called for the court. "The king has been seized in the doom of death," he said. "And behold before you Horus resident in the palace." And he slew the treacherous ministers. He called for papyrus, and he wrote a verse, and he told the scribes that they were to write about all of the land but only Atum-hadu would write about Atum-hadu. Then the Master of Largesse fell to his knees and swore fealty. Then Atum-hadu took as his queen the daughter of the daughter of the daughter of the dead king, and he moored himself to her and explored her grotto, and was well pleased.

Seventy days passed, and the Overseers of the Secrets finished preparing the mummy of the old king, great Djedneferre Dudimose. Atum-hadu sent everyone away and with his own hands carried the king's mummy to a secret place and buried him with his books and treasures and food, and sealed the tomb himself.

Illustration: A few highlights. We have here in the old king's retorts what is perhaps the first example of sarcasm in recorded history, and if this wall were more forgiving, it would be clear that the artist intended to depict the old king rolling his eyes at Atum-hadu's boastful plans, as if to say, "You do that, Atum-hadu. Tell me all about it in the underworld." One would see also the dying king's panicked frustration that the young buck was not taking the king's assignment seriously but was instead preparing to hold power for conventional reasons without taking the historical, last-man-turns-out-the-lights task to heart. Unfortunately, the artist was forced to paint on this dimpled and uneven stone, particularly bumpy here at Wall Panel C, quite difficult enough just to draw the glyphs, and was no doubt, after all this painting and composition, exhausted, hungry, dirty, thirsty, in pain, and swimming in smoke.

Analysis: Obviously, I do not know what anonymous scribe and artist decorated these walls, and the painstaking work of copying down the glyphs and translating the vast inscriptions into my notebook, all while carefully double-checking against my philology texts and the Budge dictionary, is taking a great deal of time, so I cannot say what is still to come. But I can say this: for those who are not experts, allow me to clarify what I have discovered in these wall chronicles so far: the clear determination of royal succession at the previously blurred end of the XIIIth Dynasty, an explanation for the lost tomb of the previously debatable Djedneferre Dudimose, further details of the life of the unquestionably real Atum-hadu, and a crystal-clear explanation as to why the only written proof of Atum-hadu's name had previously been found in the Admonitions written by the king himself. Carnarvon shall be the second man allowed in this chamber in 3500 years, and I will relish his dawning excitement at what all this might mean!

Sunday, 3 December, 1922

WALL PANEL D: "THE EARLY YEARS OF THE REIGN OF ATUM-HADU, FINAL KING OF THE TWO LANDS"

<u>Text:</u>   For ten floodings of the Nile, Atum-hadu made good his boasts. The Hyksos were stopped.

Where Atum-hadu ruled, business was conducted and crops gathered and the gods were worshipped and the scribes did as the old king instructed and the permanent night was held at bay and the palace was lit not by the fire of war but by the heart of Atum-hadu, a master of all things, the incarnation of Horus, but also of Atum, and with his own hand he created the world anew for the pleasure of his people.

Atum-hadu brought the wicked men of his youth to see his palace. He showed them the vast array of foods. They hungered at all they saw but were not permitted to eat, while Atum-hadu bit into a plum wrapped in a map of the night sky. The king gave his visitors a chance to apologise for rudeness delivered to the king when he was a boy. At dinner, the priest of his childhood was skewered like a veal and placed over the flame, and Atum-hadu spoke quietly to the large man, who wept in his anguish like a little boy. "Are you sorry?" Atum-hadu asked quietly. "I am, I am, master." "And do you think that your regret suffices?" "I do not know, master." "It does not. You stole something of mine, and it is not in your power to return it." "Tell me, great king and master, how I may serve you now." "Are you suffering?" "I am." "That is all the service I require of you." And Atum-hadu called for the priest's nieces and sisters and mother to be brought, and this surprised the priest, and in front of the dying priest the king engaged with the women of the priest's family in different combinations, sometimes with violence and weeping. Later the doom of death seized the priest, and when Atum-hadu deemed his flesh cooked, Atum-hadu removed him from the skewer himself and sliced pieces of the man's flesh, which he fed to the animals of the court. The priest's heart Atum-hadu did feed to the favoured royal dogs so this man's name and ka are forever forgotten.

Illustration: The wall seems to have been more forgiving here, and this text is accompanied by an illustration that again shows the artist's gradual technical improvement. In the most affecting of the dozens of scenes, the priest—naked, splayed, pierced most brutally, his muscular form no defence now against the grown and vengeful king— sobs. Atum-hadu's face displays an expression of relief, as if this exercise brought the king some measure of peace.

Analysis: This is a remarkable passage for two reasons. First, if historically accurate, it allows us a glimpse of the inner man, a man tormented even at the heights of royal power by his thirst to avenge his childhood. His soldiers were sent to gather his enemies, and his vengeance sessions (apparently more than one) were choreographed to provide him the maximum pleasure and his former tormentors the maximum shame and pain. Second, the story itself was of such importance to the king that it was included as an element of his illustrated biography to carry with him to the underworld.

Per immortality, it should be noted that the destruction of the priest's heart would mean that he could never be admitted into the underworld, where every applicant's heart is examined and weighed against a feather prior to admission. And, for good measure, Atumhadu made sure that the priest's very name would never again be uttered in this world, further insurance that immortality was impossible for the roasting, rotten priest.

Journal: Hobble down to ferry, post, bank, feed the cats. Post.

Margaret, no silence now, I beg you. You should be cabling, writing, somehow telling me all is well again. I will tell you someday of the anxiety in my belly every day that I did not hear from you, during every minute of December that you silently toyed with me, refusing to ease my pain with a word. Why are you doing this to me?

WALL PANEL E: "ATUM-HADU AND THE DAUGHTER
OF THE MASTER OF LARGESSE"

Text: After ten floodings of the Nile [1632 B.C.? — RMT], Atum-
hadu saw the most beautiful of all women. She bewitched him, and he
saw in her the spirit of Ma'at in the forms of Isis, the kindness of the
sweetest mother wrapped in the bright shining raiments of Hathor [the
moon and love goddess — RMT]. He asked for her name and was told
she was the daughter of the Master of Largesse. She approached him.
She asked for nothing, but in her magic she calmed the king, soothed
his belly, made him sleep, despite Hyksos and the memories of priests.

She enchanted his eyes so that he could look at none but her, and all
his other queens and all the women of the court wept at his absence
from their chambers and grottoes. Those women whom he no longer
needed found other men in the court, and together the men and women
who loved Atum-hadu formed a group to rival the official priests, and
they called Atum their only god, and pleasure their only practise.

Atum-hadu took the Master of Largesse's daughter as his leading
queen. That night he saw the colour of her limbs, and when her moment came she cried his name so loudly that silence fell everywhere in
the court, and she cried his name again, and again, and again, and soon
all those who had fallen silent took up the new queen's cry and the halls
of the palace echoed with a hundred throats crying his name in the
voice of pleasure, Atum-hadu, Atum-hadu, Atum-hadu, until the walls
of the palace trembled, and the hunting dogs howled in unison.

Monday, 4 December, 1922

WALL PANEL F: "ATUM-HADU IGNORES SETH'S WARNINGS"

Text: While Atum-hadu slept, troubles multiplied. The Hyksos approached. Time was not infinite, nor was the royal gold, and the Master
of Largesse had nothing to offer. Seth appeared and spoke: "Her father
is not a Master of Largesse but a Master of Betrayal. Are there not
other women who would be your queens? Look, they are littered

about, more numerous than flies on the droppings of a hippopotamus, surely another is ready to stand, bright-skinned with the neck of a white goose and heavy buttocks. Troubled Majesty, why do you resist?" Atum-hadu wept at Seth's words. He should destroy the love that bound him. He turned in their bed, lifted a knife to her white neck, and she slept in peace, and he looked at her face, and he sheathed his knife. He would not believe mischievous Seth.

Illustration: Most intriguing in this section of the wall, amidst the scenes of conjugal life tenderly depicted, is the recurring image of the Master of Largesse, a porcine figure forever lurking just out of the king's view. While Atum-hadu takes his queen's hand, her father hides behind a curtain and spies on them, his tongue wetting his lips. While Atum-hadu takes his queen to their bed and embraces her, her father hides under that same bed with carved lion-head footboards, his robes apart, and makes of himself a grotesque (and amusingly miniature) impersonator of Atum. While Atum-hadu sobs at his sleeping queen's side, his dropped knife on the floor at his feet, her father conspires behind his back, speaking to an unidentified but ominous figure. Far in the distance, the Hyksos soldiers mass.

This was not always the case, of course, and Quatrain 45 (Fragments A & C) describes Atum-hadu's trust in his adviser in earlier days, even when war with the Hyksos was pressing:

> *When two Egypts are torn apart,*
> *Twins pulled from a dying mother's cooling womb,*
> *Atum-hadu sobs and writhes at the pain in his heart,*
> *But his Master remains steadfast in the gloom.*

Journal: Post, bank. Would CCF stoop so low as to prevent the other partners from funding me? Cats, post. Have no more pre-paid cable forms, and can afford only an extremely brief cable to Margaret. The temporary abandonment of the villa is no great loss, except on days like today, when my stomach is raging against Fate and I am the innocent bystander who suffers most of all.

**CABLE. LUXOR TO MARGARET FINNERAN, BOSTON,
4 DEC. 1922, 4.13 P.M. PLSACKLVRMT.**

<u>*Margaret:*</u>   You are killing me with your barbed silence. Today I
cabled you simply asking that you please acknowledge my love. Will
there come a day when you and I compare our contemporaneous journals and I read aloud to you that on the 4th of December I was fearing
that I had lost you forever, and you will laugh at my silliness because
on the 4th you were simply asleep? Or heading by train to warmer cli-
mates? Or there was a concerted effort at heartrending chaos by the
love-hating telegraph boys of Boston, all riled up by Communist agita-
tors, viciously delivering my cable to an elderly lady while you received
orders for a million pounds of chocolate?

But if you are not waiting for me, there is nothing for me in Boston.

(*UNSENT, FOUND IN MARGARET FINNERAN MACY'S PRIVATE PAPERS AFTER HER DEATH*)

Dec. 4

Dear Ralph,

*There are things I should tell you. Daddy told me things about
you, and he made me write you to break our engagement, and so I
did. And then I slept. And then Ferrell came into my room, and he
was so happy he had done all this, had split us apart. And he said
the most horrible things about you, said you killed this boy Paul
and your friend Marlowe, all of this horrible nonsense that I knew
wasn't true, and that's when I knew that none of it had been true,
you stealing Daddy's money and lying about Oxford. Oh, Ralph,
Ferrell had been lying to Daddy and me all along and caused all
this trouble between you and me and Daddy, and I didn't know
how to make it right again, all the damage he had done, and I
screamed at him and told him what I thought of him. I was still*

sleepy, you see, from what Inge had given me to calm me down
after Daddy told me that you only pretended to love me for his
money. I should have laughed at them both, but I believed them,
at first. I am so sorry.

I should have told you what makes me ill, but I haven't. It's
not me, it's only stronger than me right now, but I am afraid that
if you knew

Dear Ralph,

Would you love me less because there are things that are
stronger than me?

Ferrell was very angry with me, at the end, when he came into
my room and shook me awake. I enjoyed making him angry, letting myself do what I am good at, which is making people angry
and then making them laugh about it, I can do that when I want
to. Everyone always says so. I could always make it OK again.

Ferrell has ruined everything, hasn't he? And I don't know
how to repair any of it, especially now that he did what he did to
me. What he did to me, Ralph. What will you think about it? I
tried to make him stop, I swear. We were alone in the house.
Daddy was gone, and Inge, too. He sent Inge away, Ralph, and
then came upstairs.

I cannot find all your letters to me. I think he took some.

It is my fault, I made him angry and could not make him stop.
It is my fault. You will not want me now.

I was wrong and I am so sorry. I am sorry I ever believed them
about you. If I hadn't believed even a little, this wouldn't have
happened. I am so sorry. He said such terrible things about you,
and I only wanted to tell him he was wrong. Antony and Cleopatra just sat there the whole time, they didn't bark or try to help me,
they just watched, and then, when he left, they just looked at me,
like they knew it was my fault.

Dear Ralph, I am writing to you bec

Dear Ralph, please forgive me for

Tuesday, 5 December, 1922

Silence at post and bank. The cats are fine and fond in our new feeding place out of view of the villa. I am sure they no longer bother visiting the villa at all, now that I meet them here instead.

Take mint tea in an *ahwa* where the waiters do not recognise me, though I have been there two dozen times before. Back to my labours.

WALL PANEL G: "THE ANNUNCIATION OF THE
THIRD BIRTH OF ATUM-HADU"

Note: The text here seems closely related to, perhaps an intentional expansion on, Quatrain 56 (Fragments A & B only):

A feast and dancing and pleasures abound.
Can they distract the king from pressing matters of state?
The agony of his ailments, the death of a hound,
This war that laps at the shore and never abates.

<u>Text:</u>   In the eleventh year of his reign, Atum-hadu's palace glowed with another feast night, beauty to be carried into eternity. The main hall was open to the air and covered with billowing linen. The high torches shed their light on the edges of the linens, and the roof seemed to burn red with a fire that never consumed. Peacocks roasted over columns filled with fire of many colours. The columns were covered with spells against the torments of the king's stomach, but to no avail. The smell of the birds brought cats and dogs into the court. Amongst them was the cat Atum-hadu loved most dearly, and she leapt into his lap.

Atum-hadu lay across his throne and stroked the cat. With his other hand he held a long spear, thin and flimsy, used only by the women in their combats where they would fight and die when Atum-hadu tired of them. He pierced a peacock and drew from its flesh a stream of juice.

He pierced a bound Hyksos prisoner and drew from its flesh the Hyksos commander's plans.

Atum-hadu's calm questions belied his fury and the boiling in his belly. The wrath of his internal cobras was visible on the surface of the king's abdomen and in the map of cataracted Nile on his bronze temple. Despite the lavish rewards he had dispensed to magicians of medicine, still he suffered. There was no reason for his pain, and there was no relief.

Until this night. Ma'at herself appeared, glowed as hot and bright as the sundisk, so that none in the court might gaze at her. All pressed their faces to the floor, all but Atum-hadu, Ma'at's ferocious lover. Atum-hadu rose from his throne and his stomach released him. Ma'at embraced him in softness, and she spoke to him in the soft language of a cobra, as she and Atum-hadu rose into the sky and conversed.

Ma'at spoke: "O Atum-hadu, beloved of the gods and of the people, you suffer because in your belly, rotting and bubbling, is your mortal past, your first childhood, the mere thought of which boils your insides. Inside you too, grows the future which must come, as the old king predicted. Great son of Atum, the end of the land will accompany the end of your second life. Your final birth approaches. You must clean your past away."

Ma'at kissed the king and disappeared. Atum-hadu descended to his throne; the dancers, cooks, and priests rose. The sounds of the court returned: twin acrobats praising Atum, women soothing their infants, small boys demanding that their fathers play with them, an old man calming his shaking son, soldiers drinking beer. The body of the prisoner drew the attention of Atum-hadu's hounds, and the cat, the king's favourite friend, lapped at the pool of Hyksos blood spreading across the floor like a map being constantly redrawn. Even in death, this display of Hyksos expansion was not lost on the king.

Soldiers entered bearing another Hyksos spy. "Atum-hadu would like them to understand," the king announced, and called for the keeper of the royal menagerie to bring a young serpent, one that carried no venom. Soldiers held the boy, and Atum-hadu seized a knife and cut a small hole in the boy's side, opened the intestine, and inserted the snake tail-first into the gap. He called for priests to sew the hole so that only the serpent's head emerged, then instructed his soldiers to carry the boy back where his own people could find him, to leave him with plenty of food and drink. "He must be found alive with Atum-hadu's sign in him," said Atum-hadu.

Illustration: Of the extensive and marvellous illustration covering the whole wall from floor to ceiling to the right of the opening into the Second Empty Chamber, some elements are particularly worthy of our immediate praise. As elsewhere, the animals are brilliantly rendered (the roasting peacock, the purring cat), as are the furnishings of what was certainly a richly but not tastelessly decorated court, where the accent was on pleasures of the bed and table. The court scenes boast oviform jars and lotiform cups and alabaster bowls, the leopard skins, the couch and chariots, the gauzy women's clothes, the king's skirt, and his ornately carved weapons and magnificent throne, the back of which bears what appears to be bas-relief in gold, showing the king in the form of a lion trampling his tiny enemies.

Journal: Post, bank, cats.

Wednesday, 6 December, 1922

Journal: Post, bank, cats.

WALL PANEL H: "THE HYKSOS RENEW THEIR OFFENSIVE"

Text: Despite Ma'at's visit, vicious beasts still caroused in the king's belly. The Hyksos chief was a quiet man but arrogant, dressed in gold. Word reached the Hyksos chief that the great Atum-hadu was weakened by his infirmity and that the better half of the country was now vulnerable again after a decade of bold defence. The Hyksos swept into the [Upper Kingdom]. The battles were fierce, and Atum-hadu led his troops when he was able. He fought like a lion, except he was often cut down by the pain in his belly or forced to turn his back and squat.

Even now, Atum-hadu could still have conquered the Hyksos. But in this time of most desperate need, the king was unable to find his Master of Largesse, that vulva of a whore. The king's enemy had vanished, stealing the queen away with him.

And soon the Hyksos victory would be assured.

<u>Illustrations:</u>   Most affecting to the viewer is the sight of the Master of Largesse, pulling the queen by her hair, imprisoning her as Atum-hadu hunts for her in vain.

<u>Journal:</u>   I have worked on translating and transcribing the inscriptions all day again. Remarkable what Budge's unwieldy dictionary does not include, and to recall that he had the gall to criticise my translations in *Desire and Deceit*. Post, bank, cats.

Thursday, 7 December, 1922

<u>Journal:</u>   Cats, bank, post.

WALL PANEL I: "THE APPROACHING END OF THE BLACK LAND"

<u>Text:</u>   The capital was silent. The people kept their heads on their knees. Desires were weak. And still Atum-hadu demanded music, joy, women. Often he returned from battle, his armour dripping red on the floors, and he strode into the palace and had two slave girls as other men have a drink of water, then demanded a brush to compose verse. He inspired those of the court who had decided to carry pleasure to the end of time, and again the court sang with desperate happiness. Hyksos spies returned to their little king and told him that the enemy would never surrender. If the army fought as his court loved, perhaps this would have been true.

"The end of everything is coming," Atum-hadu told them, and the word was passed all over the court, and there was weeping and fear and also the sound of acrobats and lovers and music. "The end of everything is coming."

Illustration: The king in battle is a magnificent sight. He stands in
a war chariot. Typical of Egyptian illustrations, he is shown much
larger than his enemies, who barely reach his knee, while in the background, the dapper leader of the Hyksos shivers with fear and conster-
nation. Also typical of Egyptian war-art, Atum-hadu is shown
accompanied in his chariot by his forebears, previous kings of Egypt,
all of whom (though smaller than he) urge him on.

Journal: Cats. Bank, post: nothing and nothing.

My father's friends were all military men, generals and high officers,
soldiers retired and active. I did not know it as a boy, of course, since I
knew them merely as Uncle Bunny or Old Lloyd, and only later would
I learn that Uncle Bunny had crushed such-and-such Khan in the
Afghan fighting. But when I knew him, he was just a fine old fellow in
hunting tweeds who thought nothing of letting me paint his face all
black so I could be Pharaoh and he my African enemy. Biographies im-
mortalise all these old warriors as lamb-gentle (despite being bloodied
in Victoria's wars all over the globe, serving as her stern viceroys, holding restive natives in their place with a firm English hand). But at Trilipush Hall the biographers were accurate. I remember one or another
eye-patched hero of the Empire on his knees in the mud with me, band-
aging the paw of one of the hounds injured in a hunt. It was as if I had
a dozen fathers in those happy years.

Friday, 8 December, 1922

Journal: Cats. Bank and post closed.

WALL PANEL J: "ATUM-HADU CONSIDERS HIS
APPROACHING IMMORTALITY"

Text: The Hyksos had become like a swollen river and could not
be kept from overflowing the banks. In one respite, Atum-hadu walked
alone in the night, high upon a cliff across the Nile. There would be no

king after him; Horus would not reside in the palace. How to preserve the writings recorded for eleven floodings, and his goods to stock his boat? Where is his queen? Where is the Master of Largesse? Seth appeared, and twelve vultures carried the king down the cliff to the ground. With bursts of fire from the vultures' mouths, Seth cut the rock. "Here, my son, you shall make your crossing in safety, and this land shall be remembered for a million million years."

Illustrations: In a series of pictures, Atum-hadu is shown standing atop a ridge of earth that is unmistakably the cliff wall separating what is now the Valley of the Kings from Deir el Bahari. The king is alone, it is night (the goddess Nut, covered in stars, stands beside him). He is lost in thought. Here he looks down on the Valley, there on Deir el Bahari, as if debating where to start his tomb and hide his immortality. In the distance, battles rage. Seth, his mythical father whose mysterious head now resembles an anteater's, and twelve magic vultures appear to the king and hoist him down to what appears to be the very path outside this very tomb. And here the vultures, spitting fire, cut an opening into the stone of Egypt itself. Seth leads Atum-hadu into the passage, unmistakably Door A and the Empty Chamber. The final drawing is of Atum-hadu standing back outside, a floor map of the tomb glowing magically on the cliff face. It is, as far as we have so far opened this tomb, unmistakably a map of the complex I am standing in at this very moment.

Analysis: We must see past the myth to the historical facts. One specific day the war was clearly and unmistakably a lost cause. And in that time of palpable but still unconsummated doom, the king most certainly realised that he needed a tomb built in secret. I would hypothesise that he—no doubt travelling alone and incognito—scouted areas where he might make safe passage to the underworld, with whatever furnishings and baggage he could efficiently transport all by himself. And, though this is plainly speculation, it seems possible that the story on the wall should be read as the happy "miracle" of Atum-hadu stumbling one night onto an open tomb, built and rejected some years earlier for some other forgotten soul, or perhaps a tomb that had been plundered and left bare, perhaps storage caverns used by another dynasty's architects or workmen, perhaps a hermitage occupied only by easily slaughtered hermits. There are several possibilities, but it seems quite likely that Atumhadu, when he needed it most, found a suitable space that could be quickly converted to his needs, without the time, trouble, and risk [see essay on Tomb Paradox] of architects, workmen, or daylight operations. I can easily imagine Atum-hadu feeling that such a fortuitous discovery could only have been effected with the timely and loving assistance of a god-father.

Journal: As soon as this chamber is completely transcribed into these notebooks, the hieroglyphs fully copied and translated, I will take the Earl of Carnarvon on a private tour, and the neat trick of changing horses in midstream will be gracefully and drily executed.

The twelve pillars of the History Chamber support marvellous illustrations as well, covering each pillar nearly from floor to ceiling in a single, giant depiction of a discrete event, with a short explanatory text. Now, observe: if the pillars were executed by the same artist as the wall panels, he had clearly grown far more confident of his abilities and materials, as they are of an altogether grander dimension and mastery than the wall histories.

PILLAR ONE, TEXT: THE BOY ATUM-HADU SETS HIS ENEMIES AGAINST EACH OTHER AND ESCAPES TO THE ARMY.

Illustration: A soldier attacks a man and a woman while Atumhadu (laughing? crying?) escapes to join the army of Djedneferre Dudimose.

Saturday, 9 December, 1922

J: Cats. P: nothing. B: closed.

PILLAR TWO, TEXT: ATUM-HADU ENTERS THE COURT OF
DJEDNEFERRE DUDIMOSE AND IS RECEIVED WARMLY.

Illustration: Atum-hadu receives a particular form of tribute from
the kneeling wife of Djedneferre Dudimose and other kneeling female
members of the court while a long-lashed giraffe gazes on, masticating
at the sight, and Atum-hadu himself looks skyward and watches acrobats fly, throwing each other high above the palace floor.

PILLAR THREE, TEXT: ATUM'S WARRIOR DESTROYS THE KING'S
ENEMIES.

Illustration: Atum-hadu, in the form of a man-headed lion, tram-
ples the enemies of Egypt, who fall in a hail of arrows. High above,
Horus, Atum, Ra, Isis, Osiris, Seth, Montu, Hathor, and Ma'at look
down with marked approval.

PILLAR FOUR, TEXT: ATUM-HADU BECOMES KING AND POET BOTH.

Illustration: Still standing on the bodies of the treacherous ministers of Djedneferre Dudimose, Atum-hadu instructs his court. He gently rests one hand on the head of the late king, and in his other he holds
a sheet of papyrus. One can just make out the hieroglyphic writing on
that papyrus in an extraordinary touch of uncommon verisimilitude
and detail in Egyptian art. It is nothing less than Quatrain 1. The detail
of the tiny black hieroglyphs on the tan sheet of papyrus must have
taken the artist hours to perfect. Considering the conditions in which
he was likely working (smoke, heat, hunger, poverty, approaching enemies), his accomplishment is nothing less than genius.

J: C. P: still nothing.

Sunday, 10 December, 1922

J: Cats, bank, post. Nothing.

PILLAR FIVE, TEXT: DAYS OF PEACE AND
PLEASURE IN ATUM-HADU'S COURT.

Illustration: This pillar is worth a moment's analysis. It was probably only natural that Atum-hadu's court was prey to nostalgic impulses, the mad desire to peer over one's shoulder for a golden age. At a
time of encroaching darkness and a pervasive sense of doom, such an
instinct was probably stronger still. That said, it is clear that Atum-
hadu (even as his scribes were engaged in the previous king's nostalgic
preservation project) was dedicated to making his era a golden age *in
itself* and his court the centre of a reborn Egypt. His was a simultaneous *anti*-nostalgic project, particularly difficult in times of defeat and
despair. But to this end, this pillar shows his court as he must have
wished it to be recalled at its peak of glory. Musicians in tunics decorated with multi-coloured lozenges perform while a woman leads several dogs in a parade of tricks. Celebrants of the cult of Atum abound,
in a vast array of mathematical combinations, from rows of solitary
worshippers to complex pyramidal arrangements requiring multitudes.
Men are tied down with symbolic chains woven of peacock feathers,
and they are lashed by nude women and, at the centre of all this activity, the unmistakable king himself, nude, surrounded by adoring
crowds of gentle, long-fingered beauties with sleepy eyes.

PILLAR SIX, TEXT: THE FALSE FATHERS.

Illustration: This curious pillar with its inexplicable title depicts a
series of executions and tortures, all overseen by Atum-hadu, whose
expression is one of stern necessity. A soldier is fed to a crocodile. A
priest is skewered and roasted alive (see Wall Panel D). A young
working man (attacked in Pillar One) is here pursued by a crowd of
what appear to be armed children, while a donkey mounts the woman
shown with him on Pillar One.

J: Post, bank—nothing. Cats. Maggie is so funny! She knows
which route I take now to bring her food, and she leads the Rameses to

meet me there, so I need not approach the villa at all. She likes her fish, we learn tonight, a little Nile perch, while the toms stick to milk and scraps of meat. I would love to have the three of them across the river with me, but it would hardly be fair, to them or to the delicate work I am uncovering.

Mr. Trilipush,

It will interest you to know that, given the apparent magnitude of Mr. Carter and Lord Carnarvon's find in the tomb of Tut-ankh-Amen, making it without question one of the great discoveries in all Egyptological history, Mr. Carter will need vast resources to complete the enormous task ahead of him: cataloguing, preserving, and removing the contents of this frankly "overstuffed" tomb. Given the tasks, which will certainly take Mr. Carter several years, the curator of the New York Metropolitan Museum has put at Mr. Carter's disposal many of that institution's resources currently dedicated to the Metropolitan's own excavations. Specifically, Mr. Lythgoe has offered Mr. Carter the services of photographers, artists, skilled workmen, philologists, chemical and criminological experts, and others. As you can well imagine, this reduces greatly the likely productivity of Professor Winlock and the amount of surface area he can profitably examine in the Deir el Bahari area, at least for the present season and perhaps much of next season as well. And so, Professor Winlock has been kind enough to inform me that if the Antiquities Service wishes to issue temporary concessions for areas that are outside his current area of investigations, he would be willing in the interest of science to consider the temporary partitioning of his concession. Considering your previous interest, I would like to offer you the opportunity to resubmit an application. While the Antiquities Service reserves the right not to issue any new concessions, any project showing a likelihood of success and professional management will certainly be considered.

With every good wish, please believe that I am your devoted and unwavering servant,

> Pierre Lacau, Director-General of
> the Antiquities Service

Monday, 11 December, 1922

<u>Journal:</u>   Cats, bank, post: and there an overdue reward to my patience awaits me in my *poste restante*, honouring my time in the wilderness when none would support me! Lacau has offered me my concession at last.

Slow down and savour these events! I raced to Carter's site, without even cleaning off the traces of my days and nights in the field. The pain in my leg was excruciating as I set off to find Lord Carnarvon. The tide has finally turned, but I turned back myself, returned to the tomb for a moment to mark this down, because in my hurry, I nearly forgot to take a copy of *Desire and Deceit in Ancient Egypt*. I have just now inscribed it, "To Lord Carnarvon, Egypt's patron, knowledge's financier, Atumhadu's Champion, Atum's most creative right hand, from his admirer and dare I say partner, R. M. Trilipush, 11 December 1922." Off again!

I am wondering if Lacau is not part of a far-flung conspiracy to break my heart. I arrived at Carter's site but found no trace of him or the Earl, no crowd of tourists, no pashas demanding unholy peeks at Tut. Instead the tomb was covered again. I asked one of the numerous native guards where his masters were. "His Lordship's returned to England with Lady Evelyn. Mr. Carter has gone to Cairo to see them off." Gone, My Lordship, gone to London on the big boat. I could hear Carter's simpering relief, squiring Carnarvon away from me just as my opportunity ripened, then quickly rotted.

Bank. Despite my rigid economies, I am nearly out of money. My backers have abandoned me. My rivals are determined to see me fail. Post: send *Desire and Deceit* and a detailed proposal to Carnarvon's estate in England, but this will take far too long. Merely what I have discovered to date would win me a new backer, I am certain. Go home? Wed Margaret with nothing to show for my time here, with no job at home, and her still under the influence of Ferrell? And even if I could refresh her affections, we would live off of what? Sit and wait for Carnarvon's word? Show him the History Chamber next season?

Carter's up in Cairo.

Sleep indoors for the first time in eleven days. I left the Victrola 50 down at the tomb, unfortunately, as I would appreciate the help in falling asleep, and there is no gramophone here.

Tuesday, 12 December, 1922

<u>J</u>:　After a fair breakfast, ferry back across to the east bank to the cats. PB: nothing and nothing. Ferry and hobble back across to Deir el Bahari. Rest often. I will finish my work, present my findings to Harvard when I return, have my job back. Or to a museum. Or a different university.

PILLAR SEVEN, TEXT: A NEWLY REVEALED QUATRAIN IN CLASSIC ATUM-HADUAN STYLE IS WRITTEN AT THE BASE OF THE PILLAR:

My Master of Largesse returns with empty hands,
Pleads illness, war, bad luck, paresse; his antics spoil all my plans.
I will take his daughter in front of him, sneer at his mingled shame and lust,
Then, finished with her, I will cut out his lying tongue and drop it in the dust.

<u>Illustration:</u>　The Master of Largesse, corpulent and shifty-eyed, pleasures himself alone in a dark room before the figurines of the temple, while with his free hand he hides the king's money. In a second scene nearer the ceiling, he speaks with a man we can safely presume to be the chief of the invading Hyksos.

The obvious rage of the king, contrasted with the illustration of the quite alive, quite be-tongued Master of Largesse double-crossing the king, demonstrates Atum-hadu's frustration: betrayed by his protector, he is unable to find and destroy him. The king blusters with weightless words.

PILLAR EIGHT, TEXT: TWO MORE NEW QUATRAINS:

He was satisfied with this one, asked for no more,
But her betrayal proved she was a whore.
He replaced her in his bed and state
With not one woman but with eight.

She's a wretched crocodile who forsakes a king,
And when she is punished he begins to sing.
She hangs from the ceiling, and sad-eyed, betrayed men come from afar
Daily to soothe themselves by viewing her weeping and her scars.

Illustration: Most remarkable. A single figure portrait, the queen, larger than life, in three-quarters. Even millennia later her beauty is undeniable. The anger in the quatrains is belied by this effortless depiction of her grace and beauty, as if she were already a painful memory rather than a living presence. It is a painting of remembered love, or a wish for some other world where they could be together without pressures of state or battle. The second quatrain seems to be more fantasy than reality, as there is no mention on the wall panels of his queen being tortured and displayed for the emotional satisfaction of the kingdom's rejected men.

PILLAR NINE, TEXT: ATUM-HADU SPIES UPON HIS ENEMIES.

Illustration: While the Hyksos general conspires with Atum-hadu's Master of Largesse, Atum-hadu himself is shown in the Hyksos general's camp, unrecognised, and in his tent, unrecognised, and finally in his home, lying in his bed, reading his most secret plans, unrecognised.

PILLAR TEN, TEXTLESS.

Illustration: Studies, perhaps, for Pillar Eight. She is shown in thirty different views, and sometimes only her head or hands. Her smile alone is attempted a dozen times. She is depicted asleep and awake, seated and striding, in a variety of costumes, with hounds at her feet, beautiful and beloved.

J: CPB. Nothing. Back across to the west. The bed is really a welcome change. I wonder if I could house the cats here.

Wednesday, 13 December, 1922

J: CPB. Someone (Carter? Finneran? Ferrell?) has poisoned the bank tellers against me, and they stage a little drama, making much of my injury and issues of hygiene, grabbing at straws to carry out some unseen enemy's illegal orders, barring me from further daily enquiries.

PILLAR ELEVEN, TEXT: THE END APPROACHES.

Illustration: Atum-hadu in distress, alone, seated on his throne, doubled over, clutching his belly. On the reverse (north) side, he is depicted with a literal crocodile gnawing at his insides. The Hyksos troops are shown massing in a hundred different directions. The dapper, smug Hyksos general stands ominously nearby and leers at the writhing Atum-hadu, perhaps with an implication that it is his magic causing the king's torments?

PILLAR TWELVE, TEXT: THE END OF DAYS.

Illustration: It is night. Atum-hadu, dead, is carried over the shoulder of a single unidentifiable friend. The friend carries him towards the miraculous, glowing tomb, where Seth and the vultures await. Meanwhile, the Hyksos rape and burn and defecate as they storm the palace. They do not notice the escaping ally carrying the dead king.

This is worth a word of analysis as, historically, it still remains to us to explain Atum-hadu's solution to the Tomb Paradox. Certainly, Atum-hadu discovered this space, and decided to make it his tomb. Probably, he furnished it secretly on his own, perhaps over the space of a year or more. Finally, abandoned by his ministers, army, priests, Master, queen, he must have had still one single, trusted friend. This friend is anonymous, perhaps someone from boyhood, perhaps only recently met and taken into the royal confidence. It must have been someone with artistic skills and with no earthly ties. Let us hypothesise a court artist whose family was killed by the Hyksos and who, in his misery, accepted a strange commission from his lord and master: in exchange for (a) painting the walls of the king's tomb (almost certainly while the king was still alive and dictating the images to the artist), and (b) assuring that the king was brought there secretly immediately upon his death the humble artist received—what? What would he value? Gold? A military-escorted escape route from the Hyksos? Some magical protection? We must continue to think.

J: CP. I am growing accustomed to beds again, a forgotten respite after the smoke and must of the tomb.

Thursday, 14 December, 1922

J: Forced to be up and out in a hurry, end of soft beds for now. Have that terrible sensation of having forgotten something, but that is not uncommon and not always true. Calm down over a mint tea at my favourite *ahwa*.

Post—nothing. Off to the cats, then.

Margaret, today brings another cruelty that I cannot even begin to I cannot control my grief. I am mewling like a child, cannot bear to write it, cannot believe it.

Friday, 15 December, 1922

How would he recognise *the* moment when the end had come? Did he simply fight until he fell in battle? Or did he know before, feel it in some specific loss, something he saw destroyed that became at that moment the symbol of everything certain to be destroyed later?

Saturday, 16 December, 1922

Work. Miserable bowels.

Sunday, 17 December, 1922

(FIG. G: THE FIRST SEVEN CHAMBERS,
ENDING WITH THE SHRINE TO BASTET, 17 DEC., 1922)

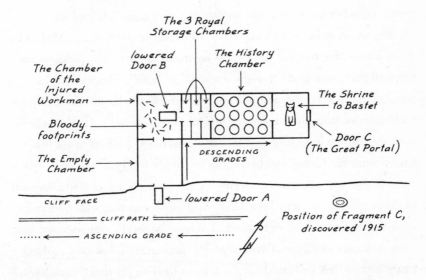

Bastet was, of course, the feline-headed goddess of ancient Egypt, and although there is no mention of her in the Admonitions, one entire chamber of Atum-hadu's tomb is dedicated to her cult. The room is, like the rest of the tomb, brilliantly decorated from an historiographical standpoint, though less successfully from an art-critical view. In the centre of the room, a symbolic union with Bastet is indicated in the form of a mummified cat. The cat seems to have been preserved in the traditional manner, wrapped in linens (emblazoned with decorative motifs of sphinxes, vultures, and cobras, as well as hieroglyphs warning of Horus's cardiovoric wrath against any tomb-robber wicked enough to disturb the shrine), and laid to rest directly on the tomb's bare floor, a comment, perhaps, on Atum-hadu's domination of the feline elements in traditional religion? A shortage of furniture in the hurried last moments, sealing in the king while Hyksos monkeys chattered in the middle distance?

The only ornament on the cat's mummy is a beautiful collar in pristine condition, black leather with a silver-and-sapphire pendant centred on the poor beast's wrapped chest. A tribute to the goddess Bastet, yes, but perhaps also a very human, very earthly desire to show a faithful animal that it was loved, that its presence and dignity and affection were appreciated, to thank her for her service in this world and the next. To let her know she was significant, that tears fell for her.

The ancients believed that at the moment the tomb was sealed, it became a hive of activity. Statues and figurines came to life, pictures on the wall grew real and three-dimensional, symbolic illustrations expanded to fulfil their meanings, and mummies (the king's, most importantly) woke from their temporary sleep, reconceived and reborn for their journey to immortality. Statues of warriors (such as those that Carter stumbled into) would have come to life to guard the king. Pictures of money, food, arms, serving girls, celebrations, concubines—all of this would have served the king. And this being the case, human or animal sacrifice, whilst not unheard of, was generally unnecessary and thus very rare in Egypt. Given that, the presence of this very real cat likely means that an actual cat died, most likely a cat that Atum-hadu would have known and loved. This was probably his very cat, described in the History Chamber. Knowing what we do, we can speculate that he would have insisted that this being, which he adored and which adored him, must of course sit on his lap purring for all eternity. He raised her to immortality, promoted her from cat to cat-goddess.

It is late. I am tired.

Monday, 18 December, 1922

WALL PANEL K: "ATUM-HADU WITHDRAWS FROM COURT"

Text: Defeat followed on defeat. Atum-hadu prepared. Under protection of Nut, he carried goods from his palace across the Nile, and a friend illustrated his life upon these walls. He returned to court. The palace was lively, the people fornicated and drank. "Flee!" Atum-hadu ordered, but they laughed. "Do you know what is coming?" he demanded. "We do, and this is how we will wait," they replied, and he loved them. The master of musicians bowed to him. "Here everything is magical." Atum-hadu loved this gentle man. He embraced him in brotherly farewell.

Atum-hadu found one of his cats choked on a fish bone. The king's sorrow devoured him, as if he were an old woman. The king wept at the implacable enemy that had chosen Atum-hadu at birth, wept like a child until sleep came.

Journal: When Carnarvon sees the twenty chambers still to come in this vast subterranean complex — even if they contain no further art- or treasure — such a mysterious maze in itself will justify a second, fully funded expedition back to Deir el Bahari. Marlowe and I were unquestionably right: the tomb is here or near, quite close, perhaps only one hill away from this temple of history, or I am doubting too much, and the full tomb *is* here, behind one more door. Enough.

I take the sledgehammer to Door C, though I can hardly stand on my burning leg, and my gut is full of fire and smoke. My arms are puny. Two hours of hammering, and all I have is dust and pebbles throughout the Bastet Shrine, powdering the cat-goddess. I fell asleep just now. I will try the door again.

Evening, I believe, and now I have this:

(FIG. I: THE FIRST EIGHT CHAMBERS, 18 DEC., 1922)

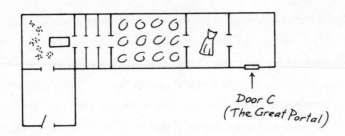

Door C
(The Great Portal)

Extraordinary find, beyond wildest dreams. The _____ Chamber, the Hall of _____. The Chamber of Mysteries. The Hall of the Magician. The

Tuesday, 19 December, 1922

<u>*Journal:*</u>   Fell asleep last night on the floor, exhausted from work, and this morning I am stiff in leg and neck. It was only from the hallooing that I realised I had been woken by Carter of all people. I was just able to reach Door A before he entered the tomb uninvited. He should know better, the old fool. I hobbled outside to greet the grand lord taking time out from his garish pit to visit the working man. He had me at a disadvantage in his efforts to sneak past me, as I was blinking, nearly blind in the sunshine.

"Hard to find you over here. So, it's true what Carnarvon said? Uncovered something quick-quick, have you?" he asked. "My God, man, are you all right?" Carter was, as always, unnaturally obsessed with my health.

"Woke me from a dead sleep, old man, is all."

"Well, congratulations to you, Trilipush. The gods seem to be smiling on us all this season."

"Quite."

"I take it you've notified Lacau, for an Inspector's visit. What do you think you have in there?"

"In good time, Carter."

He gazed at the opening of Door A in that nasty manner of his, no praise or criticism, just a calm and disinterested Eye floating disembodied, judging. "You know, I've found more dry holes in my time than I care to recall."

"Even the mighty ones guess, Carter!" I could not stop laughing at his nervous speculations. "Do just try and wait, old boy. You will have a tour with the rest of the swells."

"Of course. Well, do have the Inspector in, Trilipush. Glad to know where to find you if we need you. Do let me know if I can be of any assistance." He turned away, then came back at once, reaching into his pocket; I suspected a weapon, and cursed myself for having left my Webley inside. "Nearly forgot why I came. This arrived at my camp, mixed up with our post." He handed me a letter from my fiancée and pottered off in his superior way, not looking back to see if his arrows had landed. God alone knows how long he has been intercepting my mail, which letters he has kept.

Nov. 29

> So everything is clear to me now. Daddy has just explained it and asked me to sign a cable and write you a letter. So here it is: I release you. I must be a joke to you, Ralph. I suppose I disgust you, just a rich girl too stupid to see what's going on. So now you are free. I must even thank you, to be fair, because for all the time I thought you loved me, I was happy. And even if Daddy tells me now it wasn't true, that you wanted only his money from me, that is still not so terrible, because for a while I was going to marry an English Lord and explorer. I hate you. I hate you and I don't know why I ever didn't hate you. Ferrell and you and Daddy are all hateful. I hope you enjoy our money and your precious treasure and the hell with you all.
>
> *Margaret Finneran*

(Tuesday, 19 December, 1922, continued)

Carter's little missile was nothing at all, just an expanded version of your cable of the 29th, and no less a forgery, though it appears to be your handwriting. They must have medicated you thoroughly before that conjuror's trick. But now the best antidote to such venom is work.

The hammer blows might as well have been delivered directly to my weeping leg, Margaret. I ran through the ninth chamber and pounded against its next door until a crack appeared, and I looked, and then I wept, I think, for hours. I confess it to you. More than I have wept since I was a young boy, before I had yet learnt that tears are the most useless, most unquenching liquid there is.

A sliver of moon is enough to conjure you up, confess to you.

What might I still accomplish, if I begin again, back home. Home? Could I argue you back to me? You need success. Your father, too. Without it, I would bore you. I sparkled for you, once, I think. And with this find? The forged cable will become real after the fact. A neat trick, that.

What would she feel if I were something else? I have any number of possibilities within me. Would she be troubled if I were someone else? Of course she would: we respect the well-born, well-raised con-querors. Me.

It does not matter. I am who I am and you love that man and so he will come home to you. I will start again, take you away with me, away from your father and everything else that poisons you. I will burn all these papers, and we will start again from nothing, far away. I will sleep now, and when I wake I will throw all this away. A failed expedi-tion is not the end of anything, does not even prove that I am wrong. The actual tomb may be hidden mere yards from here. I can return, with Carnarvon or some other rich man. Margaret, you will not turn me away simply for being the man I was when I left, and for not *yet* be-coming even more. Enough. I have only to earn some money to pay my

way home and we will begin again. Tomorrow, the 20th, we begin
again. I am decided. Are we agreed? Tomorrow I will leave all of this
behind me and I will be off at first light, trekking home to you, as I
once trekked all the way from Turkey to Egypt. I will cable you that I
am coming home, I will beg you only to wait, wait, make no rash deci-
sions. Are you brave? Be brave, my sweet girl, for me. We will sleep
now, your statuette come to life next to me. Close your eyes, as I am
about to close mine, can barely hopen themhold eys morrow

Wednesday, 20 December, 1922

Good morning, darling! And what wondrous, wild, *mad* adventures
we are having here! My discovery of Atum-hadu's fabulous tomb has
become a marvellous comic farce, quite exhilarating! Wherever shall I
begin this zany tale?

A half-hour's sleep was all I was granted last night after writing to
you and all at once dreaming of you, and then a blink later I looked at
my watch before I understood what had woken me, a man shouting my
name, footsteps growing louder as he tramped through Atum-hadu's
rich and holy tomb. My heavy eyes could scarcely open, but each angry
phrase stung me to wakefulness: "Sweet Jesus' salty tears! Where's my
'mountains of gold'? What the hell is all this? Did a child paint these?"
(I must teach your father to shed that typical philistine's urge: blaming
the artist when art is not to one's taste!) I hobbled into the History
Chamber, and there was our CCF, gnawing his unlit cigar, waving his
electric torch around, a sword of yellow dust he brought down on my
face. "You there," he yelled. "Mister Carter said I'd find Trilipush here.
Where's Trilipush, eh? You speak English? Speak up, boy!" Very funny,
M., no? He thought I was a native, in the dark room, with my beard
and the robe I have been working in! I could have held my tongue,
shook my head, but that would not have brought about an understanding, which is what your father and I needed most, what we enjoy now, a
renewal of our partnership, stronger than ever from our trials.

When CCF left Boston some weeks ago, he was probably—and this is funny to us both right now, he and I, we are both laughing, he is looking over my shoulder making sure I capture all of this in my journal just the way it happened—he was probably angry at me, and you would have known that, wouldn't you?

Of course, I would prefer (as would CCF) not to mention any of this, but there is a need (CCF agrees) to clarify for anyone who may have brought CCF here, or knew he was coming. Yes, before we could renew our friendship, this ridiculous but cleansing scene had to be enacted, which it is possible someone may have heard and misunderstood, as CCF did have directions from Carter to look for me here, so I will do my best to reconstruct this quite daffy misunderstanding, precisely like one of those film comedies you so love!

"Finneran? How did you find me?"

"Holy mother of Jesus a-weeping! You? What's happened to you?"

"All manner of good news."

"Lord, that Carter. Should have invested in *him*."

"Would have been a terrible mistake, Chester. He has not accomplished a fraction of what you and I have managed here on much less."

"What's that infernal smell?"

"Well, the leg, you see, not a major injury, but—"

"Holy saints and torments, what the devil is—" Your father's light was off my face and over my shoulder now. He walked past me, following his light into the Bastet Shrine. "What was done to that cat?" he shrieked, sensitive soul.

"These are complex questions, Chester. The ancients' respect for felines, you see, was religious and—"

"You little vermin. You treacherous, gold-digging little cad. Those poisonous cables—"

"Cables?" I was baffled. He was, to be historically accurate—and he is nodding sheepishly as I write this—he was simply raving from the pressures he had put himself under. Apparently, Margaret, he has some financial problems. You knew that, but perhaps not their extent. And you should have told me much earlier. At any rate, such pressures can make a man believe anything, jump at shadows, see sharp conspiracy where there is only dull coincidence, and so it has been with your poor father: he began on some absurd tale of slanderous cables sent from Luxor. He even dropped them on the floor, one at a time, in great overwrought drama, and while he and I examine them again now, I certainly am as horrified as anyone. I only mention them as you probably already heard about them in Boston, quite terrible things, anonymous notes to church and press and police and our own partners. CCF and I will burn the nasty things now, be done with them, although there is good reason to believe—CCF and I agree—that these shots were fired by someone here trying to disrupt our success by simultaneously attacking CCF in Boston and me on the ground. That Carter is our prime suspect, with Ferrell his secret agent abroad, CCF and I are in complete agreement.

Your father was angry, as I know you know, but he had truly come here—whether or not his pride allowed him to confess it—to see our discovery *in situ,* and to put much-needed physical muscle behind his financial muscle to make this excavation a family triumph. "Some genius! You English fairy, I shoulda steered clear of you, but Margaret said you were just what she wanted, you windbag, and then you do this to me."

"Is that why you forced her to break with me?"

"Forced? Are you insane? It took no doing at all. She's got suitors by the dozen. Christ, even that little detective wants her, she's got no end of boys chasing her, and you think giving you up was any sacrifice?" Of course, your father was only trying to anger me, a natural response for the poor fellow, the pressure he was under, Ferrell's and ter Breuggen's lies confusing him. "Oh, heck, please don't write that part down, Pushy!" he has just said to me, the old devil trying to fudge the official record! He is apologising to you now for having said all that about you, and is demanding I write that down right now, too.

"Didn't you find anything for my collection?" he asked. "I had hoped you had at least managed that! And those," he yelled, waving his light behind me, again back into the History Chamber, shoving me against a wall, doing incalculable damage to the ancient masterworks, "did a drunken ape paint those? Is *that* supposed to be an orgy?" I believe he was referring to Pillar Five. "Don't make me laugh—why would he be petting a giraffe when he could have those two girls there? Blessed Mother, are the walls *wet?* My God, they're bloody dripping! What have you done with my money? Painting basement walls? Are you insane?" Now, if anyone had led Finneran here and was still lingering about outside and had heard *that*! An onlistener would have been most puzzled, to say the very least. But it is all the simplest thing, and CCF was learning about tomb preservation the hard way. You see, the paintings are glossy, of course, from the preservative celluloid sprays I have been applying to them, and the fresh, modern preservatives under CCF's electric torchlight made the ancient paintings appear to be *damp*, which is a lovely but misleading effect.

And CCF, in his confusion at what he thought he saw, was reaching out his hand to *touch* the fragile, ancient paintings on the surface of one of the pillars, and I gently, very gently, pushed his hand away with my cane, hardly at all, slightly, just enough to prevent him from touching the surface, which being desiccated and 3500 years old, would have disintegrated at the slightest touch, because while I have been copying into my notes the magnificent workmanship of the tomb, I still have not had an opportunity to complete the scientific methods of preservation that would allow even a stray warm breath on these masterpieces, let alone the mauling of a giant's paw, and that reminds me: CCF and I should be off to fetch more preserving materials today.

I had some sleep to catch up on, but that was not possible just then as there was quite a bit of tidying up to perform, on the floors and walls and whatnot, and just talking to your father was such a pleasure, as I have been toiling without company for some time. As some of the paintings had been slightly damaged by his clumsiness, he and I have agreed to restore those and deal with preservation issues next. He is eager to understand the tomb and to help me complete our work. Quite a bit to teach him, obviously, but he is a remarkably adept student of archaeology.

We finally fell asleep after that tidying up, and we were late in rising this morning, he exhausted from his travels, I from work, and we woke still laughing at our awkward reunion yesterday, and celebrating his renewed support (financial, moral, and material) of our great expedition. We certainly did work hard into the night. "Right, my boy, but hard work is good for us!" exclaimed my Master of Largesse, and sent me off to town with his petty cash for food and water, and to check the post.

CABLE. BOSTON TO RALPH TRILIPUSH, LUXOR, 12/19/22, 9:02 A.M. LEARNED FROM JP THAT DADDY IS COMING TO SEE YOU. HE MAY BE ANGRY. PLEASE FORGIVE YOUR MF.

There, sure enough, I found your cable of yesterday. Funny! Oh, my dear, if only you had been a few days more prompt, I would not have had such a surprise last night. I was right: you did think he would still be angry.

Well, you can set your mind at rest. He and I will come back to Boston together at the end of this expedition, unless he goes off to travel a bit on his own, or he decides to stay in Egypt for a spell of tourism, or meets a lady, any number of places he would want to see. No, of course, he and I must come home together, you are expecting us both, now that we are here together. And you ask my forgiveness, my darling.

CABLE. LUXOR TO MARGARET FINNERAN, BOSTON, 20 DEC. 1922, 11.17 A.M. YOUR FATHER ARRIVED SAFELY. WE ARE WELL AND BOTH SEND YOU ALL LOVE. HE IS IN AWE OF OUR FIND, WILL STAY TO HELP ME FOR A WHILE. HE ASKS YOU NOT TO WORRY. YOUR MOST LOVING RALPH LOVES YOU BEYOND ALL MEASURE.

CABLE. LUXOR TO MARGARET FINNERAN,
BOSTON, 20 DEC. 1922, 11.21 A.M.
HAVE FOUND YOUR RALPH. ALL MISUNDERSTANDINGS SETTLED,
PLEASE DO NOT WORRY, HE IS A FINE FELLA. WILL STAY FOR A
SPELL TO WORK ON EXPEDITION UNDER HIS MAGNIFICENT
TUTELAGE. YOUR FATHER, CCF.

WALL PANEL K, CONTINUED: "THE BETRAYAL OF ATUM-HADU"

<u>Text:</u> "You have betrayed me," King Atum-hadu said, calm despite his anger and pain, confronting at last the Master of Largesse in the royal palace. "I am abandoned by you whom I trusted. You would turn the queen against her lord and master, turn her heart from righteousness. You have weakened my force and my armies until we cannot do battle." The king hesitated. His pity and his love and his meek nature restrained his justified violence.

But the Master of Largesse raged, revealed ambitions, the power he craved, the envy he felt for Atum-hadu. He cried out with mischief, conflated truth and falsehood. The Master of Largesse revealed himself to be no second father to the king, but a most treacherous asp in the rush bed of an innocent child.

And in his madness, the Master of Largesse swung fists at the king and pulled a flaming torch from the wall, and swung it with fire and smoke at the earthly incarnation of Atum. "Stop, fool!" cried Atum-hadu, retreating into the shadows of the empty palace. Still the king did not wish violence against his former friend and adviser. "You do not comprehend the harm you do. You have no idea what you risk. There is still time to save all of this," the king called from the darkness. But still the Master of Largesse sought him out and attacked like a wounded lion, and so Atum-hadu had no choice, despite his wounds from fighting the Hyksos, despite the nest of cobras gnawing at his insides, spitting hot venom out behind him.

He had no choice. This greatest of all kings lifted his war hammer, and the Master of Largesse bumped against a pillar, and the flame of his torch faltered; the king brought down his weapon only once upon his enemy's head, and not with much force, and the Master of Largesse, taller and broader than the king, stood surprised as hot, red blood began to stream from his fat, bald temple. The king offered peace even now, but the villain swung at his king, and so Atum-hadu brought down his war hammer again and the Master of Largesse dropped the torch and Atum-hadu collected it and rained down blows upon the villain, alternating his hammer and the torch, and the heat of the torch blistered the villain's skin and then the hammer came down and the hot blood bubbled in the heat, and the blows fell again and again on the softening head of the traitor, blow after blow upon the deflated head and the spread limbs and the sopping clothes. Atum-hadu sat on the fallen man's stomach, one leg to each side like a woman who sits upon her lover as a hen. Atum-hadu rained down blows for many minutes until his arms failed and his eyes stuck shut from the blood. And then Atum-hadu saw that he was very alone and his stomach boiled with a pain he had not yet known.

All at once, Atum-hadu understood that the end of everything had arrived. Nothing that he loved would survive. All would be forgotten or misunderstood.

He ran outside into the light of the palace courtyard, saw the blood on his robes and on his hammer and on the torch, and he fell to the ground and struck the ground and wept at the course of all things.

Illustration: The long text beginning at the ceiling leaves little space for illustration. Copying and translating this text into these notes has taken most of the day. Explaining the hieroglyphic system and grammar to CCF as I proceeded slowed me down, but the effort was rewarded as he begins to grasp the depth of our discovery.

Then Chester and I cleaned up some of the mess in the tomb. I attended to Wall Panel K and hurried to restore some of the damaged, smeared, or stained illustrations or text that had suffered from Chester's foolishness last night. I walked a bit down the path to try to relieve my throbbing belly for a hopeless half an hour, my thoughts wandering, so many tasks clamouring for priority. Return to the tomb.

Burn a few things in the first chamber, watch the smoke sucked out the front door into the evening sky. CCF is very intrigued by how all this is done. He is a great help. He is very paternal. I have not slept more than a half-hour of last forty-eight. Really must sleep now though tormented I forgetting leaving something undone needs immed att'n. CCF, am I forgetting someth? No, go to sleep. Fine. Lie down but then right up again because I hear voices in the front chamber, but its noth

Thursday, 21 December, 1922

<u>*Journal:*</u>   Reader, my fiancée's father has arrived in Egypt to help with the expedition at the site, and this morning I assign him simple tasks I can trust him to perform correctly inside Atum-hadu's tomb while I have business elsewhere.

I find Carter's site has new facets. True to their word, the Metropolitan expedition has given him everyone and everything he needs. Miles of bandages and calico and wadding to wrap his finds as they emerge from underground. A motorcar. He is swimming in attention and help, native workers, admirers and friends (though one wonders, with sympathy, how he can distinguish the sycophants from the sincere). And there are the thronged tourists again, even dear Len and Sonia Nordquist right there in the front row, I am ashamed to write, cooing and snapping photographs side by side with the great man himself. Carter is swaddled in the trappings of a success beyond measure, but he himself is quite unchanged. He still holds over all our heads that Carter manner, that special secret knowledge that mists up your eyes when you try to look at him directly. He speaks Arabic with a local accent, no must or mould of dusty academia on him. And even in a foreign tongue his manner is unchanged. How he carries this success! "You there. Run ask Mr. Lucas if he has everything he needs," he orders me in Arabic, the moment I place my head in his command tent to say hello. I bow and do his bidding—what else can one do? Lucas is easy to find. He is the chemical specialist on loan from the Egyptian Government, yet another expert bowing down before the great leader,

feeding the insatiable furnace of Carter's ego. "Yes, thanks, all set,"
Lucas answers after I find him setting up his laboratories a few hundred yards away in Tomb 15, emptied out for King Howard's conven-
ience. And there, more excess: the paraffin and preservative sprays in
labelled and numbered red cans, adhesives and solvents, the endless
and hyphenated names of chemicals, incomprehensible in their various
combinations, skulls on labels as if Lucas were a magician or an Over-
seer of the Secrets, the wax, the excess, the horrific excess in all things:
row after row of the simplest products, tool after duplicate numbered
tool, identical backup replacement extras in every direction, a vomit of
gluttony, as if by merely closing his eyes and imagining his desire,
Carter is serviced by some snivelling jinn. "Careful not to get that one
on your skin, boy," calls Lucas in poor Arabic, handing me bottles to
tote back to his master. Even Carter's minions have it, you see, this
inner knowledge he cannot be bothered to share as he knows you could
never understand its complexity. The sooner he can stop thinking of
you the better, the sooner he can return to the altitude where his
thoughts spin in patterns you will never grasp.

Friday, 22 December, 1922

Slept on the ridge in the open air and let CCF keep the cot. Prefer
to give him some privacy down there. Quarters too close to share.

Today Carter opened his wretched hole to the Press, and I do not
know why I do this to myself, the sight of the gawking tourists, the
sound of all that blather for a minor king, I should just walk away, but
it acts on me like a siren's lethal warble, and I went in to have a look at
Carter's tomb again, escorting a sarcastic American journalist who
called me Mohammed. It really is too awful: Tut displays quite the
same excess as his dapper little acolyte. And to see the Nordquists,
back yet again for more sugary excess, looking impressed out of politeness, I could not even bring myself to talk to them, and that room, that
storage chamber of the little upstart's tomb, it is a grotesque display,
this waste pile, the leopard-skin robes, clothing crusted in gold sequins,

statues, rush and papyrus sandals, that couch with the carved foot-boards, boomerangs, lunch boxes carved to resemble trussed ducks, perfume jars, toilet tables, bin after bin of unused underwear, candle-holders shaped like little ankh-people, ornate this, oviform that, loti-form the other, golden whatnot, flails and crooks and sceptres, furniture depicting the king in lion form trampling his enemies, riding a chariot with his own ancestors, thousands of beads to string, just *one* of these items would have justified all of Carter's years, Carnarvon's money, let alone flinty Finneran's. All for this *nobody*, it is enough to make one literally sick, the messy confusion, it is enough to make one feel crushed under it, as if one could imagine all of that wealth and fur-niture just pressing down on top of one in one's own mummy wraps, crushed like a pellet of clay under the wheels of that god-awful war chariot, nauseating. The American journalist quite agreed.

Saturday, 23 December, 1922

Carter really is a megalomaniac, CCF and I agree on this. Oh no, he simply will not be satisfied until everyone admires him and everyone works for him and he makes dramas out of everything. You can imag-ine my surprise to find a police constable striding up the path toward my tomb when I came down from my cliff-top bed this morning. Mr. Carter had sent him to "make sure everything was all right up here." Yes, thanks, as if I needed Carter to keep my tomb all right. "Mr. Carter had some thefts and wanted to know if you have suffered, too?" Of course! Carter is clumsy and loses something in his unwieldy inven-tory and the police must be called in on the assumption that some crafty burglar is troubling all of Egypt's rational archaeologists as well. I laughed and waved off the officer, but he wanted to tell me all about a burglar in Carter's home and missing this and that, and stains on Carter's bedsheets. "Is everything all right here, sir?" Oh, for heaven's sake, of course it is, ducks. "Might I have a look-see at your dig? I'm something of an amateur of archaeology myself." It is all I can do to bar the great idiot's dust-kicking steps towards Door A. "Are you hurt, sir?

Is there something you want to tell me?" and other daft questions of the novice Egyptian constabulary acting as Carter's spy.

I finally see off my rival's little agent, and CCF and I debate which of our myriad tasks to take on next, much work still to be done to stabilise the interior of the tomb, correctly map it and its objects, apply the preservatives to the untreated paintings, finish transcribing the walls. CCF is a marvellous help.

I landed at Alexandria late on the 24th, Macy, and made Cairo by train the next day, Christmas, though you hardly notice in Egypt. I worked fast: our man had indeed been at the Hotel of the Sphinx and had left it on the 26th of October, holding his suite open for his return, so his reports to Boston had been truthful to that date at least. The deskman also said Finneran had been at the hotel as well, stayed the night nine days before me. I, in my turn, spent the night of the 25th, space at the inn Christmas night. No talking donkeys, though.

Sunday, 24 December, 1922

Work. Miserable bowels. The gramophone does not help. The work is hard. It makes one think about immortality. To the average man, I suppose, the Egyptian notion of immortality is the most foolish superstition. But that is only because our idea of eternal life has changed, whether we are Christians or not. Though we agree with our Nile ancestors that immortality is still man's most important accomplishment (more important than love, or a mild reputation for virtue, more pressing by far than friendship), we are not so mad as to think that our *bodies* are transported into an afterlife. We use a different vocabulary, *salvation of souls, lasting fame.* Call it what you will, but to make one's name ring out after the names of your inferiors and tormentors are snuffed out, that is something all of us still hope for. (And, most delicious of all, to have this happen before their physical lives end, so they can feel the last wisp of their names vanish while they still breathe and know—

know, ter Breuggen—that when their mouldering carcass is discovered and tossed into the ground, it will already be anonymous hair and skin, on its merry way to becoming anonymous carbon ash, while others of us will become stars and suns.) I do not know of anyone who does not aspire to this permanence, even if they claim not to. The world is littered with the arcs de triomphe and such-and-such juniors, the chattering artists nervous to know their work will last, poets committing suicide to assure their fame, last wills and testaments trying to control heirs, names annually read out in churches and synagogues, ornate tombstones and deathbed I-love-yous, bequests and named donations, money left to political parties and charities. We are all plenty Egyptian still and no debate.

I am not an idiot. When the time comes, I know that I will be *dead.* I will not be strumming a winged stringed thing, or even (as I planned as a boy) be savouring the hot, fleshy delectations of a palm-lined, Anubis-guarded, Isis-assisted Egyptian underworld. I speak of something lighter, finer, more intellectually and spiritually unassailable and inexhaustible. Immortality for us, though it will be bodiless, is not without consciousness: the consciousness at the precise moment of the expiration of our bodies that our name will carry on.

CCF agrees.

Monday, 25 December, 1922

Journal: Belly protests as if I have swallowed sharpened knives, but CCF and I continue our work into the late afternoon. Then clear out rubbish, empty pails, burn this and that.

Margaret: I have just had a visitor. It has been rather a while since I have spoken to anyone. Besides your chatterbox father, I mean.

She came to see me, the sweet old girl. I had just emptied the pails. She caught me rather tired, quite at the end of my resources, sitting outside the tomb, massaging my aching thigh.

"Dear boy, they said I'd find you up here."

I thought perhaps I was hallucinating—the sudden appearance of one of the people one would most like to see. She was so kind to me on that boat. She shielded her eyes from the glare and climbed the last steps, lifting her old-fashioned dress to scramble over a rock with surprising ease.

"Dear Ralph, you look unwell. Whatever has happened to you up here?"

"Nothing. Searching. Hard at work. Made an extraordinary find."

She sat beside me on the rock, caught her breath, took my hand. Had she been you, I would have fallen into her arms. "Poor boy, look at yourself. You're much thinner."

"But tell me about you, Sonia, what you have seen on the trip of a lifetime. The Rameses tombs? That circus down there at the Carter hole?"

"Oh dear, a bit jealous, are you? There's no need, believe me. I see these things so clearly. It doesn't matter."

"What doesn't matter?"

"All that. I've seen more than I care to of this country. It's cold and hard here." And then it was *she* crying in *my* arms, shaking, and then just as quickly she had had enough and was sitting up, dabbing her face. "I've lost my Len, you see, just two days ago. So very fast here." She looked west, at the bluffs softening into the open desert. "People seem very temporary here, all this space and history. I'm taking him home tomorrow. You look like how I feel. He liked you, you know. Oh, very much. He said so that first night on the boat. I hope those spirits haven't sent you off in the wrong direction. You mustn't take them too, too seriously. They'll have their little fun, you know. They were human once, too, and dying doesn't make you smart, I shouldn't think. Or honest. Or even interesting, now that I think of the dull conversations Len and I used to have with them. I'm done with ghosts now."

"Poor Len. Poor Sonia."

"You could come back with me, you know. I could so use the help. All the difficult work ahead. My children live too far away, too busy."

Help? "To get Len home. You could see our home, and our summer house on the lake. It's very peaceful there. In the winter, you know, there's so much snow to shovel away from the front of the house. Len used to do it, but I can't ask the kids to help. Oh, dear Ralph, do come and rescue me from all that. We'll get you cleaned up at my hotel, some clothes, have a doctor take a look at that leg, and then you'll rescue this old woman who needs you so much."

Margaret. Just a few days ago, I would have gone, just a few days earlier. And I could have cabled for you to join us there. You and I taking care of her in her rambling house, summers on the lake, gardening. The newlywed caretakers down in the other house, going to the market, cooking. Fixing this and that. Plenty of time for reading, playing tennis, taking you out on her sailboat. Would have answered everything.

"I am too close to the finish, Sonia, to my find. So terribly close."

"Of course. Of course, dear boy."

"Perhaps I might join you later, when I am done here."

"That would be fine. I'd like that very much. If you won't consider again and simply come now, right now, just walk away with me . . ."

She picked her way back down the rocky path. I sat in front of my tomb door, too exhausted to stand. She would turn and wave as she descended the winding path. When high rocks hid her, I could imagine her thinking she had seen the last of me, but then the path would turn and she would appear again, smaller, and surprised to still have me in view, she would wave again. Just once more she stopped, quite small, waved her white handkerchief, a tiny figure far beneath me. Shovelling snow.

Tuesday, 26 December, 1922

CCF and I spend the day cleaning, analysing Chamber 8, reading wall inscriptions and illustrations. Make measurements of furnishings, et cetera.

Wednesday, 27 December, 1922

Today Carter began to lift into the light what only the chosen few have seen underground, but he is bringing them up to the waiting crowds and cameras in the most gruesome fashion, as if he has become the prince of death. The stretchers, the bandage wraps: it is a vision of the War itself. I suspect from the shape that the wrapped figure now arising under Carter's command is the spear-bearing statue I saw down there, but all bandaged over, as if the ancient soldier's lungs bubbled with mustard gas and his eyes wept those brown, gritty tears. The overwrought display: the tiniest boxes emerge carried by three men on a march to Lucas's cave, every beaded slipper to be sprayed and glued and restored in this massive factory of antiquities, monument to one man's vanity, this violation of a poor boy-king's last hopes for peace.

We left for the south on a boat the next day, reaching Luxor on the 27th. By the way, Macy, feel free to add any local colour you think helps: hot weather, camels, natives, all that. No feeling for it myself, but I think it does draw a certain class of readership, and film people eat it right up.

On the 27th, I made my way to the suburban address Trilipush had given his Cairo hotel for forwarding messages. Instead of Trilipush, two American journalists were sharing the rent on this villa, their headquarters for sending dispatches on the King Tut dig. They'd taken it on the 10th of December. And had they ever heard of an archaeologist named Trilipush? One of them laughed, sarcastic: "Popular fellow." Another gentleman had come last week asking the same question. What did they tell him? "We said that if he's an archaeologist, then Howard Carter would know him, but I've never heard of your boy, chief." They told me how to find Carter's site and were happy enough to take some money: if they caught wind of Trilipush or Finneran again, they'd contact me at once at my hotel in Luxor. "Yes, boss, we sho'nuff will!"

Off I went to the big show: the mob of workmen and tourists that marked the excavation of the tomb of King Tutankhamun. Now, one of the great benefits of my career, Macy, is the wide variety of fascinating humanity it's been my happy lot to encounter. Howard Carter was a fellow of about fifty when I met him, and admirable. You know anything about him? He wasn't a toff, wasn't born into wealth and privilege like Trilipush and Marlowe, wasn't even rich. No, Carter was a gamekeeper's grandson who'd worked hard, studied hard, taught himself what he needed to excel at his field, and through intelligence, persistence, and good luck had made this quite winning discovery that the whole world knows all about now, and justifiably so. Now all the mummy voodoo and the broken furniture and the necklaces and whatnot, well that stuff doesn't interest me much, and the little bit of it that Carter showed me that day was fine, but a little goes a long way. No, what interested me was Carter himself. He was my sort of man, a self-made, honest man. And he was an Englishman, but not the type who couldn't forgive you for not being English. I could see the respect his Gippos had for him. Not to mention the mobs of journalists and photographers and tourists and would-be assistants and admirers, although none of it distracted him. As I asked my questions about his work and about Trilipush, I couldn't help but think: Here's a poor boy made good, not some toff criminal, and it's a pity that the scandal about to erupt all around here is going to pull the world's attention from Mr. Carter's work, and place it on mine instead.

Well, Carter had indeed met Trilipush several times, and in fact, Trilipush was hard at work on something, working on a shoestring budget but just on the other side of those cliffs, Carter said, pointing to a monstrous wall of this hellish valley. So even more of Trilipush's story had been true. And, Carter says, about a week earlier, another bloke, an American, had been looking for Trilipush, and Carter'd told him where to go as well, and off he'd gone with one of Carter's men showing him the way. When had Carter himself last seen Trilipush? That same day, a week earlier. That morning, a letter for Trilipush had inadvertently been included in the post one of Carter's boys had fetched, and as he was curious to see what Trilipush had found, Carter had taken the letter over to Deir el Bahari personally. And? And Trilipush was filthy, limping from an injury to his leg, a little unwell perhaps, but "wildly excited about his find." He absolutely wouldn't let Carter peek inside, and that was that. Carter returned to his own camp and a few hours later was found by an American, Mr. Finneran, asking for Trilipush. "I began to feel like the man's social secretary, and I am, after all, rather busy here with my own work."

I understood the dismissal, took it with grace, shook the great man's hand,

and thanked him sincerely for his time, sorry to have bothered him. I headed back to town to hire myself a guide to help me find Trilipush's site.

Now, Macy, what did we think *at this moment*? I'd been wrong. I admit it now and I admitted it then: Trilipush had told the honest truth: there definitely was a treasure, and Trilipush was so close to it, as of a week earlier, that he wouldn't even let the great Carter see the site. That same day, Finneran must've found him. I was behind them by exactly a week, and part of me despaired, since I didn't know where either of them was staying. Now, I didn't really credit O'Toole's idea that Finneran had come to kill Trilipush and steal the gold, though you can never be entirely sure with men under pressure. More likely, with the wealth right there glittering in front of them, the two of them would probably make amends, patch it all up, with Finneran relieved to forget everything I had so patiently helped him see, and now the murderer and his serially gullible father-in-law-to-be were already a week ahead of me on their way back to Boston, where Finneran would pay off his debts with Egyptian gold and Trilipush, bearing wealth and fame, would take Margaret's hand as his wife, though a sad sort of marriage it would be, him using her to disguise his unnatural proclivities. And he'd probably get his Harvard job back on the strength of his find. I'd probably already missed them, and now I'd have to go sailing back the way I'd just come, to interrupt family bliss once more in order to ask my troublesome questions on behalf of poor murdered Caldwell-Davies and Marlowe. I didn't relish the possibility, Macy. I don't care much for Boston, and I didn't want to go back. I'd spent enough time sailing the Atlantic Ocean, and I admit I might even have given up then, closed the case right there if these two were already on their way back to Boston with Trilipush consolidating his lies. I'd've done anything to keep the investigation near the scene of the murders.

I had to hold on for another night to get answers, and my fears grew stronger the next morning, when I finally managed to hire a local boy and two donkeys and we trotted over the rocks, past another archaeological site managed by an American, past a giant temple cut into the cliff side, past barren, brown boredom, not too different from certain rough parts of Australia. And then after a silent spell, for no particular reason I could see, the boy stopped and said, "Here." "Here? Are you sure?" There was absolutely nothing different about this bit of cliff-side donkey path than anything we'd seen in the previous hour. We were on an incline amidst some little hills, around a bend from any other living thing, and I wondered if I was about to be ambushed by this Egyptian boy. "Here?" I asked again, and the boy shrugged. I tied up my donkey, took a walk around the area, and found nothing of interest, no sign of any life at all. "How do you know it's not farther up?" I asked. The boy was adamant, he knew these hills, and this was what I had told him Carter had told me. We waited. I searched in the heat for two hours, walking up and down, finding nothing and no one. No glinting gold, no fleeing Finneran, no treacherous Trilipush, no corpse of Caldwell, no murdered Marlowe.

I was worried, and no lie. I had no other address for Trilipush, and now it appeared he'd shut down his excavations in the last week, kicked over the traces. At least I still had the post. Those cables and letters to Margaret had come from somewhere. I headed back to town and went from post office to post office distributing O'Toole's money until I heard a correct answer: I paid the Egyptian behind the counter to open his mouth—"Yes, Mr. Trilipush comes quite regularly to check the *poste restante,* and yes, he sends cables from here, and the last time he was in was probably two hours ago"—and then in my joy I paid the Egyptian behind the counter to close his mouth, and to signal my boy there in the corner the next time Trilipush appeared, and there'd be another payment coming his way.

I left my little assistant there (one of a rotating team of eight I assembled that afternoon for their discretion, instructed them in the basics of secret surveillance, and counted on them for their ability to know the streets and blend in). I stationed the boy discreetly in the post office, waiting for the mouse, December 28th, late in the afternoon. I then went to the riverboat office and disbursed more payments, billable to the Davies case, the O'Toole case, the Marlowe case, one and all of them: but the office had no riverboat reservations for a Trilipush or a Finneran on their records, and no one had travelled north to Cairo by that name today. I left my name and some money: any reservations under those names, please contact me at my hotel. I went to as many other Luxor hotels as I could find: no Finneran or Trilipush anywhere, and I scattered my clients' money behind me: should those names appear on a register, I was to be contacted at my hotel at once. I was busy, all right, but I had nothing: Trilipush and Finneran hadn't left and they weren't there: what could be clearer than that? "Patience, Macy," I urged. "Now more than ever." I'd laid the only snares I had at my disposal. I continued my circuit: to the villa, to the excavation site, to the post office to check on my local boys. The 28th. The 29th (post office closed). The 30th.

Thursday, 28 December, 1922

This morning, CCF and I stepped out to take the air and saw a man some 200 yards down the path. I watched him for hours from behind the rocks. Orange-haired, even from this distance, with some lazy native boy. He paced and sat and wandered and sat. Do you know him, CCF? "Oh, indeed, Ralph, my boy, oh yes. He is hungry to intrude, destroy, confound. He devours what other men build. He is a scavenger of lives and survives on loose ends."

It is certainly time to hurry along with our work. CCF sends me into town for food, check the post. No word from you, M. There is no need to continue pretending, my darling. Our "split" is quite forgotten.

Afternoon spent cleaning and analysing Chambers 8 and 9, copying illustrations and texts.

Friday, 29 December, 1922

There is in any scholarly effort a certain amount of guesswork, a clarification of ideas achieved only through the physical act of writing. By definition, a first draft is both inaccurate and necessary. One uses one's pen to cut through impossibilities. Now I can throw out much of what has come before, and prepare the text with more accurate analysis.

To that end, CCF and I work on measuring Chamber 9, understanding the items in relation to each other. I must quickly copy down the last translations, History Chamber Wall Panel L and the walls of Chambers 8 and 9.

Most extraordinary find of course is the complete copy of the *Admonitions of Atum-hadu.* Spend hours reading it.

I realise also that I misunderstood Pillar 12: it is not an ally carrying the dead Atum-hadu; it is Atum-hadu carrying the dead Master of Largesse. CCF pointed this out to me. Brilliant insight on his part.

WALL PANEL L: THE LAST HOURS OF EGYPT

Atum-hadu was abandoned. He left Thebes and crossed life-giving Nile and walked. Alone, he carried his goods, his Admonitions, paint, reed, ink, brushes, his cat. And he carried the Master of Largesse.

Saturday, 30 December, 1922

<u>Journal:</u>   CCF and I discuss next steps, and we are decided. We will return to this place of our glory, but later. Now it is time to go home, gather our forces and our money and our health, file new requests with the proper authorities, et cetera.

I have a few more notes to make in this journal before CCF and I return home, on Monday. All clear, simplest thing in the world: I will post these notes to my fiancée, to be sure of their safe publication should anything happen to CCF and me on our long crossing to Boston. A terrible risk to the written record of my extraordinary work otherwise, at the whim of the elements on a boat. Finneran and I will travel by boat to Cairo, stay the night at the Hotel of the Sphinx (where CCF is laughingly ready to settle my accounts stretching back to October), take the train to Alexandria, and board the *Cristoforo Colombo* for a pleasure cruise home. I will marry Margaret. CCF is 100 percent behind the idea again, will help me to cure her of her troubles. We will have children. We will be happy. Then I will return to Egypt to conduct a more complete survey of my great discovery here. My work will be studied forever. *Desire and Deceit in Ancient Egypt: The Complete Admonitions of King Atum-hadu* (2nd edition, revised and complete, Yale University Press, 1923). *The Discovery of the Tomb of Atum-hadu* by Ralph M. Trilipush (Yale University Press, 1923).

Finneran provides the cash to deal with these last details in Luxor while he prefers to stay near the tomb. "I find the place too lovely to leave just yet," he says, dozing on a cot in Chamber 8. I set off to town to arrange tickets on various boats home, hotel reservations along the way.

But that red-haired fellow is lurking about again, and CCF and I watch as he loses interest, again some 200 yards down the path from us. The strangest sort of pursuer—inefficient, purposeless, but still clumsily menacing my work. He is utterly unrelated to anything important, but he seems devotedly intent on being in my way. At last he putters off, and CCF sends me to run our errands.

On the afternoon of the 30th our patience is rewarded at last, Macy! I'm back at my hotel after again staking out Trilipush's excavation site across the river to no avail. And now, all at once, Trilipush moves from invisible to omnipresent. The riverboat office calls: reservations were made just now for Trilipush and Finneran on the boat north to Cairo for Monday, the 1st of January. A wire is delivered to me from Cairo: they've received word at the Hotel of the Sphinx to expect Messrs. F and T for the evening of January 2nd. And then a knock on the door: one of my little Luxor bandits, his palm out. "Bock Sheesh," he says, the local greeting. "Bock Sheesh," I reply. "What news?" His palm remained outstretched. Of course: as soon as his hand had been suitably weighed down with money, its connecting pulley system opened his mouth: Trilipush had come to the post office an hour before, had received nothing and sent nothing, and he was now sitting not thirty feet from my very hotel!

I ran after the boy down the stairs, out into the blinding sun, and across the street. I hid behind a palm tree. My heart was beating hard. Any moment now I would at last meet the devil who'd slaughtered the Australian boy and the English officer, the swine who'd broken the heart of that wondrous girl, your aunt. I recalled a picture of him she'd shown me, his arm round Marlowe's shoulder. Trilipush had looked an ordinary man with sandy hair, but with something greedy and immoral around the mouth and eyes. I looked now where the boy was pointing, but I saw no Trilipush. "There, he is there." The boy pointed again to a bearded man in native garb, staring at a drink at a shaded café table. "You're certain?" "Certain, yes. The man at the post said. I follow him here. He takes drink, I go to you."

And here we were, Macy, after all this time, racing so many thousands of miles across the globe, probing events of years before, chasing the dreams and nightmares of so many clients, often not even knowing myself that this man here was the man I was seeking, *this* was the man whose crimes would become famous only three decades later thanks to you and me right now.

"Mr. Trilipush, I presume?" I stood before him with the sun behind me, a tried and true method to disorient an interrogatee.

He looked up. "Ah, the dogged Mr. Ferrell. I'm a busy man. I've only a few minutes for a drink. Join me if you must, but do let's be brief about it." The effect was astonishing, Macy, I confess it. The brilliance of criminals must never be denied, otherwise it's the detective's pride getting the better of him, you see. And he *was* clever: he'd known me, a total stranger, at a glance, God knows how, and hadn't shown the slightest surprise that I was standing before him in the middle of Egypt, and had recognised him, considering.

For he looked horrible. Whatever he'd once been—in the spring of their fraudulent affair, when he'd wooed Margaret with smoke and mirrors—she never would've wanted this filthy thing, that's certain. He was dressed in a torn robe, dirt-stained and spattered with blood and tied with bits of rope knotted together, and he wore a single, broken boot, his other foot just a mass of crusted, yellowing bandages. His beard and hair were matted, and his face was tanned unevenly, and simply covered with dirt elsewhere, and one of his eyes was blackened and swollen, and his cheek and forehead bruised and cut quite badly. I nearly pitied him, Macy, but then I was put in mind of the filthy home where a promising young Aussie boy had grown up, the same boy murdered by this pom sitting in front of me. And my pity vanished.

My God, how he stank, Macy. He stank of rot, of tombs, of his own filth, I don't know. Probably of his ghastly, bootless leg. At the end of our talk, when he stood and hobbled away, he was practically a one-legged man. Yet, for all this horror, most maddening of all, most certain to eliminate any trace of pity I might possibly have felt for him, he still spoke as if he were completely unaware of his appearance, with all the dismissive bite and insane, unjustifiable snobbery of the English upper classes, all that distaste for real people, the generations of congealed hatred he'd been born with in his blood, that made him feel superior to the rest of us. You could hear what this stinking criminal thought of us Aussies: that pom bastard voice that makes colonials act like servants and servants act like blacks and blacks pick up rifles and revolt. And of course there was absolutely that something extra in his manner: the peculiar singsong of the invert, although it was greatly subdued, no doubt from the habit of hiding his nature.

The questions crowded my head, and I had to take a moment to organise my thoughts, so I told him to order me a beer, which he did in the local lingo. And then I plunged in, asking questions as they occurred to me, all my clients' interests mixed up, and the criminal answered each one so rapidly that I knew he'd been prepared for me. Finneran had betrayed me to this filthy wreck, no question. There must've been heaps of gold, that was sure.

Now recall my position as I circled Trilipush: I couldn't hope he'd quickly confess to the killings, reveal the whereabouts of the bodies. Four years on, he was too set in his lies, relying on the passage of time, the weakness of pressing physical evidence. No, instead I had to provoke him, like a bull, until in his anger he wrote his crimes on his face. Snares had to be laid, and in my words (transcribed only a few hours later, so I don't doubt their accuracy for an instant), you'll see those snares tightening around our hare. Note that I do not hesitate to transcribe his every insult and verbal charge at me: you must see in them his thrashing against the hook setting deeper in his lip. His arrogance undoes him, so I include every word, no matter what he throws at me. You must understand, as a man of the investigative sciences, that I extracted my own feelings from the proceedings, allowed him to fire off at shadows. A good lesson for you, Macy: the detective uses his own hollowed-out form as bait, makes of himself a tarman against which the criminal rages, ensnaring himself in the process.

"Strangest thing, Mr. Trilipush. I try to understand your life story, what I've heard from your friends and admirers. I can't follow it. I keep putting two and two together and stubbornly getting five. Now how do you explain that?"

"Perhaps your maths tutor spent too much of your study time buggering you, ducks."

"Very good, and an interesting choice of verb, from what I hear of you."

"Are we almost through, Mr. Ferrell?"

"Did Mr. Finneran find you last week?"

"He did. How did you know he was here?"

"Where's Mr. Finneran today?"

"We're to meet later. He's making arrangements for our departure Monday. We divided the errands."

"Departing Egypt? To points unknown?"

"If you consider Boston unknown."

"You're returning to Boston? What of Mr. Finneran's outstanding debts?"

"Everything Mr. Finneran does is outstanding, and in this case he has invested wisely, as have his partners."

"Oh, then congratulations are in order. You've had good luck on your excavation?"

"Unparalleled. You will read about it all someday and tell your grandchildren that you met me once, and they will weep with wonder. They may even love you for it."

"Where's the treasure now?"

" 'Treasure'? That's a charming term, you colonial imbecile. The *artefacts* and *obzhaydarr* and *furniture* and *manuscripts* and *mummies* are in the tomb, undergoing preservation."

"Might I have a tour of that tomb?"

"You might, yes, as soon as it is opened to the public."

To draw him out of his defensive posture, I provoked with a lie, although very near the truth: "Beverly Quint says you and Marlowe were lovers."

He stared at me a moment, then continued unfazed. "I do not know Miss Quint, though she sounds charming, so I cannot imagine what would motivate her to make such a statement. I am beginning to have the impression that you are confusing me with someone else, Mr. Ferrell. Are we nearly finished?"

Unfazed, yes, but you'll admit that this is a peculiar response: he pretends not to know his old fancy friend Quint, when there is no reason to hide that. Don't let it shake you: this sort of confusion appears often in climactic interrogations with holdout liars. They grow confused themselves, cannot remember which lies they've told to which people, so like children, they begin to throw dust all about. It's crucial here that the detective hold tight to what he knows to be true. With Trilipush's lies biting their own tails, I pressed harder: "Why's there no mention of you at Oxford, Professor?"

"I've no idea. I can only presume that you, like any number of easily impressed primitive peoples, smell great conspiracies in clerical errors."

"I see. Of course. Then can you explain to this primitive why Captain Marlowe's parents, family of your dearest friend, say they've never met you?"

And at last he was silenced. "They said that?"

"They did, Mr. Trilipush. You even know their names?"

"Of course. Priapus and Sappho. Are the old dears well?"

"Yes. No. They're named Hector and Regina."

"Are they? How odd."

"Why hasn't the British War Office got a record on your military career?"

"Haven't they? Absentminded of them."

"Not at all, Trilipush. I believe your military record was expunged by the authorities, desperate to cover over yet another Wartime English crime."

"Crime?"

He was infuriating even in his reduced and battered state, everything that is to be despised in the English. He was as visibly horrified by my presence as Marlowe's father had been; he mocked me with his voice and accent as easily as Quint had; he was as uninterested in the harm he'd done in his life as old Barnabas Davies. I wanted to crush him, squeeze his throat. I was supposed to be impressed by *him*? By a stinking, matted beggar with one boot? They're just men, Macy: killers, Englishmen, the rich: they're just men.

I approached from a different angle. "Who's Paul Caldwell?"

"I've never heard the name."

"He was an Australian soldier lost with Captain Marlowe."

"I have never quite understood the policeman's tendency to ask questions only to answer them himself a moment later."

And then, Macy, I played my ace. I showed him, simply as a spur to conversation, Tailor HQ's transcribed report from British military records (I believe I already sent you a copy of this, but reproduce it again for our readers):

Captain Hugo St. John Marlowe left base camp at Cairo on 12 November, 1918, on four-day pass. Did not return on 16 November. Searches initiated 18 November revealed nothing. Interviews with officers, men, revealed nothing of significance. March 1919, natives appeared asking for reward, having found Capt. Marlowe's identity disks and those of Corporal P. B. Caldwell (AIF), as well as an AIF Lee-Enfield .303 rifle. Natives reported finding these objects near Deir el Bahari. Renewed interviews revealed no knowledge of any relationship between Captain Marlowe and Corporal Caldwell, though AIF records show Capt. Marlowe twice took unusual step of recommending promotions for Caldwell to Capt. T. J. Leahy (AIF), Caldwell's company commander.

He looked up, pushed the sheet back to me. "And?"

"What happened to those two men, Professor?"

Watch him rise to the bait, Macy: "Oh, for Christ's sake, Ferrell, listen to me once and for all: I did not return to Egypt—surely, surely you know this, you clever little man—until December 1918. And you want me to explain your scribbled document? How could I? But fine. You purport to be a detective, so use your head, Ferrell. I can think of a hundred explanations for something as vague as this without breaking a sweat."

"A hundred? Really? I can hardly believe it, Professor." I could hear his pride, the creative criminal's pride, and this—I felt it—would be his downfall.

"Simplest thing in the world. One: captain and corporal go off, as you would plainly have it, for a *romantic* four-day weekend in the wilderness, celebrating the Armistice with a lovers' retreat. They requisition a motorcycle and sidecar, and zip their way south, where they begin to lay out a picnic, strum guitars, recite Shelley, peel grapes. However, it is only a few hours since the Armistice, and some enemy troops have not heard the happy news or some bandits cannot be bothered to care. Captain and corporal find themselves not in amorous embrace but surrounded by enemies, and the captain draws his Webley revolver. He tells his lover to run. Corporal heads for the motorcycle, hears three shots in quick succession, turns to see the mob of blood-maddened Arabs tearing the captain to pieces, and in his fear, he cannot start the cycle. The devils pull him down as well, drag him off to torture him. His identity disks and rifle are left behind. Fits your facts, yes? Again? Fine. Two: the captain is in love with an Arab girl, decides to throw everything away for her—family, country, career, Church of England—to become her Arab husband. He takes his dearest friend, this New Zealandish private—"

"Australian corporal."

"—this Os-try-lee-un cor-prill to be his manservant. They stage their own disappearances and now all live together not two miles from here, husband, wife, three children, and Aussie manservant. You can go find them right now, if you are smart enough to track them. They left their dead meat tickets in the open and hoped some idiot would presume them dead. You are that idiot. Again? Very well, three, and this one pitched to your taste: the impoverished Australian corporal was blackmailing the English captain, who was a sodomite. The English captain decided to end his compromised position by murdering his tormentor. So he invited the Aussie corporal out to the desert to show and share with him some valuable archaeological find. Over hill after hill he led him to a secluded spot. 'Here is where I happen to know we should dig,' he says. When the unsuspecting Aussie boy had his back turned and was pulling some digging tool out of the motorcycle's saddlebag, the captain drew his Webley. The corporal caught sight of this reflected in the motorcycle's gas tank, which pathetically, he had polished to impress the Englishman. There the captain's distorted reflection made him resemble an insect with an enormous thorax, tiny little limbs, and a revolver. The corporal, just a harmless would-be archaeologist, secretly drew his combat knife and turned. The laughing captain told the poor boy he was going to kill him to end the blackmail and then would dig up the promised archaeological find all by himself. The captain even had the audacity to tell the boy not to take this news badly, suggested to the poor fellow that he would be kind enough to report the death as heroic so that the corporal would have posthumous awards and pensions for his impoverished family Down Under. This was nearly convincing to the corporal, as a matter of fact, but in the end he did not believe the captain would make good on the promise, so he jumped him in preemptive self-defence. In the struggle, the captain shot the corporal just as the corporal stabbed the captain, and they both fell, quite dead. Bandits stole their uniforms, motorcycle, and belongings. Are you getting all this in your notes? Should I speak more slowly? Jackals dragged the bodies off to a cave and ate them. Metal identity disks are not digestible or valuable and were left in the desert. More, Ferrell, my dwarf red monkey? Number four: the captain, in his counterintelligence work, discovered that the corporal was passing secrets to the Turks. Confronting the corporal with this shocking discovery, the captain moved to arrest him, when all at once a British aeroplane flying overhead, mistaking the altercation for a—"

And on and on he blathered, and at least six more fanciful tales followed. I tried to interrupt, but he wouldn't allow anything to disrupt his performance: "Wait a moment, Detective. I am only getting started. You see, all of these possibilities, none verifiable or controvertible, fit your little document, and I am only beginning to stretch my muscles. Textual evidence can contain a vast quantity of pits and distortions, like a gramophone disk left in the sun. There's hardly a written report on *any* past event that can explain *anything*. We know nothing of the past, not truly, from any *single* document, but you have travelled the world, Ferrell, learning nothing, raping my reputation in certain corners, and attempting to squire my fiancée, based on *that piece of paper*!?" But, Macy! He'd made his fatal error! Did you see it? If he truly knew nothing of the missing men, if he'd truly come back to camp a month after their disappearance, then how did he—in his array of truth-obscuring hypotheses—guess that young Paul Caldwell was "*a would-be archaeologist*"? Nothing in the military record would've shown that; I only knew it from my interviews in Australia. Oh yes, our Mr. Trilipush was caught. I pounced, and we had our moment in the sun, Macy, to make our dramatic declaration and watch the wall of lies crumble:

"The truth, Trilipush, in my experience is very simple and often hidden in plain view, marked by the usual signposts of motivation: lust, greed, hatred, envy. So I suggest you calm down now and listen to what I know. To what I *know*, Professor, not to what I can imagine. In early *November* 1918, perhaps earlier, Captain

Marlowe's invert lover and treasure-hunting partner, the impoverished gentle-man Captain Trilipush, returns to Egypt from a battle in Turkey, in which he was presumed killed. He doesn't report himself to his superiors but merely lurks about, letting the British command think he's dead. In his lurking, he discovers that, during his Turkish absence, his fancy man has taken a young Australian cor-poral to be his archaeological research assistant, and how *did* you guess *that*, Pro-fessor? Well, the spurned and angry Trilipush assumes, wrongly, that Marlowe and Caldwell are also lovers, and he secretly follows the two men south to the desert when they take a four-day leave to go looking for archaeological treasure, guided by the mysterious Fragment C. Oh yes, I know all about your treasure map, Professor, don't interrupt. The two innocent men arrive unawares at the spot near the treasure they seek, but before they can even begin their digging, who should appear but the ghostly Trilipush? 'What? Are you here?' stammers Marlowe to the surprising returnee. 'Silence, you unfaithful wretch!' shrieks the wailing, weeping Trilipush, maddened by jealousy and greed and heartbreak. Using his own Webley, he kills them both, captain and corporal, the ex-lover and the innocent Australian boy. He buries the bodies but accidentally drops their identity disks and the Aussie's rifle, then simply drives off on their motorcycle, stealing their treasure map, this Fragment C that would tell him where to return when the heat had let up and he could safely come to dig for the loot. Some months later, he turns up in the USA, weeping crocodile tears for the loss of his great friend, pretending to know nothing of Caldwell, and makes his name as a scholar of the very king whose treasure-filled tomb Marlowe and Caldwell were searching for the day you slaughtered them in cold blood. So certain of your hideous victory, you even mock the family of one of your victims, sending the poor grieving parents a copy of your pornographic work, grotesquely dedicated to your murdered lover, calling them by the private, perverted nicknames you and their invert son had invented for them. In Boston, securing work through false academic pretence and a financier through equally false romantic pre-tence—"

"Wait a moment—you believe I killed Paul Caldwell?" he asked, infuriating me, as he was several minutes behind the flow of my discourse.

"Don't interrupt, Trilipush. You secured a job at Harvard by claiming to have attended Oxford, which you did not. Oh, you were there, I know, a sodomite so-cialite in Oxford's shady little underworld, a scandalous influence on a circle of young inverts who continue to sing of you to this day, and you were living off of Marlowe's money, paid to be his kept man, but you weren't a student, received no degrees, earned no right to a post at Harvard. Arriving in Boston, looking around for an easy target, you pretended to love Margaret Finneran, but only to win her father's money. With that money you set off for Egypt, having no intention of ever returning to Boston after you found your treasure, and you began to excavate in the *precise spot* where Paul Caldwell and Hugo Marlowe disappeared, a remarkable coincidence, you'll agree. Well, soon thereafter, that same potential father-in-law, realising his error of judgement, acquiesces to his daughter's wise, independent decision to break off your engagement. Maddened by this slight to your overweening criminal pride, suspecting that Finneran has understood your plan, and intending to make it impossible for him to pursue you and the gold, you attempt to ruin Finneran's reputation with a series of slanderous cables. Instead, he boldly pursues you, finds you at your dig, where you and he make a corrupt bargain: the two of you divide up your ill-gotten gains into two large heaps. Finneran intends to secretly stash most of his in Maltese banks on his way home on the *Cristoforo Colombo*, apologetically bringing back to Boston only just enough to pay off his debts, but not enough to share the find's *true* dividends with his double-crossed partners. In exchange for your silence at his treachery, and much to your sodomist relief, he will allow you to sail off to points unknown with a larger share of the gold than you are actually due, and he will tell Margaret to forget you, that you fell in love with an Egyptian girl. In reality, you will be off, most likely to refurbish dilapidated Trilipush Hall with your bloodstained Egyptian treasure, stolen from, in turn, Marlowe, Caldwell, and now J. P. O'Toole. Oh, no, I don't believe for a moment you're returning to Boston, Trilipush. Neither you nor Finneran could afford that."

The effect was extraordinary, Macy. He sat, stock-still, staring fish-eyed at me as if I'd struck him a blow. That's what the truth feels like to a liar, Macy. I understood everything at this moment, understood all there was to know of our Mr. Trilipush.

But here was our only weakness: without the bodies, what physical proof did I have? Nothing. So I quickly followed up my position of strength and made my move: if Trilipush refused to come with me *at once* to make his confession to the British or Australian consul, I had no choice but to have the local police use dogs to dig up the entire area to find Caldwell's and Marlowe's bodies. This alarmed him, and though he sputtered about damage to ancient tombs and whatnot, it was plain that his fear was more than scholarly. I had him. I knew it and he knew it. All that remained was the endgame. "Nothing lasts forever, Trilipush," I concluded, leaning back. "Your move, mate."

He decided to stall. He insulted me, reasserted his innocence, told me he was armed. Finally, he negotiated: he promised he'd be on the boat to Cairo on Monday, I could confirm the reservation that instant. And he would force Finneran to join him in answering any questions I wanted in front of any magistrate I chose when they reached Cairo. I could even walk him off the boat in manacles, if I wished. "But for now, Mr. Ferrell, my wondrous nemesis, I have preparations to attend to for the great voyage." He hobbled off, leaving me to pay for his drink. I was not concerned, as at once I signalled my Egyptian watchers to follow him, and they leapt into well-orchestrated action, spreading out, blending in, manoeuvring as I'd taught them. I went at once and booked myself on his boat to Cairo, and from there moved directly to the police station. The prospect of the police and dogs had visibly frightened him, and I meant to hold his feet to the fire. I'd no intention of letting him slide away in the coming forty-eight hours.

(Saturday, 30 December, 1922, continued)

I am back from my errands in town, my Margaret, and for the life of me I cannot understand why you and CCF did not show this lunatic the door at once. Thanks to his dust kicking, immediate clarification is now in order.

It happened thus: I hobbled over to the post, where nothing awaited me, but as I left, at least a half dozen little boys followed me out, their number growing as I walked down the street. Some of them pretended to hide and follow me secretly, but these were hardly serious efforts. Whenever I looked at them over my shoulder, they would giggle and stare at the sky or their feet. I wandered aimlessly for a while, and never with fewer than six or eight of the monkeys trailing behind. (They tried to follow me back to the tomb tonight, just now, but I simply gave them some of your father's money to go away, *imshee igaree*, which they happily did, waving good-bye to me when I stepped onto the ferry. I hired one of them, however, to come back tomorrow to run last-minute errands for me and your father before our departure, post my papers to you for safekeeping, carry away a few things we do not need anymore.)

Finally, I stopped to rest and take a tea at my *ahwa*. The children retreated across the street, and a few minutes later I was assaulted at last
by the great sleuth Ferrell. Something of a relief to see the dullard in
the flesh, to put an end to this hovering phantom secreting a slimy ecto-
plasm of lies wherever he drifts. You know him: a small, orange man,
peculiarly excited, unable to sit still, feverishly scribbling my every
word, though I can read upside-down, and I often spoke slowly for him
when he fell behind. In truth, I tried to help him with his various tasks.
As you know, he is looking for a missing Australian soldier, this amateur archaeologist you mentioned, and he also had some vague business
with your father. I tried my best to calm him down and help him. I told
him CCF and I will meet him on the riverboat on Monday. And I told
him again and again that I never knew this Aussie boy. But still he sat
there, poking at me, nibbling his raw, red lips, and generally being dis-
agreeable.

He is obsessed with the strangest, unrelated things, events having
nothing to do with Atum-hadu, or even with me, as if, at this great moment in Egyptology, when I am on the verge of revealing my work to
the world, I have suddenly been saddled with a deranged, babbling
child spouting nonsense questions: *Where is Marlowe?* Missing, presumed dead. *Where is Paul Caldwell?* The same, though I did not know
the name at first. *Where were you when they vanished at Deir el Bahari?*
Stumbling back to Egypt from Turkey. Round and round he circled
these simple facts. He was a bore, utterly without imagination, as most
critics are. For make no mistake, he is a critic of the Trilipushian project, properly to be ignored. It is almost a dictate from heaven: ignore
this man, Margaret, lest he confuse you, lest he confuse us all, lest he
distract from what great accomplishment has been granted us here in
the desert. Can we not all simply agree amongst ourselves, as rational
people, to ignore him?

Ferrell had become confused, you see, Margaret, by three documents: two missing and one incomplete. This often happens with people new to interpreting texts. They take any one document much too
seriously, when of course nothing can be understood from a single doc-

ument. When it comes to incomplete history, one needs to encircle the truth, not bound at it like an amorous kangaroo. But for men like Ferrell, if the first thing they happen to read says *x*, they believe *x* forever, and if a second document should say the opposite, they grow confused and begin shouting, "Conspiracy!" When they cannot find something, they assume it is because it never existed. Why is there no record of my career at Oxford? he demanded, as if the answer was not patently obvious: because someone misplaced the file or misspelled my name. For this, a detective has sailed across the globe and I have lost my job and my money and perhaps even your love? It does not matter, not anymore: I will have my discovery.

A small scrap of words can yield as many interpretations as there are interpreters. I tried to explain this to him. He is in a line of work not dissimilar to my own, except that he is incompetent. He has a scrap of "papyrus," an official scribe's notation—in his case a little synopsis of British Army records, telling the moth-eaten story of Marlowe's disappearance, a lacy collection of loose ends and outright admissions of ignorance. Fertile ground, in other words, for the assumptions of asses, for the annunciation of inanities. As I explained to the slothful sleuth, in the face of such spotty knowledge, how many images come to the mind of an imaginative archaeologist? A dozen or more. And with a dozen minds at work, a dozen dozen possible explanations, a hogshead of possibilities.

This is a valuable lesson in textual veracity for us all, courtesy of the doltish detective. It is only a few years since the tragic death of my friend, and it is already damned difficult to say just what happened. Now, cast our vision back three and a half millennia, and from a few such documents let us determine with 100 percent certainty what was happening in Thebes, amongst a people we scarcely understand whose language remains so much a mystery we do not even know how to pronounce it. (Gramophones! If the ancients had had gramophones— those great guarantors of immortality for countless singers today—then we could have heard them speak to us, and we would have known everything. A scandal, in a way: the gramophone has rearranged the nature of immortality in our degraded times: we may never really know how to pronounce *Atum-hadu,* but the world will remember forever the names of Daisy Montgomery, Victor Edwards and His Tuxedoed Chums, Will Wrentham and the Wellington Warblers.)

Inevitably, horrified by blunderers like Ferrell, one wonders about one's own archaeologists, certain to be drawn buzzing to our posthumous fame. What if it were me being sought, now or a thousand years in the future, by a china-shopping bull like Ferrell? What will be misconstrued or simply lost in the record I will have left behind, either knowingly or inadvertently? May the gods protect us all from excavators like Mr. Ferrell! Perhaps, like him, my future chronicler will find it *significant* that the War Office, in its infinite clumsiness, lost my dossier whilst stamping *returned* over *missing.* Thus are false lives stacked upon the crumbling foundations of real ones.

And you, my darling? Where would we be if I believed everything I heard today about you from Mr. Ferrell? Do you need the whole pathetic scene? It went like this, as best I can reconstruct it, though it makes me choke or laugh, I can hardly say which: "You and Finneran are going back to Boston? Really?" The demonic detective looked peakish at the prospect. He could not bear the thought of me returning to you, and tried several tactics to dissuade me.

"Of course," I said. "Why not?"

"But she abandoned you. Rejected you."

"No, no, not at all. You are confused."

"She told me to throw this in your face." Ferrell showed me the last cable I sent you, urging you to remain calm, telling you I did not believe the break between us was your will. He had several letters I had written you. Why did you give them to him, Margaret?

CABLE. LUXOR TO MARGARET FINNERAN,
BOSTON, 30 NOV. 1922, 9.33 A.M. RECEIVED YOUR LETTER OF 15
NOV. WILL DISREGARD FALSE CABLE OF 29 NOV. FERRELL LIAR.
ALL WILL BE WELL. ETERNALLY YOURS IN ANY AND ALL
CIRCUMSTANCES, NO MATTER.
YOUR RMT.

"She is a marvellous woman," he mused, leered, implied personal knowledge of you. "Tragic, though, her sickness."

"Curable," I said, disgusted at his intrusion into our life.

"Curable? I don't know. Opium's a difficult burden to shake, and when I saw her last, she—"

"Opium?" I admit he startled me with the vast enormity of some of his lies, and so he stuck to this one. "Don't make me laugh, Trilipush. I know men like you. I'm surprised to hear you're going back, going through with the wedding. Why bother? You have your treasure, you got Finneran and his friends to pay your way here, you're done. Why marry her now? Or is that something you need? You like her fuzzed up with opium, I'm sure, easy camouflage for your depravity. A pity. She's a beautiful woman. I left her sighing my name in her bed, you know, and I can tell you it's a waste to drug her and turn her into camouflage for you and your boys. I say, Trilipush, you look jealous. Now why's that, I wonder? Did you think the drugs alone would keep her satisfied? How little you know of women, of course."

Margaret, he described you as lovers, embracing in your room on Commonwealth Avenue, described you in great detail, your moan and sigh, your shape, the colour of your limbs. I choose not to believe this tale—how could I do otherwise? It makes no sense to me, even if, as he insisted, you have been taken prisoner by narcotics. That, too, makes no sense to me. No, I know enough about policemen and their ways. If they think you are hiding something, they will buffet you with painful lies until you dislodge what they seek. "Harry," you cried out, he said, leaning back in his seat and pressing his fingertips together, rolling his eyes and licking his dry lips at me. "Harry, you are my one and only handsome man."

I kept my dignity, though in better health I would have thrashed him for you. I could have shot him, I suppose, but we were in public, and I have not fired my Webley in years. Still, the prospect of my return to Boston—to you—brought out the devil in him: "I can have you killed, Trilipush. If I tell O'Toole you stole his money, your life is through. Stay away from her, and I'll let you live." And he tried bribery: "Pity, Trilipush. Caldwell is owed a great deal of money. If you tell me how to find his remains, we could share that money."

And so we must leave Ferrell behind. He is threatening to turn up at my work site with policemen and dogs, for reasons beyond any logic. It does not matter. I am sorry that he has bothered you, has tried to pollute the limpid truth of our lives. I will not think another moment of what he said of you. I beg of you to dispel him with a wave of your lovely hand.

But why did he have that cable? Did you really give it to him, rejecting it with a laugh, as he claims? Did you give him my letters? It hardly matters now. Once it would have. Forget it, love. Forget Ferrell's muddy footprints. This journal is the only letter you need from me.

For, observe: after all his fuss, what did this grimy archaeologist of divorce and insurance fraud want from me? My confirmation of fairy tales of murdered men and your father fleeing debts. All madness, the fantasies of fabulist Ferrell. He must be ignored, dearest, or everything will be blurred, the truth, the tomb, my immortal accomplishment.

At the end of it all, my little *tête-à-tête* with the detective almost made me happy. Having waited so long for his arrival in some anxiety, and then to find at the end that one is pursued for something having absolutely *nothing* to do with one is something of a relief. One had worried it was all going to be about something real, but of course it was not. "Wait a moment—you believe I killed Paul Caldwell?" I asked, absolutely tickled when his ravings finally sputtered to their lunatic conclusion.

But ironically, that turned out to be the single pleasure in the detective's repellent company, the one element of interest in his mad tale: the tale of the missing boy. I heard quite a lot from Ferrell, and the entire business surprisingly touched me, the history of that marvellous boy and his Father Rowley. I am only repeating what I heard from Ferrell, but there is something I would ask you.

I know that you love me. I know that our misunderstandings will be cleared up. I know all this. But what if I were not all you had dreamed of? I have a confession: I was born to this role. I did not have to fight to win it. And I confess, I am ashamed.

For, from what I have been told (perhaps Ferrell told you the same), this boy scratched his way out of poverty and mistreatment. No love, money, simple kindness, encouragement. He was born with nothing, and yet from that nothingness, he created himself. Were you to drop Hugo Marlowe or Ralph Trilipush or some other wealthy, well-educated, well-bred fellow into Paul Caldwell's youth, what would they do? Drop them in the slums of Sydney, and be sure to take their money from them. Strip them of their fine manners. Deny them everything that was not in their heads and hearts the day they were born, and what would they become? I am afraid that, without their received gifts, their internal strength would not suffice. Men like that (like *me*, it is a shameful fact) can never know with certainty what parts of themselves are truly their own. They are confused their whole lives, befogged by what they inherited. When they accomplish something (a degree, a job, a wife), they do not really know if *they* did it alone, if it was not the result of their fathers' example, their mothers' advice, their professors' pricey teachings, all the undigested bits of other people that the rich man calls his personality. But Paul Caldwell educated himself, had no family, took advantage of minuscule opportunities hardly worthy of the name, which no one else could even see, and what did he do with them? He turned them to greater advantage than you could imagine, I am led to understand, a story of self-creation worthy of Atum-hadu.

"What became of Paul Caldwell?" Ferrell demanded again and again. I do not know, but if he had not been killed in the War, what *might* he have become? In better circumstances, a fellow like that might have risen to become my assistant. Would the world have allowed him to shine in his self-made glory, and admired him for it? Or would the world require him to cover himself, lest his inferiors be blinded and confused by the glow they could never produce?

Surely, he would have done anything to impress a beautiful and sophisticated woman. And would you have been as impressed by him as he would have been by you? Could you have loved someone like him,

Margaret? Or did you, too, require someone more like me—polished, proven, endorsed? I long to know this about you.

Ferrell tells me the boy discovered Egypt in a library. Did we feel the same, he and I, as boys in love with this land? I remember the urgency I felt when waiting for new books or the next number of *Chronicles of Egyptology* and *Annals of Modern Egyptology* and *Archaeology* to arrive at the Hall. The excitement was unbearable certain days, imagining the covers, hoping for colour plates, the feel of the transparent paper over the frontispiece engravings.

From Ferrell's cold data, the inspired thinker can invest the story with warmth: early 1917, Caldwell arrives in Egypt, the land that had beckoned him since he was a boy of eight. He is tireless in his efforts to see everything. He learns Arabic, visits the pyramids, tours whenever he can win passes. After a while, he sneaks off-base when he is not given leave, as Egypt is too powerful for him, too real when compared to the unreality of his service in a colonial army, doing his bit in a war that has not the slightest bearing on him. Imagine him, Margaret, so obsessed with this land that he loses all interest in potential punishments. He knows the penalty for his repeated illicit absences, but this war seems every day less real. Perhaps in a muddy trench in Luxembourg he would have been more attentive (or dead). But in the presence of his desert, the spitting bray of camels for hire, each of them calling him to trot into the dark and touch the noseless beauty of the Sphinx, to sit at the foot of Cheops's great pyramid and consider where in this vast desert he would meet his destiny—it would have been impossible for him to fear some slow-moving, slow-thinking sergeant (losing, throughout the late watch, hand after hand of patience by the cone of lamplight in the guardhouse).

And then one day when I am injured and lost in Turkey, Paul Caldwell probably learns that a British officer visiting the Australian camp is, in civilian life, a rising Egyptological expert, even now conducting expeditions when the War allows. I knew Hugo Marlowe's manner all too well. I have no doubt that Caldwell approached him over and over, trying vainly to win his attention. And failing that, I can well imagine that he simply began to follow Marlowe (stationed fully forty miles away) out of sheer fascination with his work, but also because Marlowe knew *everything*. Caldwell must at last have won Marlowe's attention and trust, it hardly matters how. I can imagine Marlowe taking the boy under his wing, and the thrill with which Caldwell heard details, methods of scholarship and exploration, the latest research, and what topic more gripping than the latest thinking about Atum-hadu?

But of course. Of course Marlowe would have discussed Atum-hadu with Caldwell. Marlowe had Fragment C in his tent, waiting for my return. He would have told Caldwell all about Atum-hadu, and everything in that story would have made beautiful sense to the poor boy: a civilisation where a man of genius could make and remake himself every day until he was king. Perhaps Harriman had already been part of Paul's childhood reading, and Atum-hadu's fire, pale as it was in that version, had already singed him. And now Marlowe introduced them.

If he had survived the War, he would have been allowed to become, perhaps, a librarian, maybe a teacher in a provincial boys' school. He could have been as intelligent as I, as charming as I, as well-made as I, but without credentials and wealth and all the rest, he would have been an oddity, a circus freak, a poor boy who *so amusingly* knew some trivia of Egypt for inscrutable reasons of his own. Would you love me if I were that, if that were me? No, how could you. No one will remember Paul Caldwell, and no one should.

The final days of Egypt. There must have been such a day, the final day. The final hour. The final instant. There was in every cataclysm precisely such a single last moment, incredible, but true: a last casualty in the Great War, a final victim ravished by the Black Death, one last Neanderthal to parent a first *Homo sapiens*. And there must have been a last man to worship Atum and, at his death, to take with him all the mysteries of his cult. There was a last man who knew how to pronounce ancient Egyptian; a whole language died with him and all we can do now is strain to hear its echoes by leaning very close to books and wishing hard.

And for Atum-hadu there was this day when all was inarguably lost, when no escape remained, walking in an empty palace, stepping over a man with his face bludgeoned to pudding. How did the king feel that afternoon? Sleepy, so terribly tired. Wishing it could be some other way. Longing for his queen and a peaceful place they could rest together.

There was this day; this day came and then ended, snatching the whole universe with it. There was this last sunrise over pig-faced hordes at the gate under the command of foreigners and the temples burnt and the histories all burnt and the ways and the words and the stories and the aspirations and the certainty of an endless future in which honours and love are your due—merely because you live in a time of peace—all vanished. There was instead this last day, and Atum-hadu stood still for a moment, looked around him and said his farewells, though no one heard them. He was trapped by circumstances beyond the control of any man, even the embodiment of Atum the great creator. No servants, no army, no bearers, no women, no money, no time.

The "end of everything." This is the adult's bogeyman, the only ghoul that survives the nursery to rise before us from time to time and give us quaky guts. This is more than the fear of death, for at one's own demise, one clutches to the condolence that at least something else lives on that represents us or matters to us, somehow preserving us, if only it is the knowledge of the things and people that we love surviving us and enduring. *Our children's lives continue, so ours do not really end*: this is modern man's pathetic scrap of Egyptian immortality. Some, of course, will cling to their subdued Christian heaven or sternly orgiastic Allah's paradise, but for most, there is something simpler in the wings: kids, grandkids, the family business, the life's work, or just the trappings of one's humdrum affairs: the pub and the high street continue on, the football club, the Government and the Constitution and the old regiment. If one is not depressed by these institutions ploughing on heartlessly, celestially unmoved by one's death, then one is conversely heartened and they become like the drawings of food on a Pharaonic tomb wall. Oh, yes, the average man grabs at immortality with his dying breath, and he finds it—in his heirs, work, town, culture.

But the end of *everything*! How much destruction must man or nature wreak before your death becomes intolerably petty, truly mortal? Do you need an ice age or a swollen sun incinerating the Earth? Or would less suffice to end your fantasies of permanence? Your heirs slaughtered before your closing eyes? Your business in bankruptcy, your home and art in cinders? Let us say your church and all of its priests and every written or graphic mention of your god is destroyed, danced on by the sharp-clawed demons who serve some other, younger, crueller god. Let us say the city that has withstood all invaders for thousands of years, the city your family has lived in for as far back in time as you can peer, this pearl of the sea or the sands, this green and pleasant England, this eternal Rome, this pink Jerusalem or holy Mecca, this home of you and yours is dismantled, every last brick, the last bomb flattening the last house just before the last spittly drops of blood pump clear of your stuttering heart. Venice sinks into the sea. Paris burns. London howls. New York crumbles and Athens is reduced to its net ash. Not yet the end of everything for you? Every copy of every work of every author of the world's literature ignites under the watchful eyes of unquenchably pyromaniacal illiterates. The very last copy of the very last history of your country or any other changes into black smoke, and all you can hope in your last breath is for the scantiest sliver of immortality: perhaps, some generations from now, word of mouth from one long-memoried genius actor to his heir to his heir to his heir will result in a brave effort to recall *Hamlet* and write it down again . . . and what does happen at the end? Hamlet poisons himself? Thumps Polonius with a club in a darkened room? Dresses up as a gravedigger and sneaks out the back?

The following items will be irretrievably lost someday quite soon: Beethoven's works. The beer you prefer. All record of your ancestry. The place you first kissed a girl. Toffee. Coffee. The landscape you associate with peace and liberty. Any evidence of your boyhood, real or just fondly recalled. The sensation that all that stands before you and your loved ones is a series of aspirations, accomplishments, setbacks, meals, ceremonies, loves, heartbreaks, recoveries, next acts.

Will you remember me, Margaret? Will you see what I accomplished here, and will you clarify it for the world? I have no one else, you see, to trust. If you ever loved me, or only the idea of me, please, please, rid yourself of your illnesses and make my work live on.

CCF is asleep. I have much to finish, especially if mad Ferrell is coming to stamp about with police and dogs.

January 6, 1955

One likes to be right, Macy. And to be right for the right reasons, that's good, too. This morning, as I look back over what I wrote yesterday, I have the unpleasant feeling, shameful almost, that perhaps I was sometimes right for the wrong reasons. Today, reading this, it isn't quite clear to me just where and in what fashion I caught Trilipush in a lie. And yet, I remember the sensation—a sensation, Macy, as plain and real as the taste of chocolate, or the brush of wind on your face—that he was lying. And I certainly wrote then in my notes that I *knew* he was lying. But rereading it now, the certainty seems somewhat faded. I could've told Margaret about Caldwell's interest in archaeology, and she could've written to Trilipush in turn, I suppose. No matter: if it wasn't that, it was something else. Too tempting to say that hindsight brings clarity. More likely time blurs the truth. I don't question the correctness of my certainty then, only my ability to express it now. I'm no man of letters, Macy, that's your job in this partnership. So make it clear how I catch Trilipush out.

And, also, I can blame myself now, I suppose, that I was unable to convince the police to look into this straightaway. The disappearance of an Englishman and an Australian, four years earlier, during a war, didn't seem to the constable on duty to have the slightest relevance to his job. He told me to report it to the British consulate, and if they ordered an investigation, he'd look into it. I couldn't budge him, and I saw his native pride in saying *no* to me, as if I were the King of England, and not in fact yet another of the Englishman's put-upon colonials. That was Saturday the 30th.

I returned to my hotel to await word from my watchers. They did not appear. I stayed awake until midnight. Nothing. I descended to the street, looking for them. I thought I saw one of them, but when I approached, he spoke no English, and I couldn't, at the end, be sure whether he was one of my team or not. The truth is, Egyptian boys don't look terribly different from one another. I began to fear the worst: Trilipush in his desperation had done my poor boys some serious harm.

Sunday, 31 December, 1922

Dreamt I was sitting behind you, my hand on your hand on your thigh. We were sitting together in a safe, close space. I was whispering into your ear. I was holding your other hand, using your finger to point at the symbols on a papyrus, pouring into your soft ear the secrets hidden in those pictures.

The sun is already up, and there is activity on the other side of the cliff wall. I sat first on a bluff and then closer, on the balcony constructed above the entry to Tut's treasure hole, and I watched the photographer take posed pictures of the great man. It is too much, the equipment, the miles of calico and linen, the jugs of preserving fluids, the vats of photographic fixatives, the countless sifting screens and barrels and picks and carts, the train built specially for him, rail by rail out of the Valley, the dozens of admirers, the journalists pleading for a word. All of that should be enough. But no, now we must have this puff after puff, silver flash and blue flash, click after click, and "Over here, Mr. Carter, look this way, please, sir," the unblinking Eye of the world devouring him without ever reducing him. He was tireless—click, click, click, puff, puff, puff—feeding the world with his image. The great man in his tent. In front of his hole. With his minions. Pretending to oversee something. Walking some treasure up and out, into the sun of knowledge and fame. Consulting with this one or that one. Thinking. His is the tomb of the Restoration, the evidence that nothing vanishes forever, eventually everything returns in its glory. And here are the thin, temporary photographs to prove it.

And there, 200 yards down the path when I return, is Ferrell, rodential and rank, poking at the cliff face.

The next day, Sunday the 31st, in my panic, I again visited the places I knew:
Trilipush's former villa, Carter's crowded site, where I watched him pose for photographers, and the blank stretch of desert that had once been Trilipush's site.
Everywhere nothing. I returned to my hotel, praying that my little army of in-
formants would appear. Nothing. I consoled myself that perhaps they'd followed
him somewhere, and there he stayed, and therefore there they stayed. But my position felt worrisome. I went to the travel office, and they confirmed that Trilipush and Finneran were still scheduled to sail the following day, the tickets had
even been paid for. I hired a new boy to watch the rail station for anyone of the
unmistakable appearance of Trilipush or Finneran. He, at least, reported to me
after the day's last train: they had not left Luxor by rail. I prepared my next move:
I wired the details of our arrival to the British consul in Cairo, told him I was
going to bring him a suspect in the 1918 murder of Captain Marlowe for our joint
interrogation, and to prepare himself. See here: I was using every tool I had to
solve crimes no one else was even willing to investigate, Macy.

That evening, the 31st, to make certain I'd done all I could, I crossed the river
one last time to walk the Trilipush site again, but this time, as I stepped off the
ferry on the Nile's western bank, the crowd waiting to board the ferry's east-
bound return included a native boy I would've sworn was one of my missing
army of watchers. The boy was carrying a large package. When I tried to catch
his attention, though, he ignored me, just stepped on the boat, and I couldn't
reach him. I lost sight of him. I pushed my way to the front of the pier and
watched as the ferry left, but I couldn't see him until, as the boat chugged out to
the current, I spotted him suddenly, staring at me from the deck, as if he'd been
there the whole time, and I would've sworn, even at that distance, that he was
laughing.

Of course, I again found nothing at Trilipush's site, and I know enough of
human psychology at times of stress not to take too seriously those sensations of
apprehension that tickled me in the last sunlight, that suspicion I was being
watched. Even the little boy's laugh was probably more a sign of my heightened
nerves than of anything real.

(Sunday, 31 December, 1922, continued)

Atum-hadu faced the most daunting example of the Tomb Paradox in all Egyptian history. It is, at tenth glance, a puzzle with no solution. To secure his immortality, his name must survive forever aboveground and his body below it, preserved, mummified, and sealed into a minimally outfitted tomb. With nobody left to tell the tale. While the world upstairs melts in the desert sun: his name was on no king list. The XIIIth Dynasty was fast becoming a lumpy purée of fact and legend, quicksand lacunae bubbling with satisfaction where once kings had strode.

WALL PANEL L: THE LAST HOURS OF EGYPT

Text: Atum-hadu was abandoned. He left Thebes and crossed life-giving Nile and walked alone; he carried his goods, his Admonitions, paint, reed, ink, brushes, his cat. The cobras inside his stomach had died. Across mighty Nile he burnt the small boat he had captained, and he watched the silver flashes of the fire against the sky. To the east the invaders sacked his palace, and he could hear the cries of his women. He was empty of this world. He carried his goods into the tomb Seth had given him.

Analysis: The last minutes of his reign. The last minutes of Egypt. Unimaginable sorrows, regrets, but not without a certain beauty, the end of days. Surrounded by blood, danger approaching rapidly. Not danger to his life, but to his afterlife. He is abandoned by everyone. But all is now clear: the puzzle—which has tormented small minds for millennia, stymied Hyksos rampagers and ancient grave robbers and Harriman and Vassal and all those who doubted Atum-hadu's existence—unveils itself for us, Reader. We can now map, chamber by chamber, the work he performed, both that last day and in the events and days leading up to it.

We will understand why there were no seals or inscriptions on the doors.

We will understand the bodies and their placement, the bloody footprints.

We will understand the amateurish illustrations and the expert text.

We will understand how a man alone achieved his immortality, filled and hid his tomb from everyone.

To reiterate, then, we have Figure 1 — The Tomb of Atum-hadu, detail excluded:

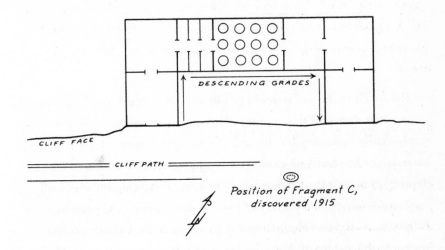

The thinness and lightness of camouflaged Door A are now explained. Even a man of Atum-hadu's prowess cannot be expected to have lifted a heavy stone door into place, sealed it on his own. So let us speculate that he built this subtle but sufficient screen himself, stone-disguised wood, plastered it shut behind him when he had everything he needed inside. With the door closed behind him, he set to work in something that must have resembled peace.

FIGURE 2—THE CHAMBER OF ATUM-HADU'S WOMEN

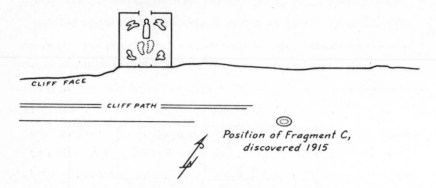

Position of Fragment C,
discovered 1915

Rebirth into the underworld required reconsummation, which required stimulation of the mummy. This chamber contained all that was symbolically necessary for the act. The beaded slippers of some beloved concubine, the scattered, multi-coloured gossamer veils of favourite dancing girls, and the extraordinary paintings covering the walls: all conceivable shape and variety of women, in activities and positions the Admonitions have so eloquently described as Atum-haduan preferences. At the instant of Atum-hadu's death, these garments would be suddenly filled by the lovely associates the king had kept all his life. The paintings on the walls would swell to three plump dimensions, then leap to the floor, giggles and sighs echoing through the supernaturally glowing chambers of Atum-hadu's voyaging apartments.

Who painted these figures? Why, observe: the same hand that had decorated over previous days the History Chamber. Sealed in his own tomb while still quite alive, he created with his own Atumic hand his own escorts to the underworld, relied on his own untrained talent to decorate the unforgiving walls, paint staining his fingers and face and robes. He would frolic in this first chamber, just as soon as he had completed the business of shedding his life and, with the ladies' touch to help him re-create himself, be reborn as his own child.

And who, more than any other, dominates these walls? Examine the small, excellently preserved figurine situated between and behind the crumbling slippers. This beautiful woman draped only in a robe, her eyes sparkling even in sculpture, her smile-sneer an invitation and a revolt—she is reproduced all over this chamber made holy by her presence, her delicate hand, each long, slender finger articulated into the graceful arch of riverside narcissi, in her drowsy languor, lounging in all manner of posture: full portraits done from the sobbing king's memory, profiles, hurried sketches, and details worried over for hours as he strained to capture on a wall all that he loved: her bursts of energy and wit, her spells of sorrow and fatigue, the angry flash in her eye when her whim was denied her, the satisfaction she took, at the beginning, merely from being with her king and knowing that he loved her. Wherever she had escaped to spend her remaining mortal years, she would spend eternity at his side.

FIGURE 3—THE CHAMBER OF THE ANSWERER

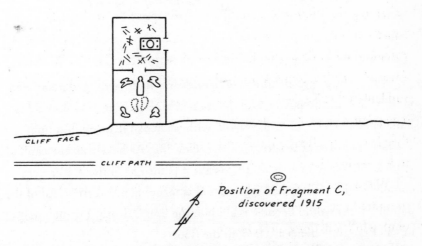

The bloody footprints and the beautiful, plain rectangular pedestal are the centrepieces of the Chamber of the Answerer. Here the *shawabti*, or "answerer," held his post. The small figurine, done in Atum-hadu's likeness, with his unmistakable mischievous grin, stands directly in the centre of the long, heavy stone pedestal, and answered for the king on his voyage to the underworld, fought battles on his behalf (with the assistance of the blood-covered soldiers standing symbolically in ranks, represented by bloody footprints). Surrounding the *shawabti* are four balls of petrified dung (presumably camel or elephant) surmounted by carved scarab beetles, symbols of rebirth for the Egyptians.

FIGURE 4—THE THREE ROYAL ANTECHAMBERS

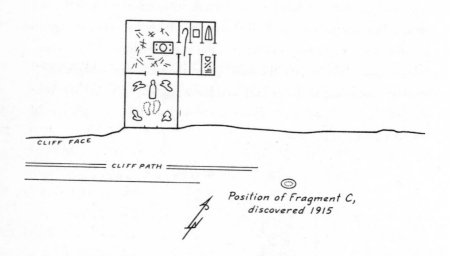

In the Three Royal Antechambers, Atum-hadu arranged items symbolic of his earthly power, and the tools with which he guaranteed his immortality. The walls are covered with scenes of feasting, hunting, warfare, pictures of wealth, treasure, clothing. As nearly as one can be sure, I would say that these, the weakest paintings in the tomb, were completed last, when the king was in his terminal exhaustion. All of the painted items would become real upon the king's death. Further, magnificent tangible items are laid on the floor:

- The carved sceptre, a curved wooden crook, inscribed on its side with the five names of Atum-hadu's titulary, and its upper tip whittled into a face of a god, perhaps Atum himself;
- A beautiful ebony-inlaid wooden coffer containing a complete copy of the Admonitions, all eighty verses on a series of papyrus no larger than the forty-eight verses of Fragment C (which I

have had with me on expedition and will be carrying with me tomorrow when I return to Cairo with CCF) but written on both
sides, forty-eight on the obverse (the same forty-eight as on
Fragment C), thirty-two on the reverse;

- A blood- and paint-spattered robe, likely the very garment the
king wore while preparing the tomb;
- The reeds, brushes, pots of paint, and cutting tools he used to
prepare the tomb's walls and furnishings.

The complete text of the Admonitions is a particularly significant find,
settling the importance of my early and devoted work on that text and
on Atum-hadu's reign. If, in the sixty previously discovered verses, we
see Atum-hadu as a strong man driven by his appetites, then we see another side of him in the final twenty. In these, he is more keenly aware
of his sufferings and of the complex questions put to him by the future.
He writes with a more marked interest in his digestive difficulties (as in
Quatrains 38–41), and the suffering caused by women who have not
returned his love (as in 62 and 69). Of particular interest here, I would
draw the reader's attention to: 68, which identifies unique marks on
Atum-hadu's body with such intriguing precision; 34, in which the
poet-king longs for an "unwinder" who will carry his name to great
heights in a restored world (Osiris would be the traditional interpretation of this, and yet I cannot help but feel a compliment sent my way by
my fraternal king); 63, which in simple, unrhymed words clarifies the
order of kings in the late XIIIth Dynasty, ending with Atum-hadu; 43,
64, and 67, which appear on Pillars seven and eight; and 14, which appears on History Chamber Wall G.

FIGURE 5 — THE HISTORY CHAMBER AND
THE SHRINE TO BASTET

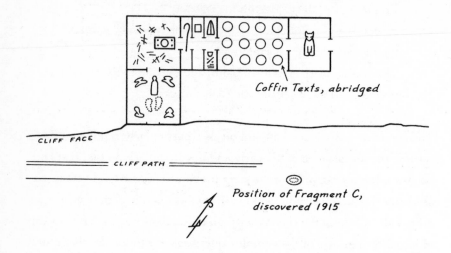

Coffin Texts, abridged

Position of Fragment C,
discovered 1915

After decorating the History Chamber with the chronicle of his life
and reign, and an abbreviated version of the Coffin Texts (the obliga-
tory guide to the underworld, which the poor man apparently had to
reproduce entirely from memory at the last moment, having just remembered to include it and not having much space), the king must
have been exhausted as well as covered in paint. But he had to proceed,
no doubt in sorrow tempered only by the knowledge that soon such
sorrow would pass. But still, for those hours in which he prepared the
Shrine to Bastet, Atum-hadu must certainly have suffered. It is not difficult to imagine that the beloved animal, choking on some ancient fish
bone, had breathed her last in his arms as he wept and pleaded with a
deaf deity.

Yet now even grislier business awaited him. He had probably begun
it days earlier, had probably been forced to consider his options the moment he came to himself straddling the pulpy remnants of his Master of
Largesse.

FIGURE 6—THE CHAMBER OF THE MASTER OF LARGESSE

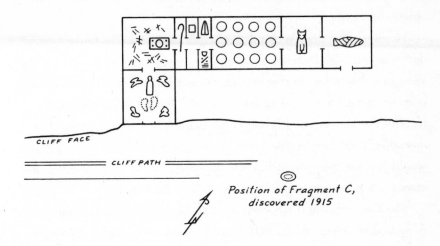

CLIFF FACE

CLIFF PATH

Position of Fragment C,
discovered 1915

I see now that further elucidation is in order, and the text which appears on the walls of the Chamber of the Master of Largesse tells the tale:

Twelve days before the end, when Atum-hadu had so unwillingly destroyed his Master of Largesse, when he began burning the Master's clothing as a first step toward preventing him from winning immortality, the king stopped [to consider].

The great king decided to make use of the Master for all eternity. The Master would make his apologies to Atum-hadu for one million years.

Atum-hadu had seen the Overseers of the Secrets at work. Though he knew their magic, Atum-hadu did not have the required seventy days. He was pursued by the Hyksos, who knew that he had escaped them. He was pursued by enemies of all sorts. He did not have time. He proceeded with haste, but according to the laws and practices.

He suffered greatly.

When his task was complete, he drew upon the linen the face of a man repentant, servile, and restrained.

Analysis: The horrific (albeit still amateurish) paintings attending this remarkable text are astonishing, showing as they do the king sickened by his task. It is worth clarifying just what the king meant by his enigmatic words.

Having killed the Master, defending himself from the fierce attack described on Wall Panel K, the king apparently came to several conclusions in quick order. At that instant he must have decided on all the actions he carried out in the next dozen days. Rather than destroy all trace of the Master and his body ("preventing him from winning immortality"), the king realised that his treacherous Master of Largesse would provide companionship and financing for the king's journey, his mere mute presence sufficient to represent vast wealth.

The Overseers of the Secrets were those priests trained in mummifying bodies, which means that Atum-hadu knew enough (or thought he did) about mummification to perform the ritual himself. The process, as we understand it, is not pleasant, and one must imagine with sympathy a man—even a man hardened by war and suffering—performing this procedure on a member of his own family—even a hated member.

The nude torso is slit along the left side and emptied of its contents. Four organs are preserved in a chemical whose exact nature is still unknown to us. They are then wrapped in linen and placed in the canopic jars, decorated with intricate sculptures of the heads of the four sons of Horus: intestines with the falcon-headed Qebehsenuf, stomach with the jackal-headed Duamutef, lungs with the baboon-headed Hapy, and liver with the human-headed Imsety. That said, it is interesting to note that there are no canopic jars in the Chamber of the Master of Largesse, an aberration that will be explained later in this preliminary summary of our findings.

The brains—irrelevant in Egyptian anatomy and religion—were generally removed from the skull by a hook or a straw and discarded. In the case of the Master, the wall illustrations would imply that his skull had been crushed in his death, and cephalectomy was therefore both speedier and less tidy.

The body was washed and filled with some sort of chemical preservative. And the mystery of this substance, which puzzles us to this day, is not explicated by Atum-hadu's tomb. At the end of seventy days, the body was deemed ready for wrapping. Now, observe: if the mummy of the Master of Largesse is not in precisely the same condition as others found under the sands, let us be clear: Atum-hadu did not have enough time to do the job properly, and had never performed this complex and mysterious ritual before, except on his cat. Further, he was the only man on the task, ill, wounded, despairing, and hunted. He had limited tools and perhaps only an amateur's best guess at the chemicals needed for the terrible undertaking. And so, if the Master's mummy looks slightly unorthodox, or has decayed along a different path, well, that is only further evidence of the unique nature of this find.

The hole in the body was sewn up. It is strange, considering what the tragic king had already gone through for this process, but it would appear from the wall paintings that this is the task which most profoundly affected Atum-hadu's delicate stomach. One group of the narrative illustrations depicts these dreadful hours: the king's face curls in horror as he begins to stitch. He drops the needle and thread, flees the tomb, stands outside, talks to what appears to be a kindly peasant woman who offers him shelter in her home, and he is sorely tempted but knows this cannot be. His throat catches, and he quietly rejects her kindness. When she leaves, he falls to the ground and weeps. He then returns to his task, stricken.

In traditional mummification, the stitched wound is then patched with a seal of the eye of Horus. Gold, jewels, amulets are laid on the body. The fingers and toes are each capped with gold. Though I cannot be certain, I believe it is safe to assume that this mummy probably lacks such gaudy accoutrements.

Normally, each toe and finger is wrapped separately in the linens. Then the arms and legs. Then the body and head, twenty layers thick. Some sort of resin glue is then used to seal all this bulky linen work, and a mummy mask covers the head. All of this is a task for several men, not for one. We can only imagine his exertions, the procedural corners cut by the hurried monarch. The king's leg was horribly wounded in one of the last battles of the Hyksos war, and it required all of his failing strength to wrap the heavy body with even five layers of linen and then roll it, centring the mummy of his onetime ally on the floor of its burial chamber.

Having completed his wrapping, the king used some ancient chemistry or linen work, the mystery of which eludes me, and emblazoned on the corpse's chest the symbol of Atum-hadu's reign—the vulture, sphinx, and cobra, along with the inscription HORUS CONSUMES THE HEARTS OF THE WICKED.

Lacking a mummy mask, the king painted a face directly upon the linen-wrapped head, re-creating the Master as a man who would do his king's bidding without argument or treachery. Linen strips are by no means easy surfaces to decorate, let alone to convey repentance, servility, and restraint. But with simple, affecting brushstrokes, the king performed an act of monumental forgiveness edging into the divine, transforming his greedy and unreliable escort into another man entirely, creating a companion and father he could trust.

The text on the wall of the Chamber of the Master of Largesse concludes:

"You are young again, you live again. You are young again, you live again." The king repeated the ritual words into the ear of his friend and earthly father, who had loved the king as a son, for as long as he had walked on the world.

Whatever the significance of my nerves at the sight of that boy on the Nile ferry, it's an undeniable fact that somewhere evil *was* being done, because, early the next day, January 1st, when I arrived with my luggage at the dock and waited to board the steamer to Cairo, Trilipush and Finneran never appeared. I stood on the dock and eyeballed every passenger as they walked aboard the gangplank with wobbly legs. I waited until the purser's last call for departure rang out. I asked him to check his list: "Yes, sir, Finneran and Trilipush reserved and paid, but not aboard." I cannot recall if I was excited or worried. I leave that to you,

Macy, to describe. But I let the boat leave without me, consigned my luggage to a porter, and set back to my work in a frenzy.

I hired a boy to watch the docks and sent another to the rail station, and then I hurried back to the police, where I was now able to rouse an inspector with the undeniable *fact* of two missing persons, not from 1918 but from that very day, an American and an Englishman, archaeologists, guests of Egypt, and now officially missing. (The tension produced by gently stretching the truth is sometimes enough to propel otherwise immobile objects along a path.)

I'm enclosing the very brief newspaper clipping from the *Luxor Times* of February 11th, 1923, "Australian Detective Helps Kena Police." That paper, a serious and reputable one, came out every three days, I believe, in those years. It's a short article, but it lays out the conclusion of these events plain enough, and the small drawing does justice to the Harold Ferrell of 1923.

I led the copper to Trilipush's villa (the resident journalists greeted us but had seen nothing), and then across the river, using a police motorcycle on the far bank. This time, another quarter-mile or so further past Trilipush's excavation site, the policeman and I found a gramophone with Trilipush's name inscribed in the lid. Odd sight: the device was just sitting on the path, a lone gramophone in the middle of the desert. A disk was still resting on its table, and I marked down the title: "I'm on the Back Swing, Sit Down, Dear." Some hundred feet farther on, there was evidence of a bonfire, including remnants of burnt clothing. Something was afoot, something very bad indeed. I guided the inspector back around the cliff face and into the Valley of the Kings to Carter's site, and there I asked Carter if he'd seen Trilipush or Finneran again since he and I spoke. He hadn't. I had the inspector ask if any of Carter's men had any knowledge of Trilipush whatsoever. The question was passed among the men, and before long, one of them—a native—admitted he'd actually *worked* for the Englishman for the month of November, and what of it? We took him aside. This suspiciously defensive Egyptian—a strong-looking, bald bloke of about thirty or thirty-five—described abandoning Trilipush's expedition at the end of November, as it had plainly failed, and he claimed he hadn't seen the Englishman since November 25th, the day he came to work for Carter. He denied knowing anything of Finneran, even the name. We took his name and address and watched him walk back to his digging work.

Events moved very quickly now, Macy, so pay attention. I had two hypotheses, which I had no choice but to pursue simultaneously, as time was ticking away very fast indeed: (a) Trilipush and Finneran had been spooked by my discoveries and had flown secretly, Finneran to Boston with his gold, Trilipush as far away as possible from my investigation of the Marlowe-Caldwell murders, OR (b) they had been set upon by someone who knew of their golden find, and foul play was afoot. I had to chase both possibilities, but I needn't've bothered with Hypothesis A, as it turned out. Still, I had someone watching the railways already, and I telegraphed the hotel in Cairo to alert me should my suspects appear up there somehow. Further, upon our return to the police station, the inspector put the word out to his men to keep their eyes open for anyone of Trilipush's and Finneran's descriptions, likely to be moving with a vast amount of luggage, which they would be very unwilling to open to an enquiring policeman. If they were seen, they were to be considered very dangerous indeed.

But, as I said, such steps were quite unnecessary, for having taken them, the police inspector then discovered in his files that this same black at Carter's site who'd worked for Trilipush had been involved in a violent incident in his previous employment on the Cairo–Luxor steamer line! For this brawl, he'd been arrested and then released, and he'd also been fired from his post on the riverboat. This had been at the end of October, after which he must have gone to work for Trilipush, who apparently was happy to hire a known thug—interesting, that. The copper and I left immediately from the station to investigate the native's home. And, behold! We arrived just a few minutes before the man himself: he'd left Carter's site in the middle of the workday, directly after we'd spoken to him. Very suspicious. We arrived just in time, for in the din of this native's arguments and fumbled explanations and wife's wailing and children's crying, I found under his bed another of Trilipush's inscribed gramophones and, right in the open on a table, a plate containing easily a dozen cigars with black-and-silver bands bearing the monogram *CCF.* That settled that. We had our suspect in custody by the afternoon of Monday, January 1st, 1923. The murders had taken place at some point between the time Trilipush left our interview and that morning. It will not surprise you to hear that our native's alibis were quite, quite feeble.

I blamed myself then for some of this, and I still do. If I hadn't let Trilipush go his way two days earlier, he would've been alive and facing a more appropriate justice than murder at the hands of his ex-employee. If I could've relied on my army of watchers, if I'd been able to find Finneran at the excavation site, I could've—well, I don't rightly know what I could've done. Trilipush was a murderer, after all, and knew he was nearly caught, so he didn't see me as his protector, though he should've done. Justice protects us as well as punishes us, Macy. Trilipush could've yet saved himself from his rough and unnecessary end, if he'd turned himself in to me, but the proud ones never do, and often they'd rather die than be caught.

The police interrogations of the Egyptian (I can't find his name in my notes—frustrating to me as a historian and an embarrassing lapse on my part as detective, I admit) were as harsh as they could legally be, and I participated to the extent my expertise in the case and in criminal psychology could be of assistance. The suspect denied any knowledge of the murders, no surprise, claimed Trilipush'd given him the cigars and the gramophone as gifts back in November. Not impossible, said one of the police inspectors, but then as questioning proceeded, the Arab's story changed, and at one point he admitted to *assaulting* Trilipush violently (more than once, he added later) and stealing the gramophone, as if these half-truths were going to bring his predicament to an easy end. All he accomplished with them, though, was losing the support of those few listeners who still generously hoped he might be innocent of the crimes. Later, he retracted even that limited confession of violence, until his compiled stories had become a stew of incompatible nonsense. Even though he nearly admitted to the killings (and if you knew how to listen, the confession was clear), he never did reveal where he'd hidden the bodies. Also, he insisted on one point with unshakable tenacity, no matter how harsh the interrogation: he maintained there'd never been any treasure at all, that Trilipush had never found a single thing. Now this claim was so far distant from the facts that it cast as unbelievable every single word of the desperate man. But he clung to this one lie so insanely that it became apparent that he was simply never going to reveal which cousin or cache he'd delivered the treasure to.

The police wanted that treasure, and you can be sure they pressed him hard on this point. But the Gippo just kept saying to me, "You have been there? Then you know it is empty." Well, of course it's empty, Abdul: you emptied it. In the end, he stubbornly refused a signed confession for any of it, which I'm certain resulted in an even harsher sentence than if he'd seen fit to cooperate.

The local authorities didn't need much convincing from me. The murder of two Westerners at the hands of a native, in this period of huge touristic interest in Egypt (thanks to Carter's good work)—shilly-shallying wouldn't be tolerated, and the Egyptian Government as well as the American and English consuls were most gratified with the fair and speedy trial and appropriate sentence.

As for me, if I was unable to answer with unshakable certainty *all* of my clients' questions, if I did not find any of the four bodies it had become my business to find, at least in this one case I was instrumental in identifying, apprehending, and escorting the malefactor to his punishment. The English and Australian consuls were also grateful for my accountings of the events of 1918.

How tidy it would be if we'd found Caldwell's and Marlowe's remains, if we had Trilipush's and Finneran's bodies, and had been present to witness this Egyptian walking away from them, his hands dripping blood! Fairy tales, Macy. Oh, no, my colleague, rare is the criminal who doesn't demand a little thought from the detective to complete the story. But there could be no doubt what had happened, the history detailed at trial and in the enclosed Press clipping: a notoriously violent and vengeful native (and not rich, to be fair), fired by his employers at the riverboat line for brawling, latched on to a Western archaeologist, in the hopes of being present when something worth stealing was found. When the expedition faltered, he left to join a different one. When he later learnt, perhaps from gossip in Carter's camp following Carter's visit to Trilipush's site, that the failed expedition he'd abandoned had suddenly turned wildly successful, the murderer returned and spied the loot guarded by two men, one of whom was injured no less. At some point between my interview with Trilipush on the 30th and the morning of the 1st, when they were due to take the riverboat north, this Egyptian had ambushed Finneran and Trilipush, murdered them, burnt their clothes, dispatched the bodies, and hidden the treasure. Had he not been so foolish as to hold on to a gramophone and the cigars, mere knickknacks compared to his hidden loot, he might've escaped justice. That he'd required confederates for his crimes—especially the transport and stashing of vast treasures—cannot be denied. But deny it he did.

But why would the killer deny it to the very end, even when a lengthy prison term was facing him? Well, the history of Egyptology, I learnt from a fellow in a club back in Cairo, is filled with stories like this: the modern Egyptian, with no real interest in the historical aspect of this underground gold, only cares about it as money. Native families often clandestinely dug up and slowly sold (sometimes over generations) these archaeological treasures, which they viewed (considering what they saw as the Western mania for them) as underground bank accounts to be disbursed as necessary. Trilipush's killer willingly went to prison to protect friends and family planning to support themselves over years by slowly dribbling out through trusted fences the vast funereal treasures of King Atum-hadu.

And, on the train from Cairo to Alexandria, my assistant Macy and I discussed another question: just who *should* have had the treasure of Atum-hadu? Did it belong to Trilipush, who killed Paul Caldwell and Hugo Marlowe for it? Or Chester Crawford Finneran, who paid for Trilipush's discovery? Or Julius Padraig O'Toole, who had loaned Finneran that money? Or the next of kin of Paul Davies-Caldwell and Hugo Marlowe? Hector Marlowe and Emma Hoyt? I suppose the heirs of this Egyptian killer had as much claim to it as anyone else in this dirty business, and I wasn't much interested in spurring the authorities to pursue them, trying to shake the tree until the confederates fell to the ground. Yet again, mere money had driven men mad, as it always does, and in the end, the cost was four dead bodies, one abandoned young woman, a man in prison, and heartbreak stretching from Sydney to Luxor to London to Boston. Money's an accelerating motivator, Macy, and when it begins to drive men, it tends to drive them right over a cliff.

I collected my fees and expenses, of course, from my clients—the Davies Estate, Tommy Caldwell, Ronald Barry, Emma Hoyt, the Marlowes, O'Toole—reported to them as much as I could of what they needed to know, and I was back home in Sydney by late July 1923, a little more than a year after I'd left. There wasn't, in the end, much coverage of the case, just the *Luxor Times*. I can't say I wasn't disappointed at this curious indifference of the World Press.

Justice was served, though, the truth was laid bare, those who'd sinned were punished. For me, of course, it'd been the adventure of a lifetime, one of the most remarkable cases of my career, the fruit of all my powers of deduction and detection at their prime. I'd travelled the globe, entered the homes of the wealthy and powerful, seen men and women in all walks of life motivated by those universal impulses that guide every last one of us, and I was never, when I reflected on what I saw, truly surprised, not truly. When you understand them, people can't surprise you, you see. Their motives are sometimes hidden, but they're not numerous. People are open books, once you've learnt how to read. That's both a curse and a delight, but it's an unavoidable result of being a dedicated student of human nature, which every good detective most certainly is.

I hope I've filled in the outlines and logic of the case with enough justice to complete your "family history" and also to let you expand it for our readers.

I look back now on this, though, and I'm a little troubled by the amount of time I've spent telling you this story. You see, I've already selected our next case from my files, my friend, and were I equipped with a recorder and microphone, I could simply dictate the tale. I shouldn't think the expense would be too prohibitive. It would, of course, be figured into our partnership agreement, if you can spare the sum in advance. I look forward to your thoughts on this matter. I await your word. I'm ready to begin as soon as I hear from you. Our readers await. Time is of the essence.

Yours in limbo,

Ferrell

Miss Margaret Finneran
2 Commonwealth Avenue
Boston

January 25, 1923

My dear Miss Finneran,

As Mr. Trilipush's employment with Harvard
concluded at the end of the autumn term, I am
taking the liberty of forwarding you the post
that has accumulated in his office during his
continued wanderings in Egypt, to wit: six journals of Egyptology and archaeology; a personal
package from England; two letters from museums;
and a few notes from students (not sealed). If
you would be good enough to forward these to Mr.
Trilipush when he returns from Egypt, that would
save us all a good deal of trouble and embar-
rassment.

With every good wish for your approaching nuptials to the great man,

C. ter Breuggen
Chair, Egyptology

PERSONAL for Professor R. M. Trilipush
In care of the Department of Egyptian Studies
University of Harvard
Cambridge, The United States of America

29 September, 1922

My dearest Ralph,

I have just spent a positively dreary afternoon (and this on one of the rare sunny days our moody, not to say bitchy, Heavenly Father has granted us of late). I was forced to pass a rather exhausting hour or two with this little Australian fellow, all spotty and orange-coloured, with a head of the most ludicrous fur. The very moment he left I set pen to paper to you, as he was kind enough to give me your address at dear, lovely Harvard. Harvard! How very grand! Of course, for old Balliol men like you and me, perhaps just a bit provincial, no? Don't I recall Marlowe calling it some rather amusing names? "The last refuge of the unemployable"?

Well, I see I've told a fib: no, I did not set pen to paper the very moment he left, dear. I waited until he was well and truly out the building and on his way, and then I had a bit of a sob first. I am no longer prone to dramatics, Ralph, not for a very long time, but wretched little Mr. Ferrell, a detective of the dullest variety, delivered me the confirmation of some very bad news. Nothing I hadn't suspected for years now, but it's one thing to know something and quite another to *know* it, if you see my meaning. When I saw your dear book autographed for Hugo's parents, well then I knew what you of course have known for years already, what I daily feared but tried vainly not to believe.

Calm down, ducks, I can imagine you running about in a frenzy. I have my grief and my grievance, but no real complaint to make to you, considering the events with fairness. Rending my garments whilst blithering to the constabulary and Hugo's dreary family certainly holds no appeal. You are free, as far as I am concerned. As long as I never actually meet you, I can imagine his face on you and tell myself he lives on in you, but there are some things you should know, before you make any more fatal errors. I should hate to see Hugo's creation meet his divine maker too soon. To begin with, Hugo's unbearable parents are called Hector and Regina, our Hugo's persistent claims to the contrary notwithstanding. Sit down, my angel, the story grows rather more surprising.

I rather overdid it for Ferrell just now, but he was quite asking for it. Normally I offer my more conservative visitors a mild and harmless atmosphere, but this one, this vile little Aussie farmer, wasted hardly a moment before loosing his Wilde references and sneering intolerably and asserting his taste in ladies. If I hadn't been curious to hear what he knew about our Hugo and you, I would have thrashed him unconscious, dressed him in skirts, and left him in the street. As it was, I did perform rather dramatically for him. The little man's face when I—preparing to ring a velvet cord which led to nothing but a curtain—asked him if he wouldn't "savour an Arab boy to go with his coffee" was all the entertainment I've had in weeks.

Also, I'm a wee bit *triste* because I have held on to the enclosed pages for years now, despite enquiries from Hugo's family and our vulgar antipodal sleuth. But what good are they to me now? You were led out of Egypt, not he.

I have become an impossible bore, these last years. I should be a hero to the youth of London, and all I do is sit in my rooms, getting daily older. I had a visit the other day from a Balliol chum, and he quite rightly chided me for becoming an old woman, something out of Balzac. Have you read Balzac? Hugo described you as quite maniacal for your field, but not much for other things. There is more to life than— Oh, listen to me, as if I have any right to urge you to expand your horizons, when mine have shrunk to a handful of letters from a dead soldier-boy.

I am enclosing five. They explain everything you need to know, except, I suppose, where it all began. Originally, at Oxford, he was a bit of a joke, you see, just some easy camouflage, a mutually corroborated name, a fellow we could all use when corresponding with the *maters* and the *paters*. It had become dogma, you see, in our circles, that we were incurable, though there were still some glum fellows amongst us who tried to resist, or curse our natures, or do as the aged parents demanded of us and speak to some horrid specialist down in London, in Harley Street, who was prescribing psycho-analysis, showers, travel, boxing. ("What about wrestling, love?" I asked him.) How *all* the parents seemed to know of the same quack is beyond me. At any rate, the boldest of us—Hugo, of course—simply said one day as the little club was dining in our apartments, "What's wrong with you girls? You submit to this? I refuse treatment. Why don't *they* seek treatment?" Delicious: the thought of our uncomfortable fathers seeking out a cure for their persistent gynophilia from some delicate doctor of our choosing. We all loved Hugo, you know. I could never have him all to myself, even then. But he was so very much what I longed to be. Women never looked at him, of course; he was not built for them, and the beasts could sniff that out from miles away, while my appearance always confounded them and had them dropping their Jane Austen novels near me with significant looks in their eyes.

"Well, I refuse," said our Hugo. But some of the younger men were not as brave, so Hugo suggested that we all tell our families that we were already cured, much better, thanks, and thinking seriously of proposing to a young woman of good family we'd met recently at a party. What was her name meant to be? Odd, now I cannot produce more than Gwendolyn, but that isn't it. And, best of all, Mother and Father, we have met the most marvellous fellow, greatest friend, just the fellow one goes up to Oxford hoping to meet, he will probably be my second should I muster the nerve to tell this lovely girl just how superlative I think she is, and he, well, he was flexible, that was his charm; he was whatever you thought your parents wished to hear. If they or that leech in Harley Street had had the audacity to discourage you from your current circle of friends, just reassure them that you were now spending your free moments in the company of a grand fellow, a tremendously trustworthy chap of good breeding who was rowing like Odysseus that season, who was running like Hermes, who was certain to take a first in Egyptology (on this, Hugo insisted for uniformity), who was engaged to Lady Mumblemumble, who was going to return to Kent and refurbish the family Hall to its previous condition, and take his estates in hand, show the local yeomen what a twentieth-century gentleman farmer looked like, and on and on, to one's taste, or one's parents' taste, to be accurate. I am sure you have heard it all, dear boy. Hugo provided an extensive biography for those fellows who weren't terribly creative, even arranged for a few of the boys to have their photograph done in sporting garb with a local man who fit the bill. We would even go to Hugo for suggestions: "Mother wants to meet *him* next month. What shall I do?" Hugo handled everything, calmed our nerves, scripted whatever tales we needed, and our parents breathed easy. Our troublesome flaw acquired at school had quite vanished at University.

I still cannot precisely make out what happened that November day in the desert. I know what Hugo meant to do, dear Ralph. I do hope you have forgiven him that, old man. Can you really blame him? No, no more than I can blame you for the result. (Or blame myself: Hugo quite misconstrued my counsel.) But might you write me and reminisce over the events? I think you owe me that filament of peace.

Did you love him, a little? I have to think you did. How could it have been otherwise? How could he not inspire love? Especially in one whose heart is open a bit, you who dare not speak your name. You knew him last. You could write me about Hugo at War, describe his days.

Now then, with a packet of letters, you are all at once educated. But do not stop being yourself! That would be, without question, the wrong moral of this tale! No, I don't mean to discourage you, Ralph, any more than I mean to hunt you, or ask the police to muck about in our lives. I am simply giving you the knowledge you need to carry on, because, after all, you are our love's labour, dear boy, and you mustn't be lost—your continued success does us honour. You are the walking expression of Hugo, his Adam outliving him, but still performing just as he built you. Oh, by all means, carry on, old Ralph, your Creator was proud of you, even if in a moment of weakness he did try to destroy you. Gods can be like that. And when I hear of your triumphs (such as this very droll little book of smut, which Hugo would have heartily admired), I shall sing to myself that in you Hugo walks the earth still, as alive as when last I embraced him.

He crafted you out of bits of cloth and horsehair stuffing, just to make me laugh, you know. Whatever you were to him, whatever he neglected to tell me, it is as nothing compared to what we were and what a gift he made to me of you, his *Guignol*, whose stage is everywhere and whose strings stretch all the way up to some tastefully *louche* paradise. I can certainly imagine you today, nameless boy, talking as much like Hugo as you can. Do you trim and stretch "good morning" into "g'd mmm-morrrrning"? Do you call people Sven when you can't recall their names? Do you bait the gynophiles and call them ducks? Of course you do, ducks.

Only, as a favour to this acolyte, give a thought, from time to time, to what you let die in a faraway desert. I do hope you were not cruel about it.

> Your admirer,
>
> B. Quint

16 January, 1918

Dearest Bevvy,

If you long for something cheering to enliven your dreary days in grey old England, then I have a tale to amuse you without fail: I am being—oh, oh! Mightn't there be a censor or two peering over your shoulder? Well, never mind. I am an officer, and I shall slip this through to you clean somehow. I know a wounded fellow heading home who can carry an envelope. Trust your Go-go.

So out with it then: I am being *blackmailed* and it is delicious, I must tell you. It has brightened my dull, dusty existence here no end. I thought I should go mad if I had to interrogate one more of these old native women suspected of some or another contact with the ferocious Enemy, as if the Egyptians aren't one and all simply *delighted* to be our Allies and top chums, from every little brown newborn to every old wrinkled labourer. Not to complain overly, though. Thanks to the work, my Arabic has grown quite good, if rather peculiar, for when I am the only interrogator in the room I am free to try out my more *recherché* phrases on the freshest quivering, treasonous youths.

But my tale.

You have no reason to know this, but here in our little home away from hygiene we are but forty miles from a suburb called Tel el Kebir, an antipodal colony, a festival of jolly waltzing matildas and swagmen, those remnants who weren't sent off to splash their insides all over the Bosporus for what, I haven't the slightest doubt, were unmistakably brilliant strategic considerations. For the most part one avoids them, of course, though some of their officers are not absolute ovinophiles and one is required to consult with them now and again whilst in the thunderous councils of war, devising devilishly clever coups to dazzle the fezzy heads of our wicked Enemy. I was even forced to spend a week billeted amongst these odd marsupials, *liaising*, as we say, though we say it in the least amusing sense of that word the Army could devise. The point: one of these dear young upside-down fellows found me in circumstances that merit illustration.

Some weeks after my return from the diggers' camp, I had quite put them out of my mind. Then, one evening—one of those nights that make this whole fancy-dress ball worth the trouble, almost make you thank the King for taking the time out of his schedule to engage in this dust-up with his cousin— I left the base for a *rendez-vous* I had arranged amongst my beloved pyramids at Gizeh, which is a longish trip from here but a pleasant one on a motorcycle late at night.

Setting please, Bev: the apex of Cheops's pyramid penetrated the silver disk of moon, rather charmingly like a head on a pike. The attenuated black shadows of the three pyramids fell behind their yellow-white selves, making a backgammon board of the desert, and I cut the 'cycle's engine. I walked towards the pyramids, sultry on this silver-black night as if they were absolutely luring me into a tryst. But for my expected guest, I was, I thought, the only man in the ancient desert, and these three proud beauties, along with their noseless pimp, called me onto the sand, where we could all be alone together. Soon thereafter, my appointment arrived, a native son I had interrogated that day, a quite innocent fellow hauled in for reasons known only to some Emma Pip or other. As I was the only Arabic speaker in the interrogation, I took the opportunity of telling him that the best way to avoid future trouble with his masterful English overlords was to meet me for a tour of the pyramids after midnight. "His Excellency does me too much honour," replied the *coquette*. "What's he saying, then?" asked the sergeant. "He says he is a submissive subject." "A likely story, the little black bastard," grumbles old sarge, and I assured him I would keep the boy's name on file and have my legendary network of spies watch him constantly.

Well, we'd placed ourselves in the shadow of the great pyramid, my interrogatee and I, making a great pyramid of our own, when I heard another motorcycle engine, but it seemed to be heading off in the other direction (damned echoes). A few minutes later I looked down and noticed I was no longer standing in shadow (damned mobile moon) but rather on moon-blanched sand, and only a moment later I heard a throat clear, and out of the dark steps this little private (whilst one's own little private remained well-concealed).

Some free counsel, Bev, should you ever be in just this situation: this is not the time to panic or show weakness. My hips absolutely continued their nocturnal travels, though my native bearer was now wide-eyed and whimpering, and his supporting arms were sagging when he was supposed to be holding up the side of the pyramid. I barked some convincing Arabic at the intruder, meaning to have him scurry off thinking he had interrupted a heavily armed Egyptian gentleman in a standard evening's pursuit: "Name yourself, accursed swine eater."

He replied in calm English with an Aussie ring: "General Allenby."

"Right then," fucking Marlowe enunciates in English. "You'd best have leave to be off base at this hour, soldier, and have a signed chit for that motorcycle I heard." You would have been proud of my rough sergeant's manner, Bev, and that I still refused to break my martial rhythms. "Name." He saluted smartly and answered. "You've not heard the end of this. I'm ordering you back to base immediately."

"Yes, sah, Captain Marlowe, sah, right away, sah." The ready use of *my* name did dishearten me a bit, as you can well imagine, and if I'd had more wit or confidence I could actually hit anything with the damned toy, I would have reached for my Webley, shot the digger, finished my engagement in peace, and found an explanation later. As it was, I heard his 'cycle buzz away, I stirruped my mount back into the shadows and tried not to think about it.

Next day, though, I admit I was a bit concerned about repercussions, but my tormentor did not keep me suffering for long. Before my servant had even finished telling me that an ANZAC was waiting outside at *my* request, into my tent strode this same jackeroo of the previous evening. "At my request?" I repeated with a tone, dismissed my servant, and set to winding my puttees myself.

"Had the impression you were unhappy with me last night, sah."

"Not at all, not at all. All you Aussies have proven to be excellent soldiers. No unhappiness at all. Anything else then?"

"If I may, sah, beg leave to enquire, what is it about the Australian fighting man that most impresses you, sah?"

I finished my puttees, sat back on my daybed, and considered the little shit, though he gazed militarily into the middle distance, where I am sure he could see the universe laying itself out very well indeed for him.

"I suppose that would be the native Aussie discretion, wouldn't it?"

"Our watchword, sah."

"Quite."

"Sah, if I may say, interesting this: the ancient Egyptians so respected this particular trait—discretion—above all others that they gave military promotions for just that."

"Funny, I can't say I recall ever reading that."

"No, sah? Well, state education down under is terribly thin, you know, sah, so it spurred me to independent scholarship."

"I see. Yes, you may be right, ancient cultures rather up for interpretation at the end of the day, aren't they? I shall look into that claim, perhaps contact an old don. Anything else today, Private?"

"Shall I write my name down for you, sah?"

"Shouldn't be necessary, I don't think."

"Very good, sah, at your service, sah."

He had me, Bev. I swallowed my dignity, and a few days later I had business again at the Aussie base at Tel el Kebir. There I mentioned to the appropriate AIF company commander that one of his number, who had some Arabic, had been of particular use on a series of counterintelligence interrogations I had been conducting, and certainly not my place, of course, but the fellow might merit a bump up to lance corporal if they had an opening in those lofty ranks. The price? I had to listen to the most excruciating stories about this captain's fiancée back in Melbourne and coo over a photograph of the most unspeakably hideous woman in the history of that sex, if she was not in fact a shaven wallaby in skirts.

Thus endeth my steamy adventure, B. I should think I'm in the clear, and have heard the last of my nasty Sven from the bottom of the earth. Of course, I shouldn't be surprised if he turns up expecting a few piastres for his continued discretion, but he should also know that I can make his life quite miserable here, have him detailed to something awfully unpleasant if not absolutely fatal.

In other exciting news from the scene of mankind's great endeavour on behalf of world peace, I found something rather extraordinary in the bazaar this past week, though I can hardly believe it is not an imposture. I bought it on the strength of its convincing appearance, better than the usual absurd forgeries. I am not done deciphering it, but it appears to be something of potential interest on a rather arcane point of Egyptology. Of course, despite meandering back into the bazaar, I cannot find the fellow who sold me it again, so all of my new questions about its provenance and authenticity are virtually unanswerable, but I wonder if you might not do me a small service, Bev? Might you ask dear, doddering Clem Wexler how best to preserve and ship to him a particular "aged document"? Be a dear and write back instantly upon his response, quite the highest priority. Also, Bev, while I do think I can pass letters to you unread, I shouldn't think yours to me will be treated with equal respect. Phrase wisely, dearest friend.

Chinlessly,

Go-go

23 April, 1918

Bev, you asinine anthrophile,

Do try not to be an absurd little girl about what I do and do not include in my letters to you. Do not lecture me on any of your newest virtues, none of which even remotely convince me. I shall continue to write what amuses me and what I believe will amuse you, my dearest friend. My method of conducting counterintelligence operations is as sound as any other I have seen. None of my young native agents have conspired with the Enemy, that is certain; I keep them much too sated, a preventive technique every security service should use. So I shall not censor myself for you, nor shall I protect what you so unconvincingly term your *sensibilities*. Do you think I write the same stories to little Theo Grahame or any of our other old dinner companions? Of course not. You are my one and only true *correspondent*. I never asked you to live like a grey Dominican friar on my account (and even they, I think, make a point to enjoy themselves more than you do, relaxing with nuns and half-wit peasant boys and such, threatening them with hellfire if they talk).

But what of Wexler, damn you? You were in such a hurry to complain (and quite indiscreetly) that you neglected to do the very simple thing I asked of you, you rotten man. Now go run across town right now before Wexler finally expires and disintegrates and the charlady sweeps up the resulting grey powder. Tell him these words: "Hugo's found some p. that seems to confirm Harriman and Vassal and wants to send it to you safely. How?" Be sure to pronounce the question mark, or he'll likely assume you're a Red Indian and have you thrown out of his rooms.

As for my other little business, it has taken a turn for the exceedingly droll. As I recall, I left off having engineered a promotion for my matilda and was then waiting for his inevitable request for funds. This never came. I began to hope that we were satisfied with our promotion, that we were most proud to show off our new lance corporal stripes and administer a bit of lance corporal punishment to those who seemed to merit or at least relish it, but no: one morning, I had instead a baffling message from an Aussie sergeant, the jolly mate in charge of his camp's front-gate guard details. He politely requested that since I was so regularly dispatching our new lance corporal out on counterintelligence missions at all hours of the day and night without, understandably, having time to issue individual passes each time, might I at least fill out some standing order for the rotating guard to have as a reference? Well here was a puzzle. I sent my batman to trek out and rustle up my pet Aussie, and that very evening in trots the colonial. Since our last meeting, explains grinning young Sven, he has adopted the habit of leaving his camp whenever he feels the urge, giving *my* name as his pass: "Intelligence mission for Captain Marlowe," he tells the guards, zipping in and out on a 'cycle requisitioned with the same words. "See Captain Marlowe for authorisation documents." A garish display of cheek, you'll agree. And what was he doing on his missions? Houris? Brawling? Not a bit of it: he has, on my good name, gone out half a dozen times to . . . wait for it, Bev . . . *explore the monuments*! He has been at archaeological sites, trying to meet the few excavators still working despite the explosive distractions of this modern War. "May I speak openly, sah?" he bellows. Of course you can, ducks, but do keep it down. Prepare yourself, Bev: it seems our little Aussie just *loves* Egypt and Egyptian studies, crazy mad for them. He does not want *anything* else from me, really, on the soul of his favourite koala, he just wants to talk to me about ancient Egypt. "How would I know anything of that?" I ask. Ah, well, he knows all about me, you will be as alarmed as I was to hear. He knows not only that I read the pharaohs at Oxford but that I am due "to go back and finish up and become a University professor," he says with stars in his eyes. He shyly confesses that having learned this some time ago, he had approached me *prior* to our first encounter in the desert, back when I spent that week at Tel el Kebir, though I have not the slightest recollection of him. When I understandably paid him no attention there, he took to following me about whenever he could, and even stole out of camp and came across to our base that fateful night, just to introduce himself again. But he saw me leaving and assumed I was off on a "walkabout to gaze at the unparalleled beauty of the

Gizeh pyramids," and off he set to catch up with me. He tells me all this as if I shall be pleased to hear it.

A cloying tale, but what the devil does he want from me *now*? Why, just what any ordinary blackmailer wants: he wants lessons in Middle Egyptian. Trembling to exhibit his hidden depths for me, he takes pen and paper from my table to prove he can already write hieroglyphs, hieratic, and demotic. He taught himself, he claims (do be sure you are sitting down for this, Bev), from books in an Australian lending library run by his first love, a woman who died tragically, breathing her last in his arms. And now he simply wants to discuss the history of the kings with me. In short, Bev, I am being blackmailed into tutoring an antipodal, autodidact, widower, criminally inclined, would-be Egyptologist. Surely you know the type, an old story. Do tell me when I am boring you, love.

My pupil is a complete *naif* but has strange, unconnected depths of knowledge, bottomless lakes of Egyptian expertise separated by vast beaches of ignorance. He is aware of this and wants the land flooded evenly. While we are at it, he would also like to learn Arabic, which he has already started to murder on his own.

He has come to my tent three times since—a forty-mile trek, Bev! Such devotion! He treats me absolutely with awe. Tales of Oxford hypnotise him, like a cross-eyed cobra swooning for a wog's warbling flute. I whisper "Balliol" very softly and he begins to grow faint, though not so faint that I am able to begin instruction in the pedagogical method I think would be more pleasurable. I tried this once or twice (one does lose count), thinking it would be amusing and would also release the young scholar's unpleasant hold over me. But I was trying to plant my seed in desert sand, I am sure you are relieved to learn, Bev: "Very koind of ye, Cap'n, but I don't wanna waste yer toim, we should troy t'discuss just serious matters." The beast. If I looked like you, of course, we would have progressed nicely by now.

Do write me of what I am missing at home. Tell me of the seasons. Tell me if my name ever comes up in conversation anymore. Tell me there is still a place for me back there. And for Christ's sake, tell me what Wexler says.

Your dusky prince of Egypt,

Go-go

29 July, 1918

Dear Bevvy,

Heartbreaking, honestly. Thank you for your efforts, and thank you for passing the news. Not that she ever thought much of me, but tell the poor widow I send my most heartfelt condolences, and that her husband meant the world to me. Say it better, say it how you would. I am not joking—he truly was important to me, really, dipsomania and senility aside. He was a pedant, of course, and his goal in teaching was to produce, before his soul seeped from its body, as many scholars as possible who thought and spoke precisely as he did. I think he probably succeeded: before I left Oxford, I had noticed a half dozen of the younger men had taken to pulling on their earlobes and saying, "Maybe so, maybe so, but I do doubt it," when they wanted to shut someone up. Poor old Clem. I truly wanted his advice on this papyrus, damn you. Damn him.

But, Bev, read on! I had just read your letter when my little orphan came in for his lesson. (Oh, yes, he is an orphan, too; the story is extraordinary, and not without some real bathos—*you*, I'm certain, would be sobbing.) He saw at once I had received bad news, and I was moved by a gust of nostalgia to discuss Wexler with him, the way he taught, his nicknames of my invention (The Ibid Ibis, I-Doubt-It, The Sic Bastard), certain methods and debates we had, including the fascinating questions of the particular historical issue surrounding that item I may have found. Of course the boy sat stock-still, agape and starved for junior common rooms, whatnot. After a few minutes, I regained hold of myself, and was prepared to start on our day's topic (religious cults of the Theban kings), but he interrupted me and asked quite simply how he could go about being *admitted to Balliol*. He is really quite something, full of surprises. "Well, do let's see," I replied, all seriousness, "did you finish your schooling in Australia, or just learn at the lending library?" He was silent. "Well, that does make it rather difficult, doesn't it, ducks?" Not to mention that moist sheep smell they all give off.

We began our tutorial (which consist mostly of me summarising certain events or themes, and giving him lists of books to read should he ever return to civilisation, some of which he has surprisingly already read, most of which he has not and which I attempt to summarise for him as well). Today, though, after only a few minutes, conversation slipped back to the glories of Oxford. This was entirely his doing, and while at first I indulged him and myself, it was becoming rather irritating, and so I said that discussing Oxford was too painful for me still, as it invariably brought back memories of (almost a reflex now to pull up his name when lying is necessary) poor Trilipush, my greatest friend there, an orphan just like you, ducks, but now missing these many months in the Bosporus campaign. (Sorry to drop the news on you so suddenly, Bev. Had I not mentioned? Oh yes, Ralph volunteered, don't you know, to lead a detachment of bronzed, broad-shouldered seamen to approach Constantinople by water, swimming actually, as Ralph, preferring not to be too ostentatious, declined a ship. Not a word from him in months. Do pray for our chum.)

The colonial, eager for any holy relic of my saintly existence in the promised land of Oxford, pleads for details.

"He was my dearest friend at Balliol, quite my inseparable mate, the golden boy, the hope of Egyptology, the orphaned son of Kentish gentry, the renowned sportsman, scholar, and soon-to-be gentleman farmer. He and I joined up for the good fight together, the pride of the Balliol Egypt men, served here with me side by side at the beginning, but he simply must insist on combat, mustn't he, and off he strode to help your countrymen in storming the empire of fezzes, our lovely lost boy." I really did go on a bit, quite sure my pupil was catching the joke, on and on I went, reminisced over our triumphs and antics in our varsity days, Ralph and I, this and that about Ralph's marvellously colourful childhood and career, really anything that came into my head to avoid our drab little tutorial, but as I went on, I saw the fool had absolutely no idea. And of course that made me curious to see how far things could go, and off I went, rather exaggerated here and there about it all, promoted into reality some things you and I would have liked, Bev, rebuilt Oxford in our image for him. I was thinking only of you in some of my additions, particularly the serving dwarves, chosen in ferocious competition for their servility, discretion, fluency in foreign tongues, and perfectly dimensioned tininess.

He has an unquenchable thirst for details, our blackmailing orphan, and I was tireless. What did we eat there? What was it like to know we were of "the fortunate chosen nobility"? As God is my witness, Bev, he asked me this. What were my parents like, and what sorts of things pleased them when I was a boy, and what methods did I use to "determine when they were about to thrash" me? That was a difficult one, I must say. You know the governor: can you imagine wee, wordless Priapus "thrashing" anyone? And, for all his self-taught and Hugo-enriched knowledge of Egypt, he really hasn't the faintest idea of how the twentieth-century world operates or who resides in it. I asked him why the War was on, why we were fighting the Germans and the Turks. Admittedly, I cannot say myself just why either, but he *really* had no idea, mumbled something about the international bankers and capitalists, but not with any conviction. Does he know how Parliament is elected or the name of the American president or what language they speak in Austria-Hungary or the rules of cricket? He does not.

I have now decided I am enjoying my blackmail, a pleasant pastime with this fawning dolt. I think you would rather enjoy it, too, Bev. "Until next time, then, sah," he says with a merry wave, gathering up his notes and hypothetical reading lists, a last worshipful wink at his private Oxonian tutor. "I'll learn all of this for next time, no question." How lovely for you, ducks. That will come in handy when you return home to breed kangaroos.

Congratulations to you, too, BQ, on completing your studies. I wonder if you've given a thought to our postwar existence, which must become a reality someday. Finally the gentlemen in charge will run out of slaughterable young men and the Belligerent Powers will have to take a rest to breed up some more. And in that interval, I, of course, shall be back at my studies, with an eye to warming Clem Wexler's chair someday. I shall need a housekeeper cum companion, and I shall insist on one with a high-level degree in Frog Letters, if you know anyone who might be interested in the post, keeping in mind, of course, my ferocious temper and Byzantine requirements.

> Educating the masses,
> Go-go

15 August, 1918

Cherished BQ,

Bit of a cock-up. Any wise counsel you care to offer would be most welcome.

You've heard these cockle-warming tales, I suppose, from up in Luxembourg or some such, where on Christmas Eve, there are little front-line truces and our men and the Boche stop shooting for the night and instead share drinks and exchange gifts and dance a bit before going back the next morning to the daily work of plunging bayonets into each other's bellies? Fine, I say, and no crime there. Well, similarly, out in an otherwise unremarkable suburb of Cairo, there is an establishment for gentlemen of refined tastes, which civilised outpost I have visited from time to time when the interrogatees brought in for questioning have for too long tended to be old women and village elders. The management of this establishment, inspired no doubt by the admirable humanism displayed in those Yuletide trench respites, does not discriminate against clientele of any particular nationality or political belief. No one thinks this inappropriate, considering the dreadful wartime conditions to which we are all submitting ourselves. And, of course, now that I think of it, what an excellent location for potential counterintelligence work, a purpose to which I shall certainly now put the facility, and have probably put it already in my previous visits, now that I think about it.

"I don't much feel like these little finishing school sessions anymore," I told my cobber ward in a fit of honesty and spite at being at his beck and call when he turned up the other night, chirping questions about Akh-en-Aten and my childhood bedroom.

"You're not enjoying them?" he asks and looks absolutely as if I have dashed his heart to splinters.

"I am not, darling Matilda."

"I see. Well, I hardly think that's your choice," he replies, tart as you like.

"Really?" I say. "You think your position is as strong as that?"

And at that, with a calm smile, he simply recited the address of that establishment I was describing above, the tiresome brute. Seeing my expression, he mentioned how long it had been since he has been promoted, despite his bold and tireless efforts on behalf of Allied counterintelligence. And, furthermore, clearing his throat, and showing a momentary hesitation rare in this magnificently confident swine, he requested—do prepare yourself, Bev, for this— that our tutorials leave the formality of the study-tent and that I take him to examine the monuments *in situ*, introduce him to archaeologists as my colleague from Oxford, a recent graduate, and give them my recommendation that they hire him after the War. Bev, I ask you. "I shall do no such thing," I am afraid I replied. "And no one would believe me if I did, you ridiculous colonial convict's son."

"I see." One minute he is quiet, smiling, presumptuously demanding. The next he has precisely that face young men in London sometimes have when you explain that they cannot come and live with you forever even if you did have rather a nice evening together the night before. It is a dangerous warning face, I know that much. And so I apologised for my short temper, excused myself by muttering something about being heartsick for poor Trilipush, from whom there was still no word, damn old Johnny Turk. I meant no offence, I said, and I will be better in a few days, if he could just give me some time to mourn and pull myself together. "Of course," he says, at once bright-eyed again. "We've been working hard, and you've lost a mate. Everyone has to let off steam now and again. Let's meet in a few days. I didn't mean to push you too hard just now. I just think we should start thinking of our situation more like a *partnership*." Yes, Bev, I can hear you nagging me for details and accuracy, but that was precisely his word; I have been careful to present all of these encounters without exaggeration. "A partnership you've been preparing me for, so after this War we can think about working together as a *team*." Quite. His mood was restored, and off he bounced.

Now then, Bev, I could rather use a bit of your calm advice, if you follow me.

HM

11 November, 1918

Bev, Bev, Bev!

Well today is quite a day, and no mistake. You have no doubt heard the news by now. The future begins again! There will be a bit of time lost before demobilisation, but I would guess I should be home well before summer. And then back to my studies, and then back here to dear Egypt in happier circumstances to apply myself to the gentlemanly pursuits of desecrating tombs and exhuming the dead. And where will Bev be, I wonder to myself sleeplessly.

As for my little problem, I believe you found an elegant solution; your counsel was subtly worded but wisely conceived: "When the War ends, things will take care of themselves. Be patient and do try at least to pretend to be kind to the boy." Trust Bev for seeing to the nut of the issue!

And so yesterday, I conducted my tutorial in a state of not entirely feigned excitement. I told him that I had something to show him, some dazzling news. I swore him to secrecy, an oath he undertook with moist-eyed Aussie sincerity, and then I allowed him a glimpse of that papyrus you failed to ask Wexler about, which document you will recall I found in a bazaar, but which I told him I had dug up before I had the pleasure of meeting him, and had held on to since, waiting for sweet Peace, when I could bring it back to England for analysis. Bless his bright convict's head: to give him (and me as his tutor) credit, he read the relic with care, and immediately came to the same conclusion I had. "Is this what I think it is?" he asked in delight. "No question at all," I declared, though the truth is quite a bit hazier; the thing could absolutely be a forgery, and even if it is real, it is still hardly conclusive as to— well, never mind, you couldn't conceivably care less, and the point of my story is elsewhere, right here in lovely, peaceful A.D. 1918. Either way, the rest of my intrigue unfolded along its own impeccable logic. "Where did you find it?" He salivated. I told him that dear old Trilipush (of course) and I had uncovered it on one of our many rambles back in early 1915 just before poor Ralph headed off to his tragic Turkish end. I was a bit drunk on my creative powers: I told him we had dug it up while under enemy fire. "Have you been back to the site since?" he asked, bursting with excitement. "If this was there, perhaps there's more! Mightn't, mightn't his tomb be near where this was buried?" he burbled.

"Dear boy, I do think so. I do absolutely believe a tomb is waiting for us down there, and I think I know where. Now listen: the War is almost over."

"Is it? How do you know?" asks my most perfect idiot-tormentor, some twenty-four hours before the Armistice was signed.

"For heaven's sake, listen. I will have to return to Oxford to finish my studies before I can come back here to conduct any full-scale excavation, but I intend to take the opportunity we shall have between now and the time we are shipped home to do a little more surface digging, to try out our glorious partnership in the field, you and me, on a preliminary expedition."

Honestly, Bev, I thought he was going to weep. He positively hugged me, a little boy on Christmas morning with a shiny new train. I was tempted to engage him in a more manly embrace, but I did not dare spoil the lovely tableau taking shape.

"Shipped home?" he said suddenly, all rapt with concern. "Can they force us to go back home? Can't one stay here?" Apparently Australia calls to him no more than it would to me or you. At least he has learnt that much under my tutelage.

Well, you should see by now how your surprisingly sage advice is playing out, Bev. Tomorrow he and I depart for a four-day leave. I showed him the paperwork, already completed, and he gazed at his dear papa with childlike wonder. Tomorrow he and I are heading south, into the very heart of archaeology in this mad, beautiful country. Carter and Carnarvon are doing interesting work in the Valley of the Kings, and I think it would do my career a bit of good to meet chaps like that now if I can. My orphan is practically wetting himself to meet them, too, but that, of course, is sadly not to be.

For down there, far from here, in the magical light of desert dusk, hills and hills away from anything and anyone, complex affairs will work themselves out simply, as you predicted they would, and I shall return to normal life free of any unnecessary weight on my mind.

Have you absolutely fallen for a life in London, Bev? I am thrilled to hear about your rooms, of course, I simply cannot wait to see them, but I hope you do not find them too, too comfortable, nothing permanent. Please do not dismiss me on this, I am utterly sincere, think hard: Oxford, you know, is where I simply must be, and then I shall be back here and back there and back and forth, teaching and digging and writing and teaching and digging and writing. Doesn't the life appeal to you, just a bit? Half your time in a don's flat in Longwall Street, and half in a tent in Egypt, a mature and tolerant country, after all. Mightn't one keep the friends one loves the best near one in such a life as that?

I shall write again on the 16th, free and light.

Eternally,

H.

(Sunday, 31 December, 1922, continued)

There is neither text nor illustration to explain the tomb's ninth and final chamber, but this should not surprise us. By now all is clear. It is asking too much to hope for more explicit illumination.

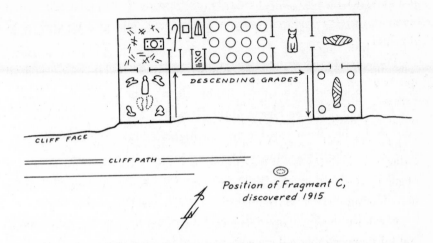

Position of Fragment C,
discovered 1915

He prepared his own sepulchre, placed the Master's donated organs in necessarily simple clay pots at the corners of his own chamber. He was no sculptor: each pot's lid was inscribed with the name of the appropriate god and an effort to draw their difficult shapes—baboon, falcon, jackal, man. He completed copying his Admonitions and to preserve his name on earth, ran back outside, buried one copy in a cylindrical jar (Fragment C, discovered 1915), another in a cloth a few yards away (Fragment A, 1856). A third, limestone copy (Fragment B, 1898) some messenger had been instructed to carry to distant lands but had in fact stashed not much farther afield. The original and complete text of the Admonitions he placed in a magnificent coffer in the Second Antechamber, an extra guarantor of immortality, as all writers merited an afterlife of a million years.

And then, with whatever strength remained to him, he turned to face the flickering torchlight, walked one last time the rooms in which he would await his admission to immortality.

What will the final moments feel like, wonders the last king of Egypt as he sets to his one remaining task. What will his last breath taste of, and the first one after it?

His hands shake with foolish fear and hunger. Some of his fingers are smashed, swollen, broken in battle or from his work on the Master.

His fingers are stained with paint, and they stink still of preservatives and his father-in-law's guts.

The chemical treatment of his feet and legs will be excruciating, but with the numbing effect of the slow-acting poisons he will have already consumed, and with the further comforting knowledge that immortality is approaching and he has thwarted his enemies for all time, he will be able to wrap his feet and legs tightly. He will remark how far he has come in this life, from how low to how high, and how high he will soar in the next, where his name will ring out forever. The preservative treatment of his groin and trunk will be almost unbearably painful. But he will bear it, and wrap himself to his waist. The embalming fluids across his cheeks feel like ice fire, and the fumes in his nose scorch his brain. The drops that fall over his parched lips and tongue gag him. His eyes cloud and burn, but he does not stop. There is no time to stop, for soon the poisons will complete their work, and he must complete his own before his departure. He tightly wraps his face and head.

He has rehearsed the solution to his final, intractable problem, prac- tised it over and over in his solitude, and while no solution is flawless, this is the best that Fate has allowed him: the long, measured strips of linen laid out across the floor. Even as the preservative's sting grows crueller, he clutches the linen in his fist. Lying on the tomb floor, he rolls, gathering the wrapping as best he can around his arms and trunk as he goes, finishing the task, he hopes, at the chamber's exact centre, precisely at the moment of his departure.

Darkness. The king's final pains recede. His breathing stops for a spell, the length of time no longer measurable. He drifts in silence. And then he awakens to music. The first face he sees is his father's, already risen and now standing over him, repentant, servile, restrained, loving. So lovingly he has with his own gentle fingers opened his son's eyes from sleep. And now the women enter the room, their almond eyes striped with malachite kohl, their copper bodies under sheer and cling- ing shirts. They approach and caress him sweetly. They love him so.

They unwrap him and anoint him with oil. And when they have prepared him, they lead her in, at last: in floats his queen, her long-
fingered hands reaching for him. She is healthy and fresh and only for
him. The food descends from the walls and fills long tables. The new,
unimaginable music grows louder, and his wife leads him away from
life's pain and loneliness. Far beneath him, mere men will daily speak of
him with awe, their honeyed exhalations of his name forming clouds
that will waft him high above the masses of rivals and pedants, above
poverty and mockery, above snobs and villains, secure from enemies
and doubt and betrayal. His mysteries and riddles remain unsolved for
millennia stacked upon millennia until another should find him, embrace him, twist and fuse with him, vanish into him, and win, for discoverer and king alike, the eternal love due an immortal name,
Atum-hadu and Trilipush, Trilipush and Atum-hadu, Trilipush, Trilipush, Trilipush.

**ARTHUR PHILLIPS GRATEFULLY ACKNOWLEDGES
THE KIND ASSISTANCE OF:**

the British Museum's Department of Ancient Egypt and Sudan (particularly Marcel Marée), Jim Forte, Norman Fruman, Daniel Goldner, the Hennepin County Public Library, Catherine Keenan, Peter Larson, Jaromir Malek and the Griffith Institute, Ross Mallett, the Moreno-Bormann Circus of Paris, Anthony Palliser, Stephen Quirke, Michael Rice, Kelley Ross, Chris Tyrer, Kristen Vagliardo, Kent Weeks and the Theban Mapping Project, and the invaluable example of Miss Vivian Darkbloom;

AND IS DEEPLY INDEBTED TO:

superstar editor Lee Boudreaux, Julia Bucknall, Tony Denninger, Peter Magyar, Mike Mattison, ASP, DSP, FMP, MMP, incomparable agent Marly Rusoff, Toby Tompkins, Daniel Zelman, and, of course, Jan.

ABOUT THE AUTHOR

ARTHUR PHILLIPS was born in
Minneapolis and educated at Harvard.
He has been a child actor, a jazz
musician, a speechwriter, a dismally
failed entrepreneur, and a five-time
Jeopardy! champion. His first novel,
Prague, an international bestseller, was named
a Notable Book of the Year by *The New
York Times*, received the *Los Angeles
Times* / Art Seidenbaum Award for best
first novel, and has been translated into
seven languages. He lives in New York
with his wife and two sons.